DRAGON SWORD

DEMON'S FIRE BOOK 1

CHRISTOPHER PATTERSON

Dragon Sword

Copyright © 2020 by Christopher Patterson

All rights reserved.

No part of this book may be reproduced in any form or by any electronic or mechanical means, including information storage and retrieval systems, without written permission from the author, except for the use of brief quotations in a book review.

Rabbit Hole Publishing

Tucson, Arizona 85710 USA

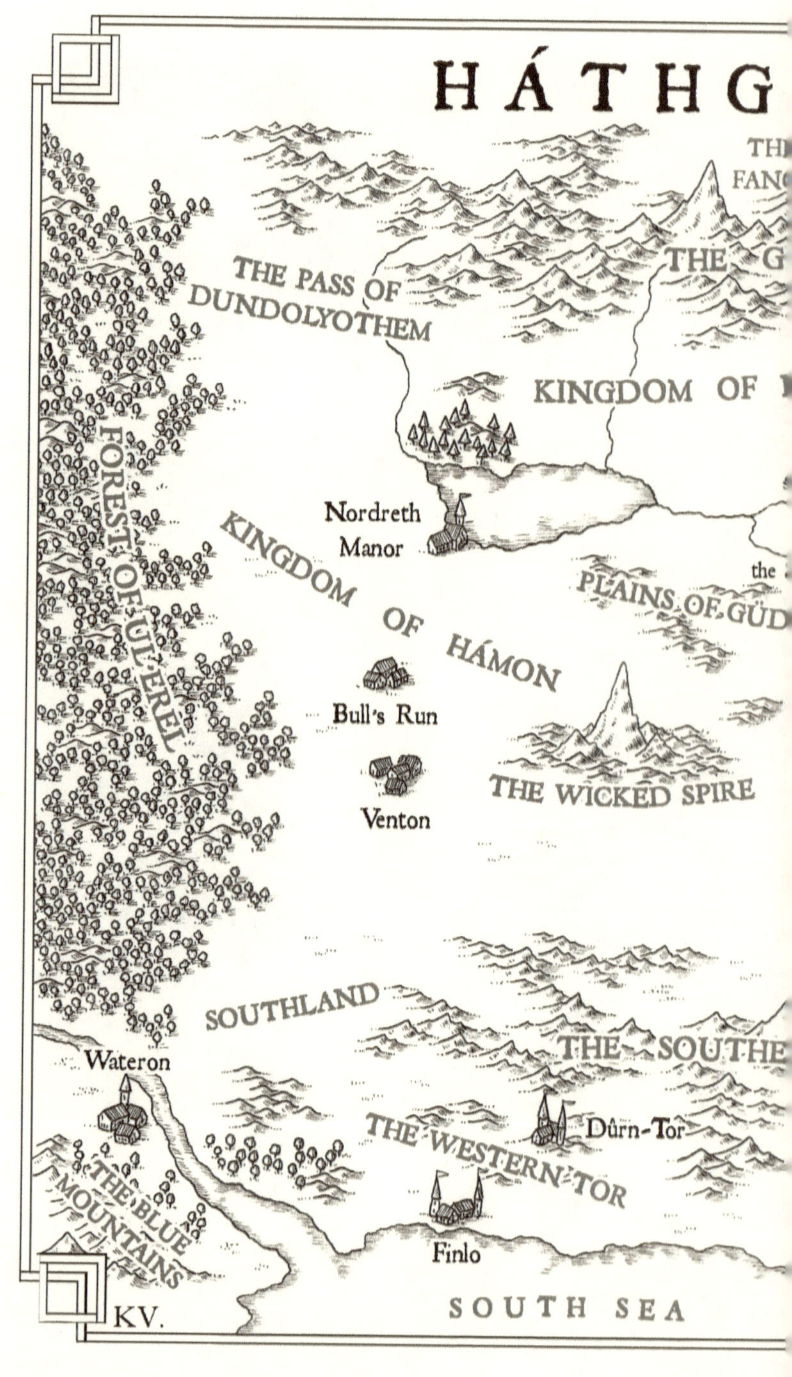
HÁTHG
THE
FANG
THE G
KINGDOM OF
THE PASS OF
DUNDOLYOTHEM
KINGDOM OF HÁMON
Nordreth Manor
the
PLAINS OF GÜD
FOREST OF UL·EREI
Bull's Run
Venton
THE WICKED SPIRE
SOUTHLAND
THE SOUTHE
Wateron
THE WESTERN·TOR
Dûrn-Tor
THE BLUE MOUNTAINS
Finlo
KV.
SOUTH SEA

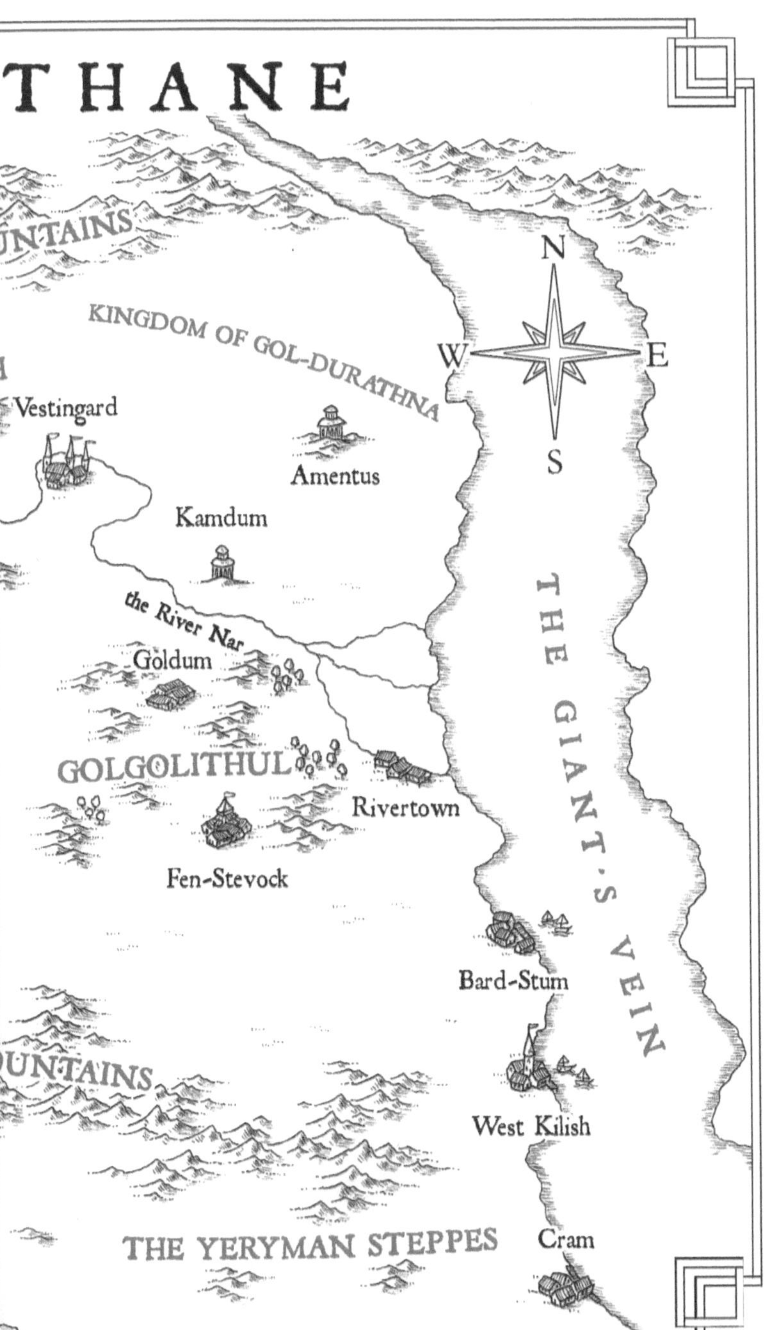

THANE
MOUNTAINS
KINGDOM OF GOL-DURATHNA
Vestingard
Amentus
Kamdum
the River Nar
Goldum
GOLGOLITHUL
Rivertown
Fen-Stevock
Bard-Stum
West Kilish
MOUNTAINS
THE YERYMAN STEPPES
Cram
N
W
E
S
THE GIANT'S VEIN

PROLOGUE

As I cut down the last of the demon's soldiers, I see him in the distance—a great shadow against the smoke-filled horizon, laughing over the carnage he had caused. He spreads his wings and they are like black clouds, blotting out the sun and casting their own, sickening red glow over the world. He cares not for the life he has spent, for his lost soldiers, for he is the Lord of Chaos and he thrives on turmoil and pain and terror.

Four shadows appear next to him—his beasts of war—the Beasts of Chaos. They are gargantuan things, laying waste to the land, the sky, and the sea. Eret Eloam—the world—burns, even the water and the clouds, and it seems that even the Creator has abandoned us. But I know that is a foolish thought. He is here, with us, even if we doubt.

I mount Ydron. I feel the power of the dragon beneath me. Is it enough, though? This Lord of Chaos and his Beasts of Chaos are even too much for dragons. I look to a brother and two sisters. We are all that is left of the dragon riders. I look down at a green, egg-shaped stone in my hand. It is light. It is magic. It is meant to be a prison. My dragon rider kin each have one as well—red, blue, and white. We are the world's last hope.

Paladins and sorceresses gather around us. They were once an army. Now, they are less than a hundred. Specifically formed, bred, and taught to fight the Lord of Chaos, this is the end of their calling. Either we win or Eret Eloam loses.

I say nothing. Most generals in my position might say a word of encouragement, something inspirational, but everyone here knows the cost of defeat. The demon screams. His Beast of Chaos roar. And an army of demon-kind, goblins, and shadow children flood over a hill and cover the earth like a plague. I look to my dragon riders and nod. They nod back. They know this is it. Ydron knows too. She tilts her head skyward and belches fire. We take to the sky.

It is carnage below. For each paladin or sorceress that dies, a hundred foes meet their fate. But they are numerous, and we are few. The dragons spit fire, but the battle below is not our focus. It is the Beasts of Chaos and the demon. If we can stop them, we can stop the war.

We get close and my heart quickens. They are horrid creatures and the Lord of Chaos is the worst of them all. I pray to El—the Creator—to give me strength in this final moment. If I am to meet my end here, let it be in faith, not fear. Let my death save the world. Let our sacrifice be the thing that brings evil to heel once again.

I feel the demon's heat. It burns my skin. It singes my hair. It stings my eyes. But I—we—press on. Together, as our bodies begin to wither to the power and dark magic of the Lord of Chaos, we hold our stones, our prisons high, and we say the words Yalathanil taught us. We say the words that will entrap the Beast of Chaos and cripple the rising of the Lord of Chaos. We shout them at the tops of our lungs, or the din of fire and roar of flaming clouds. We call them out, even as our tongues fail us our skin peels away. We call out the words, even as this world passes away and my spirit transcends to a new world.

The Lord of Chaos screams and curses. The stone, held in a hand that is now black and scarred and broken, glows a brilliant green. The others' do too—red, blue, and white. We have won. I can't smile, I can't cry, but my spirit rejoices. We have won. I cling to Ydron. Fire cannot hurt her. She is a dragon. I cling to her and I hope she feels my presence, my thanks, my love, and my hope. I hope she will carry the next dragon rider high into a sky that is reborn from this chaos. She feels me. I know she does.

As the pain of this life passes away, and as I cling the stone close to my chest, I close my eyes for the last time and I pray that the Lord of Chaos never return, for he is destruction and death.

1

————

Darius, the General Lord Marshall, marched down the hallway leading to the throne room. Reflecting his urgency, his thudding boots echoed off the cavernous walls of the capitol building of Amentus, a building hundreds of years old, built from white marble. The arched ceilings, painted to look like a crystal blue sky with puffy, white clouds, aided the acoustics of the corridor, and the ancient builders had a purpose behind such construction. One man could stand at one end of a hallway and shout anything—a command, a proclamation, or a call for help—and someone standing at the other end, some fifty paces distant, could hear him as if they stood next to each other.

As the Lord Marshall stomped by, guards placed at regular intervals slammed their right, gauntleted fists into their breastplates as they saluted. Positioned next to the pillars which formed part of a fake colonnade—they didn't hold up any weight but were simply an architect's embellishments—these men and women who guarded the capitol building were the best trained, most fearless, and most devout soldiers. As they saluted Darius, it meant more than any other salute —it was true respect.

He came to the tall, solid double doors made of a light oak leading to the throne room, each etched with the carving of a gigantic sun. The two men who guarded the doors saluted. As with all of the guards, they wore plate mail that covered every part of their bodies and made from the best steel, save for Dwarf's Iron. A sun with seven points—the symbol of Amentus—was emblazoned on their breastplates. They lifted their visors.

"Open," the General Lord Marshall said.

"Sir ..." one of the guards began.

"I don't have time," the General Lord Marshall snapped. He knew King Agempi was in a meeting with his advisors and politicians. It was an important meeting, something to do with the economic situation of their country and the steps they needed to take to rectify whatever issues they were having. It was all over Darius' head and the reason why he loved being a soldier and never accepted the King's offer to make him a senator or advisor of state. "Open the damn door."

Both men lowered their visors and stepped to the side, drawing their tower shields—painted blue with a yellow sun at the center—close to their bodies in attention. One of them knocked on the double door. They opened.

A colonnade—this one real and made of the same white marble as the rest of the building and inlaid with suns and moons and stars—led to the wide dais on which the thrones of the King and Queen of Amentus had been placed with perfect precision. Guards stood next to each column, but unlike the ones who stood at attention in the building's main hallway, these didn't salute as the Lord Marshall walked by. It wasn't for lack of respect. Darius had trained each one of these men, personally ensuring they were the most loyal and most fierce—the last line of defense if the capitol building fell in battle. They saluted no one, not even the King. It was their command. They were the Warriors of the Sun, the most elite of knights in Gol-Durathna's military, and their loyalties were to the state ... and the state only.

The king was in a meeting with several advisors and senators, but he looked up as the General Lord Marshall stepped onto the blue carpet that led to the dais, caring little for the dirt on his boots. A broad-shouldered man, the king had dark ringlets in his hair that spilled over his shoulders, and his thick beard had gray streaked through it. Despite the thickness of his beard, Darius could see his red lips and still white teeth when the king smiled. He stood and lifted his hands to silence one of his advisors before he opened his arms as if he might even hug his general.

"Darius!" the king called, "I thought you were away."

The General Lord Marshall didn't answer. He simply approached the dais and, reaching the bottom step, knelt, right fist to his left breast, and head bowed low.

"Stand, Darius," the king said, pushing past one of his advisors, "and dispense with these formalities. It is good to see you."

The General Lord Marshall stood. His eyes met the king's. Those eyes—a brilliant emerald green—were the kindest eyes Darius had ever known. He had seen rulers from other countries on the brink of war with Gol-Durathna, red-faced and angry, stand in front of King Amentus and soften simply because of those eyes.

"To what do I owe this pleasure?" King Agempi asked.

"Sire, we weren't done," one of his advisors said.

"Silence! I can interrupt a meeting with my advisors and greet one of my oldest friends if I want."

"Of course, Your Majesty," the advisor said, head hung low and backing away a few steps.

King Agempi X was a powerful man and a good ruler. He surrounded himself with well-educated advisors and politicians of character and integrity but hated the mundane nature of most meetings concerning the state. He was a man who believed his real place was on a battlefield, and his shoulders, chest, arms, and legs evidenced as much.

"As much as I take great joy from discussing taxes, the level of our wheat stores, and our economic concerns east of the Giant's Vein,"

King Agempi said, "I think I can manage a small break for you, Darius."

"I wish my presence was for pleasure, Your Majesty," the General Lord Marshall said.

"That concerns me," King Agempi replied, some of the sparkle leaving his eyes.

"It should," the General Lord Marshall replied.

"Well, then, speak, General Lord Marshall," the king said.

The General Lord Marshall shot a quick look to the advisors and senator who had been conferring with the king.

"Belisarius, you may stay, but the rest of you, leave us," the king said.

As the advisors filed out, some showing their dislike of being dismissed, the senator, an older man with curly, gray hair and a short, white beard, bowed and stepped aside, next to the king's throne. His slight frame belied the fact that he was once a soldier too ... a very good soldier. Unlike Darius, he had accepted the king's offer to throw off his armor and put away his sword for a life of politics; it had not treated him well. He was barely older than the Lord Marshall, but he looked as if he could have been Darius' father.

"We have dispatched the Atrimus," the General Lord Marshall said.

"The Shadow Men?" Belisarius gasped.

"I trust there is a good reason for this," the king said.

"There is, Your Majesty," Darius replied. "This ... this dragon attack on Fen-Stévock. We have gathered information that leads us to believe there is more to this. The Lord of the East seeks a powerful weapon; he has part of it, a scroll with a spell, but now seeks a special sword. With that he can control dragons ... even kill a dragon."

The king sat down again, resting an elbow on an armrest of his throne and his chin on his fist.

"Dragons?" the king said, as much to himself as to Darius and Belisarius. "A year ago, the mention of such a thing would have made me laugh. They were a fable, a myth, Darius. A child's tale."

The king leaned forward, resting his arms on his knees, his thick brows furling into a concerned look.

"To be able to kill a dragon, let alone control one," the king muttered under his breath.

"It is the stuff of legends," Belisarius offered.

"This would turn the tide, Darius," the king said. "The Lord of the East would no longer need to hide behind diplomacy. War would be imminent. And we would be on the losing side."

"All of Háthgolthane would be on the losing side, Your Majesty," Belisarius added. Darius felt the old soldier adding nothing of value with his comments; politics had turned him into a 'yes man'.

"The man who saved Fen-Stévock is the one who the Lord of the East has tasked with finding this sword," Darius explained, "the Dragon Sword."

"He is a man of Western Háthgolthane, yes?" the king asked.

"A pity he didn't let Fen-Stévock just burn," the senator said, and the king rebuked him before Darius could.

"He saved thousands of lives, Belisarius," the king said. "Remember that. Those people haven't a clue who their ruler is. Most of them don't care. All they care about is putting food in their children's mouths."

"How is a man from Western Háthgolthane so willing to serve Golgolithul?" Belisarius asked, his first sensible input to the conversation.

"Truly," the king added. "The men of Western Háthgolthane ... descendants of Gongoreth and Hargoleth, who stayed after the Great War and the Treaty of Bethuliam rather than returning west. They oppose the east more than we do. By the Creator and the old gods, they oppose the east more than the men of Mek-Ba'Dune."

"His service is not given willingly, Your Majesty," Darius said. "Our informant tells us that he must do as the Lord of the East bids. The Lord of the East has threatened him ... threatened his entire family."

"That is a pity. The men of Western Háthgolthane used to be

allies to Gol-Durathna." The look on the king's face was distant, staring past Darius and Belisarius as if he was remembering a sad memory. "They are the reason we won the Great War. Without them, all would have been lost, and they sacrificed much. Such a man would have been a valuable ally. Is there hope for this man, Darius? Can we sway him to our side?"

"We know where he lives, where his family lives," Darius replied. "However, at the same time, this Bu Al'Banan, self-proclaimed King of Hámon, is also after the sword. Our informants also tell us he thinks it will legitimize his claim to Hámon's throne and give him the needed power and support to conquer Golgolithul."

The king sighed, rubbing a hand along his brow as he looked down at his feet. He removed the gold crown—a simple circlet of gold studded with diamonds at regular intervals—and once more rested on an armrest of his throne.

"Does this mean we must kill an innocent man, one who saved thousands ... tens of thousands of lives to prevent the sword from falling into the hands of the Lord of the East or this King Bu Al'Banan?" King Agempi asked.

Darius felt his stomach knot.

"Can we sway him, as you mentioned?" Belisarius asked.

"To what end?" Darius asked. "The Lord of the East will surely kill his family for the man's betrayal. And this new King of Hámon will probably kill his family anyways."

"Then he must not find the sword," Belisarius said.

"But ..." the king began, but his senator interrupted him as all good politicians should.

"The greater good," Belisarius said. "A small evil for the greater good."

Spoken like a true politician. Darius glared at the former soldier, hard and cold, a moment of hatred in his eyes. But he knew his words were the truth. There was no other way.

"He must be stopped," King Agempi said. "This man from

Western Háthgolthane. And Golgolithul. And this King Bu. You know what must be done, Darius."

"The Atrimus are on their way to Hámon and the farmlands of Western Háthgolthane," the General Lord Marshall said with a bow and began to turn to leave.

"Let me know if you hear anything else from our informant in Fen-Stévock," King Agempi said.

Darius stopped and gave a half-turn to face the king again.

"I don't think I will, Your Majesty," Darius replied. "We haven't heard from him in a while. I believe he has been discovered."

"The gods be merciful to him," King Agempi said. "His death will not be quick."

"And to his family," Darius added. "His last message to us told us Golgolithul is mobilizing troops to their northern borders."

"When did things get so complicated?" King Agempi asked. "I mean, a dragon? Mobilization of troops? We have had relative peace for more than two hundred years. And now what?"

"I don't know, Your Majesty," Darius said. "Shall I garrison our southern borders as well?"

King Agempi waited for a while before looking at Darius with hard eyes, giving the General Lord Marshall a quick nod.

"Make it so."

Andragos—the Messenger of the East, the Black Mage, the Steward of Golgolithul, the Harbinger of Death—stood next to the Lord of the East, shadowed by the darkness of the dungeons under the main keep of Fen-Stévock, barely illuminated by floating red balls of magical light. The thick smell of stale blood, sweat, piss, and feces hung in the air, and a film of vaporous fungus covered much of the dungeon's stone, its spores the descendants of poisonous mold hundreds of years old. There were twenty cells in this dungeon, and the only way to get in and out was a magical portal. There were two such portals, one in the Lord of the East's quarters and the other in a hidden room in the keep of Fen-Aztûk, the sister city to Golgolithul's capitol. Magical rods of an ancient metal barred each of the cells without a door. One simply needed to know the magical word to get in and out of a cell, the bars simply disappearing and then reappearing again. Only the worst criminals—traitors, politicians inciting unrest against the Lord of the East, and people who needed to stay quiet—called this place home.

One such man hung naked from the ceiling of a cell by his hands, his feet just off the ground. Melanius, the Lord of the East's new mage and advisor, stood just inside the cell, playing the role of inquisitor. Kimber and Krista, the Lord of the East's two witches, stood just behind Melanius. Blood dripped from the prisoner's mouth as his chin dipped to his chest. This man was strong, with knotted, lean muscle ... once. Now, he was beaten and bruised, little more than an animal, his skin torn and scarred and burned. Before his physical torture, the Lord of the East would have put him through magical torture. He would have crushed organs, only to heal them just to crush them again. Magical heat would have seared the man's brain, skin, blood even. The Lord of the East, or Melanius, or the witches would have put images in the man's head, images of his wife dying, being raped, cheating on him, slitting her own throat, murdering their children, anything that would drive someone insane. Andragos knew this was what the man had endured before coming here ... because he used to be the one doing it.

The Lord of the East nodded to Melanius, who, in turn, nodded to the torturer. A large man, his upper torso as bare as his shaved head, took a curved knife to the prisoner's chest. The naked man lifted his head and screamed, jerking sideways violently as the torturer removed another piece of skin from his body. When the torturer threw the skin to the ground, the prisoner dropped his head again and wept, a low, moaning cry.

"Speak," Melanius said, his voice a croaking hiss, "or your wife and children will meet the same fate."

Andragos looked over at the smiling Lord of the East. He then looked down at the cell floor and saw a dozen squares of flayed skin; one of them bore ten scarred lines. It was the first piece of skin removed from the man's body, a symbol of his service to Golgolithul's army. The second piece of skin to be removed was a tattoo on his chest, one of a black gauntlet gripping a red fletched arrow, a symbol of his service as the Lord of the East's personal guard. Andragos frowned.

"You don't approve," the Lord of the East said.

Andragos steeled his resolve and met the Lord of the East gaze for gaze.

"He is a traitor," Andragos replied. "He deserves this and more."

Andragos tried to believe his own words, but something in his chest tightened. He had seen such punishment hundreds of times over hundreds of years. He had directed such punishments. And he had no room for traitors and liars, but something about this time, this torture, this man made him frown. It felt wrong.

Am I growing soft?

"Very well," the Lord of the East said with a smile. "But you do understand I must use him as an example. His family. His friends. His acquaintances. Anyone he did business with. They will all meet a similar fate. And then we will see who dares to challenge me. Who dares to spy for lesser men? This man must pay in full for his sins."

"Please ... no more," the man whispered through sobs of pain.

"Perhaps you should have thought of that before making a pact with that incestuous cockroach in the north," Melanius hissed, a hint of glee in his voice.

The man cried and screamed as the torturer removed another piece of skin.

Andragos closed his eyes for a moment. It would take much of his energy, but he wanted to make sure the other four wizards in the room—Melanius, those two bitch witches, and the Lord of the East—couldn't read his thoughts as he passed a message to the unfortunate prisoner.

Your family will be safe. I cannot do anything about you or most of your friends, but your family will live.

The man looked up. His eyes met Andragos'. They were swollen and bruised, barely visible through the tears and blood that covered his face. But at that moment, he smiled. As the executioner removed another piece of skin, he groaned and gritted his teeth, but he did not scream out again. He steeled his resolve and just stared on as the Lord of the East had him executed, piece by piece.

"I have things to do," Andragos said.

"You don't want to stay and watch this man break?" the Lord of the East asked.

"He won't break," Andragos replied, "and you have tasked me with the rebuilding of South Gate. It has proven an arduous task. Besides, I have seen such things more times than I can count. They all end the same."

"Very well, then," the Lord of the East said.

Andragos snapped his finger and appeared in the main hall of the Fen-Stévock's keep. Raktas and Terradyn, his two personal guards for the last hundred years, were there to meet him, and they followed him as he left the keep and met his own elite soldiers—the Soldiers of the Eye—in the courtyard. After a few words, Andragos and his guards stepped into a dark carriage that was quiet as it rolled away.

"Find Ja Sin's family," Andragos commanded, "and escort them to safety. The Lord of the East means to flay his wife and his little daughters and sons for his iniquities. I shouldn't care, but I cannot let that happen."

"Where should we take them?" Terradyn asked. "Surely, the Lord of the East will be coming for them soon."

"Take them to my cottage," Andragos said, his voice hard and his face dark. "They will stay there for a while, and then I will find a suitable place for them to live. Did Ja Sin have close friends?"

For the last two years, Ja Sin had been a high-ranking officer in the Lord of the East's personal guard. He was a powerful warrior, a dynamic leader, and a spy for Gol-Durathna. The Lord of the East couldn't prove it, but they knew he was. And he was willing to face his punishment with head held high. But to punish his family ... Andragos shook his head. A hundred years ago, he wouldn't have cared, but the increasing cruelty of the Lord of the East began to weigh on him. He grew tired as much as the Lord's actions became pointless.

"Yes, my lord," Raktas replied.

"We cannot save them all," Andragos said, "but we can save some."

"What is happening, my lord?" Terradyn asked.

Andragos didn't answer. Then he looked at his two guards, confidants, friends ... if they could be called that.

"Are you with me?" Andragos asked.

"To the death," they replied in unison.

"Just be ready," Andragos said.

"My lord," Raktas said.

"Yes."

"We have found our own spy," Raktas continued. "A man who has infiltrated the Soldiers of the Eye."

"Truly?" Andragos asked.

"Yes, my lord," Raktas replied.

"Another spy for Gol-Durathna?" Andragos asked.

"No, my lord," Raktas replied. "For the late Patûk Al'Banan."

"Does he now spy for this Bu Al'Banan?" Andragos asked.

"I don't know, my lord," Raktas replied.

"Bring him to me," Andragos said, "unscathed. And hurry with Ja Sin's family."

Both men bowed.

2

owards the end of the summer, early mornings on the
Eleodum farm were cool. The new sunlight glistened off
the dew that collected nightly on the grass and wheat and corn stalks
of the farm. A rooster's crow signified the beginning of the day and, as
if in response to the rooster's morning call, the low moaning of cows
echoed through the farm.

Erik Eleodum smiled as he put his left hand on his hip, breathing
heavily. The rising sun, so slow at first, barely a sliver of light peeking
over the eastern horizon, dared to rise more and more, its light causing
the wheat of his farm to glow as if he had planted golden thread. Life
... this was what life looked like. The world around him celebrated
the bounty of the land, the perfection of the Creator's work in nature
stood better than all the treasures of the lost dwarvish city of Orvencrest, greater than the work of the most skilled artisans.

As he twisted it in his hand, the rising sun glimmered off Ilken's
Blade, his sword, a gift from a dwarf named Ilken Copper Head, one
of the most renowned blacksmiths from the dwarvish city and capitol
of Drüum Balmdüukr, Thorakest. He smiled again. He trained every
morning and, occasionally, in the evening. As he did so—sometimes

alone and sometimes with his cousin, Bryon, or his dwarvish friend, Turk—his movements felt fluid and precise. They were a part of him, second nature now buried deep in his subconscious. As he walked or used his arms without real conscious thought, his blade was simply an extension of the movements, his body a weapon in itself.

"Thank you, Wrothgard," Erik said, pretending his friend was still right next to him. Once a soldier of Golgolithul, an Eastern Guardsman, who had become a mercenary, Wrothgard had trained Erik, but he was gone, having run away from further duty to the east and Golgolithul's ruler, the Lord of the East. Erik hoped he was safe, wherever he was.

Erik walked over to a towel that hung on a wooden fence and used it to wipe the sweat from his face and the ever-growing muscles of his chest and arms. Each day he trained, he grew stronger and his muscles bigger. Growing up on a farm, he was always stronger than most, but now, when he did work on his farm, he could do the work of two men. He didn't grow up to be a soldier, or a warrior, or a wielder of any weapon for that matter; he thought he was going to be a farmer. He grew up wanting to be a farmer ... and part of him still did. He never wanted fame, notoriety, fortune, or anything like that. But now, they were all his. People called him Erik Friend of Dwarves, Erik Troll Hammer, Erik Wolf's Bane, Erik Champion of the East ... but mostly, they called him Erik Dragon Slayer.

He didn't really slay a dragon; she was still out there, licking her wounds and biding her time. He simply fended her off as she laid waste to the southern portion of Fen-Stévock—simply called South Gate. He dispelled her with an ancient scroll containing an even more ancient spell he had found in the lost city of Orvencrest. He saw her—the dragon—often, in his dreams. She was there, as were the dead ... always the dead. They could hurt him in his dreams, but he could hurt them as well—destroy them. He could hear her at times, too. She cursed him in his mind. He sensed her, somewhere, out there. Gooseflesh rose on his arms as he thought of a question that plagued his mind every day: If he could feel and sense her, could she sense him? Most likely. She was as powerful as the greatest wizard and wielded magic more potent than Andragos could conjure up.

Putting his towel back on the fence post and pulling his shirt over his head, Erik watched the sun rise, knowing she was out there in the east, beyond the Giant's Vein that separated the continents of Háthgolthane and Antolika. She was even further, beyond the Jagged Coast and past the Sea of Knives. Even past the Isutan Isles.

He slowly turned his head and looked south. They had waited an extra month—he and his cousin and the dwarves. The Lord of the East, ruler of the Eastern Empire—Golgolithul—had commanded them to retrieve the fabled Dragon Sword—described on the same scroll that contained the spell that helped him defeat the dragon— and he gave them a year to do it. That command came two months and some weeks ago. They had agreed to meet at the Eleodum farmstead after a month of rest. When Wrothgard didn't show after a month, they agreed to wait another month. He still hadn't shown. Erik knew he wouldn't, and his heart sank a little even though he smiled at the thought of the eastern soldier. He was a good man, a good warrior, and an even better friend. But he was tired of fighting. He told Erik as much. He needed more than a month to rest. He needed a lifetime.

Wrothgard had told Erik he probably wouldn't meet them. It would mean his death because failure in service to the Lord of the East meant death. But Wrothgard didn't care. He was going to take his chances. In the coastal city of Finlo, the desert continent of Wüsten Sahil maybe, or maybe even further. If the Lord of the East sent assassins after him, and they did find him, at least he would die a free man.

With the thought of the Dragon Sword, Erik looked to the north and the looming Gray Mountains, gigantic along the northern horizon even though they were a long way away. He had grown up in the shadow of those mountains, always wondering what they truly looked like, never thinking he would get to find out. On bright, sunny days such as this, they didn't look so formidable, serene almost, painting a pleasant backdrop to the northern horizon. But on cloudy or stormy days, when the mist hung low, those mountains were the stuff of shadows ... of *the* Shadow.

In his youth's mind's eye, the worst kind of monsters lived in those mountains, which seemed to be huge, evil creatures in themselves, especially the two tall peaks simply referred to since his childhood as The Fangs. Erik gave a mirthless smile. The honesty ... the truth of youth. Now it was time. He would leave his parents again, his home, his wife—Simone—for some fool's journey he didn't care about. Erik sighed. It would be a long day. He had a lot of work to do.

Erik pushed on through the darkness, feeling the crunch of twigs and pine needles beneath his feet. The sound broke the silence of the night as the cold numbed his face, but he kept moving, pushed branches out of his way that sought to peck at his face like hungry birds. He could barely see in front of him, the moon hidden by black clouds, and what he could see appeared as ghostly silhouettes. He shivered. He rubbed his palm on the pommel of Ilken's Blade. Knowing his sword was there gave him a little comfort ... but not much. Not in this place.

Erik finally pushed past the last tree and edged slowly into a small clearing. He remembered this place; it was a long time ago. This place was from a dream he once had—now he was dreaming again. His dreams were always so vivid, so real it was hard to differentiate this Dream World from reality, but he spent so much time here —every night for long periods—and he could tell the difference now. Normally, the undead were there, waiting. They hadn't been, in a while, though, not since he had destroyed Fox. Fox was a fiery haired slaver he had killed. The man's master, a slaver named Kehl and hailing from Saman—northern most city in Wüsten Sahil—had tried to enslave Erik, his brother, and his cousin, but they failed and many of them died, along with Fox.

For some reason, the dead had elected Fox as their leader. He was anything but in life. And no matter how many times Erik killed the man in his dreams, he would always come back ... except for the last time. Now he was gone forever, his deathly form dispatched into oblivion when Erik struck him with Ilken's Blade. Since then, his dreams had been of a vast grassland and a single hill topped by a large, weeping willow. A man sat under that tree, a man Erik knew but could never remember from where or what his name was. And in his dreams, he would sit and talk with the man and wake refreshed, next to his wife, Simone.

That had been his dreams since he came home, but now, on the eve of his departure once again, things had changed. He was in a dark place he had only been to once before. Before, in stark contrast to the darkness of the surrounding forest, there had been a fire blazing in the center of the clearing, and a cloaked man had stood warming his hands. He was a mysterious and powerful man, and just the one time, Erik had peered into the man's hood and he had seen every face he had come across in his life, one after the other like the flicked pages of a book. Erik knew he was more than a man, something otherworldly.

In dreams past, the hooded man had led the dead to a golden carriage that would carry them away to heaven, or so Erik presumed. The man had also denied men access to the carriage, those such as Fox and the other slavers. The man had made Erik feel powerful, like he had control in this dream world. It was because of that man that he was able to walk in his dreams unafraid.

But now, the fire was gone, as was the man. In the darkness, Erik could just make out cold ash and charcoal sitting within a stone circle. He knelt down, sifting through the extinguished campfire, stirring the remains with a short stick and not a single ember glowed. Wind howled through the forest trees and swirled through the clearing. It picked up ash and dirt and created tiny tornadoes.

There was another clearing, just through another copse of trees. He passed through there and the open space was empty like the first. The last time he was here, this was where he found the caravan of golden carriages, waiting to carry the dead away. Now there was only darkness and cold silence as the wind dropped once more.

Erik shivered as he saw a single pinpoint of light at the far end of the clearing. It was tiny at first, a pinprick of silver, but then it quickly grew into a tall oval of blinding brilliance. It was a doorway, and a man stepped through it, cloaked and hooded, but not the hooded man from before. Erik couldn't see a face, but frail hands emerged from the wide sleeves of the cloak. They formed the shape of a cup, and another pinpoint of light floated above them. The ball of light flashed, causing Erik to close his eyes, balls of light dancing behind his eyelids like fireflies. When he reopened them, the cloaked figure held a sword, long and broad, its steel a golden color. It reminded Erik of the shape his golden-handled dagger took when he defeated her ... the dragon.

The man placed the sword on the ground, and after another ball of light flashed, he held a golden crown. It had a total of five points, and the one taller than the rest was studded with a large diamond, a brilliant gem that emanated its own light. He placed the crown next to the sword, and from one more ball of light, he produced a green stone, an emerald perhaps, that was round, almost in the shape of an egg. He placed it on the ground, next to the sword and the crown. The emerald egg flashed and the sword and crown were gone, leaving it alone in front of the cloaked figure.

When Erik stepped forward into the center of the clearing, the cloaked man lifted a finger and pointed. Erik looked over his shoulder and saw another cloaked man standing behind him. He looked almost exactly like the first figure, although Erik could see silver runes outlining the man's hood and sleeves. There was a shadow behind the man, if that was possible in the darkness. The shadow was large and looked like it had horns and wings—the dragon perhaps. But the shadow had two arms and two legs and as it moved, the second robed man moved, the shadow's puppet. A cackling laugh emitted from underneath the puppet's hood.

The first man clapped, and the forest faded away, and Erik was on his farm in the middle of the night. He heard screams as he smelled smoke and the heat of fire caused him to step back.

Erik stood in the middle of his farmstead and spiders the size of horses ran about him, spraying everything with silver silk and sinking their fangs into faceless victims they had entwined in their webbing. Giant men followed them, killing those who had not fallen victim to the spiders with clubs the size of tree trunks. Soldiers rushed in behind the giants, their skin green, their eyes blank and black, spears spilling guts and swords removing heads. Buildings burned, people screamed, and livestock lay slaughtered as, for the first time in a long while, Erik felt scared in his dreams. That was when the dead came, rising up from the ground, consuming anything still alive and pulling them down into earthen graves. That was when Erik heard distant scream. The earth shook and the fire intensified around him. The dragon.

But when he turned, there was no dragon. All he saw was a massive shadow, the same shadow that had controlled the cloaked man, only larger. It moved about without any true form, twisting, contorting, and directing the ensuing death. The shadow was over him, above him, all around him, its wings spreading and flapping up hurricane-like winds, threatening to blow him away. The shadow roared, the sound a mix of rage and anger-filled laughter. It reached out with a black, clawed hand and ripped up a whole grove of apple trees by the roots, then a grove of orange trees. The hands crushed buildings that still stood, smashed barns, and carved deep gashes into the soil.

He saw everyone he loved standing in front of his home—his parents, cousins, sisters, the dwarves ... Simone. The shadow breathed a single, fiery breath, fire consuming them, and the moment they were gone, silence descended. The air around him became stale, and he knew what that silence meant. The giant shadow hovered above him, sucking in all the air. It was the same when the dragon showered his brother in fire. He heard laughter, saw fire, felt pain like he had never felt before, and then came the darkness.

Erik awoke with a start, sitting up quickly in his bed. Sweat poured down his face and chest and back. The bedroom of his and Simone's new home was dark. Beside him, his wife groaned softly as she turned slightly in her sleep. Erik took in a deep breath and let it out slowly, feeling the beat of his heart slowing in his chest. He shook his head both in disbelief of what he had experienced, and as if to rid himself of the memories.

He knew he had been dreaming, but as of late, his dreams were just his grassland, his hill, his tree, and the man. He had come to learn that powerful men and women—and powerful creatures—used the Dream Land for communication, to send messages, to intimidate. He saw them, every night.

Something strong had controlled his dream. Was it the dragon? Was that the shadow? He could still feel it. Even now, awake, he heard anger-filled howling, malicious laughing, and it wasn't just the memory of his dream. He knew the dragon was somewhere, biding her time. It had to have been her. She desired many things, Erik had learned, but he knew one thing she truly desired was his death, and the death of everything he loved. Was his dream a vision of what was to come? Was she infiltrating his dreams and showing him what she meant to do?

He nodded slowly. Surely, that's what it was. But something felt wrong. The giant shadow—could that have been *The Shadow*? What of the two men? The sword—the Dragon Sword Erik suspected. The crown—maybe a symbol of leadership, for the dwarves or the Lord of the East or someone ancient. But what of the stone? It seemed to have no significance, and, yet, it consumed the other two.

Whatever the message, he knew it was time to leave, time for him to go in search of this Dragon Sword. Presuming he discovered its whereabouts, he did not know if he would give it to the Lord of the East as he had promised or if it had some other fate. But he could not make any such decision until he found it.

He rubbed his temples with his index fingers and then pressed the heels of his palms into his eyes, hard, trying to get the images of his dream out of his head. He pressed his hands into his face so hard he saw stars and had to stop. He sucked in a deep breath again and ran a hand through his wet, sweaty hair, pulling the last bit just to make sure he was surely awake.

"Are you alright?" Simone asked, her voice groggy with sleep.

"Yes, my love," Erik replied sweetly.

"Another dream?" Simone asked.

"Yes," Erik replied, "another dream."

Simone sat up, her night shift hanging off one shoulder. She looked at Erik with half-closed eyes and wiped a clump of matted, blonde hair away from her face. She touched his bearded cheek. Her hands were so soft and always smelled like lavender and mint.

"I am so sorry, my sweet," Simone said. "Is there something we can do?"

"I don't think so," Erik replied. "I could drink sweet wine or dream milk, but a wise man—a dwarf—once warned me about doing so."

Erik stared at his wife, making out the outlines of her facial features in the darkness of the room, the only bit of light coming in through a small crack near the window. She was beautiful, even in her sleep. His heart raced again but for a different reason, and, for that brief moment, he forgot about his dream and the mysterious shadow. But when he looked away, they were there again.

"But if it helps you sleep ..." Simone began to say.

"No," Erik said, gently, grabbing one of her hands, pressing her fingers to his lips, and kissing them. "This is my burden. My dreams have a purpose, even if I don't know what they are sometimes. Go back to sleep now; I will be alright."

"Are you sure?" Simone asked.

"I am," Erik said with a smile, touching his wife's cheek with the back of his calloused fingers.

As Simone lay back down, Erik pulled on his trousers and walked out onto his front porch. He looked out over his lands, farmland his father had given him, and to which lands Simone's father, Brok, had added. Erik could have bought three times the land again; he was a wealthy man and had more coin than any other farmer in their farmstead But that meant nothing to Erik; he had fertile lands, and he had a beautiful wife, but he was about to leave it all behind.

He stood and opened the bedroom window and stared at the Gray Mountains again, looming like shadowy giants in the dim moonlight. He knew what he had to do. There was no way around it. But what fate awaited him in those mountains? What horrors, in this world and the dream world, had yet to come?

3

———————

"I cannot lose another child," Erik's mother said, sitting at their kitchen table and staring at the wood with red-rimmed eyes. She couldn't even look at Erik, tears streaming down her face every time she did.

Erik's older brother, Befel, should have been the one to inherit his father's farm. He was the one that would carry on the Eleodum name. He would be the one to replace his father as a pillar of their community, carry on the family traditions, and bear more boys to carry on their name. But Befel was dead.

All of Háthgolthane—if not the whole world—believed dragons were gone, extinct by over a thousand years. Some even questioned whether they ever existed. That all changed when Erik disturbed a hibernating dragon in the lost city of Orvencrest. She awoke from a deep slumber and did as dragons do—breathed fire and wreaked havoc on the world. She killed many, but her first victim was Befel. Her fiery breath consumed him as he stood in front of Erik.

"Mother," Erik said, patting her hand, "I cannot guarantee that I will survive this ordeal."

His mother began crying again.

"I wish I could," Erik added. "But know this, if I do not go, if I do not do this thing that the Lord of the East has commanded me to do, he will not only kill you and Father and Beth and Tia, he will burn the whole of our community to the ground. I wish it weren't so, but it is. He is an evil man, but the Creator is with me, Mother."

"But you don't need to go my son," his mother sobbed. "If he is evil, we will leave ... all of us."

"Where will we go?" Erik asked, wrapping his mother's hands in his.

"Anywhere," she replied, the desperation clear in her voice.

"He will find us," Erik said.

"I just ..." his mother began to say and then buried her face in her hands and began to sob.

Erik reached over and hugged his mother, resting his cheek on her shoulder.

"I don't want to die," Erik said, feeling tears coming to his eyes as well. "And I wish I could stay here. You will never know how much I missed home, but I have to do this."

Erik, his brother, and Bryon had been gone for over two years. Bryon and Befel left because they wanted nothing to do with taking over their fathers' farms. They wanted money and fame and power. Erik wanted none of that but was concerned with encroaching feudal lords from Hámon. He thought that, if they did find wealth, his father could use it to pay off these nobles. Erik had missed his home and his family, the farm and the fruits of his hard work, and his love, Simone. He even thought his family dead as he envisioned them, in his dreams, burned or hanged. And now, he was back ... only to leave again.

When Erik had lost this weapon the Lord of the East sought, a scroll that explained how to control and even destroy a dragon, the ancient beast broke free from her dwarvish prison and unleashed her fury upon the world. She even destroyed part of Fen-Stévock, capitol city of Golgolithul. Even though Erik retrieved the scroll, saved the city from the dragon, and returned the treasure to the Ruler of Golgo-lithul, his future was uncertain.

Through his black magic, the Lord of the East knew Erik had lost his treasure, and for that, Erik's life was in the hands of a ruler most of Háthgolthane, Antolika, and Nothgolthane hated. Now, he had to venture into the Gray Mountains, find a lost sword called the Dragon Sword that was guarded by a mad wizard, and return it to Golgolithul. He had a year to retrieve the sword before the Lord of the East unleashed his punishment, and two moons had already passed.

"The Creator willing, I will be home in less than a year," Erik said, standing.

His mother stood too and wrapped her arms around him. He felt like a child again and could have stayed there forever.

When he walked out of his parents' home, his sisters were there to greet him. The stalwart and feisty Tia was red-faced with hands clenched. As Erik walked past her, she punched him in the stomach and then, immediately after, wrapped her arms around him.

"Don't go, Erik," she said, burying her face into Erik's stomach.

"I knew, somewhere deep down inside, you cared," Erik said with a smile.

"Of course, I do, you horse apple," his youngest sister said, letting go of him, wiping a few tears away, and punching him in the leg.

"Promise you'll come back," Beth said. She composed herself better than she would have just two years ago. She was rapidly matur-ing, becoming a young woman, and did her best to show the poise that her mother would have shown in public. But her red-rimmed eyes told Erik knew she had shed at least a few tears for him.

"I can't promise that," Erik said, "but I can promise I will do my best."

He turned to see his father. The man was as stoic as ever, but when their eyes met, the elder Eleodum smiled, and a single tear leaked from his eye. He extended his hand, and Erik took it.

"You are a good man," his father said. "The Creator asks us to honor duty, even when it hurts. I will pray for you daily ... for your return, my son."

"Father ..." Erik began, but his father held up a hand.

"Say nothing more, Erik," his father said. "I am proud of you. Proud of the man you have become, the leader, the friend, the brother ... and now the husband. You left for your family and returned to us. You will do it again."

Erik hugged his father. Rikard Eleodum wasn't an emotional man, but when he held Erik back, it was the tightest he had ever felt his father squeeze him.

Erik found Simone standing at their own kitchen table when he walked into their new home. She ran to him, throwing her arms around his neck.

"Do not leave," she said.

"You know I have to," Erik replied.

"I can't lose you again," she said.

"And I can't lose you," Erik said. "That's why I have to go."

"You will come back," Simone said.

"I can't promise that," Erik said.

"You must," Simone said. "You must ... for your son."

"My son?" Erik said, stepping back with eyebrows arched in surprise. "Are you ..."

He couldn't finish as tears flooded his eyes and streamed down his face.

"Yes, my love," Simone said with a smile wider than she wore on their wedding day.

Erik's stomach knotted, his heart quickened, and the arteries in his neck thumped against the collar of his shirt. His hands shook and, suddenly, he heard a baby's giggle in his mind, felt tiny hands on his face, smelled the smell of a newborn baby, watched a boy or girl—he didn't care which—take their first steps, say "Papa", and run to him when he finished working on his farm. He couldn't breathe. He couldn't blink. And then he imagined a child growing up without their father and Simone stretched thin like a tab of butter too small for a piece of bread. He imagined never holding his child, never feeling their arms around his neck, or never watching them smile at him. He buried his face in his hands.

Simone's soft, yet strong hands grasped his cheeks firmly, lifting his face so that he might meet her eyes. They were wet and, yet, strong and hopeful. It didn't matter how many fights he had been in, or trolls he had killed, or dragons ... Simone was stronger than him.

"How do you know it's a boy?" Erik finally managed to ask.

"I don't," she replied. "I just figured you would want a son."

"I don't care," Erik said, holding his wife tight. "Boy or girl, I don't care. It will be ours, and it will be healthy."

"So, you see," Simone said, "you have to return."

Erik looked down at her and smiled.

"Promise me," she said. "Promise me you'll return. Promise me you'll come back to your family, to your wife and child."

"Simone, listen to me," Erik said, but Simone grasped his face in her hands again.

"No, you listen to me," she said through her tears, "you must come back. Promise me."

"Please, listen to me," Erik said, looking away for a moment and then grabbing her wrists and lowering her hands.

She didn't say anything. She just watched Erik.

"The money from Orvencrest is in the chest under our bed," Erik said. "It is everything—gold, silver, gems, jewels."

"Why are you telling me this?"

"It is enough to buy a thousand farms," Erik continued. "If I do not return ..."

"No," Simone said, looking away and crossing her arms across her chest.

"Listen to me, Simone," Erik said, gently gripping her chin and forcing her to look at him. "If I do not return, you are to take that money, take my family and Bryon's, and head to Waterton. It is a small town situated on the Blue River. You will find a man there named Del Alzon. Tell him you are my wife. Tell him they are my family. Show him the gold. He will take care of you. He will make sure you are safe."

"It doesn't matter," Simone said, "because you will come back to me."

"Simone, did you hear me?" Erik said, his tone stern. "Simone?"

"Yes," she replied, nodding, weeping, and falling into Erik. "Promise me you'll come back. Please. Promise me."

He didn't want to make a promise he couldn't keep, but those eyes, the smell of lavender and mint, her soft skin, her tears.

"I promise," Erik finally said, as his stomach knotted even tighter.

Bryon Eleodum, Erik's cousin, and Erik loaded supplies onto their horses. Erik's father had offered them several of his packhorses so that they might carry more, but Erik declined. They were heading into the Gray Mountains, and there would come a time when they would have to let their animals go. They packed bows and spears so they could hunt and extra water skins, as snow would be plentiful the higher they climbed into the mountains, especially with winter on the horizon. Erik frowned as he stuffed bag after bag of dried fruit and meat into the saddlebags. That had been his main source of subsistence for almost two years, after having left his family the first time and traveling with mercenaries and dwarves, and having real food for every meal of every day had spoiled him. Now he would have to get used to jerked meat and dehydrated fruit all over again.

Erik stared at the mountains, looking intently at the two peaks that disappeared into the clouds. The Fangs. He heard the dwarves refer to them as Hora Tesak and his father once, when Erik was young, referred to them as the Voiceless Spires, for all the people who had attempted to travel through them and never come home. Nevertheless, as they rose into the sky, scratching the underbellies of clouds, they looked imposing, even though he really knew nothing about them. He had a general idea about where they were going. The instructions the

Lord of the East had given him spoke of the Fangs, traveling north of them and then east. He knew they were looking for an ancient keep named Fealmynster and the instructions mentioned Eldmanor, a small town north of the Eleodum farmstead, standing at the foot of the Gray Mountains. But none of that helped him know what to expect.

"Are you ready, cousin?" Bryon Eleodum asked as he finished loading the supplies onto his horse.

"No," Erik said with a simple shake of his head.

"I suppose I'm not either," Bryon replied.

"Where are the dwarves?" Erik asked.

Four dwarves had been staying with them and their families. They were more than just companions and adventuring partners. They were friends. Brothers even. Their own brethren had died for Erik and Bryon. Demik Iron Thorn came to Erik's mind. He was a ferocious fighter, stubborn dwarf, and a good friend. He had always been suspicious of men, according to the other dwarves with whom Erik had traveled, but Erik had broken down barriers and gave Demik cause to trust, so much so that he taught him Dwarvish and eventually gave his life for Erik.

These dwarves had traveled with Erik and Bryon to the lost dwarvish city of Orvencrest. Despite the Lord of the East being a sworn enemy of the dwarves, they had helped Erik and Bryon recover a powerful weapon for the Ruler of Golgolithul. They bled with them and cried with them and defeated trolls and wolves and a dragon with them. Despite an offer from King Skella, the King of Drüum Balmdüukr—the dwarvish kingdom of the Southern Mountains—to protect them from the Lord of the East and his assassins, the loyalty of these dwarves—Turk, Nafer, Beldar, and Bofim—to Erik and Bryon was so strong, they refused. They denied their own people to walk alongside these men and continue a task commanded by the Emperor of the East.

"I don't know," Bryon replied. "They seem to wander off quite a bit. They are rather taken by our farmlands, you know."

"It makes a difference," Erik said.

"What does?" Bryon asked.

"Being able to grow your crops in the sun," Erik replied.

Dwarves built their vast cities underground, in great mountain caverns. One of the greatest dwarvish innovations, and one of the inventions Erik found the most fascinating, were giant mirrors strategically placed throughout tunnels and caverns to reflect the sun's light onto a dwarvish city, mimicking the sun. It allowed them to grow crops and livestock as if they were on the surface, almost.

"Being from the south, I don't know if they have ever seen soil this fertile," Erik said.

"Are we truly leaving without Wrothgard?" Bryon asked for perhaps the fourth time in as many days while their final planning and preparations had taken place.

"He's not coming, Bryon," Erik replied, showing no sign of any irritation about his cousin's persistence. "He's probably not even in Háthgolthane anymore."

"Smart man," Bryon muttered.

"Perhaps," Erik said.

Erik stared at his parents' home. His mother stood on the front porch, his sisters—Tia and Beth—clinging to her. Tears streamed down her face. She spoke with his wife, Simone, who held his mother by her elbows and, even though he couldn't hear her, knew she tried to comfort her. His father was in front of their barn, tending to some of the animals. He had gone about his daily business as if nothing was happening, but when Erik greeted him that morning, his father had red-rimmed eyes. He had been crying.

"We have to go, Erik," Bryon said. "The longer we wait, the harder it will get."

"I know," Erik replied, but he didn't move.

"Erik," Bryon said.

Erik nodded.

"Very well."

"Or do you want to run away?" Bryon asked and his voice was serious. "We could go live in Thorakest, with the dwarves."

Erik shook his head, although he had thought of the alternative multiple times.

"No. We have to do this. For them, for our families."

4

———

Erik didn't look back. He knew his wife, parents, and sisters were there, behind him, watching and waving, but looking back at them would only make his departure harder. His Uncle Brent was there too, along with his aunt and cousins, all waving and bidding farewell to Bryon. Other people came to see them off, some gathering in front of the Eleodum household and some just gathering along the road leading out of the free farmlands of Northwestern Háthgolthane and to the north. As stoic as Erik tried to seem, he couldn't help but smile and wave at a few of the people cheering for them, throwing white flowers in their path.

"You would think we were heroes," Erik said.

"We are," Turk Skull Crusher replied, "at least, you are."

"No, I'm not," Erik said.

"Did you save thousands of people in Golgolithul?" Turk asked.

"Yes," Erik said.

"And did you return home with more money than the whole of these lands has seen in two hundred years?" Turk asked.

"Yes," Erik replied.

"And did you give much of your money away," Turk asked, "to

other farmers who were struggling? Even to Farmer Jovek, who I heard you complain about more times than I can count on our travels."

"Yes," Erik said with a quick shrug of his shoulders.

"Then, you are a hero," Turk said, and when Erik began shaking his head, he added, "at least, in their eyes."

The recent weather had been fairly temperate—warm during the day and cool at night—but as soon as they passed the last farm and a final grove of trees at the edge of the fields, the air carried with it an uncommon chill. It was as if the farms held in all the land's warmth, and there was none to share in the north. It was windier, and the looming Gray Mountains cast longer shadows. The first night was cold enough for a thin layer of frost to form on the grass, and Bryon built a suitably sized campfire, but despite the flames, the air still had an uncomfortable chilly bite to it.

"Your people are kind," Nafer said.

On their previous travels, Erik had soon taken the time to learn the Dwarvish language. Bryon, in his stubbornness, refused, but after suffering an injury—a poisonous wound from a dragonling in Orvencrest—he found himself living amongst the dwarves for a time and was forced to also learn their language. So, now, when they were just around one another, they normally spoke in Dwarvish.

"Normally," Erik replied.

"At least they don't harbor any ill will against dwarves," Beldar said.

"No," Erik agreed. "Dwarves are not so uncommon in our lands, although those of you I met in Finlo were the first I ever spoke to."

"That would include Demik," Nafer said, sadness in his eyes as he spoke the name of one of their fallen friends, Demik Iron Thorn.

Nafer touched the handle of a thick broad sword hanging from his hip, the scabbard covered in ornately worked iron, formed to look like thorny vines scrawling up the leather. It was his friend's sword, once. The dwarf had given his life for Erik. A lump caught in Erik's throat as he thought of the dwarvish warrior, stubborn and cantankerous and kind all at once. He didn't trust men and would watch all the ones they traveled with suspiciously, but he eventually warmed to Erik and Bryon and Befel. And when he recognized they were friends, his true nature showed, a warmed-hearted, kind soul, willing to give his life for a brother in arms, taken by the forked spear of a froksman—a frog-like humanoid.

Nafer later explained this froksman originated from the Shadow Marshes, driven from their lands by both goblins and Golgolithul. Erik hated himself for delighting in the froksman's later death, consumed by dragon fire. He was, after all, following orders just as they were, trying to retrieve the Dragon Scroll they meant to give to the Lord of the East and bring it to Gol-Durathna. To what end, Erik didn't know, but perhaps to simply keep such a weapon out of the hands of the Ruler of Golgolithul.

"A toast," Erik said, and he lifted a cup of water, "to Demik. I know we don't have wine or ale to give a proper salute, but we miss our friend dearly."

"Yes," Nafer said, "a toast to our fallen comrade. May he wait for us and save us a seat in the halls of heaven as he basks in the glory of An."

They drank, and then they sang, Erik joining in by playing his simple wooden flute, a gift from an old gypsy friend, and the instrument always seemed to give him comfort whenever he needed it. As they played and sang, the bitterness of the cold night faded away and the warmth of the campfire spread. It felt like old times ... good times.

When Erik first left his farmstead with his brother and cousin, everything was different and frightening. Most days, thoughts of home consumed his mind and visions of dead parents and imprisoned sisters plagued his dreams, but there were nights, in the company of mercenaries and dwarves, when Erik felt normal, as if he was sitting at his mother's kitchen table drinking hot tea or fresh-squeezed orange juice. For all the fighting and death and fear and anger and sadness that filled a two year journey from a farm, to a dirty, seaport bar, to a dwarvish city, to the east, and back to the farm, those nights around a campfire, singing and playing the flute and drinking apple rum were good.

Now back on the road, they traveled for three days past the free farmlands of Háthgolthane, each night much the same, singing and playing and remembering before they came to the small town that sat at the foot of the Gray Mountains. They might encounter other outposts and small villages along the way, clusters of homes built and settled by people shying away from the business of cities, but Eldmanor would most likely be the last sign of real civilization before they reached the Keep of Fealmynster. The fabled resting place of the Dragon Sword, and the residence of an old and mad wizard, long ago banished from Gol-Durathna for practicing his dark magic on people, was said to be far away from any other habitation.

Eldmanor was a simple town with little more than a wooden fence for a wall. The streets were dirt, and the homes and buildings were mostly made of timber and turf. A manor house stood off to the east of most of the town, a two-story structure made of stone and surrounded by a stone wall, and a chapel to some local deity stood off to the west, also made of stone and surrounded by a complex of wooden and stone buildings. A tall mill stood next to a small stream running through the town, and several long houses sat towards the center marketplace.

"This place reminds me of Stone's Throw," Bryon said.

Erik remembered the little village in which they stayed. It was a place of escape for many of the people who survived a troll attack on the mining camp of Aga Kona, full of superstitious, simple people. Erik and the others had helped the sick and injured while they were there, where he had met a woman, Mari, and her son, Willy. Remembering them put a smile on his face.

I hope you are well, little Willy.

"Yes, I suppose it does," Erik replied, "maybe a larger version of it. I wonder if this is what it would look like if we returned to Stone's Throw ten years from now."

Also as with the town of Waterton, which sat in the center of the

Abresi Straits just as Háthgolthane gave way to the wilds of the west and the continent of Nothgolthane, the people of Eldmanor were used to adventurers and travelers, including dwarves, and didn't even bother to glance at Erik and his companions as they rode down what they presumed to be the main street of the town. An alehouse, a home that had been converted to an inn and tavern, stood between two long houses. Erik looked to Turk, and the dwarf nodded.

The instructions the Lord of the East had given them said they would go to Eldmanor. There was someone in this place who would help direct them to the key that would then lead them to the hidden keep of Fealmynster; supposedly, they would know this messenger when they saw him. But that was it apart from a piece of parchment that appeared to show Fealmynster being north of the Gray Mountains, in a plain of frozen tundra.

The dwarves were much more travel-worn and battle hardy than Erik, but in his short time as an adventurer, he had come to learn that alehouses, taverns, and inns were excellent places to discover mysteries and find out much-coveted information. They tied their horses to a hitching post in front of the building, which looked as if, in a good wind, it might fall down. The smell of animals hit Erik's nose as soon as they opened the door, and when they looked around, they saw the alehouse shared space with a small stable, two mules eating lazily from buckets hanging from a wooden fence that separated the animals' space from the eating and sitting area.

"How can anyone eat or drink when all you can smell is chicken manure," Bryon said, covering his nose and groaning.

Chickens ran about between the legs of the two mules, pecking at the floor and chasing after one another, squawking loudly and a rooster—a large breasted fellow with almost black feathers save for a brown spot on his chest and a large, red topnotch on his head—found a perch atop one of the stable's fence posts, eyeing Erik and his companions warily. The familiar sounds of pigs oinking filled the air as well, bringing Erik back to a time when his job was to clean pigsties in Venton. Four sows and a hog lounged about in hay that covered the floor, three piglets playing and bugging the adults until the hog grunted and snapped at them, causing them to retreat to a corner of the stable until they regained the courage to harass their elders once again.

Despite sharing space with animals, the sitting area was quite large, with long tables and benches for seats. Only two other people sat on the benches. Two men, looking like typical villagers who may have stopped in for a quick bite to eat or decided to get a drink at the end of a hard and early workday, talked loudly and joked, slapping the table at an especially funny jape. A fireplace sat in the wall opposite the stables, two chairs in front of it, one occupied by another man haphazardly plunking notes on a lyre. The minstrel wore a feathered burette and a red blouse with billowing sleeves. His bright blue tights clung to well-muscled legs, leading into soft, ankle-high calfskin boots, curled at the toes. He started by playing a jig with which Erik was familiar, although he didn't even know if the tune had a name, but then he stopped, trying his fingers at another song, seemingly struggling to find the right notes.

A barrel with a spout sat on a table next to the musician, and a short bar stood on the other side of the barrel. Two more men stood in front of the bar, talking quietly and drinking from large mugs. One of them had a large, black, bushy beard that spread out like a broom that had been used for too long. The hair crawled up his cheeks almost to his eyes. The robe he wore hung from his large belly that poked out obtrusively like a pregnant woman, and his eyes were small and piggy.

The other man wore a heavier, cloth hauberk studded with iron discs and a conical helm. His face showed a lean figure, and as he spoke with the bushy-bearded man, he rested a hand on the pommel of a long sword. The swordsman drained the contents of his cup, went to the barrel, and filled it back up with whatever drink the wooden cask contained.

"Do you think he's a guard of some sort?" Erik asked.

"Do you know of any dung heaps like this that need guards?" Bryon asked.

"A militiaman, perhaps," Turk offered, "stopping in to get his drink."

Erik nodded and shrugged.

"Sit wherever you like," a younger woman said, passing by Erik. She carried a plate with bread in one hand and a pitcher in the other.

Her blue dress was dirty and stray strands of her red hair stuck out all around her face, otherwise contained within a bun, loosely pulled at the top of her head. She was tall and broad-shouldered and, when she went to deliver the plate and pitcher to the two men sitting at the bench, rather than taking their order, they ignored her and continued to talk. She practically slammed the plate and pitcher on the table and rushed back to a door, presumably the kitchen.

"I don't normally prefer fiery-haired women," Bryon said with a smile, "but her spirit matches her hair. She might be fun."

"Bryon," Erik hissed, "compose yourself. Remember why we're here."

"Of course, fearless leader," Bryon replied, and, even though there was a hint of mirth in his cousin's voice, Erik was still irritated by his cousin.

"Either sit or leave," she said, walking past Erik when she quickly reappeared again. "Don't just stand there."

"Will you sit with me if I sit down?" Bryon asked, trying his best to flash a boyish smile in her direction.

The serving woman simply rolled her eyes and began to turn and walk away, but Erik cleared his throat, elbowing his cousin in the ribs at the same time.

"How much for the ale in the barrel?" Erik asked.

"Do you need cups?" the woman asked, turning back around, her serving tray rested on her hip.

She looked at each one of them, squinted eyes and pursed lips stopping at Bryon. Erik could see, through a sidelong glance, that his cousin was still smiling, and then gave the girl a wink. She tried not to, but as she continued to glare at Erik's cousin, the slightest of smirks touched the corners of her mouth.

"No," Erik replied and then wondered how his cousin did it.

"A penny a piece," she replied.

"A penny?" Bryon asked, almost exasperated. "Surely, a penny is not nearly enough for something as fine as you ... I mean, your ale."

The slight smirk on her mouth disappeared, her faced turned bright red, and the serving girl turned and walked away with heavy feet.

"Bryon," Turk said, shaking his head. "You bring too much attention to yourself."

"Not you too," Bryon said. "I can handle my cousin's derision, but you as well? It's been so long since I've been with a woman."

"And it will be even longer," Erik said, throwing six pennies on the table and grabbing his companions' wooden cups. "I'll fill them up for you."

"Be careful of that minstrel," Turk said as Erik took his cup.

Erik gave the dwarf a confused look with a cocked eyebrow.

"I've been listening to him," the dwarf said. "He struggles to play the simplest of tunes. And when was the last time you saw a minstrel as muscled as he?"

"A good question," Erik replied, now as alert as his dwarvish friend, realizing and agreeing with Turk's observations.

"He is in fine clothing, with a well-crafted instrument, in essentially what is a border town, and he can't play that well. Just keep an eye on him."

"That's why I have you," Erik said with a half-smile, but Turk didn't respond.

Erik filled the cups with the liquid from the barrel, presumably ale. It looked dark and frothy, but when Erik sniffed at it, smelled old. He supposed that's what they would get for a penny a piece and unlimited refills. As he filled the cups, Erik could feel eyes watching him intently. He looked to the swordsman and the fat man talking and drinking. They seemed consumed with their conversation. He then looked to the minstrel. He only paid attention to his lyre, trying to, quite unsuccessfully, plunk through a new song.

He set the cups in front of his companions.

"Keep an eye on mine, Bryon," Erik said with a smile. "You never know how thirsty Nafer is."

The dwarf laughed while Erik approached the two men speaking in front of the bar. As Erik approached them, the fat man squinted, and his eyes seemed almost invisible under his bushy eyebrows, causing him to wonder how the man could even see. The other man, the swordsman, didn't bother to look at Erik, but he caught the armed man looking at him through sidelong glances.

"Can I help you?" the bushy-bearded man asked before Erik could say anything.

"Perhaps," Erik said.

"Well," the man said, huffing hard enough that the black hairs of his mustache fluttered.

"We're getting ready to travel into the Gray Mountains," Erik replied.

The fat, bushy-bearded man shrugged.

"I am from the free farmlands south of here but am unfamiliar with the Gray Mountains. This is as close as I have ever been."

"Congratulations," the rotund man said, rolling his eyes.

"Is there a road that will lead us north of the Fangs?" Erik asked. The tall peaks that rose up like sharp teeth from the Gray Mountains were so large they could be seen from leagues away even though they stood towards the northern borders of the mountain range.

"Why would you want to travel north of the Fangs?" the bushy-bearded man asked.

The armed man turned towards Erik and glared at him, his hand sliding from the pommel to the handle. The hairs on the back of Erik's neck stiffened, and he felt the gooseflesh along his arms rise. He didn't mirror the armed man and left his thumbs tucked inside his belt. He didn't know this man, or how adept he was at the blade, but

Erik knew his own hands were quick—quicker than most—so he pretended not to notice the show of force.

"We are traveling with dwarves," Erik said.

"Don't they know the way?" the fat man asked.

"They're southern dwarves," Erik replied.

"Why are they traveling in the north, then?" the man asked.

"To see distant cousins," Erik replied.

"Most northern dwarves don't live that far north," the fat man said, cocking an eyebrow and tilting his head to one side.

"What's it matter?" Erik asked.

"We get a lot of adventurers coming through here," the armed man said. "Most of them are traveling through the Pass of Dundolyothum or into the Gray Mountains, even seeking the dwarves, but no one ever wants to travel that far north."

Erik looked over his shoulder, to his companions. They pretended to drink their stale ale, but he saw Turk's eyes, and Bryon's, staring at him, over the lip of their cups. Then he looked to the two other men sitting, eating and drinking. They paid no attention to him or the two men standing at the bar. He watched the musician, plunking out of tune notes. There was something about this fat man and the armed man in front of him. They were searching for something, a clue or a key word.

"I wish to get lost in the mountains," Erik said. "My wife left me, and I lost my home to Hámonian nobles. I don't give a shite about this life anymore, and I just want to die. I figured what better way to go than search the wilds of the Gray Mountains."

"I think you're lying," the armed man said.

Erik looked at him, squinted as his glare bore into the man. He heard the dissonant music behind him. It faltered for a moment and then stopped. He could hear Turk's warning in the back of his head.

"I am," Erik replied. "I am supposed to meet a man who can lead me to the hidden keep of Fealmynster."

The fat man groaned, and the armed man reached across to the handle of his blade with his sword hand. Erik heard the slightest of noises to his left. He felt the air around him move, and he jerked his head back just as a knife passed in front of his face and thudded into the wall. Drawing Ilken's Blade, he turned to face the musician who no longer held his lyre, but two short swords. He attacked Erik.

Erik grabbed the front of the fat man's robes and pulled him into his attacker's path and pushed the other armed man away, just in case he tried to attack as well. Benches and tables flipped as his companions ran to his aide, and the serving woman screamed and ran back into the kitchen from where she had just emerged.

The musician was an adept fighter, moving with precision and speed as he jabbed his short swords at Erik. Erik found himself taking several steps backward, but only for a moment. He blocked one attack with Ilken's Blade and then swung out with his left fist, catching the man on the jaw before he knocked the other blade from the man's hand with his own sword. Erik's would-be attacker stumbled backward into the barrel and knocked it over where it broke, and the beer spilled across the floor. One of the pigs started lapping it up.

Erik saw Bofim and Beldar run to the two men sitting eating and drinking. They didn't look like they wanted to join the fight, but just in case, the dwarves grabbed the men's collars and pushed their faces to the table. Turk and Nafer rushed to the kitchen door, making sure no one, not even the serving woman, emerged, ensuring there wouldn't be some sneak attack. Meanwhile, Bryon drew his magical elvish blade and rushed to Erik's aid.

The musical assassin picked up his lost short sword and crouched, eyeing Erik as he steeled himself, Erik gripping Ilken's Blade with both hands. The attacker slashed left then right with his blades, Erik jumping backward both times, the last time right into the swordsman from the bar who hadn't gathered the courage to draw his blade yet. Erik elbowed the man backward and heard him fall, emitting a deep groan. As Bryon came upon the minstrel, he turned, throwing one of his short swords at Erik's cousin. The blade flew, end over end, but Bryon easily dodged the attack, the would-be assassin drawing a knife at the same time and turning back towards Erik.

Erik blocked one attack and then slashed the attacker's wrist, causing him to drop his knife. He then brought Ilken's Blade across the man's thigh. He faltered, just for a moment, but it was enough. With another angled strike, Erik brought his steel down on the musician, cleaving a deep mortal wound from shoulder to hip.

Before the first would-be assassin hit the ground, Erik turned, the tip of Ilken's Blade touching the skin of the armed man's throat.

"Unless you want to end up like your friend," Erik said, glaring at the armed man, whose eyes were wide and sweat pouring down his brow, "don't move."

"He's not our friend," the fat man said.

He had fallen when Erik pushed him into the musician and had just climbed back to his feet, breathing heavily.

"Who was he?" Erik asked as his companion came to his side, Beldar and Bofim escorting the other men out of the alehouse.

"I don't know," the armed man replied, throwing up his hands in submission and almost crying as he spoke.

"An assassin," the fat man said.

"Is that so?" Erik asked.

The fat man nodded.

"He showed up a week ago," he explained. "He said two men and two dwarves would come looking for a road to the cursed city of Fealmynster. He paid me in Durathnan gold to let him stay here. He either sat there and played the lyre or stayed in his room. That's it. A few days ago, two other men showed up. They also said they were looking for two men and two dwarves, but as soon as they had paid for a room and sat down to drink some ale and eat some stew, that fellow there," the fat man said pointing to the dead minstrel, "slit their throats and had me bury their bodies out back. When I was done, all he asked of us was to get rid of your bodies as well when he had killed you. Please don't hurt us. You can have the gold."

"I don't want your gold," Erik said. "Draw your sword and place it on the floor."

The armed man complied. Erik lowered his blade. The dwarves

surrounded the fat man and his companion. Erik looked to the kitchen, seeing the red-headed serving woman peering out, red-eyed.

"You have nothing to fear," Erik said. "We will not hurt you, or these men, as long as they behave."

Erik looked at the helmed man.

"Are you going to behave?"

"Yes, sir," the man replied.

"You see," Erik said to the woman. "Come now, clean up this mess, and we will forget this ever happened."

The woman slowly emerged from the kitchen and went to standing toppled tables and chairs back on their feet. Her hands shook while she cleaned up, and Bryon went to help her. Erik could hear him whispering to her while he helped, causing a gasp and then a giggle. He rolled his eyes at his cousin.

"We were supposed to meet a man who could lead us into the Gray Mountains," Erik said again. "I need you to show me where you buried the other bodies."

"You think this assassin killed the Lord of the East's man, or men," Nafer asked in Dwarvish, "the one that was supposed to lead us?"

"I do," Erik replied.

The fat man led them out a door in the back of the alehouse, all but Bryon, who continued to help the serving woman clean. Behind the alehouse, the man pointed to a small mound covered with hay. Erik nodded to the dwarves, and they all, even the fat man, began digging.

The graves were shallow and, even though there were signs of decay on the two men's faces, it was cold enough that they were still mostly intact. They had the look of easterners with short-cropped, straight black hair and soft jaws. They both wore breast-plates under their clothing, bearing the emblem of a gauntlet clenching an arrow.

"The Lord of the East," Erik said.

"Aye," Turk replied.

"These are the men we were supposed to meet then," Bofim added.

"I think so," Turk replied.

"Damn," Erik said, kicking a bit of dirt back onto the dead bodies. "Now what?"

"All we have are half-finished directions," Nafer said. He pointed to the bodies. "They were supposed to know the way."

Erik looked back at the fat man who, clearly nervous and shivering, both from the cold and his nerves, just stared at the dead bodies.

"Is there a man in Eldmanor who would know of a road that leads past the Fangs? Is there a man in this town who would know the legend of Fealmynster?"

"I don't know, sir," the fat man replied. "As the gods of the north are my witness, I have no idea. I barely leave Eldmanor. I run my bar with Edgar and his sister. We barely make ends meet. When a man comes and gives me ten times what we would make in a year ..."

"You don't need to explain yourself to me," Erik said. "There is no one else in Eldmanor or nearby, other than these dead men, that would know how to get to Fealmynster? Someone old who might have been a child when men still traveled that far north?"

"I know of such a man," the serving girl said. She was standing at the back door, Bryon just behind her.

"Hush, Emma," the fat man said.

"No, you hush," Bryon said, pointing an accusatory finger at the fat man. "Speak, Emma. Tell them what you told me."

"There's a hut, north of Eldmanor," the girl said.

"There're a lot of huts around Eldmanor," Turk said.

"Not like this one," she replied. "You'll recognize it. The old man that lives there raises goats. And it sits north of all the other homes. He's old ... older than my great grandmother who passed when I was just a girl."

"Maybe that is the person you need," the fat man said before he led them back inside, where the tables and benches had been set upright and most of the spilled ale had been mopped up.

"You say this man was from Gol-Durathna?" Erik asked, standing over the dead minstrel.

"I don't know," the swordsman, Edgar, replied. "He paid with Durathnan coin. That's all I know."

"You will dispose of the body," Erik said. He retrieved a small sack from his belt and handed it to the fat man. It wasn't heavy, but it had enough coin in it to make any man happy. "What is your name?"

"Hagmer," the fat man replied.

"If any more Durathnans come, Hagmer, we were never here. Do you understand?"

Hagmer nodded, eyes wide as he stared inside the sack.

"And if any more Golgolithulians come, we were never here," Erik said.

Hagmer nodded again.

"I will know if you betray me," Erik said.

After a simple meal, but probably the last served to them for a while, they led their horses through the northern part of the town, past the wooden fence that surrounded Eldmanor, and through a small cluster of huts.

"How will you know if he betrays you?" Bryon asked.

"I won't," Erik replied.

"Then why say you would?" his cousin asked.

"He's a simple man who has converted his home into an alehouse," Erik explained. "He is scared enough to believe anything I say."

They walked a little further.

"Was that assassin sent after us?" Beldar asked. "The fat man said two men and two dwarves."

"That's all that held audience with the Lord of the East," Erik replied. "Turk, Nafer, Wrothgard, and me. You two were in hiding, and Bryon was in Thorakest."

"If Gol-Durathna had spies in the Lord of the East's court," Turk said, "which I suspect they do, they would have reported seeing two men and two dwarves."

"And this wouldn't be the first assassin Gol-Durathna has sent after us," Erik said. "Right Nafer?"

"Aye," Nafer said, "although, I don't believe that man and froksman who stole the scroll were assassins."

"Three years ago, I never would have thought Gol-Durathna was capable of such a thing," Erik said. "Amentus is the golden city, after all."

He remembered a tale that an old friend, dead and gone—a gypsy named Marcus—once told, of his time imprisoned in the dungeons of Amentus, the Golden City and Capitol of Gol-Durathna. It was a tale of murder and rape and all sorts of horrible things, and the first time Erik realized that even supposedly noble and righteous countries have dark underbellies.

"While their goal is, I'm sure, to stop the Dragon Sword from reaching the Lord of the East, you have to remember it is ruled by men," Nafer said. "It is capable of anything. We will need to travel with caution. Who knows which rulers know of our mission?"

"Durathnan assassins are concerning," Turk said, "but what is more worrying is the men who were supposed to lead us to the key of the Keep of Fealmynster being assassinated. Surely, the Lord of the East and the Black Mage will know of this? Will they see it as failure?"

Erik just shook his head, mounted his horse, and led the way further north.

5

———————

In only a short matter of time, they came to a solitary hut sitting as far north as any structure could sit before being built onto the side of the mountains. Smoke rose from a hole at the center of the hut's roof, while goats, sheep, chickens, and pigs roamed about the outside of the hut freely.

"He's not worried about wolves or bears?" Bryon asked.

The entrance to the hut was dark, small rabbit and chicken bones scattered about.

"I'll stay with the horses," Beldar said, as there was no place to tie them.

Erik nodded, and as they handed Beldar their reins and stepped towards the dark entrance of the hut, a voice cut into the darkness.

"Only Erik, Friend of Dwarves, may enter."

Erik looked to his companions as gooseflesh rose along his arms. The voice sounded like it was in his head.

"Did you hear that?"

Bryon nodded and said, "That's not a good idea."

"I agree," Turk added.

Laughter came from the hut.

"You are scared of an old man," the voice said. "Hagmer may have a need to fear me, but you do not, Erik Troll Hammer."

Erik looked to his companions one more time.

"Wait here," he said and then moved inside.

The hut was small, and the scent of burning cedar and rain leaf and other herbs filled the air as a thin layer of smoke hung just above Erik's head, slowly escaping the hole cut in the top of the ceiling. A fire blazed in the middle of the hut, two crossbars and a spit holding a thick cauldron of black iron. The fire flickered, and its shadows danced on the thatched walls of the dwelling. The only furniture in the hut was a small, three-legged table standing against the far wall. Several wooden bowls sat on the table along with a wooden spoon and a dull, rusted knife stuck into half a loaf of bread that had started to mold.

A man sat on the ground next to the fire. He wore a heavy, dark wool robe that spilled off his thin and frail shoulders. Tatters and tears riddled the edges of the wool robe, and several holes dotted the fabric. A hood hung low on the man's head, so Erik could not see his face, but he could see the thin, scraggly strands of a white beard, frizzy and frayed like the ends of a cut rope. Two, frail hands, thin and liver-spotted with pronounced knuckles, poked out the robe's sleeves and held another wooden bowl, stained and warped. The hands lifted the bowl to the hood and Erik heard the slurping sounds and smacking lips of satisfaction. They then set the bowl on the ground.

"Come in Erik," a small, shaky voice—an old man's voice—croaked with a hint of glee, "Dragon Slayer."

"How did you know my name?"

Erik took a step back

"The wind," the old man replied, "words on the wind, Wolf's Bane. The wind speaks."

"The fat man, Hagmer, from the alehouse," Erik said more to himself than to the old man.

"Tsk, tsk," the old man clicked. "I thought Erik Friend of Dwarves would have more faith than that. Hagmer will not step within a hundred paces of my house. He fears me, as he fears you. You are a forgiving man, are you not, sparing the life of one who harbors your possible assassin?"

"I don't know," Erik replied.

"I told you," the old man said, "you have no reason to fear me."

"I am not afraid," Erik said sternly, taking a few steps forward, farther into the light of the hut's fire.

"Just as I thought," the man said aloud, but not to Erik, "bold, not wanting to show fear, not wanting to show weakness. The Friend of Gypsies wants to prove to me he is not afraid, but who am I? Just an old man."

As he said his last words, he squealed with a sort of malevolent glee, as if he understood something, some hidden joke that Erik could not have known.

"I said I am not afraid," Erik reiterated, his voice getting louder, agitated.

"But you are," the old man croaked with a sneer. "It is not myself I refer to; trouble surrounds you. Misery follows you. You fear what you do not know. You fear what might happen to your friends. You fear never seeing your mother and father again ... your sisters ... your baby. You fear what they think of you. Have they truly forgiven you for Befel's death? Such torment. You blame yourself for your brother's death, don't you Dream Walker?"

Erik swallowed, but his throat was dry. He felt a small tremble in his hands and rubbed them together to get rid of it. He stepped forward, dropping to one knee on the other side of the fire to the robed man, his face sweaty and his palms clammy.

"How do you know these things?" he asked, his voice cracking slightly.

The old man lifted his head towards Erik, showing a face riddled with wrinkles and tiny, white scars ages old. He stared at Erik from two sunken sockets with blank, milky white eyes, void of pupils. He smiled a wretched, yellow-toothed smile.

"I only know what the wind tells me," the man said with a hiss. "I only know what dreams tell me. What do your dreams tell you?"

Erik did not reply. His hand trembled stronger as he remembered the dream in which the dragon consumed him with fire. Before that, he saw two cloaked figures, and now he couldn't help but think that this blind, old man, was the one who appeared behind him.

"The world of dreams can reveal much, yes?" the old man questioned and then waited for Erik's response, but it never came. Erik remained silent, staring at the fire, trying to still his racing heart.

"Now then," the man cackled, almost laughing at Erik's fear. "*My* dreams tell me you seek something powerful, but for a man you hate. A powerful weapon, but this boy does not know, does he? He does not understand what it is he carries with him already. He does not know what it will eventually lead him to."

"Know what?" Erik finally asked. "What do I carry with me? Lead me where?"

The old man laughed.

"It is powerful, this weapon you seek," the old man said, "and the man who protects it is also powerful ... very powerful. As powerful as the Black Mage, the Dragon Slayer wonders? Perhaps. Perhaps not. And for what? Why do you seek this weapon? To save your family? To save your friends? You cannot save them."

"I can and I will," Erik replied. "I will save them by any means necessary."

"How do you save a man, or dwarf, who has free will?" the old man said. "Foolish boy. He does not know, does he?"

"Who are you speaking to?" Erik asked.

"The wind," the old man said.

"I am done speaking in riddles," Erik said, standing up again. "You know why I'm here. I seek the key to Fealmynster. The man who was supposed to lead me there is dead. Do you know where it is? Do you know the way?"

The man hissed like a snaked and then laughed.

"Foolish boy," he said, slowly pushing himself to his feet and whispering in a language Erik had never heard. When he stood, he revealed a crooked, broken man, bent over and hunchbacked. As the man slowly trudged around the fire towards Erik, he stepped back and winced almost, as if the man smelled.

The cloaked man lifted a shaky arm, pointing a single finger at Erik.

"The one you serve is mistaken," the old man said. "There is no need to search for a key."

"The Lord of the East lied," said Erik, his question rhetorical.

"He is a liar, yes," the man said, "but he did not lie to you. He does not know. You see, you already have the key."

"I don't understand," Erik replied.

"Of course, you don't," the old man said. "The key is not to find Fealmynster. No, the key is to reveal the weapon. And then the weapon is a key."

Erik shook his head. Too many riddles.

"Do you know the way to Fealmynster then?" Erik asked. "The map the Lord of the East gave us is incomplete. Worthless without the men who were supposed to lead us there."

He retrieved a folded piece of parchment from his belt, holding it out, as if the man, clearly blind, could see it. The parchment caught fire in a bright flash. Erik yelped as he let go of the parchment, floating to the ground, little more than ash.

"Worthless indeed. Fealmynster, the cursed city, home of Sustenon the Damned, Sustenon the Warlock, Sustenon the Necromancer. Beware, Dream Walker. He is a dream walker too."

The old man chuckled, and he looked less evil, now a simple, crooked, blind man. He stared past Erik.

"You have loyal friends," the man said. "They would follow you to the ends of the world if you asked them."

Erik continued to just stare at the old man. The man chuckled again.

"This journey you choose to take," the old man said, "will cause your friends great pain and anguish. They will follow you, and their loyalty will be the death of many of them. They will be glorious deaths, but deaths nonetheless."

"They are all adept warriors," Erik said.

"I know," the old man said, "but they will die to save you."

Erik just stood there, and the old man groaned as if he had grown bored.

"The road into the mountains will eventually fork," the old man said, "at the tree made of stone, dead, yet, still alive. That is called the Forlorn Pass. You will follow the Pass through the Fangs. As the Fangs disappear in the mist, look for the serpent and let it swallow you. Enter the serpent's belly and beware of its venom. After you pass through the snake, you will find another path. This road is ancient and rarely traveled and brings a giant problem. Cross the bridge of ice, and that road will eventually lead to Fealmynster."

"A snake? Venom?" Erik asked. "You mean to kill us."

"You must trust me," the old man said. "You will see when you get there."

"How can I trust you?" Erik asked. "I don't know you, and you speak in riddles and talk of my friends losing their lives."

"Search your heart, Troll Hammer," the old man said. "You know you must trust me."

Erik waited a moment, squinting and watching the old man.

"How do I save my friends?" Erik asked.

"You cannot," the old man said.

"I will try," Erik said.

"I know you will," the old man said.

"Should I even be seeking this sword?" Erik asked.

The old man laughed.

"What choice do you have, Dragon Slayer?"

"None, I guess," Erik replied.

"Then your choice is simple. Take care Wolf's Bane. Guard your heart, guard your soul."

Erik emerged from the hut, his companions waiting for him, and as he took his horse's reins from Beldar, he heard laughing coming from the hut.

"I will see you in your dreams," the old man's voice said.

6

————————

Andragos sat at a table in his home, a large but simple cottage located in a meadow hidden away, no other dwellings within many a league. He preferred his other house, one closer to Fen-Stévock, and surrounded by stone walls, but he was sure this one was unknown. He stared into a bowl filled with water that showed him visions. First, he watched a middle-aged man—a former soldier from Golgolithul—ride into the coastal city of Finlo. To what end, Andragos couldn't tell. The city was under martial law, but he watched the man frequent taverns and whorehouses until he grew bored. He shook his head.

"Fool," Andragos muttered.

The Lord of the East's assassins would find him eventually, assuming some other assassin didn't. His spies told him that the General Lord Marshall of Gol-Durathna had dispatched the Atrimus. The Northern Kingdom hated admitting they had such assassins, but they did, nonetheless. King Agempi must have truly been worried to dispatch his Shadow Men.

This man in Finlo, Wrothgard was his name, was a good soldier, but he would not die in battle. His demise would come through poison, or a slit throat, or a blade in the belly in some coastal city alley. Such a waste of good fighting talent.

His vision turned to a young man from a small farmstead in Northwestern Háthgolthane. Four dwarves and another man accompanied Erik Eleodum as they traveled along a road leading into the Gray Mountains. He saw Erik step into a hut on the northern edge of a town called Eldmanor. He knew that place, and when Erik stepped into it, the vision disappeared.

"Bah, you old witch doctor," Andragos huffed in irritation, but then he heard a cackling laugh, and the candles in his cottage dimmed, causing Andragos to smirk. "You're nothing but a riddler and trickster."

Looking at his bowl of water again, the liquid swirled, and he saw another man—Bu Al'Banan he called himself as well as being the self-declared King of Hámon —leading armored horseman into the Gray Mountains.

"Another fool," Andragos muttered. He sat back. "We're all fools."

A knock came at his door.

"Enter," Andragos said.

Raktas entered.

"They are here," his manservant said.

Andragos stood and walked outside. Terradyn stood behind two dozen people. Ja Sin's wife and their children. The man's brother and his family. His nephew and two nieces. A few more friends.

"The Lord of the East had his whole unit executed, my lord," Raktas whispered.

"That's a hundred men," Andragos said, "a hundred good soldiers."

"An example of what happens when men betray their country," Raktas said.

"Stupidity," Andragos whispered. "Please tell me he at least gave them an honorable death?"

"He had them burned at the stake," Raktas replied.

Andragos just shook his head. A waste of resources. A waste of good men and good soldiers.

"My lord," a woman said amidst sobs.

"Be quiet!" Andragos said, his voice hard and stern. "No harm will become you as long as the Lord of the East doesn't know you are here. Pray it stays that way. You will stay inside. You will do as you are told. Failure will result in your discovery and the death of you and your children. Do you understand?"

The woman nodded, tears still streaming down her face.

"I have much to lose keeping you and your family here," Andragos said, his expression flat as he looked over the several dozen people before him, "and if you are discovered, I will have no choice but to hand you over. Terradyn, take them inside."

Terradyn did as he was asked, and Andragos turned to Raktas.

"Any other news?" Andragos asked.

"The Lord of the East has summoned the Bone Spear," Raktas replied.

"Specter?" Andragos asked. Then he shook his head.

Specter was an assassin from the Isutan Isles, the same homeland of Melanius, the Lord of the East's new advisor. More commonly known as Bone Spear for his main weapon of choice, the shaft of his spear was made of the vertebrae of his victims. It was tipped with the tooth of some poisonous creature—some assumed a dragon—and when he was tasked to killing someone, he never failed. He protected his name and reputation well, but his price was high ... and always in blood. He was also called Specter for several reasons: his white hair, his wistful ways, but mostly, his ability to move like a ghost. Many from the Isutan Isles were adept in such magic and other arcane arts.

"That Isutan warlock has poisoned his brain. Now, he summons an Isutan assassin. To what end?"

"Something to do with the Eleodum man, my lord," Raktas said, and Andragos gave him a questioning look. "A mistranslation with the Dragon Scroll. Melanius thought it said they needed a key, and I guess they do, but they now believe Eleodum already has it."

"Already has the key?" Andragos asked, as much to himself as his manservant.

He thought for a moment, and then his eyes went wide.

"The dagger," Andragos said.

"I would believe so, my lord," Raktas replied.

"What is Specter tasked with?" Andragos asked.

"Follow Eleodum to Fealmynster, wait for him to retrieve the sword, take it and kill him and Sustenon," Raktas explained.

The name of the wizard of Fealmynster made Andragos shudder. He knew the man, once, and might have even called him a friend. Now, he was a shadow of his former self.

"What do you want to do?" Raktas asked.

"Nothing for now," Andragos replied. "For now, we wait."

7

_S_itting in a throne-like wooden chair that suited his ego, Fréden Fréwin watched his warriors—_His_ warriors—train in the courtyard of an ancient castle in El'Beth-Tordûn. Men had bastardized the name and started calling it The Wicked Spire. There was nothing wicked about this place. Fréden ignored the fact that part of this place's name was Elvish. He contemplated renaming it, making it a bastion of everything that was dwarvish.

The castle had been abandoned centuries before and, when they found it, was in drastic disrepair. It still had a long way to go—crumbling walls, gates nothing but rusted dust, and unsteady defenses—but they were well on their way to restoring its former glory. They were the true dwarves. The patriots. The nationalists. Those who believed in everything dwarvish. They didn't necessarily believe they were better than everyone else. No, they simply believed they should concern themselves with their own kind first.

A time of isolation was needed to repair a lost culture and, when the time was right, they would make themselves known. They would join in the leadership of the world, and they would help everyone else

—men, goblins, ogres, antegants, dwarves who had lost their way, even elves (if they still existed)—be a better version of who they were. And if they didn't accept the dwarves' help ... Fréden clenched a fist. Every other creature—trolls and giants to name a few—would feel the wrath of dwarvish steel and bravery.

He didn't really understand what his warriors were doing. He wasn't a soldier or even a fighter. He never was because he didn't need to be. Others took that mantle upon themselves. He was a politician, born to be a leader, and that's what the dwarvish people needed right now. They needed someone to lead them ... not into battle, but into the future.

Fréden thought it was foolish how his race prized the leadership of generals and military tacticians. They knew how to lead people in battle, but what about times of peace? Those were the people who had gotten them to where they were now, lost, disenchanted, and forgetful of who they really were. It was time for a new era, a time when those born and bred to lead should take charge and others would follow. Sure, the warriors and generals and tacticians had their place. Fréden would need capable dwarves to lead them into battle when the time came, advise on military matters, construct defenses and defensive plans, but what did they know of infrastructure and diplomacy? They were not visionaries as Fréden was.

He watched, pretending to know what his newly appointed generals were doing and saying, but really not caring. He could have been doing something else, but his advisor, Nalbin, suggested he watch the army's training for a while. The warriors' morale had been low. They had begun questioning their motives for leaving the north and the south and joining Fréden Fréwin in his conquest to a new, dwarvish future.

"I still have a hard time believing the attack on Fen-Stévock was a dragon," Fréden said, not bothering to look at Belvengar Long Spear; he knew he stood there, obedient as always, standing slightly behind Fréden's chair.

"My lord, as hard as it is to believe, there is no denying it," Long Spear said. "What else could have destroyed the whole of South Gate?"

"Perhaps it was an army of siege weapons," Fréden said. "The Durathnans are resourceful people."

"It was not Gol-Durathna," Belvengar said.

"Black magic, then," Fréden said.

"Most definitely, my lord," Belvengar replied. "What else are dragons made of, if not black magic?"

"How is it that for years, centuries, millennia even, dwarves were able to subdue dragons and keep them hidden away in the deepest parts of the earth," Fréden asked, "and now, when the power of the dwarves wanes, a dragon once again emerges?"

"I do believe the answer is in your question, my lord," Belvengar said. "And you must remember, my lord, that the elves trained them—kept them as pets."

"Bah," Fréden hissed. "The elves. Flighty fools. And supposedly this man ... this farm boy, had a piece of paper, a spell that subdued the dragon?" Fréden asked.

"Aye, my lord," Belvengar replied.

"A man who was in the city of Thorakest," Fréden asked, "who broke bread with King Skella?"

"Aye, my lord."

"That fool of a king," Fréden hissed, slamming his fist on the arm of the chair. "And I hear Lord Balzarak was there when this man found the spell."

"That is true, my lord."

"We have truly lost our way, Long Spear," Fréden said. "And our spies say this man, this Erik Dragon Slayer as he is being called, is now tasked with finding a weapon, a sword, that could slay a dragon?"

"Aye, my lord." Fréden saw, through a sidelong glance, Belvengar step up closer to him. He added, "An elvish weapon, legend says, crafted by dwarves and enchanted by the sylvan people."

"Our ancestors would have never conspired with the elves," Fréden said, looking to Belvengar quickly. "The sword must have been stolen."

Belvengar shrugged.

"And this man, he is with your friend, Skull Crusher?" Fréden asked.

"He is my friend no more, my lord," Belvengar replied. "He chose man over his own kind; man over his own battle brother."

"Where is it they search for this sword?" Fréden asked.

"North of the Gray Mountains, my lord."

"Ah, yes. That is right. Do we have dwarves that are loyal to us in Thrak Baldüukr?" Fréden asked.

"We do, my lord," Belvengar replied. "We have more support in the south, but there are those in the north loyal to our cause."

"Send word," Fréden said. "They must be stopped ... and the sword must be mine." He saw the raised eyebrow Belvengar gave him and realized what he had said sounded ambitious and power hungry. "So it might rest with the dwarvish people once again, of course."

Belvengar nodded and bowed, and Fréden caught the movement out of the corner of his eye, but he didn't acknowledge it.

"The power," Fréden mused when Belvengar left. His brows furrowed deeply, and he knuckled his chin as warriors continued to train, their commanders barking orders and the soldiers responding with increased intensity. He tried to ignore them.

The power to kill a dragon ... to control a dragon.

He almost salivated at the thought. He would unite the dwarves and not just those of Háthgolthane, but those dispersed afar, in Nothgolthane and Wüsten Sahil. They would once again rise to where An intended them ... rulers, leaders, the ones helping the rest of this backward world to be better.

As he pondered his role as the true savior of his people, he watched one dwarvish soldier continually lose at sparring. It didn't matter who he went against, even the dwarves that looked smaller and weaker, they would always best him. Every time he made a mistake, a commander would come over and correct him, but then he would go back to performing the same movements incorrectly. As he screwed up his fists, Fréden was filled with hatred for this weakling and any others like him. He would crush those that didn't want to better themselves.

8

———————

Bu rode Warrior, his—Patûk Al'Banan's—old gray warhorse, through the dense forest of the Gray Mountains. His men, easterners and those who had once fought for Patûk, followed him without word. His knights followed him as well, not without complaint, of course, but he had begun to drown them out. They were weak, and he often wondered what made them nobility. Was this the way of the world? He had so little exposure to it. Were nobles in Golgolithul this soft? They couldn't be. The east was a hard place; at least it was for him.

Supposedly, these were the best knights that each of the dukes and barons of Hámon had to offer, but any one of his normal foot soldiers could run circles around these fools. He began to curse himself for not bringing more than a dozen of his men, on top of which, he had a dozen Hámonian knights. In addition, he had Sargent Andu and his personal guard, Bao Zi. The old, grizzled soldier with one eye and a wound to his shoulder that would have killed anyone else—truly, Bu believed death was too afraid to take Bao Zi—was worth all two dozen men.

Bu had already lost one of his own men when the fool fell from his horse and broke his neck. Then, as they rode along the ledge of a steep slope that ended in a windswept, rocky, barren valley, he lost one of the Hámonian knights. The fool was trying to show off his horsemanship, to whom, Bu couldn't figure, and prodded his horse into a wrong step, and both beast and man slid down that slope to their deaths. Well, what eventually would be their deaths. They could hear both screaming and the man calling for help, but after a quick look at the situation, Bu would send none.

"Let that be a lesson to all of you idiots," he said, as the other knights protested his order to keep moving.

"He's a knight," one said, refusing to get back on his horse. "He deserves to be rescued."

"It'll take a dozen men," Bao Zi had croaked, "and they could lose their lives in the attempt."

"A hundred of these peasants," the knight had said, pointing to Bu's regular soldiers, "aren't worth a single knight."

Bao Zi immediately reached for his sword, and Bu had to step in front of the old warrior.

"If you want to rescue him, go yourself," Bu said. "We're not stopping."

"There are cannibals in these parts of the Gray Mountains," another knight said.

"Better him than me," Bao Zi said as he spat at the feet of the knight. "Maybe he'll do the honorable thing and put a dagger in his throat."

At that point in their journey, Bu had believed he had a good idea of where they were and where they were going. The map that his seneschal, Li, had copied from the Dragon Scroll before the man named Erik Eleodum stole it was easy enough to follow. Their quest for the Dragon Sword was going well, and Bu tried to contain his excitement, the thought of holding a sword that could kill a dragon was almost arousing. Now, two days later, they were lost. Somewhere they had gotten off track, and Bu cursed himself for it. He was an expert tracker, but the forest in these parts of the mountains was so dense, they could barely see ten paces in front of them. And the weather was so cold it chilled a man to the bone. Bu tried finding a path, but the constant snow, sleet, and rain made that impossible.

"We're lost," Bu told Bao Zi in confidence.

"Don't tell the men," Bao Zi croaked, and Bu nodded.

Riding made it difficult for both horse and rider, with the hidden roots and undulations and divots in the earth, masked by the thick carpet of snow, and Bu started leading Warrior through the forest. He suggested the others do the same—actually, he commanded it and his men obeyed—but the knights grumbled and complained, so he told them they could do what they wanted. Several of them complied, but most kept on riding as if they knew best, as if they had been the best of all scouts and spies and assassins for the largest resistance move-ment against Golgolithul.

Bu knew it would happen. He heard a yelp. A screaming neigh from a horse. The sound of something snapping. The thudding of bodies. The thrashing of an animal that had just broken a leg. The cry of a man stuck underneath that animal.

"Gods be damned!" Bu shouted. "I told you to walk your horse."

"What good is a horse if you can't ride it?" the knight asked, several of the others helping him up as the horse screamed, its right foreleg bent in an unnatural angle.

Bu backhanded the man, sending him into a tree. The air rushed from the man with an oomph before he bounced off the trunk and then landed on the ground, face first.

"I am getting tired of your insolence," Bu said, pulling the man up by his collar and looking at him face to face. This Sir Robert was a flippant man and had been a nagging gnat, almost as bad as Count Alger's man—Sir Garrett—since they left Hámon. His beard was a pathetic thing of wispy, blond hair, so much so that he should have just kept his face clean-shaven, and his straight bangs and bobbed hair that hung just above his shoulders made it hard for Bu to believe that he was one of the best knights and warriors Hámon had to offer.

"I ... I ..." Sir Robert began to say.

"I am your king, you pile of troll shit," Bu said, "and unless you want to see what your intestines look like and know what your balls taste like, you'll remember that."

He let go of Sir Robert and the man fell on his ass.

"Kill that damn horse," Bu said as the poor animal continued to whinny pathetically and thrash about, "and skin it, gut it, and portion it out."

"You mean to eat the horse?" Sir Garrett asked.

Sir Garrett actually looked like a soldier, with a stern jaw and broad shoulders. He kept his light brown hair short, in the fashion of eastern soldiers, even though he was a westerner through and through. And, like many of his kind in the east, he thought his noble blood made him better than everyone else.

"Unless you wish to stick your manhood in it first! There will come a time when you might consider boiling your leather boots, *Sir Garrett*," Bu said, his voice hard and flat. He spoke from experience, but the knight turned away with an arrogant shake of his head.

They hiked through the dense forest for another two days before the terrain began to open up. It didn't make traveling that much easier, for with the wider open space, the snow fell more freely. Most of the knights mounted back up, but Bu, Bao Zi, and the rest of his men continued to lead their horses. There was no point in riding them when they would travel at the same speed either way. And this way, they saved their horses, if only a little.

Of course, Sir Robert continued to complain about not having a horse. His voice was whiny, and he sounded like a petulant little girl. It grated on Bu, and he found himself gripping the handle of the sword he had inherited from Patûk Al'Banan's death.

"What is that, my lord?" Bao Zi asked.

Bu hadn't been paying attention, simply concentrating on not removing Sir Robert's head from his shoulders.

"What is what?" Bu replied, his voice hard and short.

He hadn't meant to be short with perhaps the most trusted man in his employ, but the old soldier continued as if Bu's voice was no different than any other time.

"Look, my lord."

Bu followed Bao Zi's hand to the trees where the forest began again up ahead. Dusk had started to settle on the mountain, and in the intermittent combination of sun and moonlight, something glimmered between two trees.

"I don't know," Bu replied, squinting and straining to try and see what it was.

"It's over there too," Bao Zi said, pointing to another tree.

"It looks like a spider's web," Bu said.

One tree trunk was all white, and the branches, which were all clumped together, were also white, but not with snow.

"Either, there's a million spiders up there," Bao Zi said, "or that's one, big, damn spider."

"When are we stopping?" Sir Robert whined. "My feet hurt."

"Damn the gods," Bu hissed.

Bu stopped, handed Warrior's reins to Andu, and walked towards Sir Robert. He was complaining to another knight, Sir Caleb—his red hair kept in the same fashion as Sir Robert and with a thin mustache and small bit of red hair on his chin—when Bu unsheathed his sword and drove it into Sir Robert's gut. Everyone stopped, several men gasped, and one man even let out a cry that didn't sound like it came from a hardened soldier. Sir Robert stared at Bu in disbelief. He removed his sword, and the knight collapsed at his feet, dead.

"Shall we skin him, gut him, and portion him out as well?" Sir Garrett asked.

Bu looked at the knight, a smile on his face.

9

———

Boulders and wooden poles marked the road leading into the Gray Mountains, and slabs of stone marked some of the road, preventing it from washing away during snow and rainstorms. Signs of travel were evident and Erik and his companions even passed a small group of northern dwarves traveling to Eldmanor and northwestern Háthgolthane.

Despite the passable nature of the road, often cutting a wide path between rising peaks and trees, travel was slow. The Gray Mountains didn't have gently sloping foothills like the Western Tor of the Southern Mountains, and the trek into the range was steep, and even the horses had to tread carefully.

"We will eventually have to let the horses go," Beldar said as they reached an especially treacherous part of the mountain road, with a steep ascending slope on one side and a sharp drop to the other.

That made Bryon's heart sink, and he patted his horse's neck.

"It's all right," Bryon, ever the horse lover, whispered to the animal when no one was looking. "You'll be all right."

The skeletal remains of a mule lay to one side, and Bryon suspected the animal had been part of a supply chain and had taken a misstep farther up the mountain; that was all the confirmation needed to know they would, eventually, have to let their mounts go, hoping they made it home safely. He now understood why Erik had turned down his Uncle Rikard's offer to give them his best horses and extra ones to carry their supplies.

Even though it was late summer, a thick fog hung in the air of the early mornings in the Gray Mountains. Whether they were camping in the forest or alongside a mountain path, it was as cold as winter on the Eleodum Farmstead. As the day wore on, the sun would melt the fog away, and by noon, if Bryon stood directly in the sun, it could feel hot. By dusk, the fog would come back, accompanied by light rains, often not much more than a gentle mist, sometimes sleet and soft snow that melted as soon as it touched the ground, and more cold weather. A light frost would form on the ground or grass by midnight, meaning the horses would slip and stall the next day, making travel even slower.

The mountain road cut through forest for four of the first five days of their journey, and when they were in the forest, they hunted every night. Food was abundant, and they could walk but ten paces and at least find a squirrel or rabbit to bop on the head, let alone the small deer, raccoon, berries, nuts, and mushrooms that were readily available.

"The old man in Eldmanor said we already have the key?" Bryon asked as he and Erik took a walk after eating.

"Yeah."

"Where is it?" Bryon asked. "Better yet, what is it?"

Erik just shrugged.

"Do you trust him?" Bryon asked.

"As much as I trust the Lord of the East," Erik replied. "He knew things. I don't know if he was a mage, but I don't think he was false."

"If you lead us to our doom ..." Bryon began to say.

"Did you embark on this journey thinking it would be a merry, joyous one, full of safety?" Nafer asked, to which the other dwarves laughed.

"Things are always joyous and merry with dwarves," Bryon said sarcastically and his comment brought on even more laughter.

"We'll be dead before you have a chance to kill me," Erik said, joining in the dwarves' amusement, and Bryon eventually lost his scowl and chuckled a little bit too.

They were camping along a mountain ledge on the fifth day of travel from Eldmanor, Bryon staring out over the edge just before they set out for the day.

"Does this remind you of anything?" Bryon asked Erik.

"Leaving Thorakest I'd say," Erik replied. "The Southern Mountains."

Bryon nodded his head.

"Is it odd that I miss it?" Bryon asked.

"What do you miss?" Erik replied.

"The Southern Mountains. Thorakest. Orvencrest. The journey. The fighting," Bryon said. "All of it. Do you feel the same?"

"I don't know," Erik said. "I suppose I haven't thought about it much recently."

"You have Simone," Bryon said with a smile, "now you have something else to think about."

"She's pregnant," Erik said.

"I didn't know, cousin," Bryon said. He actually looked happy. "Congratulations. Your equipment works. That's good to know."

Erik elbowed his cousin with a laugh.

"Boy or girl?" Bryon asked.

"Who knows?" Erik replied. "Whichever the baby is, they will call you Uncle Bryon."

"But I'm no uncle to your child," Bryon replied. He gave Erik a serious look.

"It doesn't matter," Erik said. "You've been like a brother to me ... and you'll be an uncle to my child."

Bryon felt a flutter in his stomach and couldn't help the small smile that touched his lips.

"I am honored," Bryon finally said.

"Think nothing of it," Erik replied.

They let a few moments of silence pass between them, just watching the mountain.

"I don't know if it is so odd to think about the journey and the fighting," Erik finally said. "It gave us purpose."

"Maybe that's what it is," Bryon said. "Maybe I feel like I don't have purpose."

"Well, we have a purpose again," Erik said, staring out into the darkness of the mountain night.

Next morning, as they rode slowly along the carved out road that took them through the Gray Mountains, they came to a wide, white tree. It wasn't a broad trunked pine like most of the mountain's trees, but an old oak with branches spreading out like the channels of a river but no leaves. The road diverted sharply to the left at the tree.

"A tree made of stone," Erik said, more to himself than anyone else, dismounting, "dead, yet, still alive."

Erik touched the white bark of the tree. It looked cold and hard and smooth, and Bryon watched him with a furrowed brow. He was speaking nonsense.

"It's petrified," Beldar said.

"What?" Bryon asked.

"It's dead," Beldar explained.

"Then how is it still standing?" Bryon asked.

"It's made of stone," Turk explained. "Dead, long ago, and its bark replaced by mineral and stone."

"This is the landmark we are to look for," Erik said, "to take the Forlorn Pass."

"I don't see any other roads," Nafer said.

Bryon followed Erik as they walked around the tree. The forest was especially dense, with bushes and creepers and other trees, but just behind the petrified tree, tucked in between two white roots, Bryon saw a wide, flat rock.

"Look," Bryon said.

He pushed aside the bushes that grew over the flat stone to find similar rocks, all lined up one after the other. It was a road, or at least marked as one.

The way ahead was overgrown with foliage and narrow in most places, as far as Bryon could see, tucked in between broad pines and dense shrubbery.

"We found it," Erik said, walking back to his companions. "This is where we must leave the horses."

"They'll die if we leave them here," Bryon said.

"The path is too narrow," Erik said. "We can tie them to the tree and hope that someone finds them before wolves do, or let them go and hope they find their way back home."

They opted to let the horses go, Bryon intently watching the animals, their heads hung low. At first, they didn't know what to do, the one Bryon had been riding nuzzling his hand. He had to push the creature away and finally slapped it on its ass to get it to leave.

"Unless you'd been told, you'd walk right past this road not even realizing it's here," Bryon said as he crouched low to duck under a thick branch and then stepped over a high arching root that was as thick as the branch.

They had walked only a few paces when the petrified oak was lost to the dense forest foliage. Bryon wondered if there really was a road as they pushed aside thick bushes and creepers, ducked under branches, and crawled through narrow deer paths. But every once in a while, he would see a smooth slab of stone marking a road he presumed was once heavily traveled and guessed that meant they were still traveling in the right direction.

It felt like they had trekked leagues, but with the density of the forest, Bryon knew they hadn't even traveled one. But as night fell, which happened early in the Gray Mountains with its tall peaks, Erik decided they would bed down in a small patch of greenery, the ground cushioned by thick knots of vines and fallen pine needles. Nafer tried building a fire, the chill of the mountain air biting them all the way to the bone, but there was nothing for kindling, and the ground was too wet. Bryon leaned back, pulling a bearskin his father had given him around his shoulders, but even that did little to stem the freezing temperature of the mountain night.

As a wind came up, the bushes and branches around them rattled and shook with the growing shadows, as distant wolves howled, and the growling of predatory cats pierced the air. Bryon suddenly felt as if he was a naïve boy leaving home for the first time, nervous and scared of everything and anything that moved in the darkness.

"Did you bring your flute with you?" Turk asked, and Bryon looked to Erik, making out his silhouette in the darkness.

His cousin rifled through his haversack, and, in the blackness of night, Bryon could see him put the instrument to his mouth and blow.

Bryon never really figured out how Erik could play this particular flute. He never had an affinity for music. Mardirru, son of the gypsy Marcus, had given it to Erik as a parting gift, and, coming from gypsies, Bryon just figured it was magic. At first, he was a little jealous of the gift. He actually knew how to play the flute and pipes. But after a while, it seemed to fit Erik.

The tune Erik played was somber. When his cousin did play, which was sparingly these days, Bryon liked to lean back and close his eyes and imagine what the music might be if it were a dream or a vision. This one was a small pond at night, the moon reflected in the dark water that shimmered when the ripples of a fish trying to catch a nocturnal bug spread outwards.

Crickets chirped, and a frog croaked from a thick patch of grass. A long-legged heron stood at one edge of the pond, while a nightingale sang, its song a rapid succession of chirps and clicks. In the distance, an owl joined in, hooting loudly to add to the clamor of nighttime sounds. It seemed as if all of life was portrayed in this song Erik played ... this scene of nature and life and the world around them, unaware of war or death. Unaware of political intrigue and lying and stealing. They sang their song to the water and the grass and the night and the Creator ... and it was beautiful. Bryon kept his eyes closed as he leaned back and smiled, watching the birds, watching the tiny ripples of waves in the water, and, finally, watching a bullfrog leap into the pond, barely escaping the sharp beak of a long-legged heron.

Shortly into the next day, the dense forest gave way to a valley path, cutting through tall peaks that shadowed the gorge regardless of the time of day. Where trees and greenery consumed much of the Gray Mountains they had hiked through so far, this valley was stony and gray. Loose rock constantly slid down the rising peaks on either side of them and, with no trees to provide a shield, the mountaintops funneled any wind right in their faces, causing somewhat permanent pinched expressions as the temperature dropped. Not only had the wind picked up, but so did the light rain they had been experiencing, turning into a downpour, leaving the ground an almost muddy river.

"I can see where Forlorn Pass gets its name from!" Bryon yelled, trying to speak over the howling wind, rain, and thunder booming overhead. "Not many people have come this way because they choose not to travel it because of this."

"We need to try and build a fire tonight," Erik shouted back as the sky overhead darkened, but the wind and rain made it impossible.

"Damn this," Bryon muttered to himself, huddling closer to his cousin and wrapping his thick bearskin more tightly around his shoulders.

"This is why I prefer the Southern Mountains," Turk added with feeling.

"I can't argue with that," Erik agreed.

They all leaned into one another, trying to stay warm and sleep, but it was all for naught. The howling wind, the rain, and the rough ground prevented any hope of rest.

"To the nine hells with the Lord of the East," Bryon muttered, his teeth chattering as he shivered next to Erik.

"I think I could spend the rest of my life in the Eleodum Farmstead," Turk added.

"You would be more than welcome," Erik replied.

"I bet you're cursing yourself for leaving a warm bed and a good woman right now," Bryon said.

"I miss her," Erik said, staring at the cloudy sky.

"We could have stayed hidden in Thorakest," Nafer said. "King Skella would have protected us."

"Or we could have gone west," Bryon said, "past Waterton. We still can. It's not too late. We return home, pack up our families. The Lord of the East isn't expecting us for another ten months."

"He would know," Turk said. "The Black Mage is probably watching us right now."

"I am most certain of it," Erik said.

As Erik and the dwarves tried to pass the time by making small talk, Bryon felt the gooseflesh on his arms rise. It could have been an errant gust of wind finding its way through his bearskin, or the rain soaking his hair, but it wasn't. He leaned forward as if he could see anything in the blackness.

"Hush," Bryon said, putting a hand up.

He couldn't hear much over the wind and the rain, but nonetheless, he strained and leaned forward. Erik and the dwarves stopped. Beldar sniffed at the air.

"Do you smell that?" Beldar asked.

"Something stinks," Bofim replied.

"Men," Nafer said.

"Look to the slope," Beldar whispered. "Do you see the shadows?"

Bryon was sure the dwarves with their keen eyes saw them better than he did, but in the darkness of the mountain night, he saw shadows, darker than the surrounding environment. There were two dozen of them. Men.

Bryon put a hand on the handle of his elvish blade, slowly. He felt a shadow just behind him. He smelled it as he closed his eyes and listening intently he heard the man breathing.

Bryon stood, unsheathing his blade, the purple steel flashing and brightening, and bringing it across the man's chest all in the same motion. The leaping attacker's legs failed him, and he crumpled to the ground in an ungainly heap, letting out a gurgled scream before he fell silent. All at once, shadows appeared across the valley. There were audible gasps from several of them, presumably as they saw the magic sword, and then, as if under instruction, each man yelled an animalistic cry.

"This is going to be a hard fight," Turk said, readying his battle axe.

"We've had harder," Erik replied.

Both Beldar and Bofim produced torches smeared with pitch. They flared up, despite the rain and the wind, and revealed at least two dozen men—seemingly mountain bandits that looked ragged and hungry. With gaunt faces, barely more than clubs as armaments, and little more than thick furs for clothing and armor, it almost seemed as if screaming wildly was seen as their greatest weapon and show of strength. There were no speech patterns to the cries, simply squawks and screeches that made Bryon think of demented birds.

He threw Erik his hunting bow who deftly killed two of the bandits while Nafer used Demik's broadsword to kill two more. Bryon brought down another man, his steel easily passing through makeshift armor and flesh, as did Beldar and Bofim with their long spears. Turk took on yet another two bandits, dispatching them easily.

"They're little better than animals!" Bryon yelled, the rain hissing as it struck his burning blade.

"Hungry animals!" Turk added.

"They mean to eat us?" Bryon gasped, almost taking his eye from the fight.

"Most likely," Nafer replied.

"Oh, by the Creator's beard," Bryon said, cleaving one man in half and then removing another's head, "I think not."

They only had to kill a few more of the wild men before they started to retreat.

"I know our supply of resin is sparse," Nafer said, "but I say we keep these torches burning tonight."

"I wholeheartedly agree with you," Bryon added.

Erik turned a dead man onto his back with his boot. Bryon looked over his shoulder, staring at a thin and sickly looking fellow. Dirt smeared his face. His trousers were tattered, and he wore a heavy bearskin over a vest made of wood and rock—a makeshift shirt of armor. Bryon patted his dwarvish mail shirt.

"Not so hard," Bryon said, patting his cousin on the shoulder.

"You're right," Turk said, looking at Bryon. "They are little better than animals."

"We did them a favor, then," Erik said.

"Perhaps," Turk said.

"Does this remind you of the slavers from the Blue Forest?" Bryon asked.

Bryon thought, for a moment, of a gypsy caravan they had traveled with, once. That hadn't been half a year ago and, yet, it seemed so far away. A troupe of slavers had attacked the caravan and had managed to kill its leader, a mighty man by the name of Marcus. Bryon hadn't liked Marcus at first. He hadn't liked the gypsies in general, but looking back on that group of people, and their leader, they were good and kind, and he shook his head as he thought about how poorly he had treated them, especially Bo and his wife Dika. Life on the road—especially recuperation in the dwarvish city—had taken the edge off his temper, and he liked to think of himself as more tolerant and easy-going. If he hadn't changed, he probably wouldn't have survived.

"Not really," Erik said with the shake of his head. "Like you said, these men were animals, driven by hunger and, possibly, madness. Let's keep moving. We don't know how many of them are out there."

The sun had finally crested the tall peaks of the valley. Bryon looked up and saw one, gigantic peak extending towards the sky so high, that its top disappeared into the clouds, which had stopped depositing rain for at least a moment.

"The Fangs," Erik said.

As they walked, Bryon felt his foot catch on something, and, looking down, he saw a piece of cloth hooked around his boot. The cloth clung to what looked like flesh, and following it, he saw it was the remains of a horse, most of the muscle and tissue gone. What remained was black and covered in dirt, and the cold had staved off the normal beetles and maggots that might aid in consuming rotting flesh, so it had decomposed more slowly than might be expected.

"Is that a horse?" Erik said.

"One of ours?" Bryon asked, his voice giving away his concern.

"No, you fool," Erik said with what was becoming a rare hint of laughter, "they're probably almost to Eldmanor by now if they found their way back. This is fresh, though."

Bryon crouched and gingerly touched a bit of muscle still clinging to a bloody femur.

"The cloth looks like a tabard," Erik said.

"What fool tried to bring their horses through this valley?" Bryon asked.

"I don't think they did," Turk replied, looking up the steep slope leading into the valley in which they traveled. High above them, they could see tall trees peeking over the ledge. "I suspect the horse was traveling up there and lost its footing. I don't see any sign that it slid down the slope, but it has been raining and probably would have washed away any evidence of a fall."

"Its femur is broken," Beldar said, crouching next to the horse.

Erik inspected the cloth that had caught Bryon's foot. It was tattered, but as he held it up, they seemed to realize, at the same time, it was a tabard, one that someone would drape over their horse. Even though there were only bits and pieces of the tabard, Bryon saw yellow triangles.

"Hámon," Erik said.

"What was that?" Turk asked as Bryon nodded his head in agreement.

"It could be something else," Erik said, "but if this tabard was all white and covered in yellow triangles, it might have belonged to a Hámonian knight. A white flag with four yellow triangles is the standard of one of the lords of Hámon. I don't know which one."

"What would Hámonian nobles be doing in the Gray Mountains?" Bryon asked.

"I don't know," Erik replied.

"The man who calls himself King Bu Al'Banan, who is really a former soldier of Patûk's," Turk said. "Could he have seen the Dragon Scroll? He might have even been one of the men we fought when Erik killed Patûk. It is possible they copied the scroll, and if they did, it's likely they know as much as we do about the sword and all it is supposed to offer."

"Are you saying Al'Banan is in these mountains too?" Erik asked, sounding as incredulous as if Turk had said the dragon was there.

"I would suspect so," Turk replied. "At least, those he commands."

"If he is anything like Patûk Al'Banan, he is with them," Erik said.

Bryon shivered. Patûk Al'Banan—a name that struck fear into men ... once. The former general of Golgolithul's famed Eastern Guard defected when the Stévockians took control of the Eastern Empire, launching an all-out underground war against the Lord of the East's family. There were others like him, but he was the most powerful, the most cunning, the strongest, and he led the largest force of resistance fighters ... and Erik killed him.

"This horse has not been dead for long," Bryon said, "and it must have had a rider. How did it decay so quickly in the cold? And where is the knight it carried?"

"Wolves," Erik replied with a shrug, "or a cougar."

"I think we fought what happened to them," Nafer offered, "a day ago. Remember, they were hungry and little more than animals."

A sour look crossed Bryon's face, and he looked as if he was going to gag.

"We need to be cautious," Turk said. "The man who took Patûk Al'Banan's place would truly be a ruthless and cunning man."

10

———

"What now?" Bryon muttered, staring at boulders stacked on top of one another.

"I suppose we climb over," Turk said with a shrug.

"Looks like the leftover of some landslide that happened recently," Erik said.

"Be careful," Turk said, sliding a finger over one of the larger rocks. "These are icy."

Erik nodded, stepping onto a smaller rock and then climbing up a boulder. He looked over his shoulder, nodding for his companions to follow him, then he took a wrong step. The rock below his feet moved, and he slipped and fell backward, landing with a thump on his back as he hit the ground.

"Damn it," Erik muttered, standing and rubbing the back of his head.

"Are you all right?" Turk asked.

Erik nodded and looked up. The rock that had moved under his foot sat underneath a boulder that jutted outward and upward. The top boulder had formations on it that looked almost like ... teeth. As

Erik looked closer, he could see that the two rocks looked like an open mouth ... an opened, snake's mouth.

Let the serpent swallow you.

He climbed back up and pushed on the bottom rock. It moved, teetering and revealing a dark space towards what would have been the throat of the snake. He pushed on the back of the rock and tried to hold it open, even though it was heavy.

"Give me a torch," Erik said, reaching out but keeping his eyes on the dark space between the two rocks.

Nafer handed him a lit torch, and Erik tried to illuminate the darkness. He saw nothing.

"What are you doing, cousin?" Bryon asked.

"This is where we must go," Erik replied.

"You are joking?" suggested Bryon. "More tunnels full of monsters. What a great day this is turning to be!"

"Are you sure Erik?" Turk asked, his voice more level.

"The old man was clear. And I believe we have to trust him, so yes. This is the way we go."

While Turk nodded, Bryon still looked unsure, but he knew he was alone in protesting. He folded his arms, his hands tucked away in a vain effort to keep them warm and watched his cousin.

Erik breathed heavily and sat on the bottom rock, feet towards the dark space.

"Light your torches," Erik said, and then pushed himself towards the snake's throat. The boulder teetered, opened up, and Erik slid inside.

Erik landed hard on the ground of a dark tunnel, his torch the only source of light. He could hear his companions yelling for him. He stood and yelled back, his voice echoing into the darkness of the tunnel. He felt a tingle at his hip.

I wouldn't be so loud.

"What's wrong?" Erik replied quietly, looking at his dagger.

This place is dangerous.

"I have no choice."

Another boulder above Erik moved, letting more light into the tunnel. He stepped out of the way as Bryon slid through, landing hard on his stomach, his sword and torch skittering along the floor of the tunnel.

"You could have caught me," Bryon said, pushing himself up and retrieving his things.

"Hush," Erik hissed.

The dwarves slid down the boulder, one by one, Bryon and Erik trying to help them as much as possible, so they didn't land too hard. Last in was Nafer, and he caught his foot as he slid into the tunnel, causing him to fall headfirst. He naturally extended his arms to brace himself and cursed when a loud snapping sound echoed off the tunnel walls. He struggled to sit up and immediately cradled his left arm.

"It's broken," Turk said, making a sling for the dwarf.

"What do we do?" Beldar asked.

"Turk, can you heal him?" Erik asked.

"I will set the bone," Turk replied, "and I can take away the pain, but completely healing a broken bone ... that is beyond my ability."

Turk knelt next to Nafer.

"Stupid," Nafer said as he looked down at his now deformed arm.

"Better you landed on your arm than your neck," Turk said.

Turk produced a vial of sweet wine, but Nafer shook his head and refused.

"So be it," Turk said, pushing back Nafer's sleeve.

With one hand on Nafer's upper arm, and one on his wrist, Turk pulled on the arm and with a loud pop, and an even louder groan from Nafer, the bones moved back into place, and most of the deformity was gone, save for a good deal of swelling. Turk huffed and retrieved a jar of salve, which he spread over Nafer's arm.

"It smells like mint," Bryon said.

"It has some mint in it," Turk replied. "Mostly to remove the otherwise unbecoming smell."

"I presume that's for the pain?" Bryon asked.

"It will dull it," Turk replied. "Not like sweet wine, mind you, but my stubborn friend here is refusing to drink, so this will have to do."

Nafer glared at Turk, and Erik laughed.

"At least you're not the only stubborn ass down here," he said to Bryon. His cousin just rolled his eyes.

When Turk's treatment was finished, he bowed his head and prayed quietly, holding the broken arm in both hands. In the darkness of the tunnel, Erik could see a slight glow around Turk as he whispered his prayer, and the light traveled along Turk's arms and then surrounded Nafer. Nafer closed his eyes and breathed deeply as a look of serenity crossed his face, a small smile touching his lips.

"Thank you, brother," Nafer said to Turk when the moment had passed.

"This will hold you over for now," Turk said, "but the pain will return and then I will have to do this all over again, and soon."

Erik looked at Turk, and the dwarf looked back and nodded.

"We move," Erik said.

The tunnel's walls were smooth and straight, the floor void of any stalagmites and the roof tall and void of any stalactites.

"Is this man-made—or dwarvish made?" Erik asked.

"I don't know," Turk replied. "I suspect that someone might have made it but wanted it to look like it was formed naturally."

The air inside was stale, and it seemed warm when compared to the temperatures outside. It was nothing like the tunnels of the Southern Mountains that led to the city of Thorakest; they were comfortable to travel through, but this one was barely wide enough for Erik and Bryon to stand shoulder to shoulder. Erik had never been afraid of closed in spaces, but he felt anxious in this place, his brow sweating and his palms clammy.

They hadn't gone a hundred paces when in the black distance came the sounds of scratching and scuffling.

"Did you hear that?" Bofim asked.

Erik's dagger tickled his hip again, although it didn't say anything.

"Be ready," Erik said.

They walked another hundred paces, and the sounds grew louder. Erik heard growling and animalistic arguing, like dogs quarreling over scraps. He leaned forward and squinted, seeking to make out what was beyond his torch's light, but saw only shadows.

Erik jerked backward as something flashed from the darkness. He felt a searing pain on his left cheek, felt blood trickle from a wound. He grabbed Ilken's Blade and swung upward, as fast and as hard as he could. He felt his steel hit something other than stone. The weapon shuddered in his hand as whatever he had struck fought against the blade.

"More light!" Erik yelled, and Turk rushed forward with his torch, but the dwarf's head barely came to Erik's shoulder, and even with an extended arm, his torch couldn't illuminate the roof.

Erik retrieved his blade, heard growling above him, and swung upwards. He struck something again, this time Ilken's Blade cleaving through flesh. He heard tendon and ligament and bone break, and a limb fell in front of him as a screeching howl echoed through the tunnel. As quiet returned, he could hear whatever had attacked him running away, and, at the edge of the torchlight, in the distant shadows, he caught sight of the thing running up and down the tunnel walls.

The sound of dripping water echoed off the stone walls. Erik tried to take a deep breath, but the air was so sour and stale that each breath made him want to cough. He gripped his sword with white knuckles, pushing his torch out into the darkness as far as his left arm would extend. It had been hot just moments ago, and now the tunnel was cold, almost freezing. Nevertheless, sweat poured freely from his brow, and he anxiously brushed a stray strand of hair from his eyes, escaping the leather cord that held the rest back, away from his face. He looked back at Nafer, who still cradled his left arm in his right, despite the sling Turk had made. His face looked pale.

Erik looked over his other shoulder at Turk. He was calm, holding his battle axe in his right hand and his torch in the left hand.

"What, by the Creator, was that?" Erik asked.

He looked at the arm—at least, that was what it looked like, with sinewy, knotted muscles and fingers that had no nails but ended in sharp points, nonetheless. Erik wiped a bit of blood away from his cheek with the back of his hand ... testimony to how sharp those long, bony digits really were.

"Tunnel crawler," Beldar replied, standing beside Turk, the broad blade of his spear poised and ready.

"This is a dark place," Bofim said, looking all about, his spear ready as well but not as calm and collected as Turk and Beldar. "An evil place."

"As evil as Orvencrest?" Bryon asked.

"Perhaps," Bofim replied. "With tunnel crawlers, maybe even more evil."

"What could be more evil than the Shadow?" Erik asked.

"Things born of the Shadow," Bofim replied. "Things that challenge the Shadow."

Erik felt a shiver crawl up his spine.

"They have no eyes," Turk explained.

"How do they hunt then?" Erik asked.

"Sound and smell. They can smell blood, and sweat, and the warmth of your skin from a league away. They crawl on the walls and roofs of the tunnel, hunting any poor creature that accidentally happens into their environment."

Erik nodded his head to signal advancement, and the party slowly inched forward. The darkness of the mountain tunnel was so dense that their torches lit only the space where they stood; ahead and behind them was like a black wall. Erik could only think of his dreams. There were places in this world where the land of dreams and reality crossed over, and Orvencrest was one of them. This place looked as if it was another.

The tunnel had no features, no stalagmites or stalactites. There were no undulations or curves. Just straight through the mountain, with solid floors, and a roof so high, Erik had to stretch his torch upwards to see any semblance of it. The sounds of their boots on the cold floor resounded off the walls of the corridor like a chorus of drums. Tiny drops of water falling from the roof of the passageway clanked off Erik's armor. The flame of Turk's torch fizzled, and he heard the hissing of moisture against Bryon's elvish blade.

The adventurers walked another cautious hundred paces. They made sure to shine their lights on the walls and roof as best they could as they walked, ensuring no tunnel crawler waited for them, clinging there with its claws, ready to ambush them as they passed by.

"They are out there," Turk said. "They travel in packs, like wolves."

"Oh, just great," Bryon said, his eyes flicking left, right; up, down.

When the first one had attacked, it was like a shadow reaching from the blurry edges where light and darkness meet. Erik never really even saw the thing, it simply melded with the darkness, becoming one with it. It was truly a thing of the Shadow.

As Erik inched forward, Turk's hand caught his shoulder and stopped him. He looked to the dwarf, who put two fingers to his eyes while looking at Erik and then pointed in the direction they were walking. Erik squinted and strained to see what he saw and stepped back when he saw it, more torchlight revealing more of the tunnel.

A long, spindly, gray figure hunched over something, its back to the party. It was so skinny that the ridges of its spine poked through its skin. It moved from being on all fours to sitting back on its haunches, picking at something, tearing at it with its hands and what seemed to be its mouth. It picked whatever it was tearing apart up and shook it viciously. The men and dwarves heard the sound of bones breaking and of tendons snapping.

Then, suddenly, it stopped. The thing dropped what it had in its hands. It put its face to the roof and began to sniff. The sound of air sucking deep into the thing's nostrils sent chills up Erik's spine. It was a low, scratching sound, like teeth on raw bones. It turned its head slightly and then spun around rapidly.

Their torches flickered off the tunnel crawler. Its face had no eyes, only a smooth dome running from two slits that served as nostrils to the back of its head. A small ridge of bone ran around where the creature's nose would be and down to its mouth, which covered half its face. Long, razor sharp teeth filled the mouth, and every time it opened, green drool spilled out. A long, forked tongue lashed about the air like a snake, taking in tastes and warning signs its nose could not pick up.

The tunnel crawler was so thin, its ribs poked through the skin like its spine, and its knees and elbows looked too big for its body. It looked to be bipedal, but at times moved on all fours. Its arms were as long as its legs, and the creature standing straight up might have been as tall as a dwarf. Its muscles looked sinewy and knotted, a tortured mess of flesh and skin.

The tunnel crawler hissed before it screeched and then sniffed at the air again. The creature scratched its claws against the floor of the tunnel and then, moving to all fours, ran at the party. Erik moved shoulder to shoulder with Turk, gripping his sword with white knuckles. Bryon was still at the back, and Nafer moved next to him, as far away from the fight as possible. Bofim and Beldar moved close to Erik, standing almost on his heels and extending their spear over Erik and Turk's shoulders. Erik could feel their breath and hear it quicken as the sound of claws got closer.

Just as the faint torchlight illuminated the sickening grey figure, it was gone, fading like a shadow banished by the disappearing sun. Erik could still hear the scratching and sucking, but the creature was no longer there.

"Where did it go?" Erik cried, peering into the darkness.

"Damn it, more light," Turk added.

Everyone thrust their torches farther into the darkness, and yet, nothing was there. As Erik poked his head forward, squinting, straining to see anything, he smelled and felt hot, putrid breath. It reminded him of his dreams, of the dead who dwelt there and their stink of death, the smell of carrion and offal ... the smell of evil. Erik recoiled at the stench, leaning back and looking away, and as he did, the face of a tunnel crawler snapped at him from the darkness above. It clung to the roof with its sharp claws, hanging there like a grey, ugly monkey, whipping its tongue about, salivating and hissing.

Erik fell back into Bofim, swinging in retaliation. The blade scratched against the tunnel's wall, barely missing the tunnel crawler's face and sending sparks into the darkness. The creature hissed and snapped again. As Erik tried to regain his footing, Turk jumped in front of him, swinging his axe. It missed, too, and thudded into the ground sending up shards of stone. The tunnel crawler's claws screeched along Turk's mail shirt, and he left his axe in the ground, using his torch like a club and smacking the beast on the shoulder with it. Its skin hissed as it burned, and with a wild scream, it batted the torch away, sending it into the darkness.

In the light of the other torches, Turk retrieved his axe and with both hands, swung again, this time his axe hitting the wall. At the same moment, Bofim jabbed with his spear, also missing. Erik stood firm again and swung, but the tunnel crawler ducked his attack too and rolled back onto all fours, flailing its drooling tongue and hissing. The monster was like smoke, shifting with the movement of the air, always whirling away just in time, always moving too soon.

It snatched at Erik's legs. The man jumped just in time and swung his sword at the monster's arm, nicking it. It drew back momentarily and howled with pain, but quickly lashed out with its other arm. It caught Erik's ankle and pulled hard, its claws trying to dig into his steel greaves. Erik fell backward, and in seconds, before any of his companions could react, the beast was on him, its tongue licking about with excitement, and its breath rapid.

"*Erik!*" Bryon yelled.

Bryon knocked Nafer out of the way, sending him into the wall.

He pushed past Bofim and Beldar, both about to raise their spears in an attack. The tunnel crawler raised its head, mouth open, ready to bite into Erik's face, and as it did so, Bryon rushed in with his whole body, backhanding the creature and sending it into the wall and off Erik. As it bounced against the stone and hissed, mouth open and baring its teeth, Bryon punched his elvish blade through the open maw. Blood and brain matter and skin sizzled against the heat of the sword, and the magical steel even dug into the tunnel wall as if the rock became molten lava. The purple hue the weapon gave off brightened until the light was almost blinding, and, in a single, brief moment, the tunnel crawler caught fire, flared into a ball of flame, and then fell to the floor as a pile of ash.

"Have you ever seen it do that before?" Erik asked, staring at the elvish sword as it returned to its normal brightness.

"No," Bryon said, shaking his head and staring at the pile of ash with wide eyes.

"Well," Turk said, "praise An for your sword. Its strength seems to be growing, especially in your hands, Bryon, and I fear we will need more of its strength ... and soon."

Erik sighed deeply.

"Are you all right, cousin?" Bryon asked.

Erik nodded, now back on his feet.

"We need to keep moving," he said.

They saw the thing that the tunnel crawler was ripping apart when it first attacked them. It was the first tunnel crawler, the one whose arm Erik severed. Its intestines spilled out of its gaunt stomach. Even the stalwart Turk covered his nose with his arm at the smell of the dead thing.

"Wretched things eat each other," Beldar spat. He kicked it as he walked by.

"Hungry animals," Bryon said, "just like those men."

They walked for a while before stopping for a quick rest. The monotony of the tunnel wore on Erik, and he could tell it did the same to the others. He had no idea how long they had walked the underground pathway, but it was the same. Smooth walls, roof just out of torch light, simple floors void of any rocky formations but also a little too rough to have been carved by human or dwarf hands. There were no side tunnels. There were no changes in the inclination of the tunnel. There were no changes in the temperature. Everything was the same. Erik thought this place could be the work of the Shadow, but he also guessed it was part of the protection surrounding the dragon sword.

"This has to be one of the nine hells," Bryon said, echoing Erik's thoughts. He was helping Nafer along, as his broken arm seemed to sap as much of his energy as the walking did.

"You may be right," Beldar replied, "with these demons down here."

"Will there be more?" Erik asked.

"Undoubtedly," Turk replied.

"Great," Bryon added.

"Then we should stop," Erik said. "Put the torches in the middle of the tunnel. We can lean against the walls."

"You mean for us to sleep?" Bryon asked. "With those things out there?"

"I will stay awake," Erik said.

"I'll never be able to sleep in this tunnel," Bryon said, but moments after he leaned against the tunnel wall, he was snoring.

Bryon was soon joined by three other dwarves, Turk the only one staying awake with Erik.

"Go to sleep," Erik said.

"I will stay awake," Turk said, "with you."

"I will be fine," Erik replied, "and when we stop next, you can stay awake, and I will sleep."

But he knew it was a lie. He would never sleep in this place, one where his dreams wandered the realm of the living, where the undead dared to tread past the boundaries of the mind's fantasy. He felt them as soon as he entered this place. He even felt them outside the tunnel, in the valley of the Gray Mountains, as they passed through the Fangs. They were there, just out of the light's reach. He could smell them, hear them, feel them.

He had destroyed Fox and Patûk Al'Banan—men he had killed in his world, cursed to haunt Erik in his dreams. While he stayed in the Lord of the East's keep, he saw them, in a waking dream. They came to him, and he knew it was one of the few times they could actually kill him. But Ilken's Blade was with him, and when he struck them down, they burst into a thousand points of light, and he knew—how, he didn't quite know—they were gone forever.

So, Erik wondered which man he had killed would be leading the undead now. He heard their breathing, their shuffling about, and their cursing, but they weren't quite as aggressive as they once were. Perhaps the Shadow had yet to find them a new leader. It didn't matter. Erik would stay awake and keep them at bay, and when they woke, they would not only face the undead but living demons as well.

11

―――――――

$\mathcal{E}$rik awoke, the torches in the middle of the tunnel waning, flickering with the last bit of light they had to give. He rubbed his eyes. He hadn't meant to sleep, and his slumber was dreamless. He stood. The tunnel looked so pale, the waning light against the gray stone. His companions still slept, and rather soundly. They didn't even snore. They didn't move, not even the lifting of the chest with each breath. He touched his cousin's shoulder. It was cold. His skin was pale. He was dead.

His slumber wasn't dreamless. He was dreaming now.

"When will you realize that I know I am dreaming?" Erik asked the darkness. "This doesn't scare me. They are alive, in my world, in the land of the living."

He spoke to the darkness, and he could feel the presence of the dead, but his dream felt different somehow.

"For now," the hissing chorus said, coming from the darkness in all directions.

"Shall we do this, then?" Erik asked, drawing Ilken's Blade. "Will we fight until I wake? How many of you will I destroy tonight?"

They said nothing. They were scared. Erik smiled, but there was no mirth in the gesture, and his smile quickly faded as a shadow extended across the palely lit space in which he stood. He turned as he heard footsteps, and a figure came into the faint light.

"You," Erik hissed.

Rotten flesh hung from his face, and tattered clothes and broken armor hung from his body. Both an arm and a leg looked as if they had been sown back on, and, around the stitching, his skin had turned black and rolled with the swarm of maggots that ate at his dead flesh.

"You remember me, do you?" the dead man said. His voice was ripe with the condescending tone of nobility.

"I do," Erik replied. "I remember trying to give you mercy. I remember you being a fool. I remember you sending men to their deaths without care." Erik looked at the stitching about the arm and leg. "It seems the trolls did get to you, yes?"

The dead man scowled, revealing a mouth of blackened teeth.

"You are a pompous little shite, aren't you?" the dead man asked. "They warned me about you."

"Who? Them?" Erik asked with a laugh. "I must be really getting under your skin, at least, those of you who still have skin."

"Laugh all you like," the dead man said. "You think you are so powerful. You remember me, but do you remember my name?"

Erik tried to think, but he couldn't recall it. He remembered despising the man, thinking him a coward and cruel man, but he had never thought to commit his name to memory.

"Sorben Phurnan," the dead man said.

"Sorben Phurnan," Erik repeated. "Puppet of Patûk Al'Banan."

"I was no puppet," the man sneered and then began to laugh. The chorus of the dead joined him. "Remember my name well, for it is the name of the man who will spell your doom."

It was Erik's turn to laugh. Sorben Phurnan meant for his threat to be bone-chilling and scary, but Erik couldn't help but think it was the pathetic attempt of an even more wretched man trying to act strong and powerful.

"Is the Shadow so desperate for broken souls to lead his undead that he chose you?" Erik asked.

Sorben Phurnan's smile faded. He was once a lieutenant in Patûk Al'Banan's army of defectors. Erik knew little of the man, but from what he saw at the battle of the green glen, he wasn't a very good leader.

"It looks like you became troll dung," Erik said with a smirk. "It's too bad you aren't wandering the dream world as a pile of scat. That might be rather entertaining in what has become rather droll dreams."

"Joke all you want, Erik Eleodum," Sorben said. "Your time is coming."

"That's what Fox said," Erik replied, "and now he's gone forever."

As soon as he mentioned that about Fox, Erik remembered what someone had told him about his dreams. Most of the time, he dreamed of a wide-open grassy field with a single hill. A weeping willow stood atop the hill, and a man sat under that willow tree. Erik knew the man, from somewhere, but he could never tell and, just as he thought he remembered who the man was, he would awake. But that man warned him, once, about taunting the dead.

Erik's smile faded.

"Are we fighting or what?" he asked. "I need to get back to my world and fight more tunnel crawlers."

"No," Sorben said, "no fighting today."

Erik heard the sound of hissing and clawing in the darkness. It wasn't the undead. Sorben looked scared and the shadow in the pale light deepened.

"The Shadow Children," Sorben hissed. He looked scared as he backed up into the darkness. "They will have their fun with you. I will see you soon enough."

Sorben cackled, although his laughter sounded forced, and the undead that followed him joined in. The walls of the tunnel shook with their enjoyment, and the dead man continued to back up into the shadows until Erik could no longer see him.

Erik awoke, sweat beading down his forehead. His cousin and the dwarves were already up, sitting around the circle of torches they had made to shed light on their makeshift camp.

"So much for our fearless leader staying awake and watching out for us while we slept," Bryon said, smiling.

"Why didn't you wake me?" Erik asked.

"We know you don't normally sleep," Turk said, "so we figured you deserved it."

"I guess I didn't realize how tired I was," Erik said. "Are you ready?"

Turk nodded.

They hadn't walked but a league when Nafer grabbed Bryon's arm and stopped him.

"I hear something," the dwarf said.

"What is it?" Bryon asked.

"I hear it too," Beldar said.

"It sounds like scratching," Turk explained, "and growling."

"Great," Bryon muttered cynically.

"I can't see a thing," Erik said.

A deafening screech echoed off the walls, and all six of them winced at the sound.

"More tunnel crawlers," Turk muttered indignantly.

"Son of a whore," Bryon whispered dejectedly.

A scratching sound slowly crept through the tunnel. It was followed by a high-pitched grumble, then several bird-like chirps. Another chirp and grumble, different from the first, answered the first sounds. The noises of heavy sniffing filled the stale air around the company. The noise rose to a chorus of noises inspecting the air. The sound was like a myriad of nails scratched against stone slab, grating at ears and sending shivers up the spine.

"There is more than one this time," Turk said, a worried edge to his voice.

"Get ready," Bryon said from the back of their group.

Erik turned to see his cousin gripping his sword with both hands, an adrenaline fueled look on his face that showed a combination of both fear and excitement. Just for a moment, Erik was taken back to their childhood and Bryon's expression as he prepared to jump down into a deep waterfall. Then the sniffing stopped, and a tense silence filled the tunnel. It was so quiet, Erik wondered if he had gone deaf.

Then, in an instant, an opus of shrieking, gurgling, and screaming erupted that jangled every nerve in Erik's body, and as that quieted, he heard the scratching of claws against stone. As thin, gray shadows flickered in and out of sight at the edge of the party's firelight, Bryon pushed his way to the front of the party.

"*Bastards!*" he seethed, "we'll kill them all."

Four tunnel crawlers appeared in the torchlight, all scampering across the walls like giant, four-legged insects. When one of the creatures closed in on them, it jumped from the wall to the floor, growling and snarling on all fours, back arched like an angry cat. It leapt at Erik, but as soon as it was in the air, Turk swung his axe. It dodged that attack, curling itself into a ball initially, but soon reverted to its normal shape and landed on all fours. It screamed and spat at Erik, but the sound changed to a manic gurgling as he brought his sword down upon the monster's head, and Ilken's Blade cleaved through its face down to its shoulders.

Erik breathed heavy, almost gagging on the smell of the tunnel crawler's blood. His own adrenaline kicked in again with the kill, and he felt his heart speed up even more as he knew others were coming. He turned and saw them bounce from wall to wall to roof, lashing out with their hideous, snake-like tongues and sniffing the air around them. Spears and swords jabbed at the monsters while Turk's axe swiped back and forth, but shadow and speed and a seemingly supernatural sense seemed to thwart every attack. And then the creatures' own assault would come, quick and then gone, scratching to draw a drop of blood there. It was nothing mortal, but enough to wear down their prey.

One tunnel crawler jumped out of sight onto the roof, and Erik could hear it skittering along above them, in the darkness. He tried to follow the sound and keep his eyes on the other two in front of them, but the thing finally moved out of the darkness above, leaping down onto Beldar's back, clawing at his throat and face. Beldar dropped his spear and screamed, punching backward. Every time he swung, the tunnel crawler jerked its head sideways only to bite at the dwarf's knuckles and wrists. Nafer rushed forward and managed to grab the monster around the neck with his good arm. He pulled hard, choking the beast. It gagged and hissed, then threw its head back, throwing its hard, gray skull into Nafer and breaking his nose.

Nafer immediately let go of the tunnel crawler, his eyes watering and blood flowing from his nostrils. As he stepped backward, stunned and clutching his nose, the tunnel crawler released Beldar's neck, put its feet into his back, pushed him forward so that he fell on his face, and turned to Nafer. It growled, its tongue flicking and salivating as it smelled blood. Nafer knew it was there, but he couldn't see because of his watering eyes. Just as the tunnel crawler was about to attack, it paused for a moment, and that was enough; Bofim rammed his spear into its ribs.

As he retracted the blade, blood and other body fluids spilled onto the floor. Nafer kicked out at the injured tunnel crawler, and the toe of his boot, capped with an iron plate, shattered the monster's teeth. Bofim jumped over Beldar, who was still lying on the floor, and brought his axe down onto the creature's neck several times until the head rolled from its body, and it slumped to the floor in a gray heap.

Bryon blocked another attack with his sword, the heat of his magical blade burning the tunnel crawler's hand. The monster hissed and jumped up into the darkness of the roof. Bryon lifted his sword, the magic flaring and the light brightening until they could see the creature up there, clinging to stone. Now thrown, Bofim's spear flew at this one, but it easily dodged the attack, the spear ricocheting off the roof and into the darkness.

The creature appeared in front of Bryon again, and he snapped his sword down hard, with an angry grunt. The tunnel crawler grabbed at the blade with both hands, seeking to push it away, but the momentum of Bryon's attack was too much, and the steel cleaved through its face. The blade's magic flared again and, before the creature realized it's injury, its hands and head caught fire. As flesh and bone burned away, it screamed and howled, frozen from pain. Bryon brought his sword down on the thing's head several more times until nothing was left but its burning torso.

The last tunnel crawler had reached out, grabbing Erik's ankle and catching him by surprise. He expected the creature to leap on him, but apparently it had learned from its comrades' deaths and stayed in the darkness, its clawed hands wrapped around Erik's ankle, the rest of its body in the darkness. For such a thin, emaciated thing, it had immense strength, and Erik felt himself being pulled rapidly along the tunnel floor. He had lost his torch and, even though he still held Ilken's Blade, once he entered the darkness, he would be in this monster's realm ... he would also be in *their* realm.

He could hear them laughing, cheering, and crying out in victory, their voices so distant and, yet, so loud. He could hear Sorben Phurnan. But still, the dead man's laughter sounded forced, afraid even.

"*Turk! Bryon!*" Erik cried out.

He could hear the tunnel crawler growling, hissing with glee. At first, he tried kicking out, but then, he felt paralyzed, as if the dead were holding his arms and legs still from the other side, reaching through to him from the dream world. He didn't smell their stink, or sense the chill of their presence. Rather, he felt hot, like fire blowing against his face, and if shadows could grow darker, they did.

He saw a flash of light, and a small hand axe twirled by before a spear flew overhead. He heard footsteps and shouting, and a quick scream and hiss before he felt the grip on his ankle release. He then smelled burning flesh before the intensity of the light began to increase, as did the stink of burning.

As the light faded again, Erik started to get up, knowing his companions were there, watching him, waiting on him. Bryon had even offered him his hand, but he needed just a little more time to gather himself, to make sure he didn't piss himself and accept he wasn't dreaming, but truly still alive. He sat up, staring at the pile of burning tunnel crawler, its body rapidly turning to ash as had those of the others who had felt Bryon's blade. Erik took a deep breath and shook his head; he hadn't been that frightened in a long time, and they—the dead—would have felt it. He had felt them, but they weren't close. They were distant, waiting. Erik raised an eyebrow.

"Erik, are you all right?" Turk asked, putting a hand on the man's shoulder.

Erik looked up at his friend. Despite his shorter stature—although rather tall for many dwarves—he had gigantic qualities about him. He was well-muscled, even more so than the strongest-looking men, and his beard had grown even longer, forcing him to twist it into four braids and then twist those braids together. But the dwarf had a warming smile, and the biggest thing about Erik's friend was his heart. His concern was genuine as his eyes looked down at Erik, just sitting there, and, at that moment, Erik felt blessed to be amongst these warriors. He pushed himself to his knees and then his feet. Now, looking down at his dwarvish friend, he put a hand on his shoulder and nodded.

"I am now, thanks to you," Erik said with a smile.

"I didn't do much," Turk replied. "It was mostly your cousin and his elvish sword."

"How hard is that, giving your thanks to something that is elvish?" Erik asked, and Turk answered with a short laugh.

Even though the elves had retreated into the vast forests of Ul'Erel long ago, a contempt and almost hatred between them and the dwarves existed. It was ages old and deeper than any wound.

"As I have learned to love men as much as I love my brother dwarves," Turk replied, "I think I have also learned to let go of my disdain for elves. Of course, I have never met one, but I do hope, if given the chance one day, I would give him or her the opportunity to prove themselves deserving of respect as one of An's creations ... even if they do have pointed ears."

Turk and Erik laughed together, and it felt good to experience some semblance of happiness in such a dark and evil place.

"Disgusting," Bryon said, his nose wrinkled in a look of repulsion. He spat on the pile of ash that was once the tunnel crawler trying to carry Erik away into the darkness.

Turk stared into the darkness, a scowl replacing his recent smile.

"What did you see from the sword's burning light? Were there more?" Erik asked.

"Many more," Turk replied. "There must have been two dozen lurking in the darkness, but when Bryon struck the one that had a hold of you, his sword flared, even brighter than before. It was as if it could sense the presence of the Shadow." The dwarf pointed to the pile of ash that was once Erik's attacker.

But what Erik had felt was something different, something just as dark and evil, but not the Shadow. It wasn't cold and distant, but hot and suffocating and, even though the dead were there, they waited, in the distance, far away, just as afraid as Erik was.

"Before that one caught fire, several others came to try and get the body, no doubt as a meal later," Turk continued, "but they were consumed by the flames. Several ran as they caught fire, setting alight more tunnel crawlers and so on until the whole tunnel was alight with burning monsters."

Erik looked to Bryon, and his cousin just shrugged.

"Not a bad time to find out it could do that, I suppose," Bryon said.

"No," Erik replied, "not a bad time at all."

12

─────────

*B*ryon wiped more sweat from his forehead and rubbed his eyes, sleep, dreams of his dead cousin Befel, still fresh in his mind. Turk crouched over Nafer, rubbing more of his salve on the dwarf's broken arm and then some of it on his face and nose, which had already started to discolor with bruising.

"I am running out," Turk said, and then chuckled. "You are not allowed to get any more injuries."

Turk closed his eyes and prayed over Nafer. He had offered to tend to Beldar first, who had several jagged cuts along his face and throat, but the dwarf refused, insisting that Turk tend to Nafer's more severe problems.

As Turk prayed, the faint glow silhouetted him and Nafer again. When he stopped, breathing heavy as his healing sapped much of his energy, most of the bruising around Nafer's cheeks and under his eyes was gone, although his nose was still swollen and misshapen, and he was clearly breathing through his mouth all the time.

"You need to rest," Nafer said to Turk.

"No ... I have a bit more energy I can ... spare," Turk said, his eyelids half-closed, his head lolling back as if he was about to pass out.

"You have done enough for now," Erik said, helping Turk to the ground so he might get some rest. "If there are more tunnel crawlers out there, we will need you as strong as possible."

Bryon looked at Nafer.

"You look like the nine hells," Bryon said with a smile.

Nafer forced a quick laugh, but Erik shot him a dirty look.

"My poor friend," Erik said, "you look so uncomfortable. I am sorry."

"I have seen better days," Nafer replied with a mirthless chuckle, "but I have also seen worse."

They had placed their torches in the center of the tunnel again, each leaning against the wall, save for Turk, who already slept and snored.

"I wonder what Wrothgard is doing right now," Nafer said.

"He's probably sitting somewhere, just waiting for the Lord of the East and his assassins," Erik said with a mirthless smile on his face.

"I think not," Nafer said, "I imagine him to be sitting by a blazing fire with a glass of spiced wine and a tray of cheese and bread. He is somewhere far away, where the Lord of the East can't find him."

"He might be already dead," Bofim said.

"Well, thank you very much for making our cheery situation even merrier," Bryon said. "Leave it to the dwarves to put a damper on our conversation."

Bofim just shrugged.

"The Lord of the East can find you wherever you go," he said. "He could find us in here if he wanted to."

"Well, wherever he is, I think I hate Wrothgard right now," Bryon said. "You know why? Because I think he is drunk. I think he's drunk on the best ale or wine all that Shadow be damned dwarvish gold can buy. And he's in bed with a whore. Or two. And they're the best money can buy also. Prick."

Now everyone laughed out loud, drowning Turk's snore for a moment.

"Joking aside," Bryon added, "we could use his sword right about now."

"He was the best," Erik said.

"At least the best we had ever known," Bryon added.

"We could only hope he is safe and happy," Nafer said. "He was a good man ..."

"For an easterner," Beldar said.

"No, for anyone," Nafer replied. "I wish him well, and I do hope he remains hidden. He deserves more than an assassin's knife in his back."

"Well," Bryon said, lifting his waterskin, "here is to our friend who cannot be with us in body, but will always be with us in our hearts."

Everyone else lifted their waterskins and toasted with Bryon. When his eyes met Erik's, he saw a mixture of joy and sadness in them. Thinking of the past did that, especially to his little cousin. It was as if he missed the simpler times, and Bryon supposed a part of him did too. And not that his cousin was little anymore.

They sat there for a while longer, talking and reminiscing, as they had done around a fire many times. However fleeting, those moments provided familiarity, and as they conversed around their torches, they could briefly forget about the constricting tunnel and darkness that surrounded them. As they fell silent, each sleeping or with their own thoughts, Bryon closed his eyes and imagined he was on his farm, before he found himself swimming through a mountain of gold hidden away in an ancient dwarvish city. He finally ended up in bed with a beautiful woman ... or three. These memories—or daydreams—of better times, faded, and the cold darkness with the apprehension of creatures of the Shadow waiting for them became their world again. The blackness weighed on Bryon's shoulders like bundles of wood and anxiety seemed to replace the blood in his veins. He knew the others felt the same way.

Erik waited a while, but eventually, he nodded to Bryon, who nodded back and stood to rouse Turk. Once the dwarf nodded he was ready, without a single word, Erik walked into the darkness, dimly shrouded by torchlight, before following his cousin. After too many moments of silence, the dwarves tried to sing, but their echoing voices and melodious tunes carried on into the abyss without the normal joy they sent into the open sky on a starry night. When the dwarves finally stopped, Bryon whistled some tunes he remembered from days on the farm, but his cheeks grew tired and his lips dried, and his whistling became more maddening than the dripping water.

"What about your flute?" Bryon asked Erik.

Erik looked at him over his shoulder.

"What about it?" Erik replied.

"It always seems to lighten the mood," Bryon said.

Erik walked awhile before replying but eventually looked back at Bryon again.

"Not now," Erik replied. "I don't think there is anything cheerful about this place, and we can't make it such."

Bryon kept his mind busy. That was how he passed the time ... thinking. He imagined things from the past, even stories his uncle or the dwarves told him. He imagined things that might have been, if he stayed on the farm, if he grew up in the east rather than the west; if he was the son of a noble knight, a duke, or a king even. Losing himself in thought always brought Bryon's cousin Befel to mind. He recalled the memories he had of his cousin; Befel walking in a field of golden wheat, or laughing and drinking his father's orange brandy behind his barn, or seeing who could get a kiss from some girl at a Peace Day celebration first, or being mighty warriors ... or being consumed by a fire hotter than the nine hells. Bryon missed Befel at Erik's wedding. He felt awkward standing with his cousin, as his nearest kin supporter as was the tradition, but he was glad to do it, honored even, but that place was meant for Befel. And what of Erik's baby? Erik told him his child would call Bryon uncle, and that made him smile, but he really wasn't the unborn child's uncle. Befel was.

The torches started to falter. Erik blew gently on his, trying to keep it going, but the stale air was a hindrance, and the black pitch began to burn away. Every step into the tunnel seemed like a step away from the outside world, as if they would walk in darkness until their last breath. With every pace forward, air was a little fouler and a little more stagnant. Each breath Bryon took stung his lungs, and he began to feel like gagging. Perhaps the end would come sooner than expected.

No one really knew whether it was day or night, they just stopped to rest after they'd begun to slow down. Bryon could only guess now but thought they'd been in the tunnel for several days. He'd be very happy to get out not only for fresh air and sunlight, but also some fresh meat cooked over an open fire.

"Thank the heavens it seems as if there are no more tunnel crawlers," Bryon said, no doubt voicing what everyone was thinking.

"Aye," Turk responded, "foul beasts they are. I have never seen anything like them; they are almost not even animals. Even a dog can be reasoned with. Not even a bear would attack a group of well-armored warriors, even if it were starving. You would have to be threatening one of its cubs for it to do such a thing."

"Shadow Children," Erik said. "That is what they are called, yes?"

"Yes," Nafer replied. "How do you know this?"

"My dreams told me," Erik said.

"I remember my grandfather, and even great grandfather, talking of them, telling scary stories about these creatures when my grandmother and sisters weren't listening," Nafer said. "Their beginning goes back to the Age of Darkness, the time of ignorance, not evil, and even we Ervendwarfol and the Elenderel were primitive to some extent. Many of the evil creatures that inhabit our world today were born of the Elder Days, ages past the Age of Darkness when the Shadow tried to imitate An, and those creations reigned in Háthgolthane until the end of the Great Darkening."

Nafer took a breath and rubbed his bald upper lip, not much wanting to think of such things.

"The tunnel crawlers are an older abomination, an older evil,"

Nafer continued. "Even before the Age of Darkness, even before time was time and morning was separate from night and the sun and moon shone in the heavens and the world was nothing, a great battle waged against good and evil, against An and the Shadow. An has always been, but no one really knows where the Shadow came from. We dwarves, as many men in the west do, believe he was one of An's creatures who became jealous of An's power. However he came to be, the Shadow raised an army of wicked spirits, the twisted remnants of their once beautiful forms, and they fought viciously to control the heavens. Some of these demons, through victory and wickedness, through treachery and deceit, became generals in the Shadow's army, and he gave them powers upon powers, powers that were almost god-like."

Nafer coughed and spat out dust that had collected on his tongue while he spoke. He rubbed his upper lip again and wiped a simple trickle of sweat that had collected just above his left eyebrow.

"One such demon was Yebritoch," Nafer said after taking a moment to wet his mouth with a drop of water. "In many ages past, and the armies of the Shadow began to lose, and then An, the Almighty, created the world, and a new battlefield was formed. Yebritoch was appointed High Commander to the Shadow's armies and the earth, trying to thwart An, the Creator. His powers were so great that he created his own army—like An had created dwarves and elves and men—only his minions were sick and distorted; the tunnel crawlers.

Back then, they were not just mindless animals, and Yebritoch would lead them into battle riding on a chariot of elvish bones pulled by four great monsters, the Beasts of Chaos. An was too powerful, is too powerful, though, for some fool demon. An crushed Yebritoch's demonic forces, threw him back to the realm of the Shadow, imprisoned each of the beasts of chaos in a gem—the Emerald of the East, Sapphire of the South, Ruby of the West, and Diamond of the North —and spread them to the corners of the earth. He took the intelligence from the tunnel crawlers and drove them into the darkest parts of the mountains, making them the mindless scavengers they are today. The demon, Yebritoch, returned to the realm of the Shadow where he was punished for his failure. He now opposes both An and the Shadow from his own domain of earth and fire and is worshipped by many of the alfingas—goblins—as well as others secretly in Háth-golthane."

"Did you say fire?" Erik asked.

"Aye," Nafer said. "He is said to control fire as his chosen element."

Bryon could help but notice the pensive look on Erik's face.

"So, what are these tunnel crawlers then?" Bryon asked. "Are they demons?"

"In a sense, they are. They were demon spawn, horrible crossings of men with demon blood, twisted and tortured over time," Nafer replied.

"So, are they evil?" Bryon asked.

"Some would say so," Nafer replied. "Some would say that wickedness is in their blood, being the children of the Shadow. Some would say that despite their mindlessness, evil still courses through their veins, and what they do is in the service of evil. Others would say that enough time has passed that they are now simply animals. Nonetheless, they are also known as Shadow Children."

"Great," Bryon said, his voice dripping with sarcasm.

The tunnel began to change as the roof brushed errant strands of hair on Bryon's head, and they had to walk in a single file line. The walls looked more like those of a natural mountain tunnel, cut away by water and earthquakes over millennia, and there were different signs of life. Insects skittered and scurried away when caught by the torchlight, and albino rats with mottled white fur and red eyes squeaked and spat as they hurried back into darkness.

"Will this tunnel just eventually close in on us?" Bryon asked. "Are we going to walk for days and days and find ourselves looking at a dead end?"

"My father sought to get me to accept things always get worse before they got better," Turk said. "I never believed him, but now I know what he meant."

"The man in Eldmanor said this was the way we must go," Erik added.

"That does not make me feel better either," Bryon said.

"Me neither," Erik said. "I'm beginning to wonder, is this the only way to get to Fealmynster, and if not, then why send us this way?"

"Let's just hope whoever, or whatever made these tunnels made an exit."

13

———

Bu had gone to take a piss when he heard something hissing and rattling from within the forest. He quickly finished, and when he was moving back towards their fire, something white shot out from the darkness and struck one of the Hámonian knights on his breastplate. Bu froze as the man stared down at his chest, a silver line leading from him to the trees.

"What, by the gods?" the man said, his expression one of annoyance as well as surprise.

He reached out to the strange substance to pull it away, but as he touched the thin, silvery thread, his eyes widened when his hand became stuck. A moment later, the knight flew through the air towards the dark forest that surrounded them, screaming as he bounced off the trunks of the trees with a series of sickening thuds. Bu heard the man scream again, seemingly in agony, and two of his men meant to make for the trees, but Bao Zi grabbed both soldiers by their wrists and held them fast.

"Stay where you stand," the old man croaked.

Another scream was cut off in mid breath, and the sudden silence was filled with the sickening sound of something tearing flesh, a man gurgling, and then slurping. Bu wasn't a squeamish man. Growing up on the streets of Fen-Stévock, a beggar and the son of a whore, he saw plenty a boy shouldn't see. But the knight's final scream, and the sounds that followed ... Bu would remember those for a long time.

At the edge of the firelight and with his back to the forest, one of his soldiers stared in the direction the knight was pulled. He was a stalwart man, all the eastern soldiers were, especially when compared to these Hámonian knights, but the look on his face told Bu he might piss himself. He held his spear tight with his shield pulled close to his body.

Something behind the soldier hissed, then a clicking sound, followed by a rustling and a chattering, came from the darkness. The man slowly looked over his shoulder as if he didn't want to turn to see what was there. As he did, his eyes went wide, and he screamed.

"What is it?" Bu shouted, but the soldier gave no reply.

Something long and black and tipped with a claw-like blade stabbed out into the light from the flames. The soldier lifted his shield, but the claw shattered the wood. The man gripped his spear with both hands as several other soldiers started running to his aid, but another long, black claw appeared, this time stabbing the man in the shoulder. The leather breastplate did little to stop the barbed appendage from piercing the man's flesh, and he cried out as he fell backward.

Bu stopped breathing, and his skin went cold when he saw what it was that attacked his soldier. A spider, its body round and the size of a large dog stepped out from the darkness to the edge of the firelight. A sharp claw tipped each of its eight legs, and it thrust them into the ground as if exerting its dominance over these men. The soldier it had attacked tried to stand, despite the blood rushing from his wound, but the spider lifted its head and two huge pincers before it spat a thin line of webbing from its abdomen, striking the man in the face. He dropped his spear and clutched at the white silk, screaming.

"It burns!" he cried as his hands got stuck to the webbing when he tried to peel it off his face.

The spider rushed the man, and the others now backed away, not willing to risk their lives for this soldier who was as good as dead. The creature jammed two of its forelimbs into the soldier's chest, pushing him back to the ground. As everyone else just watched in horror, unable to move, the spider drooled on the man and stabbed him with one of its pincers. The soldier screamed and kicked and gurgled as the spider picked him up with both pincers and rushed back into the darkness of the forest.

"Get out of here now!" Bu cried.

He grabbed Warrior's reins, ready to mount the mighty warhorse and ride away as hard and fast as he could, but he saw another Hámonian knight mount up and, even though at least four of his soldiers surrounded the mounted man, he was the target of another spider's attack, this one from the tree branches overhead.

A line of webbing entangled the horse's forelimbs, and the beast toppled over with a desperate whinny. Before the knight knew what had happened, the huge spider landed on the horse and jammed its fangs into the horse's neck. The animal struggled under the spider for a moment, but the poison soon took effect, and it went still, foaming at the mouth.

Much to the knight's credit, he stood, producing a flail with his left hand and drawing his long sword with his right. He might as well have been holding two sticks. The sharp claw of one leg stabbed one of the knight's legs, his plate mail doing little to stop the appendage. He swung down hard with his sword and must have done at least a bit of damage as the spider hissed, bristles on its legs straightening and rattling. At that moment, the knight turned to run, but the spider crouched, bending all eight of its legs, and launched itself onto the knight's back, pushing him to the ground, and jamming its fangs into his back and neck. Bu couldn't hear the man's screams, muffled by the mountain floor and snow, but at that moment, he realized that riding Warrior made him a larger target. He turned to his horse.

"*Run, Warrior!*" Bu yelled, smacking the horse's rump. "*Run faster than all these bastards, back to Hámon!*"

The horse didn't need any more encouragement, and the great destrier galloped away in the opposite direction.

"Release the horses," Bu commanded. "Hopefully, they will serve as a distraction."

Bao Zi began slapping rumps, sending horses in various directions. It seemed to work, at least for a moment, as they heard the sounds of the spiders moving away from them, supposedly giving chase after the fleeing animals.

"Now is our chance, Bao Zi," Bu said.

As they ran, Andu held a torch, and Bao Zi and Bu followed him. Just when Bu thought they had escaped this nightmare, he heard hissing and rattling and chattering again. He could see other torches in the forest, some close and some far away. One torch disappeared, followed by the sounds of struggle and a scream. Then another ... and another. The torches started veering towards them.

"Stay away, you fools," Bu hissed. "Draw these demons away from us."

"Shall I kill them as they come into view?" Bao Zi asked, his voice even and calm even though they were running for their lives.

Bu just shook his head as what was left of his men and the knights joined back up with him.

They ran until they had to stop, but as soon as they had caught their breath, they set off again, running for most the night. It was hard to tell when daybreak was actually coming in the Gray Mountains, with the tall peaks and thick clouds, but Bu saw the intermittent pinks and oranges of an early morning casting lines of light through spaces in the branches of the tall trees; he had never been so happy to see a sunrise. He normally welcomed the night; he was an agent of the darkness, a creature of the shadows. It was his realm for his years as a spy, a tracker, and an assassin, but he learned to love the night when he was a boy, when his mother had gone out working; when she was away, it meant she couldn't beat him.

Bu stopped, and so did his men, now less than half the number who had set out with him from Hámon. They weren't really in a clearing, although the trees were a little less cramped here. He put his hands on his knees, trying to catch his breath once more, his thighs burned, and his stomach cramped.

"Water, my lord," Andu said, and Bu snatched the waterskin out of the man's hand, drinking all of its contents and throwing the skin back into the easterner's chest without so much as a thanks. He looked around and shook his head. As usual, Bao Zi understood his master's thoughts.

"We have lost some of the best men."

"It's not good," Bu replied.

"We're alive. That's all that matters."

"It is," said Andu.

Bao Zi turned hard on the man. Andu had once served the Lord of the East, as sergeant of a small contingency that guarded the largest mining camp in Golgolithul's employ—Aga Min. He came from a small but wealthy house in the east, and his father was a cripple. He was the only male heir, so when Patûk Al'Banan commanded his trolls and men to attack the camp, killing its old and broken master, Cho, Andu turned traitor to save his own life and agreed to serve Patûk. The general had broken the man. He was little more than a dog, but, under the tutelage of true eastern training, he had become an adept fighter, and he now served Bu with unwavering loyalty. Still, neither Bu nor Bao Zi could really stand the man, and the moment he lost his usefulness, Bu would dispose of him.

"Not you, you yellow-bellied rat turd!" Bao Zi croaked, and Andu ducked at the man's words. "No one gives a troll shit about you. Just keep the king's waterskin full, and I won't gut you like the neutered coward you are."

"Yes, my lord," Andu said with a quick bow.

"We should keep moving," Bao Zi said, turning back to Bu.

"Any idea where we are?" Bu asked softly, so the others couldn't hear.

"None, my lord," Bao Zi replied, "but I wouldn't feel good about staying here. Not with *them* still out there."

"Truly frightening," Bu admitted.

"I've never seen anything like it, my lord," Bao Zi said. "They were maybe one of the most terrifying things I have ever seen in my life."

For Bao Zi to say something was terrifying meant it truly was; normally nothing scared the old hardened warrior. Bu nodded in agreement.

"My legs ache," one of the knights said, a man named Sir Caleb. Both he and Sir Garrett had survived the ordeal with the spiders. "Are we going to stop and rest?"

Bu saw Bao Zi grind his teeth, his hand going to his sword. Bu grabbed the man's wrist.

"Stay here all you want," Bu said, "and become spider droppings. I'm going to keep moving lest I wind up a cocoon with my guts being sucked out."

They kept moving. It was just before noon, and the snow had started again.

"We need to find out where we are," Bu said as they finally stopped for a short break.

"Aye, my lord," Bao Zi replied.

The old soldier looked at the map for a moment and was about to hand it to Bu when he stopped, lifting his nose and sniffing at the air. Bu knew what that meant, and he crouched, squinting and trying to peer through the trees. He punched his hands through the snow, feeling for the ground, seeing if he could pick up on any vibrations. He caught a whiff of what he suspected Bao Zi smelled—strong body odor, rancid sweat, and bear fat.

"What is that?" Bu asked, sniffing at the air.

"Dwarves," Bao Zi grumbled.

"Dwarves don't smell that bad," Bu replied.

"What is it, my lord?" Andu asked.

"Shut up, you idiot," Bao Zi cursed.

They looked all about. Bu's men knew something was wrong, just by seeing their leader, and they readied their weapons, but the knights hadn't a clue, and they continued to talk and jape.

Bu heard the sound of wood crack accompanied by the heavy crunching of snow as a fallen tree crashed through the forest. The smell grew stronger, causing Bu to almost retch. A deep growl reverberated through the trees when a giant of a man burst through the space between two tall pines, pushing them aside as if they were simple saplings.

This wasn't a man. It ... he looked like a man, in certain ways, with two arms and two legs and a torso and head, but there the true resemblance ended. Its arms were almost as long as its legs, and it stood at least twice the height of most men. It looked as if he had no neck, and his jaw was abnormally wide with big, bushy eyebrows and a sloping brow. He had a wide, bulbous nose that resembled a dwarf's, and his hair was black and wild and knotted into tight, dirty clumps; his beard was as bad. He wore a simple vest of some animal hide, and it extended down to his knees. As this giant man-creature stood there, surveying Bu and his men, it roared, clutching both of his dirty hands into tight fists. He didn't carry a weapon but grabbed a thick branch from one of the trees he pushed aside and easily ripped it away, his intentions clearly to use it as a club.

One of Bu's men ran to the giant creature. A noble move, but a stupid one. The giant man swung its new club hard, crushing the man's skull like a grape. Where Bu's men moved in front of him, most of the Hámonian knights moved to run, but two more of these giant men burst through the forest. They could have easily killed them, but rather, they started grabbing soldiers and knights as yet another giant stepped through the trees, a large bag in his hands.

"What do we do?" Andu asked.

"Shut up," Bao Zi said.

"We run," Bu said, but as he began to run, he felt a hand clamp around his arm and pull him hard, throwing him to the ground.

As the giant man held Bu there, he twisted, his shoulder on the brink of dislocating, retrieving a dagger from his belt and jamming it into the meaty part of the beast's inside arm. He howled and let go of Bu.

Bao Zi came to his king's rescue, sword unsheathed, but a giant kicked out at him, sending him into the trunk of a tree. That would have stopped most men, but Bao Zi wasn't most men, and he got to his feet, coming to Bu's side once again. The giant Bu had stabbed fumed and cursed in a language that sounded oddly like Dwarvish.

Bu watched as the giants subdued his men. The easterners that were with him tried to form a small wall in front of him, their loyalty unshakable, but not a single one made it. They were all hit over the head with a makeshift club or held underfoot until the giant with a bag could tie them up and throw them in his sack. The knights fought back as well, caring little for their king and more for themselves. Bu saw four of them, the giants' attention elsewhere, take the opportunity to run, and Bu followed, knowing Bao Zi and Andu were right behind him. His stomach twisted, a little, as he knew his men were still back there, in the clutches of those creatures, bundled up in a sack. They had given their lives for him, something he would have done for his general, Patûk Al'Banan, and these Hámonian knights could have cared less about what happened to him. He scowled.

"We need to rescue them," Bu said when they stopped.

"How?" Sir Caleb asked. "They are gone. We should just go back to Hámon."

"We stay the course," Bu said, grabbing the knight's tabard and pulling him close and then pushing him away with a disgusted grunt. "Those men gave their lives for me. It is the least we could do."

"Did you see those creatures?" Sir Garrett asked.

"Of course, I did," Bu replied. "It doesn't matter. Find your balls because we are following them. Bao Zi."

The old soldier nodded with a grunt.

14

———

The tunnel through which they traveled narrowed so badly, Erik found himself crouching and, at times, walking on his hands and knees. With so little space and so little air, the torches waned and flickered, and several times, someone's went out.

"When do we start heading back?" Erik asked.

"Yesterday," Bryon said.

"When was yesterday?" Turk asked.

"You tell me," Bryon replied. "You're the dwarf. You live in environments like this."

Bryon chanced a laugh, and Turk joined him, even if it was forced. This was a hopeless place. Clearly, the old man in Eldmanor was crazy ... and wrong. They would have to turn back soon, lest they get stuck and live out the rest of their miserable lives caught underneath a mountain.

Erik was just considering they discuss turning back when the ground beneath him gave way. He slid down a wet slope, giving a quick yelp. His torch flared up, as fresh air struck it, but then it skittered away, struck something, and it was gone, along with its light. He seemed to slide for a long time, but then his head struck something hard, and he went dizzy for a moment.

"Erik!" Turk called and, when he had regained his wits, Erik looked up and saw a distant torch.

He stood quickly. The roof was clearly tall enough for him to stand. But it was dark, the only light the distant torch. Erik's pulse quickened. He felt sweat trickle down his face and, as hard as it was, he tried to control his breathing, but failed. He drew his sword. The sound of steel on leather echoed throughout whatever space he was in.

"Erik!" Turk called again.

He saw a torch and the distant purple light of Bryon's sword.

"I'm fine!" Erik called back, and his voice echoed.

He heard rocks shifting somewhere in the darkness, and he turned, Ilken's Blade out and ready. His breathing quickened even more, and he gripped his sword in both hands, staring into blackness. He couldn't see anything, save for the distant light of his friends' torches above. He heard laughter and thought he felt something brush his cheek. He didn't know if it was his imagination, or the mountain playing tricks with him, but he sensed they were there.

"To the Shadow with this," Erik muttered.

He patted his golden-handled dagger.

Do you think you could spare me some light?

The tingle at his hip was all the confirmation he needed. He drew his dagger, and as soon as it left its golden scabbard, it blazed with a golden light that spread out in the darkness like a beacon. Erik heard hissing and the shuffling of feet. They were there. It wasn't a figment of his imagination. He felt a vibration in his left hand, and the vision of a silver circlet with a sapphire studded in the middle popped into his head; Lord Balzarak's gift to him. He retrieved the circlet from his haversack and placed it on his head. It wasn't quite an exact fit—his head was too big—but it fitted well enough, and as soon as it rested there, the sapphire lit up like a blue beacon. Erik heard more hissing.

"Not today," Erik said.

He expected to hear Sorben Phurnan's voice, but instead, he simply heard a hiss and felt heat against his face and smelled burnt wood and coal. He tilted his head, pensively.

"Erik!" Turk said. "We see you. Don't move. We're coming."

"Carefully," Erik called. "Come down on your ass, and slow your descent with your feet."

As Turk descended the wet slope, Erik turned about, his illuminated dagger extended. He was in a giant cavern. A stalagmite had stopped him, although the ground evened out where he stood. When he looked up, he couldn't see the roof, and when he looked side to side, he couldn't see the walls. Looking straight forward, he also only saw darkness, and he turned around, feeling childish and foolish about being scared.

Bryon came next, followed by Beldar. Nafer slid down with Bofim, Bofim hugging Nafer to him, seeking to protect his injured arm. They crashed into another stalagmite and seemed shaken, but only for a moment. They lost another torch, but between Bryon's sword and Erik's dagger and circlet, they had enough light.

"Shall we go," Erik said with a smile.

"You need to be more careful," Turk said. "A wrong move in a dark place like this can mean your death ... a very dark and lonely death."

"I didn't know your dagger glowed," Bryon said as they marched through the wide-open cavern.

"I didn't either," Erik said, and as he felt a tingle in his hand, he smiled.

"And the circlet?" Bryon asked.

"A gift from Balzarak," Erik replied. "I figured it might glow like the one he wore."

"Well, thank the Creator for Lord Balzarak, but you might have tried it out a bit sooner!" Bryon said, and after everyone had chuckled, he asked, "Do you know where we're going?"

"Forward," Erik replied.

"Well, that's comforting," Bryon said sarcastically, but as they walked on, Erik heard laughing behind him.

The great dark cavern through which they traveled reminded Erik of Thorakest and the Southern Mountains. The temperature was mild, and the air was fresher. They twice came to small, subterranean rivers, no more than knee-deep, and both were full of small pink fish, with white bubbles where their eyes should have been. Nothing needed eyes in this place. The water though was freezing and the rock under the rivers slippery. Bofim fell in the first river, emerging shivering, and Bryon was soon second, although he popped up much faster, and his response was to curse everything he could, including his cousin and the dwarves. He didn't get quite as wet as Bofim.

"Are you all right?" Erik asked as Bofim's lips trembled with the cold.

"Just keep moving," Bofim said. "There is nowhere to stop, and moving will keep me warmer."

"Bryon?" Erik said.

"I'll be fine," his cousin said testily and stomped off.

The ground sloped downward again after the second river, but not as steep as before. In places, water escaped the river and created tiny streams, flowing haphazardly past and before they trickled into the darkness. They finally came to a different part of the cavern and found the tiny rivers snaking their way around rocky formations, which rose abruptly from the ground.

"Would you look at that?" Erik said, lifting his dagger up and casting more light on the cavern.

As if his dagger knew what he was trying to do, it brightened, and everyone gasped. Some formations looked like shrines or temples, and others looked like tiny mountain peaks and ranges. They were different colors, blues and purples that looked like the dusk of a summer day and the yellows and reds of a blazing fire. There were also ones with greens and silver, and Erik wondered how they had not lost their brilliance in the everlasting darkness. As the small streams flowed in between each small mountain of stone, rock pools had formed and become home to tiny fish that created bubbles as they gulped at the surface, plucking at some unseen organism for food.

A small, slimy creature emerged from one small pool. It looked like a frog at first, but Erik realized it was a salamander, its skin slick and wet and, not the white or clear most of the animals in this underground cavern had, it was a dull brown with black spots. It licked its face with a long pink tongue and bit at a few of the invisible insects that fluttered quietly above the water hole it called home. When Erik got closer, put his dagger down towards the puddle, it waddled away back into the puddle, and Erik could see it floating about in a deep hole amassed with other salamanders and small, white larvae bouncing about, avoiding the snapping jaws of their adult counterparts.

Wherever there was a puddle, blooms of fungus covered the floor, even reaching up the sides of the rocky formations the pools lay next to in silky, spider web-like strands.

"Stay away from those," Turk said, walking by Erik as he bent down to look at one cluster of mushrooms that glowed with an almost fluorescent pinkish color. "Many of them are toxic or venomous ... deadly to anything that dwells down here, including men and their dwarvish companions."

Not all the rocky formations ended in mountain-like peaks, but some were flat plateaus, the height of a man's chest, and clusters of brilliant crystals sat atop them, white or clear, and they seemed to steal away the light the torches gave off. At the base of several rocks that only rose knee-high, steam rose from small geysers, and Erik could hear more in the distance. Wherever the geysers erupted, they found veins of emeralds and sapphires.

"This is a dwarf's dream," Bryon said.

"Now you can see how the dwarves have amassed so much wealth," Nafer said. "In the surface world, these rocks are rare, but in the deep places of the world, they are commonplace."

"This dark place seems so evil and, yet, look at all this life," Erik said, illuminating another crystalline formation with his dagger and watching translucent insects mill about.

"An finds a way to give life in every place," Turk said.

"Those tunnel crawlers weren't from An," Bryon said as he walked by. He looked irritated.

"No," Turk agreed. "The Shadow corrupts."

15

______

The giants weren't hard to follow. Their stink permeated the forest wherever they had been. Bu's diminished band of followers tracked them to a small camp at the edge of a wide, circular clearing in the forest. Several haphazard and primitive lean-tos sat at the opposite end of the clearing from where Bu and his men hid. A large fire blazed in the middle of the clearing, and the giants sat around it, joking and laughing. A huge sack containing some of Bu's men sat behind one giant, and, as it moved and a sound emanated from the makeshift prison, the giant reached back and smacked whoever was in there causing commotion. It went still.

A spit stood next to the fire, a sharpened stick running through something baking in the heat, its skin cracked and blackened and its flesh red. When Bu dared to lean closer, his eyes widened, and he gagged. It was a man ... probably one of his men. They were cooking them and eating them. Just to confirm what Bu already knew, another giant reached over and pulled a large chunk of meat from what would have been the man's side and threw it into his large mouth.

"Is that a ..." Andu began to say.

"Shut your mouth," Bao Zi hissed.

Bu had seen cannibalism before. East of the Giant's Vein, it wasn't so uncommon, a custom of the barbarians from Mek-Ba'Dune, thinking they would gain the strength of the person they ate. As Golgolithul pushed east and established trading posts and outposts in the vast plains and grasslands of Antolika, it was a constant fear and one of the reasons why most soldiers were hesitant to bring their families east. Of course, he never saw a man-eating man firsthand, but he had seen the remnants—leftover bones, people who looked like they had been chewed upon—when he was a young scout.

He had also seen the remains of cannibalism and heard about it, on the streets of Fen-Stévock, among the hungry and destitute poor of the capital city. It was a last resort to starvation when all the rats and pigeons had been hunted, the scraps were all gone, and the boots had been boiled. And it was one of the few things in Fen-Stévock that would earn someone an immediate and very painful death. The ruling class could have cared less if the poverty-stricken trash of the city sold their children to brothels, stole from one another, raped one another, or killed one another ... but eat another man or woman, and that was a capital crime.

This wasn't necessarily cannibalism, but it was close enough, and it churned his stomach. He had seen all sorts of awful things in his life—burnt victims, dismemberment, brains and entrails—and he barely noticed them, but this ... it affected him differently. Perhaps it was because he knew these men, whored with them and drank wine and broke bread with them. These men, most of them, had willingly given their lives for him and, even though he shouldn't have cared, he did. He hadn't ever really felt that way about the men who served him ...cared much for them, and now that he did, that bothered him as much as the sight of a human meal. He shook his head and made a decision before he turned to Bao Zi.

"My lord."

"We need to leave," Bu replied.

"But they're going to eat them," Sir Garrett said. "They're eating them now."

"Really? I hadn't noticed," Bu replied.

"My lord, we can't just leave them," Sir Garrett tried again.

"Listen, you prick," Bu said, pointing a finger at the man, "you didn't want to rescue them at first, and now you do. Your lack of conviction sickens me. Most of the world doesn't ransom off nobles and respect your station as a knight. They could give a rat's ass. Everything in these mountains wants to eat us. I plan on my body remaining intact, and when I do die, I want to be burned so the carrion feeders can choke on my ashes. We're going. Pray to whatever gods you pray to for these poor bastards. I know I'm sending prayers to the Princess of Pain for my men. Hopefully she finds their sacrifice pleasing."

Bu didn't bother to wait for his remaining men, not even Bao Zi. He slowly backed away from the thick copse of creepers and bushes behind which they'd hidden and hiked into the forest. At that moment, he thought of Ilsa—her body, her lips, her breasts. The thought aroused him, and he tried adjusting himself without anyone else seeing. But it wasn't just their time in bed that he thought of. He thought of someone sitting beside him while he ruled Hámon. She was a fickle woman. He could tell that much. And power-hungry. If he showed weakness, she would find another man to stick with her and convince him to kill Bu. As much as that might sicken another man, it made him smile. She was his kind of woman. Surely, she knew that he would do the same to her.

Then he thought of Li, that spineless, burned, poor excuse for a man. He had better be keeping an eye on Bu's wife. Her father still lived, an unfortunate result of honoring the Hámonian culture and custom of keeping captured nobles alive after battle. What a foolish idea. Nobles fought to the death in the east, if for no other reason than to save themselves from the certain torture they would experience when caught and imprisoned. In the west, they willingly gave up, allowed their peasants and subjects to be killed and raped, and expected soft pillows and fine meats in their prison cells. Hopefully, Kan, once Patûk's second in charge and now a Duke of Hámon,

Pavin Al'Bashar—former resistance leader much like Patûk and also a newly appointed Duke of Hámon—and Ban Chu—Bu's personal guard and second only to Bao Zi—were keeping a proper eye on everything, especially his wife and Li. He trusted those men, as much as he could trust anyone.

Bu's lip curled. A man who cared so little for those that served him was no man at all. It was what disgusted him about the Lord of the East, and why he eventually defected into Patûk's services. The Lord of the East cared little for his subjects. When South Gate burned under the dragon's fire, he probably celebrated as the poorest parts of Fen-Stévock burned away rather than mourning the loss of Golgolithulian citizens.

It wasn't that Patûk was a kind man. He was far from it. He was cruel, ruthless, and hard. In all truth, he was a bastard, but he respected the men that served him and served them in return. He fought alongside them, drank with them, whored with them, and bled with them. That was who Bu wanted to be.

"Where to, then?" Sir Garrett asked, finally catching up to Bu as the huge campfire of man-eating giants faded away behind them.

Bu looked to the sky. The stars barely blinked, trying as best as they could to twinkle through the wispy clouds that consumed the heavens over the Gray Mountains. He didn't recognize any of the constellations and wondered if they were different in the north. Then, he caught the slightest glimpse of something in the sky, a subtle glow. He had heard of such a thing in the far north—lights in the sky. This glow was green and reflected against the bottoms of the clouds. It meant something.

"North," Bu said. "We follow that glow, and we keep going north."

$\mathcal{A}$ blind lizard, its skin pink and thin, ran about the crystal formation, snatching up what insects it could. When it sensed Erik's presence, it darted away, behind a patch of fungi and mushrooms growing in between two small geysers. He heard a quick chirp when the reptile disappeared and saw rustling among the fungi as if it were grass shuffling in the wind.

Erik crept around one of the geysers and found the lizard there, dead and curled up into a ball. A spider stood next to the lizard, and, when Erik leaned forward, he saw two large puncture wounds in the lizard's side. The spider moved, its abdomen large and fat and as big as a man's hand and its legs as long as fingers. It was aware of Erik and faced him. It was black with no other markings, and, in Erik's dagger and circlet light, the arachnid's eight eyes twinkled.

The spider tapped on the ground with one of its forelegs, sending a clicking sound out into the darkness. It bounced its abdomen up and down and then moved side to side. Erik took a step forward, and so did the spider. He took a step back, and so did the spider. He moved right, and the spider mirrored him. He moved left, and so did the spider. Erik stopped moving, and the spider crouched. Erik thought he heard the arachnid hiss.

"Turk, come here," Erik said. "Look at this."

He pointed with his sword.

"Ah, those are tinsy mushrooms," Turk said. "They are highly poisonous. Stay away from them."

"No," Erik said, almost smiling as the spider followed his every movement. "Look at the spider. If I move left, it does too. If I move ..."

"Stop," Turk snapped.

"What's the matter?" Erik asked, but did as he was told.

He watched the spider for a few more moments. The thing hissed and tapped with its foreleg again, and then its whole body shook, exposing bristles on its legs. They rattled as it quivered. Turk put a hand on Erik's chest and moved him backward.

"What are you doing?" Erik asked.

"Move away," Turk said, "slowly."

The spider finally took a step forward, and then another; first, it moved slowly, but then sped up. It crawled up onto a tinsy mushroom, and then to a taller one. It tucked its abdomen underneath itself and spewed some of its silk towards Erik. It didn't reach him, but Erik cocked an eyebrow.

"Is it trying to attack us?" he muttered.

He looked to Turk as if it were some sort of joke, but the dwarf's face was all seriousness. Erik looked back to the spider. It was closer. It rattled again, and then they heard chirping and clicking overhead. Erik thought he heard fluttering, and, out of the darkness, great leathery wings spread, sharp claws extended forward and dug into the spider's abdomen, and the spider and its attacker were gone, high into the darkness of the cavern.

"Bats," Turk said.

"Big bats," Erik added.

"We should keep moving," Turk said.

"You look worried," Erik said. "What was that?"

"A spider," Turk replied.

"A big spider," Erik said. "Was it trying to attack us?"

"Yes," Turk replied. "Come on. There will be time to talk later."

Turk poked about the cluster of mushrooms. Erik pointed out the lizard the spider had killed, which wasn't too alarming. He had seen large spiders kill smaller lizards before. But, then, they saw another bat. It was twice the size of any bat Erik had ever seen, and if it had been able to extend its leathery wings, they might have extended as far as a man's arms. But it couldn't extend them. They were tightly wound in spider's silk, and the bat wasn't the deep black and brown colors Erik suspected it normally was, but a mottled gray. Turk nudged it with his boot, and it sounded hollow. It was a husk.

"This is not good," Turk said. "Let's move."

As they walked, they heard fluttering above them, in the unseen darkness, followed by chirps and clicks and clacks.

"It must be night," Beldar said.

"Aye," Nafer agreed.

"Why do you say that?" Bryon asked.

"They are gathering," Beldar replied, "the bats. They have a way out of this cavern, and they are about to converge on the surface world and feast."

"There's not enough in this cavern for them to feast on?" Bryon asked.

"The creatures in here are probably wary of the bats," Nafer replied. He pointed to the hidden roof. "And there must be thousands up there. Maybe hundreds of thousands."

They had gone only a little further when Bryon stopped, staring out into the darkness, straining to see.

"What is it?" Erik asked.

"I heard something," Bryon replied.

"More bats," Erik said.

Bryon didn't reply. He just stared forward, squinting, pushing his elvish sword out farther.

"Lend me your light," Bryon said.

Erik lifted his lighted dagger up.

"There," Bryon said, pointing, "just at the edge of the light. Do you see it?"

"I don't see anything," Erik replied. "It's the darkness and the cavern playing tricks with your eyes and ears ... and maybe mind a little too."

Bryon shook his head.

"No." He stepped forward, ever so slightly. "Something is there, just beyond the light. It has been following us. Don't you feel it?"

"I feel the chill of a mountain cavern and the constant numbness of eternal darkness," Erik said. "Come on, Bryon."

Erik stepped forward, but Bryon reached out and caught his arm and squeezed hard.

"Don't move," Bryon said.

"What has gotten into you?" Erik said.

"What's going on?" Turk asked, walking up next to the cousins. "We're waiting for your lead, Erik."

"Bryon thinks there is something out there, watching us in the darkness," Erik said, "and now he won't let me continue."

"There is something there," Bryon said.

"What is it?" Turk asked.

"I don't know," Bryon replied with a shrug. "I heard it. Saw it. Sensed it."

"Keep moving," Turk said, "carefully. Slowly."

They hadn't walked another hundred paces when Bryon stopped again. Erik heard it this time—the sound of tapping and clicking. The rustling of leaves and the slightest hiss. It was above them, but when Erik lifted his dagger up, he saw nothing.

"Tighten up," Turk said.

Erik heard something like a sack of flour drop behind them.

"Beldar, Bofim, face the rear and be ready," Turk commanded. "Erik and Bryon, take point. Extend your magic light as far out as you can. Nafer, take the middle with me."

"What is it?" Erik asked.

"I hope I am wrong," Turk said, "but if it is what I think it is, we are in for a hard fight."

As Erik took a step, he felt something crunch under his foot, like dried leaves or small twigs. The sound was so slight, but in the vacuous darkness, it was like a war drum and echoed through the cavern, but not as much as before. The walls had closed in on them.

Erik looked down, and whatever it was that dangled from his boot had small bones and dried, stretched skin. It looked as if it was stuck in webbing of some sort. He shook his leg, trying to kick the remains away, but they clung tightly. He scraped his foot along the ground, but when he stopped, something in front of him was making the same scraping sound.

Erik drew Ilken's Blade and took one step forward, extended his dagger.

"Are you with me?" Erik asked.

"I'm here," Bryon replied.

The magical light caught something silver, a strand of something in a mountain wall in front of them.

"Is that Dwarf's Iron?" Erik asked as the light glinted off several silvery strands.

"I don't know," Turk said.

Erik took another step forward and then reeled backward with a quick yelp.

"Son of a whore," Erik said, breathing hard as he backed into his cousin.

"What?" Bryon said, moving Erik aside and stepping in front of him.

"Tunnel crawler," Erik said.

Its mouth was open, baring its rows of sharp teeth, and both hands were out, fingered claws ready to strike, but it was frozen in time. Thin, white threads stretched across its face and consumed the rest of its body, hiding it in a silky cocoon. As Erik brought his dagger closer, the tunnel crawler's skin wasn't its normal gray, but a pale white and its skin looked stretched and worn, like old parchment.

"Get away from that!" Turk yelled.

"What is it?" Bryon asked.

"Spider's webbing," Turk replied. "Look."

He lifted his torch, as did the others, fanning out slightly. The wall in front of them was barely visible, but they could make out the silver thread that mummified a myriad of creatures of all sizes, some ages-old and some fresh.

"This is part of a horse," Erik said, pointing to two hooves poking out from a webbed cocoon lying on the floor. "And look at this."

He knelt down, inspecting cloth poking from another web casing, much smaller than the horse and in the shape of a man. The cloth was once white and, from what Erik could see, had a blue square on it. A tabard.

"It's another Hámonian noble," Erik said. "How? A tunnel crawler, a man, a horse."

"The ártocothe," Turk said, shaking his head. "The spider you saw before, among the tinsy mushrooms, was an ártocothe. Aggressive and intelligent. This is truly the realm of the Shadow."

"That was a big spider," Erik said, "but not big enough to take down a horse, let alone a man or a tunnel crawler."

"Or a huge elk," Bryon added, looking at another webbed cocoon, gigantic antlers poking through the web.

"That was just a spiderling, I'm afraid," Turk replied. "And with the way you said it was moving, it was hunting you."

"Hunting?" Erik asked.

As if on cue, they heard several loud taps behind them. Then they heard clicking and several hisses as a spider, its body the size of a wild boar, stepped into the light, the hardened, pointed exoskeleton at the end of each leg clacking against the stone floor. Its body was as black as midnight, its eight legs longer than spears with bristling, long spines along their whole length. Two large, bulbous, black eyes sat atop the ártocothe's head accompanied by three smaller eyes on either side. Four feelers, dripping with green saliva sat underneath its eyes, each tipped with a single claw. The same spittle drooled from the two large fangs underneath the ártocothe's feelers.

The ártocothe reared up on its back four legs. Beldar and Bofim both jabbed with their spears, but it was as if the spider knew what they were going to do. Beldar's spear shattered as one of the forelimbs came down on the shaft. Bofim's spear tip struck black flesh before it broke in two, and a yellowish-greenish fluid flowed from the wound, but the ártocothe seemed not to notice. Then, as they tightened up around the injured Nafer, Erik heard a deep hiss and smelled the wretched scent of decaying flesh behind them.

He spun around as another ártocothe attacked, jabbing at him with one of its forelimbs. He barely dodged the attack, grabbing Bryon's shoulder and turning him around. The arachnid struck out with one of its forelimbs again, Erik twisting and turning as he sought to evade the attacks. One leg struck the ground so hard in front of Bryon, and such was the power that the exoskeleton claw at the end of it sent shards of rock up into his face. He swung out hard, his elvish blade glaring a bright purple as it struck the hardened exterior and then sliced through the leg. Yellow fluid spilled from the wound, and the ártocothe had to catch itself, off-balance for a moment.

It hissed deeply as it reared up and tucked its abdomen underneath its body, its spinnerets twitching, and spewed silk at Bryon. He instinctively held out his sword, and as the web struck the blade, it caught fire and burned away, pieces of the webbing floating gently to the ground. The spider hissed again and spewed more silk at Bryon. A stray strand struck Erik on the cheek, and where the webbing struck his skin, it burned and stung.

The ártocothe behind them shot webbing out as well, at Bofim and Beldar. Both dwarves avoided the silk, but it struck the injured Nafer square in the chest, so hard the dwarf fell backward. Another thread of silk wrapped around Bofim's legs, and he too crashed to the ground. Turk rushed in front of both Nafer and Bofim, blocking strikes from the ártocothe's forelimbs as it tried to skewer to the two fallen dwarves with its exoskeleton claws.

The spider to their front rushed in towards Bryon, ignoring the elvish sword for a moment. Bryon brought his blade down on the spider's head, slicing it open, but the force with which the ártocothe hit Bryon, like a battering ram, threw him to the ground. Clearly badly hurt, the spider crawled over the top of Bryon and reared up. With fangs bared and dripping with poison, it came down hard. Erik lashed out with Ilken's Blade as Bryon rolled to his side, the spider's fangs slipping off the ground. Erik's blade struck deep into the side of the ártocothe's abdomen. Yellow fluid erupted from the wound, and with the damage to its head, that was enough, and the spider jerked sideways before it curled its legs over on top of itself as it died.

Erik turned to face the other ártocothe as it jammed one of its forelimbs into Bryon's chest. His mail shirt stopped the claw from penetrating flesh, but he still cried out in pain as the spider spat poison at him, some of it striking him in the face and neck. He cried out again and, where the poison struck him, his skin turned a bright red. Erik stepped over Bryon, who had dropped his sword and covered his face with both hands. As the spider tried to rush Erik, as it had done with Bryon, he lifted his dagger up. The creature seemed to shy away from the light and tried spitting poison at him as well.

The spider reared up, and Erik batted its feelers and forelimbs away with his sword. When the spider came back onto all eight legs, Erik jammed his dagger into one of its big, black, bulbous eyes. The eye sizzled and then popped. The ártocothe reeled and ran backward, hissing and screaming and rocking from side to side. Erik took his opportunity and rushed in. When the spider tried regaining its feet, Erik jammed his sword into the other eye, driving his blade all the way to the crossguard. The spider spun web frantically, covering the ground underneath it, and Erik felt his feet stick to the floor, but it wasn't enough to hold him.

He retrieved his sword and then jammed in unison with both his dagger and his sword into two smaller eyes, each strike causing yellow fluid to splash against his face. He tasted some, and it made him want to wretch. Eventually, the ártocothe stumbled backward. It seemed the spider had lost its will to fight, but it still stood there, challenging Erik. He saw a space between the ártocothe's feelers, keyed in on that spot, and jabbed forward. His blade struck that small space, and the spider collapsed to the ground, rolled to its back, and curled its legs like the other one.

Erik helped his cousin stand up, but as soon as he got to his feet, Bryon collapsed again, clutching his chest. Something had happened to irritate an old wound, a wound that almost killed him; the poison from a young dragonling in Orvencrest.

"It's my old wound," Bryon said through clenched teeth. "I don't know what happened, but it burns. I'll be fine. Go help the dwarves."

Erik hurried over to them and tried cutting the webbing with his sword, but the silk simply stuck to the Dwarf's Iron, so he used his dagger, and the webbing burned away. Bofim rubbed his shins and groaned in pain even though he wore greaves and boots. Nafer looked groggy and couldn't even sit up on his own.

"By the Creator, you dwarves are heavy," Erik said, helping Nafer up as Bofim kicked one of the dead creatures. "And I'm glad those two are dead," Erik added.

"There will be more," Turk said, facing Erik, "be ready."

Bofim helped Nafer along while Turk helped Bryon, but they only took a few steps before their torches and magic light illuminated a scene that caused the dwarves to groan and Erik's stomach to twist.

"By the Creator," Erik muttered.

A cavern wall stood in their way, as wide as the light would reveal and as tall as the darkness. White webbing covered the whole wall, holding thousands of cocoons, the horrifying prisons of any number of different creatures. It was a haphazard web, much like the black spiders Erik would find under wood piles back home, not the symmetrical and beautiful creations that a garden spider would build in between two rose bush branches. The spider silk was thicker in some areas and in others, where it wasn't as thick, he saw holes, perhaps where the ártocothe would sleep or wait for unsuspecting victims.

Erik saw movement along the strands of web and realized they were the ártocothe's young. There must have been thousands of them.

"This is the stuff of nightmares," Bryon said through labored breaths.

Erik remembered what Bryon's elvish sword had done to webbing, and he picked it up and touched it to the web on the wall. The silk flared up where the sword touched, igniting the web around it as well. The white spiderlings scurried everywhere as Erik cut a hole in the web big enough for them to pass through. The webbing was like dried tinder, catching fire quickly and lighting up the whole of the cavern. Husks and cocoons hung from the high roof, and the wall in front of them extended all the way to the top.

"If that thing could bring a horse or an elk in here, we can't be that far from finding the way out. This is our chance," Erik said turning to Turk. Both Bryon and Nafer couldn't walk. The spider poison, present in its silk, had infected them and they could barely maintain consciousness. "I'll carry Bryon. Beldar, you carry Nafer."

Erik carried his cousin through the hole, emerging on the other side, again into darkness. They had lost all but one of their torches and, the waning brightness of Erik's dagger told him that its energy was faltering and, just as before when he had used the dagger and its extraordinary magic, it would need time to regenerate. But, even in the faintness of the light, he could see they stood on a ledge giving way to a wide chasm. A long and wide land bridge connected the ledge on which they stood to the other side. They crossed the bridge as quickly as they dared, and after a while, they finally stopped, hoping they'd seen the last of the ártocothes.

"Do we have more torches?" Erik asked.

"I have two, in my haversack," Turk replied.

They lit them and sat, letting Nafer and Bryon sleep.

"We need to help them," Turk said, "and soon, or they will die."

"Do you have medicine," Erik asked, "or the power to help them?"

Turk was always the self-proclaimed healer of their party. At first, Erik thought it was simply because he knew how to mix herbs and medicines and different liquid concoctions to stem headaches and stop bleeding and take away pain. But as they escaped Orvencrest, Erik learned that Turk was more than a simple doctor or alchemist, he had the gift of healing, even without potions and creams. He called it a gift from the Creator. Others called it magic. Whatever it was, it had saved Bryon's life once before, among others.

"Not in this place," Turk replied, "and not against this poison. I need to forage if we ever get out of here. I need charcoal and the oil from the witch's brush. If I find lavender, that will help as well, and pine needle oil. I will give them something to stem their pain, but if I try to help them now, it will completely drain me, and then we will have three incapacitated adventurers."

They lit the other two torches Turk had and rested, the dwarf giving Bryon and Nafer some sweet wine and another tincture on their lips that he said would remove their pain and slow the poison's progress through their bodies.

"An be good," Turk said, sitting back against his haversack, "and we will be free of this hell soon."

17

———

*E*rik stared into the darkness. Bryon stirred, sweating and feverish, and Nafer didn't look much better. Bofim complained about his legs hurting where the webbing had struck him.

"We need to leave," Turk said, "and soon."

"Bryon and Nafer," Erik said.

"We'll just have to carry them," Turk replied, and Erik nodded his agreement, thinking again of the old man in Eldmanor.

I am a fool. He has led me astray, and my friends are going to pay for it. And they are here.

He could smell them, hear the shuffling of their feet, and sense them. As Erik thought about the dead that haunted his dreams, he wondered if, the next time he closed his eyes, a dead ártocothe would meet him there. His dreams didn't usually scare him, but then he remembered the last nightmare he had back in his own home, and the giant shadow burning his home and his family. Surely, the Shadow could use spiders and tunnel crawlers in his dreams, but it was something more than the Shadow. He thought of the Shadow Children, this place—so cold and, yet, at moments he felt heat like a billow. It could be the realm of the Shadow. It could be something else. Some other evil minion. A demon perhaps, if what Nafer had told him about spiritual and cosmic battles was true.

He felt them closing in as gooseflesh rose on his arms.

"With only three torches, what of the fairies' gift?" asked Turk, breaking into Erik's reverie.

The moon fairies—chaotic, ancient, primal, beautiful. As Erik, along with his mercenary companions and a coalition of dwarves from Thorakest, camped in an old forest of the Southern Mountains, evil had crowded in on them. Much like now, the dead surrounded them. All hope seemed lost. Doubt was darker than the night, or a mountain cavern, and then moon fairies appeared, chasing the darkness and evil away. The fairies had given Erik a bag of dust. Just a single speck of the dust was like a beacon and chased their enemies away.

Erik nodded, digging into his haversack and retrieving a simple, brown bag. He opened it, and the contents glowed, splashing white light across his face. He smiled, but then heard tapping and a subtle rattling, followed by hissing and more tapping. He felt heat on the back of his neck and heard laughter, although it wasn't the laughter of the dead. It was something different, deeper, and more evil.

"Your death has arrived," a dark voice said.

Erik grabbed a handful of the fairy dust and threw it into the air. The specks floated in the air, casting white light throughout the cavern. Erik saw shadows running away, fluttering in an unseen wind like black sheets caught in a springtime breeze. Even the fairy light didn't fully illuminate the cavern, but, in combination with the light from his circlet, Erik saw something move in the distance and could make out yet another giant spider about to attack. Then he saw something else. It looked like water moving, flowing through the mountain, all white and blue and silver, and then he realized it was something uncoiling.

"Is that a ..." Erik began to say but couldn't finish as a monstrous snake completely uncoiled itself.

It lifted half of its body up, its head poised and its white eyes unblinking before it hissed and then struck, the movement so quick it was only a blur. Thinking one of his companions was gone, Erik turned his head in the direction of the snake's attack and saw it snatching the ártocothe up, opening its mouth, and swallowing the spider whole. It then turned towards Erik and the others, its massive forked tongue flicking in and out of its mouth.

"Move quietly," Turk said, "but move quickly."

Erik hoisted Bryon up on his shoulders while Beldar lifted Nafer, and Turk helped Bofim along as he limped. The giant snake didn't seem too interested in them, and Erik didn't know if it was because of the fairy dust that still floated in the air or if they simply were too unimpressive to bother with, but whatever the reason, he was glad.

"Giant spiders and then giant snakes," Erik huffed as they hiked through the mountain, the fairy dust creating enough light to dispel the choking darkness of the cavern.

"A nadre," Turk replied. "They are extremely rare. You could understand that they control massive territories, and they are solitary creatures, coming together only to mate. They can be found in deep forests, in the ocean, and, of course, in deep mountain caverns. That was a very large one. It must be very old."

"It didn't seem too interested in us," Erik said.

"We are far too small for it to worry about us," Turk said. "I am sure it ate the ártocothe because it was more of a threat than anything else."

"Thank the Creator for that," Erik said.

"Indeed," Turk added.

They continued onwards, and now it seemed as if the fairy dust was leading them somewhere. After a while, both Bryon and Nafer had awoken and, even though the ártocothe's poison still affected them, they were able to walk on their own. Then, as the dust seemed to dissipate and fall away, Erik saw a distant light. He walked faster.

"Do you see it?" he asked.

"Aye," Turk said. Erik could sense the elation in the dwarf's voice.

The opening was large enough for a man to pass through but was frozen over, a thick layer of ice separating the mountain cavern from the outside world. They could hear the wind howling through several cracks in the icy door and, putting a gloved hand to the ice, Erik could feel the biting cold.

"It's a blizzard out there," Erik said.

"I don't care what's out there," Bryon said, "let's just get the hell out of this mountain."

Erik looked to Turk and nodded. The dwarf gripped his axe tightly and swung at the ice. After three hard smacks, it began to crack. Several more and the ice chipped away. After a dozen strikes, the ice covering the opening shattered and wind gushed into the cavern, howling, drowning out their cheers, and bringing with it an instant chill that caused Erik to shiver. Hail and snow covered the ground at Erik's feet.

"Well?" Erik said with a shrug of his shoulders. "From a dark and poisonous hell to a cold and white one."

"Just go," Bryon said, his voice fading as his eyelids hung half-closed.

The snow was knee-high, and the winds and snow beat against Erik's face stinging him like angry bees. The mountainside curved away to what Erik presumed was the north, and the ground slowly sloped downward to the south. The trees of the forest, for which Erik was glad, were large, red-barked pines, tall and strong, their tops disappearing into the clouds. They grew away from one another, allowing snow mounds to build in between them.

It was past noon, as the sky darkened a bit, the sun barely a glimmering orb mostly hidden behind the thick, gray clouds.

"Where do we camp?" Beldar asked.

Erik looked around and then looked back at the opening to the mountain cavern.

"No," Turk said, looking at the dark opening as well. "I am sorry, Erik, but I am not going back in there."

"I agree," Bryon said as his consciousness waned again.

"Then we walk until we can't walk anymore, and then we sleep," Erik said.

Erik shivered and looked up at the night sky. It was void of stars or the moon, but a pallid, faint light still spread out over the plain. The ground was covered in snow, but here and there, a blade of knee-high grass managed to escape. Erik had been here at night before, but then the stars twinkled overhead with magical brilliance. The place was usually warm and pleasant, but now it was cold and unwelcoming.

His hill was still there. He could see the weeping willow, its branches extra droopy under the weight of snow. The man was there as well. Erik could see him even though he was several hundred paces away. He walked towards the hill, the snow crunching under his boots, when the ground shook, and the sound of thunder rolled over him.

Erik turned to see a distant range of black mountains. From time to time, they were there. They were the realm of the Shadow. He knew that much, and when they were present in his dreams, the dead were strong.

Black clouds normally hung above the mountain range that existed in his nightmares, but they weren't there this time. Still, thunder rolled, and Erik saw a flash of purple lightning brighten the sky; it took on the shape of a spider's web, cracking the blackness like a shattered mirror.

"What is going on?" Erik asked himself. "Is the Shadow growing stronger?"

"Yes and no," a voice said.

Erik turned to see the man who normally sat on the hill standing there. He had never seen the man away from the hill.

"How are you here?" Erik asked.

"What do you mean?" the man asked. He smiled and, as always, Erik couldn't quite place his face, although he knew he knew it from somewhere.

"You are away from the hill," Erik said.

"Yes," the man replied. "I may go where I please. I simply choose to sit under the tree most times."

"This place has become corrupted," Erik said, turning back to the black mountain range.

"Not quite," the man said, standing next to Erik. He folded his hands behind his back.

"Is this place corruptible?" Erik asked.

"Yes and no," the man said. "What you see is a world man has created. Some, like yourself, are more conscious when they are here. Others simply understand it to be a dream. But anything man creates can, and often times will, become corruptible. Time is short, Erik."

Erik looked to the man. He smiled again and then pointed to the black mountain range. Erik stared in that direction, and he saw flame erupt into the sky—the dragon. In the distance, a vast shadow crossed the horizon; an army.

"The Shadow is growing powerful indeed," Erik said.

"Yes," the man said, "but there are other evils at work in the world, things of the Shadow and things outside the Shadow's control. I don't know how much longer this place can last."

"What can I do?" Erik asked.

"Do as you have always done," the man said. "Fight."

An army of the undead sped towards Erik. When he looked to one side, he saw a dwarf. On the other was another dwarf. He had seen a dwarf in this place once before, going through a rite of passage that was part of their baptism.

"You lead," one dwarf said, "and we follow."

"It may be to our deaths," Erik said.

"A glorious death," the other dwarf replied.

Erik drew Ilken's Blade and charged, the dwarves behind him.

Fire scarred spiders, mutilated tunnel crawlers, decaying mountain men, slavers, trolls, a Durathnan assassin, and Sorben Phurnan ... they were all there. The battle would have lasted an eternity, every time one undead soldier burst into oblivion, another replacing it. After a long while, one dwarf disappeared.

He passed his test.

Then, the other disappeared.

Good for them.

The army surrounded Erik, giving him a little space as every nature of creature waited to tear him apart. Laughter came with a clap of thunder and Sorben Phurnan, his skin turning black, stepped into the small circle where Erik stood.

"Your time has come," the undead lieutenant said.

"So be it," Erik said. "I'm ready. I'm not scared."

Sorben must have known he was lying. He laughed, the whole army laughing with him.

Kill him.

It was a thought in Erik's head, but it was the dragon's voice, evil and oddly feminine commanding Sorben. How had Erik heard that?

"Know this," Sorben said. "I will visit your wife in her dreams. I will ravage her. My army will ravage her. And then I will rip your offspring from her belly and feed it to the darkness."

Erik screamed as he ran for Sorben, and the army converged on him. But, just as every undead hand, claw, tooth, and fang should have reached for him, they stopped and the undead were gone. Despite the snow on the ground, Erik felt warm, hot even as sweat dribbled down his cheek. Off in the distance, he saw a cloaked figure, cowl pulled low so that he couldn't see the figure's face. Erik cocked an eyebrow and tilted his head.

"Who are you?" Erik asked, gripping Ilken's Blade tightly, but the figure only cackled.

Erik held his sword in both hands and grunted, ready to fight. The figure reached into its own robes and withdrew a long, black blade.

"So be it," Erik said, but as he stepped forward, the world around him shifted. He was waking. He stood tall and sheathed his sword. "Next time."

His eyes opened to a clouded sky silhouetted by tall pine branches.

18

The Lord of the East sat in his chair upon the dais in his hall. He watched the naked people lounging about in his presence caressing and fondling one another. It bored him. He snapped his fingers, and they turned into monkeys, now climbing the trellises of vines on his walls. That made him laugh. As soon as they reached the top, he snapped his fingers again. The monkeys turned back into people, and they fell, crashing into the stone floor. That made him laugh even louder.

The door into his hall opened, and a man in tight-fitting black leather armor entered, preceded by the Lord of the East's personal guard. The man's hair was pale white and fell to his waist, all tied back into a tail. He was a lean man, but the Lord of the East knew he was strong. He was tall, too, a half head taller than the Lord of the East. A large, oval shield hung from his back, and he carried a spear that was made from vertebrae. This was a legendary weapon of the Isutan Islands, and he was Specter, wielder of the Bone Spear. It ended in a wide-pointed blade made of tooth, its edges sharpened, and its tip poisonous.

"Specter," the Lord of the East said, standing as the Isutan approached his dais.

Melanius had recommended the assassin, a fellow Isutan. The Lord of the East knew this man—if that's what he was—and had used his services before. He needed him now, more than ever. Erik Eleodum had killed the two agents he sent to travel with the young man, and he—the Lord of the East—had read the Dragon Scroll incorrectly. Gods be damned, so had his witches and his advisor. Part of him wondered if he should have let Andragos read it, but he shook the idea off. Andragos was growing annoying and even a little soft.

The Lord of the East remembered something about Erik Eleodum, the man who had dispatched a dragon and saved Fen-Stévock, something magical. He carried an elvish sword. He admitted that much. It was a fine sword, with powerful elemental magic. But this magic was different. He couldn't place his finger on it until Erik had left. He had something hidden. He had the vision of a weapon, a golden handled dagger encrusted with jewels. And when Melanius came to him with their mistake, a mistranslation: "One must use a powerful weapon to find a powerful weapon," or something to that effect, he knew what Erik possessed. But how? Surely, the young man knew it too, had somehow figured out what he possessed and what it meant? A remarkable young man. It was too bad he had to die.

A part of the Lord of the East wanted to send his whole army after the man, but the moment Erik stepped foot from Fen-Stévock's keep, he was a hero. How would that look, the Lord of the East chasing down and killing the man who saved the capitol of Golgolithul?

When word of the Lord of the East's agents—the ones that were supposed to meet and lead Erik to Fealmynster—being murdered reached the keep of Fen-Stévock, its ruler raged. Who else could have killed his agents but Erik Eleodum? He must have realized what it was he had and now intended to keep it for himself. Traitor. The Lord of the East's Isutan advisor told him that fortune was smiling on them as Bone Spear was in their country. The Lord of the East had sent for him, right away. That was weeks ago. Arriving in a timely manner wasn't a strength of the assassin. That was the way of Specter. He thought so highly of himself, and such an ego annoyed the Lord of the East intently.

"Syzbalo," Specter said, standing in front of the dais, slamming the butt of his spear into the stone floor.

Specter had many striking features: his long, white hair, his lean and strong frame, his yellowish-tan skin, his almond eyes, and even the paint he wore around them, but the most striking feature about the assassin were his pupils and irises. His pupils were almost a translucent gray, and his irises practically white. The Lord of the East knew the man could see, but he had the eyes of a blind man.

"If you are in my hall, the least you could do is address me with some respect," the Lord of the East said. He felt his face growing hot; he hated people using his name.

"You are the one who called me here ... Syzbalo," Specter replied.

As the Lord of the East inwardly seethed, the Isutan looked at the nails of his left hand with lazy eyes. His smooth face belied his age, a result of the magic of the Isutan Isles. He rubbed his fingernails on the front of his leather breastplate, shining them. He blew gently on them, and then began shining again. When Specter finally looked up at the Lord of the East, he rolled his eyes at the man's pained expression.

"Fine," Specter said with a mocking bow, "Your *Majesty*, what can I do for you?"

"I need someone killed," the Lord of the East said.

"Clearly," Specter said, "if you are summoning me. You couldn't have just sent me a name or a description of the man. I had to come all the way to Fen-Stévock for you to tell me that."

"Your insolence is trying my patience," the Lord of the East said through clenched teeth. "Besides, Melanius said you were already in my country."

"And you are wasting my time," Specter replied.

The Lord of the East felt his temple throb.

"I want you to kill a man who I sent out to seek the Dragon Sword of Fealmynster."

Specter laughed.

"A myth."

"So are dragons," the Lord of the East said, "but clearly, you saw what was once South Gate."

Specter shrugged. The Lord of the East walked down the steps of his dais so that he stood right in front of the Isutan.

"He was supposed to meet my agents in Eldmanor, to receive instructions from them concerning a key to finding the Dragon Sword, and then locate it in Fealmynster. I now realize, as he must have, that he already has the key, and he is on his way to the lost keep. When he retrieves the sword, you are to take it from him, take a golden-handled dagger he also carries, and then kill him and anyone with him."

"In that order?" Specter asked with a smirk.

"*Damn it!*" the Lord of the East screamed, and his voice echoed around the walls of the hall. His guards shook with fear, but Specter didn't move.

"Is this the man named Erik Eleodum?" Specter asked.

"It is," the Lord of the East replied.

"Why didn't you kill him when he was here?" Specter asked.

"I didn't know then what I know now," the Lord of the East replied, "and, besides, he was being heralded as a hero."

"And what is it that you know now?" Specter asked.

"A dagger that he carries," the Lord of the East said, balling his hands into fists, "is special. He hid it from me. If it is what I think it is ... I must have it."

"This will cost you," Specter said.

"You know I will pay," the Lord of the East said.

"You had better," Specter said, pointing the Bone Spear at the Lord of the East's face.

No one dared talk to the Lord of the East in such a way, but Specter wasn't anyone. If the Lord of the East wanted someone dead,

Specter would do it without question. He never failed. But his payment was always steep, and never in gold. Blood—Specter's fees were always paid in lives.

"I need his family dead as well," the Lord of the East said.

"Sure," Specter replied. "What do I care?"

Specter turned to leave but then turned around again.

"Dragons and such," Specter said. "These are dangerous times."

The Lord of the East nodded.

"After this, do not call on me again," Specter said. "I think I will spend some time away, let this dragon ravage Háthgolthane, and reappear in a hundred years after its over. If you're still around, then, Syzbalo, I'll call on you."

The Lord of the East watched as Specter left his hall and fumed silently; he could not remember when he'd been so angry. He pointed a finger at one of the naked men, and immediately a knife appeared in his hand. He looked at the woman he was with and then grabbed her hair and slit her throat. As the other women screamed, Syzbalo's expression softened, and he began to laugh.

19

*E*rik awoke to five mounds of snow—his companions. As he brushed the white stuff from his hair and beard, he nudged the mound closest to him. A dwarvish grunt came from underneath the icy blanket, and Turk sat up.

"At least it's stopped snowing," Erik said with a shrug as he awoke Beldar.

"I think the snow actually kept us warm during the night," Turk added.

"Aye," Erik replied.

Bryon barely woke, sitting up and then promptly falling backward. Nafer wasn't much better. His arm didn't hurt as much anymore, the icy cold numbing it, but his face was pale and sickly, with sunken cheeks and red eyes.

"I don't know if they can keep going," Erik said, whispering to Turk. "Isn't there anything you can do?"

"I don't think so," Turk replied, rifling through his haversack and retrieving a bottle of sweet wine.

"What good will that do?" Erik asked.

"We'll have to carry them," Turk replied, "but the sleep will be good for them. Beldar, Bofim, help cut down one of these trees so we can make a litter."

All three dwarves went to work on felling one of the giant redwood pines. It was an arduous process, the bark not only iron-hard but toughened by the cold and ice.

"What ... what are they doing?" Bryon asked, his teeth chattering as he lay next to Erik, his arms wrapped around his own body.

"Making you a litter," Erik replied.

"Here we go again," Bryon said, "me infirmed and you having to take care of me."

"We're all hurt," Erik said, "just you and Nafer more. It's not your fault. We'll make you a litter and you'll drink some sweet wine, and then maybe you'll regain some of your strength."

Turk took a quick break from chopping at the hard wood to retrieve some water. Even in the cold, he sweated.

"They will die if we continue," Erik said, looking to both Bryon and Nafer, who had both fallen back asleep.

"The only other option is to leave them," Turk said. "Beldar or Bofim could stay with them, find an old wolf's den or cave, and just watch them and wait for our return. One of them could go out each day and look for a dwarvish outpost or small village, although I doubt there are any near here."

"*Watch out!*" Beldar cried as the creaking of wood turned to the thunderous sound of a trunk breaking and snapping.

Erik looked up to see a tall red-wooded pine falling, snow and ice trailing after it. It was taller than he had thought and seemed to fall for a long time. When it finally struck the ground, falling in the opposite direction of where they had slept the night before, the ground shook.

"It will be a good source of wood as well," Turk said.

The dwarf picked up his battle-axe, ready to join their dwarvish companions as they chopped wood for both a fire and a litter, when the ground began to shake, just as it had when the tree fell. Erik heard more cracking and rock, from a peak far away, breaking.

"*Avalanche!*" Beldar cried, rushing back to Turk and Erik, Bofim just behind him.

Erik didn't have time to think. He grabbed his cousin, hoisted him over his shoulder, and looked to Turk. The dwarf did the same with Nafer as the sound of crashing and smashing neared. He didn't know to where they would run, and, as he looked to Beldar, he saw defeat in the dwarf's eyes.

The ground shook harder and faster. A wave of cold wind hit Erik's face. The snow under his boots shifted. Beldar stopped and looked over his shoulder. He turned back to Erik and smiled.

"Get behind a tree!"

And then he was gone.

It was really only a few moments, a dozen maybe, but it seemed like hours as the white wave of rushing snow and debris burst past them, taking everything with it that lay in its path—trees, rocks, animals ... friends. Erik felt a force stronger than he had ever experienced before hit him from behind as he tried to find shelter in front of a tree. Bryon flew from his shoulders and then felt the weight of snow as it piled on top of him. It was freezing. It was dark. He was lost.

20

———

The new crop of recruits walked in front of Fréden as Kizmit, one of his new generals, and Belvengar led them on a march. Only two dozen had shown up—the reason why Fréden continually chewed on his lip—but as much as the number of dwarves coming to his call of unity dwindled and irritated him, one of these new recruits, a stout and experienced warrior and leader, had access to the northern kingdom of Thrak Baldüukr.

The vast majority of Fréden's forces hailed from Drüum Balmdüukr. Some came all the way from the Black Mountains east of the Giant's Vein, and very few came from Thrak Baldüukr, and those that did were hardly useful, dwarves that were once criminals, lowly birthed, unskilled, or destitute and poor. As much as it pained Fréden to see impoverished dwarves, he had little use for them in his planned new world. But this dwarf was a skilled practitioner of the martial arts, and obviously a soldier.

The name he had given General Kizmit was false. Fréden couldn't prove it, of course, but he suspected as much. Fréden wasn't sure why the dwarf would give a false name—perhaps to protect his family back home or his reputation—but it worried him at first. The dwarf warrior who called himself Mungrun Flint Toe—the name of a famous dwarvish assassin dating back to the Elf Wars—quickly proved himself to Fréden's liking.

When Fréden had asked him his usual prospective questions—why are you joining the cause, why have you left home, what do you feel about the current leadership in the dwarvish kingdoms—Mungrun grew red-faced, his rage almost uncontrollable. Fréden was a little perturbed that Kizmit didn't catch the faked name—he was never known for being an overly well-read dwarf—but this new dwarf seemed zealous. Now, it was time to test his skills in battle.

Plenty of dwarves came to Fréden wanting to fight—fight men, goblins, trolls, other dwarves—but many of them didn't have the aptitude for battle. With his advisers and counselors, Fréden had developed a system of ascertaining a dwarf's strengths and weaknesses so they may better place them in a job that would suit their contribution to the new society, hidden away in El'Beth-Tordûn. Certainly, some dwarves became upset with Fréden's assessment, but it wasn't his fault. The testing had been created by the finest minds, and, as a dwarf argued that he or she wished to fight, Fréden would simply explain to them it was for the greater good.

He had only lost a few recruits due to the results of the test, and none since the last defector had openly opposed the outcome. He began shouting at Fréden, and he met a quick demise under the spear of Belvengar, testimony to his inability as a warrior. Since Belvengar's example had been set, whether a dwarf was placed with the builders, engineers, agriculturalists, or cooks, they didn't complain.

These new recruits marched to the warrior proving grounds. It was one of the old training grounds of the fortress at El'Beth-Tordûn and, even though Fréden Fréwin could have cared less about the physical tests Kizmit and Belvengar put new recruits through, his general insisted he come so he might learn what made a qualified soldier, and to show his new followers that he cared. He did care; he just didn't care about fighting or a dwarf's prowess in battle. It was a necessary evil, but the truly intelligent and worthy dwarves were better off spending their time learning policy and procedure, and politics and history.

These two dozen dwarves entered the proving grounds, a dilapidated arena that once contained racks of weapons and armor and training dummies.

"I know it doesn't look like much," Belvengar said, "but as soon as we have the time and resources, we will repair the proving grounds."

"We have more important things to spend our limited resources on, Long Spear," Fréden said.

"Yes, my lord," Belvengar said with a quick bow.

"This should be a priority," Kizmit said, "if we want to truly assess our new recruits, and if we want to properly train them."

General Kizmit was always so combative. He thought the military was the most important aspect of their new kingdom, but Fréden knew otherwise.

"I would think the ability to train our recruits rests with the trainer," Fréden retorted.

Kizmit looked at Fréden evenly, but he said nothing. The insult hadn't fallen on deaf ears, but, for as combative as Kizmit was, always seeking more resources and more bodies for their growing military, he was loyal.

"Get on with it," Fréden said. "I have matters of the state I need to get back to."

Both Belvengar and Kizmit bowed; the rest of the recruits simply stood at attention and readied themselves for the ensuing physical test. As he waited, Fréden couldn't help but think this new Mungrun gave him a quick, smirking look.

The first phase of the testing was a simple test of endurance—a run that started and ended in the proving grounds. Two of the recruits failed that one. Then, a test of strength, lifting boulders and pushing weight carts and carrying loaded wheelbarrows and baskets; after that one, Kizmit disqualified five more dwarves from military service. The third assessment, one Fréden had thought pointless and silly, but Kizmit insisted upon, was a mental test of knowledge, history, and arithmetic.

"They need to be able to throw a spear and swing an axe," Fréden had said.

"We need thinking warriors, my lord," Kizmit had replied in protest.

Fréden figured he would give his general this little victory, perhaps appeasing him and making him less likely to fight him on other army policies. Kizmit was a military genius, but Fréden was lord and knew what was best for his people as a whole.

Only a dozen dwarves were left after the mental assessment, and Fréden selected two of those to work for the engineers since their scores were so high, leaving ten. Knowledge of martial weapons eliminated two more, and hand-to-hand combat eliminated yet another two. Mungrun was one of the last six that stood before him that day. Kizmit looked over at them and shook his head.

"My lord," Kizmit said, and Fréden already knew what he was going to say, "two dozen came to fight, and we now have a quarter that number."

"But they aren't soldiers," Fréden said.

"I can make them soldiers," Kizmit replied, "Belvengar and I."

"We are not having this conversation again, General," Fréden said. "We need men to rebuild and cook and take care of our crops."

"And soldiers can do that, my lord," Kizmit said. "It is the way we have always done things. *Everyone* is trained to fight."

"Enough!" Fréden shouted, causing the remaining potential soldiers in his army to stare. "We are creating a new world and, therefore, doing things a new way. I will hear no more of it. Now, continue."

Kizmit bowed quickly.

"My lord."

The final test was actual combat. Fréden thought there was something special about this Mungrun, and he had always heard of the battle prowess of the northerners, and the dwarf did not disappoint.

It seemed that only one of the other dwarves gave the warrior any sort of challenge, and that was hardly.

"Have I pleased you, my lord?" Mungrun said.

"We'll see," Fréden replied. He rubbed his chin, eyeing Belvengar. "Long Spear ... fight this dwarf. I want to see what he can really do."

"My lord," Kizmit said. Fréden could see the apprehension in his general's eyes.

"No arguing," Fréden said, putting up a hand. "Just do it."

Belvengar bowed and crouched into a fighting stance, his namesake spear held in both hands. Mungrun chose a sword that was broad-bladed but short and a round shield. Kizmit was, of course, afraid Belvengar would hurt this new recruit who had so much potential, but Fréden wasn't so sure.

The fight lasted far longer than either Fréden or the general thought it would, ending with Belvengar finally besting Mungrun by disarming him with an elbow to the nose and then the butt of his spear to the dwarf's wrist. Fréden wiped sweat from his brow.

"That was exhausting, was it not?" Fréden said, slapping Kizmit on the shoulder and smiling, almost like a child. "And exciting."

Belvengar helped the other dwarf up and shook his hand, but Fréden couldn't help but notice two things. Firstly, he noticed the scowl on Mungrun's face as he accepted Long Spear's help. He was a fighter and a competitor; that was good, and he didn't like losing, so he would be a valuable asset. The second thing Fréden noticed was the look Belvengar gave Mungrun when the northern dwarf wasn't looking. It wasn't the same look of derision the northern dwarf had given. It was a look that consisted of scrunched eyebrows and questioning eyes as if there was something off about the dwarf. But, then again, Belvengar was also a competitor and a great warrior. He was probably just irritated it took him so long to defeat this recruit.

"You are from the north?" Belvengar asked.

Mungrun just nodded.

"Where?" Belvengar prodded.

"Near Ghrâg," Mungrun replied, wiping blood and snot from his nose with the back of his hand. It left a smear across his cheek that looked like war paint.

"Were you a soldier in the northern armies?" Belvengar asked.

"Please, Long Spear," Fréden said, "must we continue with the hundred questions?"

"It is all right, my lord," Mungrun said. "My last post was at Stangar."

"That is a large outpost," Kizmit said.

"Are there others there that might heed our call?" Fréden asked.

Mungrun thought for a moment.

"Possibly," he finally said, and Belvengar gave the dwarf another questioning look.

"Welcome to El Beth-Tordûn and Düum Wastûk," Fréden said with a smile—his name for his *resistance* movement—before Kizmit had led the six recruits away."

"My lord," Belvengar said then.

"What is it?" Fréden asked, wanting to get back to more important matters of state.

"Beware of that new recruit," Belvengar said, "the one from the north."

"Are you irritated that he gave you such a hard time in battle?" Fréden said with a laugh.

"He is well trained, surely," Belvengar said, "but that is not why you should keep an eye on him."

"Then why, Long Spear?" Fréden asked.

"There's just something off about him," Belvengar said.

Fréden gave another short laugh and patted Belvengar on the shoulder.

"You worry about our soldiers and our spies, Long Spear," Fréden said, trying not to be too condescending, "and let me worry about reading our new recruits and their intentions."

Belvengar bowed.

21

———

*E*rik was in an air pocket where debris was mixed with the snow, but he could see only white, and did not know how much of it was above him; his air wouldn't last long. One arm was trapped beneath him, and he pushed his other hand through the snow, scooping it to one side, and tried to leverage himself up with his legs. His body moved only a bit, and he began to push snow away again. His nose and cheeks were numb, but eventually, he broke through and looked up, seeing nothing but falling snow. He wiggled his other arm free, and eventually, he freed his torso, which made completely escaping his snowy tomb all that much easier.

Erik found Turk easily enough. He was curled up under the broken trunk of a pine tree.

"Are you all right?" Erik asked.

Turk nodded, sitting up. His face was bruised and scratched, and, as he stood, Erik could tell he was sore, but he looked relatively unscathed.

"Have you seen Bryon?" Erik asked.

Turk shook his head.

"I lost Nafer as well," Turk said. "I tried to hold on to him, but ..."

Turk's gaze trailed off, down the steady slope of the forest. Erik followed his gaze and bore witness to the destructive force of fast-moving snow. Many of the trees were broken in half or uprooted, and amidst the snowy remains of trees and boulders, he saw animals—large elks, deer, a bear, and a cougar—frozen and dead.

"We have to go searching for them," Erik said. His heart quickened as he thought of his cousin out there, buried under who knew how much snow.

In his condition, Bryon wouldn't last long. If the cold and poison didn't kill him, he would be easy prey for some scavenging predator, picking through the remains and looking for an easy meal. And Nafer was in the same situation.

"Just give me a moment," Turk said. He put his hands on his knees and breathed long and hard.

"You are hurt," Erik said.

"I am afraid so," Turk said, trying to stand up straight. I think I've cracked some ribs and twisted an ankle."

"You stay here then," Erik said. "I have to go and look for Bryon."

Erik turned to leave.

"And the dwarves," Turk said.

"Yes, of course," Erik said, looking at the dwarf over his shoulder, "and the dwarves."

Erik found Bofim right away. The dwarf was lodged up against a large boulder and part of a tree. He was unconscious with the same scrapes and bruises on his face that Turk had borne. His mustache and beard were matted with blood, and one cheek looked swollen, but when Erik shook his shoulder, he slowly came to.

"Turk is back that way," Erik said as Bofim rubbed his face and winced when he touched his cheek.

"Where are you going?" Bofim asked. "What about the others?"

"I am going to go look for them," Erik replied.

"I'll go with you," Bofim said.

"No," Erik said with the quick shake of his head. "You're hurt, and so is Turk, and I am not. You'll just slow me down, and I need to find Bryon ... and Nafer and Beldar."

Bofim nodded. Erik helped him to his feet and sent him in Turk's direction while he continued his search for any signs of his cousin ... and the dwarves. Erik felt bad for not thinking of the dwarves at the same time as Bryon. They were like brothers, closer than brothers, but the thought of losing both his brother and his cousin ...

Erik searched the whole day, zigzagging back and forth, looking for signs of his cousin and the dwarves—clothing, weapons, body parts, anything. He saw dozens of animals, all broken and shattered against trees and rocks, but no sign of his friends. As the day waned, Erik thought of going back to Turk and Bofim, but then how long would it take him to reach this place, so he found a felled tree, dug some of the snow out from underneath it, pulled his bearskin tight, and did his best to sleep. It seemed that as soon as he closed his eyes, he opened them, but it was the morning. The night had passed without any dreams, and the snow had stopped.

"Thank the Creator for that," Erik muttered as he stood and brushed snow off him.

Erik had barely walked a hundred paces when the snow under his boots moved. He jumped to the side, retrieving Ilken's Blade from its sheath. The snow moved again, undulating as if it were a bubble trying to burst. He sheathed his sword and began to dig. At first, he saw the links of a mail shirt. Then, the toe of a boot and the tip of a sword scabbard.

"*Bryon!*" Erik shouted, his heart beating ever faster, and his digging quickening.

Within moments, Erik uncovered a beard and a bald upper lip. The nostrils above the upper lip moved and sucked in air jealously. He pushed the snow away from Nafer's face, and the dwarf, hurt and sick and half-conscious, stared up at him with a smile.

Erik's heart sank. He cursed himself for it, but he thought Nafer was his cousin. He helped the dwarf emerge from the snow, sitting him up and then finding a tree to lean him against.

"How do you feel?" Erik asked.

"Broken," Nafer replied, his words slurred and slow.

"Your arm doesn't look good," Erik said.

His sling was gone and, even as Nafer cradled it, it undulated in spots it wasn't supposed to. His shoulder hung oddly as well, and Erik knew it was dislocated. And with the way Nafer was breathing, he certainly had broken ribs as well.

"I am going to set your shoulder," Erik said. "It is dislocated, but it's cold, and I am sure it's numb so you won't feel it ... at least for now."

"Wait," Nafer said. "Have you ever set a shoulder before?"

Erik paused a moment.

"No, but I've seen it done," Erik said.

"We should wait for Turk," Nafer said, putting up his right hand. "He has set hundreds of shoulders."

"He's a day's walk from here and in no condition to heal anyone but himself," Erik said, grabbing the dwarf's arm.

"Wait, wait," the dwarf said, but Erik tugged on the arm hard, and it slid into place with a quick clicking sound.

"See, right as rain," Erik said with a smile.

Nafer leaned his head back and passed out.

"Stay here," Erik said to the unconscious Nafer. "I am going to go find Bryon and Beldar, and then I'll be back to get you."

Erik didn't go far when he came across another giant elk, its huge head exposed from its snowy tomb, its antlers spread out large and wide. A fallen tree lay next to the beast, its branches broken and scattered about in large piles. Much of the snow had melted away under the fallen branches, and icicles hung from both branch and antlers. He stepped over the elk's head, and his foot broke through a small web of branches covering a shallow indentation in the ground. He felt his boot hit something hard and he heard a low groan. He retrieved his foot quickly, found solid ground to get his balance, and hurriedly put his face to the small hole. He found Bryon there, buried underneath dirt, wood, and half-melted snow, lying on his back with a large piece of tree trunk across his chest and both legs stuck underneath the dead buck.

"*Bryon!*" Erik yelled once more, starting to pull away the smaller branches he could easily break with one hand. A low groan was the only response he got.

Erik bent down to pull larger branches away with both hands. Once the hole Bryon laid in was clear of wood, he began to lift the piece of tree trunk off his cousin's chest. It was heavy, and as Erik stepped on both sides of Bryon and bent to lift it, he felt pangs of sharp pain shoot down his hamstrings and up his spine. It wouldn't move.

He stared at Bryon, stared at the tree trunk with perplexity written on his face. Bryon moaned again, tried to move but never opened his eyes. Erik figured he really wasn't conscious. He was, rather, in some dream, or moving simply out of instinct.

"I have to get you out of here," Erik said and looked again at the scene. An alternative idea came to mind.

He sat down, his bent legs against the log and his back against the elk's chest. He took in a huge breath and pushed, his vision growing red as blood rushed through bulging arteries on his neck, and he was sure his face turned the same color. The log moved slightly, and Erik yelled, trying to give himself extra power. He pushed again, and it moved a little more. Another yell. A little more.

You're going to kill me, cousin.

Eventually, Bryon was free of the tree, but still trapped, his legs stuck under the dead, frozen elk. He moved so that he was behind Bryon, standing halfway up the small bank of the ditch Bryon rested in. He set his torch down and scooped his arms under his cousin's shoulders, counted to three, and pulled. Immediately Bryon came to as if cold water had been splashed across his face – or pain shot through his whole body – and gave out a sudden, blood-curdling scream that caused Erik to jump.

"Bryon," Erik said, tapping his cousin's chest with an open palm, "it's me, Erik. I'm here."

Bryon winced, caught Erik's hand, and gave him a one-eyed look.

"Yes, I see that, but stop … stop pulling me. It feels like … like my ribs are broken."

His voice was strained and labored. He had to catch his breath after only a few words, and it seemed he used all of his energy just to simply open one eye and look at his cousin.

"Sorry," Erik replied. "I need to get you out of here, but this dead elk is lying across your legs."

"So that's what it is," Bryon said. "I came to … I don't know how long ago … but I tried moving my legs … I couldn't. I wondered if … if my back was broken. I guess this is better."

He tried to smile but coughed instead, and when he did, he clenched his teeth and groaned loudly in pain, his lips curling back over his teeth in almost a snarl revealing a mouth that was blood-stained. Erik saw that, saw blood squeeze through his teeth as he gritted them, and knew his cousin was bleeding internally.

Erik stared at the elk and wondered what to do. He could chop it up, carefully, avoiding his cousin's legs. But even a sword made of Dwarf's Iron was no match for the frozen muscle of this giant beast. And then he thought of Bryon's sword.

"I need to use your sword," Erik said.

Bryon just groaned, he might have been conscious, but barely, as Erik gripped the elvish blade in both hands and began to chop. At first, the muscle and fur and fat were so tough and frozen the strikes sent pains up into Erik's arms. But the sword began to flare a brilliant purple and more easily seared through the animal, even melting the creature's massive femurs.

As Erik freed his cousin, Bryon shivered violently, and even though his groan was soft and low, the look of pain that crossed his face said anything words could ever say. Erik slung his cousin over his right shoulder, cautiously stepping out of the snowy hole in which Bryon was entombed and then trudging through the snow, towards Nafer. He stopped, as the shadowed light of an overcast day began to wane and turned, looking farther down the mountain. Beldar was still out there, but Bryon wouldn't last another night without Turk's attention. Neither would Nafer.

"Creator be with you," Erik said.

His stomach knotted, and his heart sunk, but he couldn't lose his cousin.

He found Nafer where he had left him. He looked the same, and his condition mirrored that of Bryon's.

"How am I going to carry both of you?" Erik asked the two unconscious warriors.

He carried Bryon and dragged Nafer through the snow, and from somewhere, Erik found the strength to struggle on. The going was slow and became a matter of a mere few paces before Erik would have to stop and catch his breath again. When he finally began to recognize the carnage of the avalanche as he drew closer to their original campsite, night had come upon him again, and the light of a new day began to fight the clouds of the overcast sky.

"We're almost there," Erik said. "And then, I promise, Beldar, I will come looking for you. Hang on Bryon. We're almost there."

As Erik smiled and began to thank the Creator, he heard a loud roar, like some deranged man screaming, the voice low and booming. And then he heard Turk's voice.

"*Etenweird!*"

22

$\mathcal{B}$ofim sailed through the air and landed a few paces in front of Erik as he stood, wide-eyed, scared, and confused. The dwarf was clearly unconscious, and Erik watched as Turk too wobbled on his feet, gripping his battle-axe in both hands. A giant of a man—at least, it looked somewhat like a man—stood in front of the dwarf. It was twice the height of any man, even taller than the one-eyed antegants of Finlo, and much more muscled. The creature had the features of a man or dwarf, but it looked primitive and didn't wear any shirt or armor, only an animal skin vest.

The giant, the etenweird, swung a fist at Turk, who ducked the attack and tumbled forward, struggling to come to his knees. He swung his axe, catching the back of the giant's leg. The creature screamed, turned, and grabbed Turk with a single hand, lifting him up and shaking him violently.

"Hey! You ugly son of a whore!" Erik yelled.

"Run!" Turk croaked, struggling to speak as the etenweird squeezed him.

The etenweird threw Turk to the ground, and the dwarf's body went limp, although Erik suspected it could have done far worse. He had at least prolonged the warrior's life for a little while. The giant turned to Erik, took one step forward, clenched its fists, threw its head forward, and roared.

It ran towards Erik, surprisingly nimble and quick for its size and in the snow. Erik dropped Bryon and let go of Nafer's collar, gripping Ilken's Blade with both hands. He felt weak, having walked all night, but he stood over his cousin and waited for a hard fight to ensue.

The etenweird swung at Erik, stepping over him as it did. It wore simple leggings made of the same fur its vest was made of, so Erik rolled forward, came to his feet, and brought his blade up into the giant's inner thigh. It screamed as the steel drew blood, but it was more of a pinprick than anything. It swung with the back of its hand, a knuckle connecting with Erik's shoulder. He thought his joint would be dislocated as he flew backward. The strike was an errant one. If he had received the full force of the blow, he'd probably be dead.

Erik did little more than avoid the etenweird. As it tried to step on him, he moved out of the way and chanced a glancing blow with his sword. When it swung, he rolled underneath it, staying close enough that it made it difficult for the giant to track him. The giant moved one way, Erik stepped the other, and then it turned hard, its initial movement false. It caught the man off guard, and Erik fell backward, looking up as a giant foot came down on him.

The snow was thick and the ground soft and wet enough that as the giant sole pressed down, Erik sunk into the mountain soil. The foot stunk, and as the etenweird pressed down hard with a grunt, he felt several joints in his body pop. The giant lifted its foot and reached down to pick Erik up, and he shook him as Erik struggled against the grip, seemingly getting tighter with each breath he took.

"Dwarves," the etenweird grumbled, speaking Dwarvish.

It looked irritated, a low gurgling rumble coming from its throat, but then it gave a gruesome grimace that might have been a smile. It had almost all its teeth, but they were more black than yellow, and its breath smelled worse than its feet.

"And men," it croaked, looking between Erik and Bryon. "I haven't tasted man flesh in many moons and, lucky me, I get it twice in the same week."

The etenweird's command of the dwarvish language was astonishing, and rather contrary to its look. It looked primitive and dumb. The giant threw Erik to the ground and walked over to Bryon, lying face down in the snow. It reached down to grab Erik's cousin when Bryon rolled over and jabbed upwards with his elvish sword. The blade glowed brightly as it pierced through the giant's palm.

The etenweird's fist slammed into Bryon's chest and he went limp, his sword sizzling and melting the snow around him. The giant screamed.

"I will eat you raw," it said, "and when you wake."

Erik tried to push himself up, his sight blurry, his head pounding, and his whole body throbbing with pain. The etenweird walked to him, slowly and intently, when its body jerked to the side. It yelled and turned hard. Erik saw the shafts of two spears protruding from its back. He saw four blurry figures rush towards the giant, and then a dozen more converge on it from either side.

Erik could make out very little, but the battle was short as the etenweird screamed and fled. The blurry figures came into view, and he saw that they were dwarves. He smiled and held up a hand, but his gesture was met with shouts and the steel blades of spears being pointed at his face.

"I'm a friend," Erik said in their language, but three dwarves jumped on him, roughly brought him to his knees, pulled his hands behind his body, and tied his wrists together with a bit of rope.

"We are friends," Erik tried again.

The pain in his head intensified, and his vision grew worse.

"Please," he said. "We are hurt. One of our companions is still lost in the avalanche."

"Quiet," one of the dwarves said as he stood Erik up.

But as soon as Erik was on his feet, he felt nauseous. The world around him began to spin, his vision narrowed, and he felt as if he was falling. The ground rushed up to meet him, and the world went black.

Erik woke with a start, and as he drew in a deep breath, a sharp pain shot through his ribs, and his stomach tightened, making him cough. He felt himself moving and could see a roof rather than sky above him. It was the rocky roof of an underground tunnel. He let his head fall backwards. Not again.

He felt bumps and heard rattles and realized he was in a cart being pulled—after an upwards glance—by an armor-clad dwarf. Torches sat on each of the four corners of the cart, illuminating the air around him, brightening the tunnel he traveled through. He lay on warm furs, soft as down pillows. He was naked, save for a short sarong that covered his waist and thighs.

Erik lifted his head again, enough to see Nafer asleep in another cart next to him. Snoring loudly, he too wore only a sarong, and the cart was pulled by a woman, and she was moving her cart faster than Erik's

"Thank you," he said to her in Dwarvish as he turned his head in her direction.

The female dwarf didn't say anything, didn't smile, but she gave Erik a slight nod of her head as she moved past.

He could hear other wagons, behind him, hopefully carrying Turk, Bryon, and Bofim. And Beldar ...?

"Beldar," Erik muttered, "where are you?"

"I'm right here," the dwarf said, as he appeared at Erik's side.

Erik was startled at first, but let out a huge sigh of relief as he looked up at the dwarf. His face was bruised, and one eye looked puffy and discolored, but otherwise, he looked relatively unscathed compared to the others.

"What happened to you?" Erik asked.

"These dwarves found me," he replied. "The avalanche carried me to its very edges, a long way down the mountain. Apparently, the commotion alerted this patrol. Avalanches are common in these parts of the mountain, making for easy hunting, with all the animals that get picked up and killed in the snow slides."

"I wouldn't think dwarves would want scavenged animals killed in an avalanche," Erik said.

"No," Beldar said, "it is the etenweird come scavenging, maybe some other creatures they wouldn't want to roam about their lands too. They dispatch their patrols to clear out any giants they find foraging. They found me unconscious. I told them of you all. I thank An that I was able to warn them, they tell me you were about to become an etenweird's dinner."

"I'm sorry I didn't find you, Beldar," Erik said, resting his head back again. "I found Bofim, and then Nafer and Bryon. But I had to turn back, to get them to Turk. I had to carry one and drag the other."

Erik still felt ashamed he hadn't done more. How much more would he have had to travel? A half day? Less? He left his friend for dead, concerned only for Bryon. A good leader puts relationships aside, and does what his best for the whole, all of those who follow him. He heard Wrothgard say that once. He was proving a poor leader.

"You would have never found me, Erik," Beldar said, patting Erik on the shoulder. "Yora, that's one of the dwarves here, told me I was at least a league from where the avalanche had started. It would have taken you two more days to find me. You did what was right, saving the ones you could."

Beldar smiled and now rested his hand on Erik's cart.

"I thank An for this patrol, and I thank An for you, Erik," Beldar added. "You saved Bofim and Nafer and Bryon. Yora also said you fought the etenweird. If it wasn't for you, it would have killed Turk and Bofim. I can tell you are worrying about not being a good leader, Erik, but you should never do that."

"No, I'm not good," Erik said.

"Oh, but you are," Beldar reiterated, "I will follow you to the ends of the earth. Erik..."

The dwarf gave Erik a long, deep look.

"I would give my life for you," Beldar said.

Erik shook his head.

"I am not worth your life," Erik said.

Beldar patted his shoulder.

"You are too humble," the dwarf said, and Erik knew it was pointless arguing anymore. He didn't believe he was worthy of such dedication.

"What are these etenweirds?" Erik asked. "Giant men? Giant dwarves?"

"Yes and no," Beldar explained. "They are a race unto themselves, like antegants and ogres. Most men simply call them giants. They are brutal and cruel, wicked and primitive. You won't see them in the south, but they are plentiful here in the north. They live in small tribes and are always hungry, constantly scavenging and foraging for anything they might eat. They are dangerous to a single dwarf, but no match for a patrol like this. Oddly enough, our shorter stature makes it difficult for the clumsy etenweird to fight us. I hear you fought one well, staying close to it, underneath it even, thus making it hard for it to maneuver."

"Aye," Erik said, "but while I was underneath it—or him, I guess I should say—I saw things I will never forget."

Beldar gave a short laugh, and Erik changed the subject, some other questions that he wanted answers to.

"They were watching for that long before they did anything?" Erik asked.

"The patrol?" Beldar replied. "Yes."

"Were they waiting for us to die?" Erik asked.

"I don't know," Beldar replied, "but I think when they saw you fight with bravery and saw your cousin's elvish sword, they thought you worthy of risking their lives."

"So worthy they tied my hands behind my back," Erik said.

"Your hands are free now," Beldar said. "They are suspicious of men who travel into their lands. And, apparently, you are not the first to do so in only a short number of days."

"The etenweird said something about eating man flesh twice in a week," Erik said.

"Aye," Beldar said. "I am curious to learn what these patrols have seen lately. It may help us in our quest."

Beldar walked for a while longer, hand resting on Erik's cart. Finally, he looked down at the man.

"Rest, Erik," Beldar said. "We have a long journey ahead of us. Take this opportunity to rebuild your strength."

23

"Do you want some rain leaf?" asked Yolli, one of the dwarves escorting Erik and his companions.

"I don't know," Erik said as he walked.

He was feeling better, even if his body still ached and his ribs were still sore. Turk and Bofim were back on their feet too, but Nafer and Bryon hadn't stirred.

"I haven't chewed rain leaf since I was a boy," Erik said, "and when my father found out, he made me chew so much I threw up."

"Well," Yolli said, "your father isn't here and you're a man now. So, do you want some? It's the best in Háthgolthane. Most don't realize you need a cold climate to grow good rain leaf, and the best grows in the Gray Mountains."

"Okay," Erik said, taking a pinch of the wet, green leaf and stuffing it inside his lower lip.

"You're both going to rot your teeth," Turk said.

"You sound like my mother," Yolli replied with a laugh.

"Your mother sounds like a smart woman," Turk said.

The rain leaf was refreshing, even if it burned the inside of his mouth a little. Erik had heard that black root and kokaina tasted awful but gave the user a euphoric feeling that kept them coming back for more. The rain leaf simply made him feel energized and clear headed.

"Stop pawning that stuff onto people," Yora, who was the female dwarf, said, passing by Yolli.

"You want some?" Yolli said, but Yora simply scowled at him over her shoulder.

"I've never seen a female soldier," Erik said.

"Ah, yes, you don't see them in the south, or in Háthgolthane for that matter," Yolli said. "Although, the women of Hargoleth know how to fight. Tall, broad shouldered beauties and their big axes and their big ..."

Yolli trailed off, seemingly staring at nothing.

"Here we go. Dreaming about Hargolethian women again, Yolli," another dwarf said, a warrior named Tûkgad.

"He knows me too well," Yolli said, laughing.

A call came from somewhere in front of Erik, and the small train of dwarves stopped. Erik turned to ask Turk what was happening, but the dwarf simply shook his head and Erik knew that meant to be quiet.

They waited there, still and quiet, for a while. Suddenly, the low pitch of a horn rumbled through the tunnel and all the dwarves—there must have been two dozen northern dwarves in all—snapped to attention, shields coming up under their chins, spear hafts snapping into their shoulders, heels clicking together. Another call came from the front of the company of dwarves and the procession started moving again, albeit slowly and silently. As they moved on, the low, grating sound of metal on rock reverberated through the tunnel. The sound stopped, and a wash of light flooded into the tunnel.

"Stangar," Yolli said. "The outpost we are stationed at. You will stay here, for a while."

"While our friends heal?" Erik asked.

Yolli gave a concerned look to towards Bryon and Nafer; it wasn't a comforting look. He turned back to Erik and smiled.

"We will do our best," Yolli offered.

They entered the outpost, and while Stangar was bigger, it reminded Erik of Ecfast, an outpost in the Southern Mountains in which they stayed before reentering the lands of men. A stoutly built dwarf with reddish gray hair approached Erik and bowed. He was armored from shoulder to toe, holding his helmet under his right arm, showing that he was no threat. A brown cape fastened to his pauldrons flowed behind him and pooled around his feet when he stopped.

"When I first learned that men were coming to Stangar, I was rather upset," the dwarf said in Westernese, "but when a raven reached us, telling us one of the men was none other than Erik, Friend of Dwarves ... or perhaps I should say Erik, Dragon Slayer, I was honored."

The dwarf bowed again and then extended his hand and Erik took it firmly in his, also grasping the dwarf's forearm with his other hand as a show of respect.

"Lieutenant Güthrik," the dwarf said. "I am second in command at Stangar. Our captain, Captain Khâmuth, is in Ghrâg, attending the funerals of several of our fallen warriors. I apologize."

"My condolences to the loss of life."

"They died fighting the etenweird," Lieutenant Güthrik said. "They have been quite active lately. They were glorious deaths. That is why the captain honored their families by traveling with the bodies, even though their spirits are certainly with An as we speak."

The lieutenant walked with Erik for a moment.

"Might I ask," Lieutenant Güthrik said, "but how was it you were north of Stangar? Finding two men north of our outpost was one of the things that alarmed my patrol and, well, treated you unkindly at first. They were naturally suspicious."

"We embarked from Eldmanor and were told to travel through the Fangs and into a tunnel passage," Erik explained. "Its entrance looked like the open mouth of a serpent."

Lieutenant Güthrik gave Erik a concerned look.

"I have always lived in these mountains," the dwarf said, "and explored them without reserve, and I know of no such tunnel passage."

Knowing that dwarves lived lives that were at least three times as long as men, Erik knew that when the Lieutenant said he had explored these mountains his whole life, that would have been a long time.

"Nonetheless, my lord," Erik said, "it was there. And in there, we fought Shadow Children, found a nest of ártocothe, and snuck by a nadre—one that Turk said must have been ages old."

"Shadow Children?" Lieutenant Güthrik gasped, his voice deep with suspicion. "Are you sure of this? I have only seen one tunnel crawler in all my years, and that was many winters ago. It was a sight which still gives me nightmares."

Erik nodded. His brow furrowed deeply and his lips pursed; he tugged at his beard.

"What is the matter?" Lieutenant Güthrik asked.

"It's just ...well," Erik said. He stopped and stared at the dwarf.

Lieutenant Güthrik moved to one side as the others moved past and folded his hands behind his back as he turned to the man.

"What is it?" Lieutenant Güthrik asked.

"We plan on heading north of the Gray Mountains," Erik said.

"Why would men, even dwarves, want to travel into the frozen tundra of the north?" Lieutenant Güthrik asked.

Erik breathed in deeply, closed his eyes, held his breath for a moment, and then slowly let the air out of his lungs.

"We are traveling to Fealmynster," Erik replied.

"I see," Lieutenant Güthrik said. He looked concerned, his eyebrows lifting at first before pushing together, his eyes trailing towards the ground as if he was thinking.

"The man who gave us directions," Erik continued, "I feel he gave us wrong directions, sending us the way he did. If not, it could have been to stop us achieving our goal, or as some sort of worthiness test. Whatever the reason, we could have come through here and saved ourselves a lot of trouble, including demon spawn, giant spiders, and giant men."

"No, you couldn't have," Lieutenant Güthrik replied.

Erik cocked an eyebrow.

"Firstly, there is a range of peaks that run south to north, just east of the Fangs," Lieutenant Güthrik said. "You, seemingly, went under them, but you would have had to firstly travel along the feet of the Gray Mountains, along the northern borders of Nordeth, to reach Wyrma, the first dwarvish fort east of that range. That would have taken you at least a fortnight from Eldmanor. Assuming the dwarves at Wyrma let you pass into our lands, your travel north would have been slow. There are no surface roads in these parts of the Gray Mountains. They are all underground and maintained by us. No, I do believe the path you took was—or would have been—the fastest route to Fealmynster if you had been able to continue on your way. The forest opens up just northeast of where we found you, and then, from there, you would cross the ice bridge and enter into the southern parts of the Northern Tundra. But now ...”

"My lord?" Erik said. It now looked like the lieutenant was hesitant to let him continue on his way.

Lieutenant Güthrik put up a hand.

"A conversation for another time. We will have our surgeons look at you and your friends, but I do need to speak with you alone, where errant ears cannot hear our conversation."

"Why not Turk?" Erik asked.

"Not taking your fame into consideration," Lieutenant Güthrik said, "Turk Skull Crusher told my warriors that you are this group's leader. Was he incorrect?"

Erik stopped and looked at the floor. He thought for a moment. Then, with a smile, gave his head a slight shake.

"Yes, I suppose I am their leader," Erik replied.

"Well, then," Lieutenant Güthrik said, "I will let you get settled in, and then I will meet you in our dining hall. I would meet you in my quarters, but, despite your reputation, there would be warriors that might question me meeting a man in the privacy of my own room."

Erik watched his cousin sleep, Bryon barely moving. Every now and again a dwarf medical attendant would come in and check up on his cousin, look him over, change a wet cloth lying on his forehead, and adjust him in his bed so he didn't get bedsores, but for the most part, they were in there alone.

"Will he be all right?" Erik had asked during the last attendance.

"I think so," the dwarf said, somewhat taken aback by Erik's ability to speak his language. "His leg has some serious muscle damage and is swollen. He has broken ribs and a broken nose. He mostly just needs some rest."

"What about Turk and Nafer?" Erik asked. "My dwarf companions."

The attendant just looked at Erik, didn't say anything, and walked out of the room.

"Well, since you're going to be all right," Erik said to the sleeping Bryon, "and as much as I would just love to sit here and listen to you snore, I need to go speak with this lieutenant."

He patted Bryon's foot as he left his room and made his way to Stangar's dining hall, escorted by one of the other dwarvish medical attendants.

Lieutenant Güthrik was waiting for Erik in the dining hall—a wide, square room with several dozen long tables and matching benches—presumably finishing up with his supper.

"Ah, Erik Eleodum, Friend of Dwarves," Lieutenant Güthrik said with a smile and then dabbing his mouth with a napkin. He presented a space across from him on the opposite bench. "Please. Sit."

Erik sat after a quick bow. Lieutenant Güthrik looked at the medical attendant that had accompanied Erik to the dining hall and then nodded to the two dwarvish guards, armored head to toe, standing on either side of the entrance to the hall. All three dwarves bowed and left.

"I apologize about the clandestine nature of our meeting," Lieutenant Güthrik said.

"I understand," Erik replied.

"It is unfortunate that people have such suspicions," Lieutenant Güthrik added.

"I agree," Erik replied. "If my journeys have taught me anything, it is that everyone, regardless of race or culture, is suspicious of anyone that doesn't think, look, or speak like them."

"True," the lieutenant said.

"Not that I am in a hurry to do anything," Erik said, resting his hands on the table in front of them, "but what is it you wish to speak with me about, Lieutenant?"

"I have several questions," Lieutenant Güthrik said. "Firstly, why are you traveling to Fealmynster?"

"We are searching for something," Erik said. He leaned forward a little. "I will not lie to you, Lieutenant. It is a task that was given to us by the Lord of the East."

He saw the look that crossed the lieutenant's face and put up a hand.

"I hate him as much as you do, perhaps more," Erik began. "These names that people insist on giving me—Friend of Dwarves, Troll Hammer, Wolf's Bane, Dragon Slayer—as much as I don't care for them, they are because of another journey taken in his name. To explain it all, we would be sitting here for days, but something happened on this journey, something that displeased the Ruler of Golgolithul."

"The dragon?" Lieutenant Güthrik asked. "The destruction of South Gate?"

"Yes and no," Erik replied. He knew the Lord of the East cared little for the citizens who lived within his city, save for those who gave him money and more power. "But, because of this mistake, he tasked me and my companions with another mission."

"Why not refuse?" Lieutenant Güthrik asked.

"You know as well as I do that one does not simply refuse a command given by the Lord of the East," Erik said. "I have a family. We all do. If I disobey, they all die."

The lieutenant nodded with understanding. As they spoke, two new guards came to the dining hall, standing at the entrance to the eating room. Lieutenant Güthrik saw them and nodded. They were armored head to toe as well and carried long spears and wide, tower shields. One took position just outside the room, facing out, while the other took position just inside the room, facing Erik and the lieutenant.

"And what is this mission?" Lieutenant Güthrik asked.

Erik looked at the two guards standing at the entrance to the dining hall.

"You can trust them," the lieutenant said.

"The Dragon Sword," Erik replied.

Lieutenant Güthrik tried to keep his face as stoic as possible, but the way his eyes widened and his mouth dropped, just a little, was obvious. Erik thought he heard one of the guards cough, and the other one shifted uneasily.

"The wizard of Fealmynster guards the weapon, and the Lord of the East wants it," Erik said.

"And you mean to deliver it to him?" Lieutenant Güthrik asked.

"Right now, it doesn't seem we are doing a very good job of finding it," Erik replied. "But I would do anything to protect my family."

"By doing anything the Lord of the ..."

"Before you start telling me about how dangerous and wicked the Lord of the East is," Erik said, cutting the lieutenant off, "I know. I have seen it first-hand. I have seen, personally, his wrath, his magic, and his cruelty."

As he watched the lieutenant, Erik wondered if he would let

them leave and continue on their journey. When they spoke before, it didn't seem the lieutenant would.

"I don't know if I can let you go," Lieutenant Güthrik said. "Success of your mission would no doubt mean defeat for my people."

"I love the dwarvish people," Erik said, straightening his back, "but I will continue on."

Erik stared at the lieutenant intently, his eyes hard and cold. The dwarf finally dropped his gaze, unable to match the man's intensity.

"What if I offered you safety?" Lieutenant Güthrik asked. "What if I sent a platoon of warriors with you, to your homeland? I would fully supply you. The warriors would stay with you, protect your family and loved ones."

"Dwarvish warriors are formidable," Erik said, "but what good are they against the full force of the Lord of the East? He has powers no one can overcome."

"What if I suggested you could bring your family here?" Lieutenant Güthrik asked.

"King Skella offered me the same thing," Erik said. "Can you offer me the same safety that the King of Drüum Balmdüukr can offer? The same protection the walls of Thorakest can give?"

"We could petition King Stone Axe," Lieutenant Güthrik said.

"Even since I am a personal friend of Lord Balzarak," Erik said, "there is no guarantee that the king will protect us. And, even then, can anyone save me, or my family, from the Lord of the East's black magic."

"The Black Mage," Lieutenant Güthrik muttered.

"Perhaps," Erik said, "but two witches now also serve him. And another wizard. King Skella knew that even the walls of Thorakest were no match for the Lord of the East, his dark magic, and his assassins. In reality, I am as good as dead. It is my family I wish to protect."

"I cannot persuade you otherwise?" Lieutenant Güthrik asked.

Erik shook his head.

"I will have to wait until Captain Khâmuth returns," Lieutenant Güthrik said, "before I can let you leave."

"How long?" Erik asked.

"Four days," Lieutenant Güthrik replied. "Your two companions —the other man and Nafer Round Shield—are in no condition to travel, so you could not leave yet anyway."

"And you will continue to do everything you can to heal them?" Erik asked.

The Lieutenant nodded with a smile on his face, and Erik felt like he could trust him. Probably.

"Tell me Erik, Friend of Dwarves," Lieutenant Güthrik said, "what was Orvencrest like?"

"Broken, dark, lonely," Erik said, remembering the lost city and the death he felt in that place. "I could tell that it was a faint shadow of what it once was, cast aside by a wall of flame."

"That is too bad," the lieutenant said. "What about the treasure room? You found that, didn't you?"

"Magnificent," Erik replied. "I have never seen anything like it, and I will probably never see anything like it again."

Erik stood slowly, taking care of his ribs. The guard facing them snapped to attention and, even though he couldn't see the dwarf's face, he knew the warrior watched him intently.

"If you have nothing more for me," Erik said, "I would like to rest and then check on my cousin."

Lieutenant Güthrik nodded before speaking again.

"What was it like? The dragon?"

Erik stopped and stared at the ground for a moment. Most days, he tried not to think about her, or the sound of fire burning children alive, the hurricane winds her wings created destroying everything or her malicious voice that still invaded his mind. He lifted his head and looked at the lieutenant.

"Just imagine the most terrible thing you could ever consider, and that will come nowhere near how terrifying she was."

Back in Bryon's room, he found Turk by his cousin's bedside.

"How is he?" Erik asked.

"It's his old wound," Turk replied. "The dragon's wound is

festering again. I don't know why exactly, but I suspect it has something to do with the spider's venom."

"Poison strengthening poison?" Erik asked.

"More like, evil strengthening evil," Turk replied, and the intensity in his voice made Erik shudder.

"Will he be all right?" he asked, but Turk could only shrug his meaty shoulders.

They watched as one of the medical attendants changed a cloth patch resting on Bryon's chest, where the young dragon had wounded him. It was red and swollen again, and the cloth the dwarvish attendant removed was soaked with yellow puss. Bryon stirred a little, mumbling something incoherent while he slept. One of the dwarves tending to him said he had awoken for a little while and was able to drink some water. But then the dwarf gave him sweet wine, and he fell back asleep.

"We have to hope he will recover," Turk said. "The surgeons here aren't as good as the ones in Thorakest, but they are good. And when they are finished, I can probably heal him some more. It is Nafer that I am more worried about."

Erik gave his friend a questioning look.

"His condition is worsening," Turk replied. "His arm, nose, and most of his ribs are broken, but they can heal in time. It is the poison I am concerned about because they can't remove it from his blood. He has a terrible fever, and I fear for his life."

"If Bryon will recover," Erik said, "then use your strength on Nafer."

"I can try, but you have to remember my powers have their limits."

With that, Turk walked away, his head bent low as if in shame. Erik wanted to reassure his friend but knew the dwarf would probably prefer to be left alone with his thoughts.

The next day, Erik met Turk outside the infirmary where Bryon was being cared for. When the dwarf appeared from the room, he was covered in sweat and breathing hard.

"He is awake now," Turk said as he wiped his brow with the back of his hand.

"That's good, but how are you?" Erik asked.

"Tired," Turk replied. "Dragon poison. Ártocothe poison. They don't just poison the body. I need to rest ... for a while."

"You have no idea how much I appreciate you," Erik said.

"Yes, I do," Turk replied, looking at Erik and then the door to the infirmary. "Bryon is as much my family as he is yours. Now, if you'll excuse me."

Erik entered the room to see Bryon sitting up in his bed.

"Are you done wasting everyone's time and energy?" Erik asked with a smile.

"I think so," Bryon replied, also smiling. "Turk says I will be all right."

Erik nodded.

"How are the others?" Bryon asked. "How is Nafer?"

Erik shrugged and shook his head.

"What can we do?" Bryon asked.

"Wait," Erik replied. "All we can do is wait."

24

———

afer lay in a large bed covered with several layers of blankets. A short towel lay across his brow, and a washbasin full of soapy water sat beside his bed and his chest rose and fell with short, choppy breaths. He looked a ghost of his former self; his shallow cheeks showed too much bone beneath the pale skin, and his normally well-tended beard was unkempt. An unpleasant smell hit Erik's nose. It wasn't one of trash or rot, but a stale smell of sickness.

As Erik sat on a short stool next to the bed, Nafer's breathing suddenly became stuttered and then stopped altogether for a long moment before starting up again, just as shallow as before. Erik realized he'd been holding his breath, and he let it out with a long sigh of relief as he reached under the blankets to grasp Nafer's limp hand. The muscles that once rippled through the dwarf's thick forearms were now all but gone, and Erik winced at clammy skin, cold despite the layers of blankets the physicians had piled on top of Nafer.

"I am sorry, brother," Erik whispered, tears filling his eyes.

He rested his head on the bed and closed his eyes. He remembered words Demik told him as he died, jumping in front of Erik when a spear was meant for him.

"There is no greater love than for a friend to lay down his life for another friend," Erik whispered. "I would trade places with you, Nafer, if I could."

Truly?

The voice running through his head startled him; he hadn't heard from his dagger in a while. Erik stared at the dwarf lying so still. If it wasn't for his chest, he might already be dead.

I would. He and his people have given me so much. His best friend gave his life for me.

But what about your wife? Your child?

Erik considered that for a moment. The thought of Simone and his unborn child hadn't even crossed his mind as he spoke to the unconscious Nafer. The idea of a child—boy or girl—bouncing on his knee, running away as he playfully chased after them, and laughing as he tickled them seemed too hard to comprehend, but he knew they would be precious times. The thought of watching a boy grow into a man or a girl grow into a woman filled him with a sense of pride. Was that how his father felt? Would Erik want to miss out on that? That thought triggered another.

Could I look at my child with honest eyes, knowing I didn't do everything I could to save my friend? Could I ask my child to be coura-geous and brave, upright and honest, knowing I hadn't been any of those things?

Erik felt a strong tingle at his hip.

You amaze me. I wish I had known you before.

Erik's mind was silent for a while as he watched Nafer again. Then he questioned what the dagger had said.

Before what?

His dagger didn't reply.

"Are you there?" Erik asked aloud, looking down at his dagger and touching the hilt.

Unsheathe me and place me on your friend's chest. Leave me there, and do not touch me.

Erik did as he was told. He'd learned not to question the dagger's instructions.

If we do this, you will not be able to use me until we get to Fealmynster. Do you understand? Is this your choice?

Yes.

This will not be like before. I will not just be tired or drained. If you attempt to use me until I say you can, it will destroy us both.

"I understand," Erik said aloud.

Erik sat there and waited. His dagger began to glow, faintly at first and then with a mixture of colors as it started to hum. The whole room seemed to vibrate as the dagger glowed brighter and brighter until what looked like multi-colored flames danced on the blade and then along Nafer's blankets, but nothing burned. The humming turned to more of a screech, a low moan at first and then louder, its increasing pitch forcing Erik to cover his ears. Now, the whole room shook, and knocking and shouting came at the door, but it seemed it was now locked the way the handle rattled.

Nafer levitated, floating just above his mattress as magical fire consumed him. The light was so bright, Erik could no longer see his dagger and could barely keep his eyes open. The noise became even louder, and the room shook so violently Erik thought the ceiling and walls would cave in.

Nafer opened his mouth and screamed, and as he did, so did Erik. The sensations of the light and the sound and shaking became so intense he felt like he was going to lose his mind. And then it was over.

Erik looked up as half a dozen dwarves burst through the now open door, all ready to fight someone, but they all froze on the spot in astonishment as Nafer sat up in his bed. He looked to the physicians and then to Erik, and then to his lap.

"Erik, why is your dagger here?" he asked. He looked around, his eyebrows scrunched, and his lips pursed. "Where are we? Who are they?"

"What do you remember?" Erik asked.

Nafer rubbed his brow and then scratched his chin.

"I remember the tunnel crawlers and the ártocothe," Nafer replied. "I remember fire ... the ártocothes burning. And then all I remember is white."

Nafer shivered.

"And cold," he added as he lifted his left arm.

"I thought my arm was broken," Nafer said.

Erik laughed.

"It was," he replied.

"Have I been in a coma for several months?" Nafer asked. "It doesn't feel like my arm was ever hurt ... ever."

"You were dead, my friend," Erik replied. "Well almost, but now you're alive."

As the dwarves sheathed and belted their weapons, Erik slipped the dagger back into its own gold scabbard. It felt cold, and he didn't sense the presence of whatever entity dwelt in the blade, as he normally did. For a moment, his stomach knotted, and his heart sank.

"Erik," Nafer said, and Erik looked up at his friend. He looked the pinnacle of health. His bruises and cuts were gone. His color had returned. He looked strong and vibrant. "Are you alright?"

"I am now," Erik said with a smile.

25

———

*E*rik spent most of his time in Bryon's room over the next four days. The dwarvish physicians couldn't stop talking about what had happened to Nafer, and Erik decided he would rather avoid any incessant questioning. Bryon was getting better, staying awake for longer, and his color returning.

"I see you are doing much better," Lieutenant Güthrik said, hands crossed behind his back after stepping into Bryon's room.

"Yes, thank you," Bryon replied.

"Your friends are healing quickly," Lieutenant Güthrik said to Erik, "quicker than any of our physicians expected. It seems we misdiagnosed Nafer Round Shield with a broken arm ... and a broken nose ... *and* broken ribs. Bones do not heal that fast."

The lieutenant didn't look especially upset, more curious than suspicious of strange happenings.

"I suppose so," Erik replied.

"Well, I am happy your friends are healthy," Lieutenant Güthrik said. "Captain Khâmuth has returned and would like an audience with you, Erik."

Erik looked to his cousin.

"I'll be fine," Bryon said.

Erik followed Güthrik, and the two guards that had watched them when they first spoke in the halls of Stangar, once again to the dining hall. Erik recognized Yolli and Tûkgad and Yora from among the dwarves who had saved them from the giant. They stood next to another dwarf, his hair uncommonly dark for a northerner, but it was splashed with white in places. It fell back into a braid as his beard followed suit, parted into four such braids. Captain Khâmuth stood armored in decorative plate mail, a red cape attached to his pauldrons pooling on the floor around his feet. His right eye, white and useless, stared in one direction while he watched Erik with his left. The long handle of a sword poked over his shoulder, and the dwarf wore two short swords on his girdle, one on either side.

"Erik Eleodum, Friend of Dwarves," Khâmuth said in Westernese with a quick bow.

"Captain Khâmuth, I am honored to make your acquaintance," Erik replied, speaking in Dwarvish and returning the bow.

"It is I am who is honored," Khâmuth said. "Word by way of raven reached me while I was in Ghrâg that you were here, a letter from Lord Balzarak himself."

"Isn't he in Fornhig?" Erik asked.

"Aye," Khâmuth replied. "That he is."

"How did he know we are here?" Erik asked. "Can a raven really travel that fast?"

"We have other ways of communicating across long distances," Khâmuth replied with a smile.

"I would like to speak with Balzarak," Erik said.

"That will most likely be impossible, but we can try," Khâmuth said. "Such communication is draining on our resources and is often used only in rare circumstances. Erik Dragon Slayer finding his way to our front doorstep happens to be one of these circumstances. I would be honored to seek to send a message via raven to Lord Balzarak for you."

"I would appreciate that," Erik replied.

"The Most Respected Lord Balzarak said he does not know when he will see you next, Erik," Khâmuth said, folding his arms across his chest, "or if he will ever see you again. For this, know that he is sad. But he has given me a great honor."

"Oh?" Erik said.

Khâmuth looked to another dwarf standing to his left and nodded. The dwarf retrieved a large, round shield. Where most shields were made of wood, this one looked metal, and on the front, etched above the domed boss that centered the shield, Erik saw dwarvish runes. Pictures of a mounted knight fighting a fire-breathing dragon, also expertly etched into the metal, ran along the circumference of the shield, four images in all—north, south, east, and west.

"Thank you, Hragram," Khâmuth said to the dwarf, took the shield, and presented it to Erik. "This is yours. Made of Dwarf's Iron. A gift from Lord Balzarak."

"This is a great, great honor," Erik said, looking at the shield. "I don't recognize the runes on the front," he added.

He had studied and knew the dwarvish alphabet, but their ancient languages didn't use an alphabet, rather runes that Erik had only begun to learn.

"They say Clan Dragon Fire," Khâmuth said. "It is your clan. King Stone Axe has decreed that Erik Eleodum, Friend of Dwarves, would be given a proper dwarvish clan, one that you may pass down to your descendants, in essence, making them dwarves."

"Truly?" Erik said, and Khâmuth nodded. "I don't know what to say."

"As you said of the shield, this is a great honor," Khâmuth replied. Erik couldn't tell if the captain approved or not, his face the visage of stoicism. "Across our long history, there are only a few men who have received such a gift from the dwarves."

"I will wear the name proudly," Erik replied.

"I have also been instructed to baptize you," Khâmuth said, "as Erik Dragon Fire, if you wish to receive this offering."

Erik thought for a moment. He had seen dwarves in his dreams when the field of grass was brown and dead and the sky was red and the distant, black mountains were looming and thundering. And he knew of the mark all dwarvish warriors wore on their left breast.

"Yes," Erik replied, "I accept."

"Good," the captain said, "And I hear your friends have healed up well ... and rather quickly."

"Yes," Erik replied. "Thank you. I guess there were several misdiagnoses."

"Surprising," Khâmuth said. "Our physicians are some of the best."

The dwarf gave Erik the same look Güthrik had given him, but now there was a hint of a wry smile.

"No matter," Khâmuth added. "I am just happy they are well. Lieutenant Güthrik."

The lieutenant stepped forward.

"We will prepare Erik Dragon Fire for baptism tomorrow," Khâmuth said.

"Yes, my lord," Lieutenant Güthrik said with a bow.

Erik Dragon Fire.

Erik couldn't help but smile. Gooseflesh rose along his arms, and he felt a quick shiver of excitement. Then, his smile disappeared. He remembered the dwarves in his dreams. The dead. The feeling of evil and the presence of the Shadow. It would be nothing new, but Erik wondered if, this time, it might be different enough.

26

———

*B*elvengar bowed before Fréden, handing him a rolled piece of parchment.

"A raven brought this today," Belvengar said.

Fréden Fréwin grabbed the piece of parchment and unrolled it. It was a long letter, and the seal had been broken, so he knew Belvengar had already read it.

"I am pressed for time, Long Spear," Fréden said, rolling his eyes at one of his construction officers. The dwarf hid his laugh, and Fréden chanced a smile. "Just tell what is in the letter."

"As you wish, my lord," Belvengar said. "I have several spies in the north. They are not in prominent positions, but they are there watching, nonetheless."

"Yes, yes," Fréden said, rolling his eyes again, "all things I know. Please, get to the point."

"Yes, my lord," Belvengar said, standing. "Erik Eleodum is in Stangar."

"What?" Fréden said, standing faster than anyone could have expected him to.

"He is in Stangar," Belvengar said again.

"What is the nature of his stay?" Fréden asked. "Does he have the Dragon Sword?"

"I do not know the answer to either question, my lord," Belvengar replied.

"Well, what do you know?" Fréden demanded with a scowl.

"He is there, and he is being heralded as a hero," Belvengar said.

"A hero," Fréden hissed.

"Yes, my lord," Belvengar said and paused, just staring at Fréden.

"What is it?" Fréden asked.

"King Stone Axe has decreed that this Erik … well, he … he is …"

"Spit it out," Fréden said.

"He is to be baptized. In the ways of the dwarvish warrior," Belvengar said, his eyes wide and full of worry as if Fréden would think it Belvengar's idea.

As Long Spear spoke, the council around Fréden gave an audible gasp and then went silent. Fréden was never baptized. He wasn't a warrior. But Belvengar and Kizmit and many of the other dwarves who served in his new army were. It was a sign of passage, the ritual all warriors went through to join the ranks of others. Fréden didn't know what happened after a dwarf was branded and fell into a coma. No one spoke of his or her baptism; it was a warrior's code. But what Fréden did know was that not everyone survived his or her baptism. If they didn't, they were deemed the unworthy, better to die in their coma rather than bring dishonor to their family and clan on the battlefield.

In truth, Fréden thought baptism a pointless ritual, but as silly as it was, it was reserved for dwarves, not men. King Stone Axe had lost his mind.

"He is to be given the clan name, Dragon Fire," Belvengar added.

"Kizmit," Fréden said, and his general stepped to his side. "Send for Mungrun."

Shortly, Mungrun knelt before Fréden as he dismissed all of his advisors save for Kizmit and Belvengar.

"I know your true name isn't Mungrun," Fréden said, "but I don't care. You keep your real name secret for a reason. I am sure, with time, you will see you can trust me."

Mungrun simply looked up at Fréden.

"I need you to travel back to Stangar," Fréden said.

"My lord," Mungrun said, "may I ask why?"

"There is a man there," Fréden said. "His name is Erik Eleodum. I need you to kill him."

Fréden looked at Kizmit and Belvengar with a wide smile, but neither one of the warriors returned the gesture. Was it such a complex concept? This so-called Mungrun was from Stangar, so he could move around freely and kill Eleodum. If he had the Dragon Sword, Mungrun would bring it to Fréden. If not, Mungrun would bring the directions, and Fréden would find it himself—at least, he would send his best warriors to do so.

"Consider it done, my lord," Mungrun said, and Fréden dismissed him.

"My lord," Belvengar said, "I don't think this is a good idea."

"You don't serve me to offer your thoughts on such matters," Fréden said, his brows furrowed. "You elicit information, spy for me, and carry out assassinations."

"I happen to agree with him, my lord," Kizmit added. "We know nothing of this Mungrun."

"I will hear no more on it," Fréden said, standing, wanting to retire for the day. "It is a good plan, and we will carry through with it."

"Let me go with him," Belvengar said.

"Out of the question," Fréden said. "Relax, Long Spear. In a fortnight, Erik Eleodum will be dead, and I will either have my hands on the Dragon Sword or know where to find it."

27

———

Bu clapped his hand roughly over Andu's mouth.

"You fool," Bu whispered. "You gave away our position."

The dwarvish patrol—six dwarves, all armed with spears, bows, and armored in leather, scouting breastplates—stood back to back, in a circle, peering out into the forest. Bu, Bao Zi, Andu, and his remaining men crouched behind an especially large, oval-leafed, purple-flowered bush that dared the cold, as it grew wider and taller. It was all that divided the scouting party from Bu.

Bu squeezed his hand further against Andu's mouth, digging his dirty and broken fingernails into the skin and on his cheeks. He could feel his sergeant's groans against his palm, but Andu made no attempt to stop Bu. He was little more than a broken dog, and now he'd messed up royally.

They had been traveling due north, towards a strange green glow in the sky. The green light eventually disappeared, leaving Bu nothing to follow, so he just remained on the same course, until they came to a tall and steep range of mountain peaks made of black rock. They spent two days looking for a way over, through, or under them but found nothing. Bu knew the keep of Fealmynster was towards the northeast, but so were the giants, so they searched for a path to the west. They searched and searched, and had traveled for the better part of a week—the hiking slow going through the heavy snow and thick forest of the Gray Mountains—when the black-rocked range finally subsided and gave way to a more gentle mountain slope that allowed them to continue north at a better pace.

Bu had even found traces of several roads, following one until it ended at an abandoned trading post, finding another that just disappeared without any obvious reason.

They had seen the dwarves—at least, Bu did—a half-day before and decided to take a wide birth. They seemed to be moving in the same direction, and dwarves were good trackers and scouts, but Bu was better. He didn't think they were actually after them. He knew the northern dwarves patrolled their lands with an almost zealous diligence, and after running into giant spiders and giant men, he could see why. As Bu instructed his men to move out, Andu relayed the command to the Hámonian knights, but Sir Garrett just stared at Bu's sergeant rather than move.

"Didn't you hear what I said?" Andu had asked.

"I don't speak dog," Sir Garrett replied.

In a rare form of aggression and bravery, Andu screamed and attacked the knight. But, as much as Bu hated these Hámonian pricks, they were all adept fighters. Andu wound up on his back, Garrett beating him senseless until Bu pulled him off the man. That's when Andu retrieved a knife from his boot and tried to stab Garrett in the back, again, with a mighty yell. He was a loyal dog, but not at all stealthy.

Bu grabbed Andu, and Garrett turned on the sergeant with his sword drawn. That was when Bu sheard dwarvish shouting, and he knew they had alerted the patrol to their position. His glare at the knight told the man this matter would have to be settled at a later time, and that's when he pulled Andu behind the large bush and muffled his curses.

In a way, he was happy to see his broken sergeant show a bit of balls, but it was misplaced and at the wrong time. Garrett would have killed him, and he gave away their position.

"What do we do?" Bao Zi asked in a croaking hushed voice.

"These little hairy pricks won't stop looking for us now they're here," Bu replied. He finally let go of Andu and gave the man an angry look that caused him to whimper like the dog he was. "We'll have to kill them. That's all there is to it."

Bu looked at Garrett.

"Wait here," Bu said.

"What am I waiting for?" Sir Garrett asked.

"When I slit the first dwarf's throat," Bu said, "attack."

Bu jerked his head sideways, and Bao Zi, Andu, and his last remaining eastern soldier followed him. They crawled on their bellies for a long time, and Bu suspected the knights of getting restless, but there was no indication they would disobey their orders. For as long as they crept along the mountain floor, the dwarves stared out into the forest, muttering to one another. They broke their circular rank and stepped away from one another, fanning out and inspecting trees and bushes.

Bu would have much rather continued without a fight. He was low on resources and, if this wizard of Fealmynster was as crazy and powerful as Li said he was, he would need all the strength he could muster, but these dwarves would not let that happen. The northern dwarves were aggressive and unkind to intruders in their lands. Once they saw several easterners, fighting would be inevitable. If Bu had tried to sneak away, it would never have worked with the useless idiots he had in his party.

Bu stopped and looked over his shoulder. Bao Zi stared back, waiting. Bu nodded. He could smell the bear fat on the closest dwarf, and a deep musky smell. It disgusted him, but he sought to ignore it. Bu crouched behind a tree, pressing his back up against its trunk hard. It was wide enough that it covered his whole body. He withdrew a dagger from his belt.

As he waited there, dagger in his right hand, he saw the tip of a spear pass by, then the whole blade and part of the shaft. It was slow, as the dwarf gingerly tiptoed forward. Bu was certain that this dwarf, no doubt chosen to be a scout for his tracking abilities, knew they were in the forest. As about half the shaft of the spear passed in front of Bu, he grabbed the wood, pulled the dwarf forward, grabbed his hairy chin, jerked it up, and plunged the dagger blade into exposed flesh.

"Now, Bao Zi!" Bu shouted, and his personal guard stood and threw his own dagger at the next nearest dwarf.

The loud grunt said that Bao Zi hit his mark, but he wasn't sure if the dwarf was dead. Bu stared at the bush behind which the knights hid.

"Now!" he shouted again, and Garrett and four other knights emerged from the bush, swords drawn, shouting like madmen. Fools.

A spear sailed through the air and struck one of the knights in the chest. He went down, dead. Bu drew his sword. The dwarf Bao Zi had attacked wasn't quite dead, so he brought his steel—Patûk's steel—down on the scout's head. Four more.

He hadn't seen one of the dwarves rushing him from the side. His last eastern soldier rushed from cover and swatted the dwarvish spear away. The dwarf dropped the weapon, drew a short sword, and thrust it—hilt deep—into the eastern soldier's gut. Bu pushed the soldier aside and brought his own sword down on the dwarf's neck. Blood sprayed him across the face.

Garrett actually proved his prowess in battle, blocking one spear strike with the simple bracer on his forearm and, in the next motion, removing another dwarf's head with a precise sword strike. He wounded his first attacker with a sword to the scout's leg, and another knight brought his sword down into the dwarf's chest.

That left one dwarf. Bu knew the scout wouldn't surrender, but he could possibly run and try to alert whatever outpost from which he came. Dwarves didn't normally retreat, but to withdraw here wouldn't really be capitulation. Andu flicked a knife towards the dwarf as the scout turned to run. It struck the dwarf in the leg, enough to make him stumble. Bu was on him quickly, tip of his sword buried in the back of the dwarf's shoulder.

"Where's your outpost?" Bu asked, turning the dwarf over so he could see his ugly face.

"Easterner dung," the dwarf said in Shengu with an angry groan.

"Where's your outpost?" Bu asked, this time in Dwarvish.

The dwarf didn't answer. Bu jabbed his sword into the front of the dwarf's shoulder. The dwarf gritted his teeth.

"We are looking for Fealmynster," Bu said.

The dwarf stared back with wide eyes and then narrowed them.

"Speak, and I will give you a quick death," Bu said.

Bu slid his sword into the dwarf's flesh deeper.

"Almost directly north of here, there's an abandoned road," the dwarf said with a groan. "It leads to a surface tunnel that runs through the northern range that separates the Gray Mountains and the northern tundra. From there ... from there, it's a fortnight or more to Fealmynster."

"Are there more patrols?" Bu asked.

The dwarf laughed.

"Of course," the dwarf replied.

Bu frowned and brought his sword down on the dwarf's neck. He looked at the dead knight and his dead soldier. This was a costly battle.

"Bao Zi, let's move," Bu said.

28

____

Specter watched from the corner of the tavern as two men
jostled for position, each trying to impress a young prosti-
tute who clearly had not been working in the business for very long.
She looked nervous, scared even. A veteran would have recognized
the opportunity for extra coin. This girl simply wanted the night
to end.

These men were Durathnan. It made sense. They were in the
northwestern edges of Gol-Durathna. They were soldiers, but not
ordinary ones. Specter recognized Dragon's Teeth, the elite of the
Northern Kingdom. Specter laughed. They were supposed to be
upright, righteous, merciful, kind, generous, chivalrous, and here they
were, bullying a young girl barely past her sixteenth winter. He
thought it was funny how people viewed the world. Northerners
were inherently good. Westerners were inherently strong. South-
erners were inherently free. People from Wüsten Sahil were exotic,
Mek-Ba'Dunians were barbaric, and Isutans were mystical. Easterners, like Syzbalo, were simply arrogant.

They were all men. They were all wicked—some more than

others. They were all selfish. They were all cruel. Specter wished people would just realize that. It's what made his job so easy. He preyed on man's natural habits. And when he drained their life, he didn't feel bad. They would have done the same thing to him, given the opportunity.

Most would say they wouldn't. Drink someone's blood and live forever? Lunacy. Despicable. But any man, when his back was pressed against the wall and death was knocking at his door, would make that deal.

The two men finally convinced the girl to take both of them upstairs, all for the price of one. The tavern owner just shook his head as he stood behind the bar. He got his cut no matter what. He didn't care that these men were about to take advantage of this girl and probably traumatize her for the rest of her life.

After a few moments, Specter stood and followed. While they began to walk up two flights of stairs, Specter waited in the shadows and then began to climb, testing each step for creaks. The girl opened the door to a room, and the first man—his hair dark and curly, his shoulders wide and his chest broad—pushed her in. The other man, also wide and strong with long, blondish hair, laughed as he followed, and the door shut behind them. Specter stood and listened.

"No! Wait!" the girl pleaded.

"No! Wait!" one of the men mimicked in a falsetto voice. "We made a deal. You're not an oath breaker, are you?"

"I changed my mind," the girl said.

"No changing your mind in this business," the other man said.

"Hey, what are you doing?" the first man said. "I go first."

"Hog's piss," the other said. "Last time, there wasn't nothing left for me. She was all spent and couldn't even stay awake."

"What do we do then?" the first man asked, all the while, Specter could hear the girl sobbing softly.

"You take one end, and I'll take the other," the second man suggested.

"Deal," the first said.

It wasn't that Specter felt bad for the girl. He didn't. She had chosen her course ... perhaps. She might have been forced into the brothel, sold by her father, or an alley rat with nowhere else to go. Specter shrugged. He had killed younger ... drained younger. But she was Isutan; at least half. He could tell by her tanned skin and her almond eyes. It was probably what appealed to these pasty pale northerners so much.

Specter didn't open the door but stepped through it. It took energy to do it, took a year or two off his life, but he would get that back ... soon.

The men didn't see him. They had both pulled their pants down, and the curly-haired soldier pushed the girl's face into the mattress of the bed, her underclothes simply pushed aside. She tried to scream, but the blankets and sheets muffled her cries. Then, she turned her head to the side, and she saw Specter. She stopped struggling.

"She's already broken," the blond-haired man said, a hint of disappointment in his voice. "I was looking forward to more struggle."

The other man shrugged. He was about to stick the girl when the blond man gasped.

"What, by the bloody gods, is that?"

Specter stepped from the shadows into the light. He knew his appearance was jarring—his white hair, his white eyes, his black, leather armor. Both men pulled up their pants. He let them. He had no desire to kill men with their pants down. He extended his hand, and the Bone Spear appeared.

"Black magic," the first Durathnan said.

"The blackest," Specter said with a smile.

The curly-haired man drew his sword and charged. Fool. Too eager. Too ambitious. Specter side-stepped, kicked out and watched the man trip and fall into the wall. He gave him another kick to the ribs. Bones broke.

"What are you doing here?" Specter asked.

"None of your damn business," the blond man said, unsheathing his sword.

"Tsk, tsk," Specter said. "Such language around a young girl."

The blond man gave the girl a mocking look.

"She's nothing but a whore."

"An Isutan whore," Specter replied. "She's one of my countrywomen."

"What difference does it make?" the man asked.

Specter kicked out as the first man tried to get up. He felt the man's balls crunch under the toe of his boot. Specter leaned forward.

"It makes all the difference."

He jabbed with the butt of his spear, hitting the blond man half a dozen times all over his body before the man could even move. Specter was like smoke, shadows, or the wind. He was behind the man, punching him in the solar plexus. When he turned, he was behind him again, his boot to the back of the man's knee. A fist to the back of the head. A hammer fist to the side of the face.

"I yield," the man said, already bruised and bloody.

He dropped his sword and threw his hands up.

"What are you doing here?" Specter asked, pointing the bony point of his spear at the man's throat.

"Whoring," the man said.

Specter rolled his eyes. Men from the west were simpletons.

"No, here, in this town," Specter said, looking around the room, "in ..."

He looked at the girl.

"Bardsville," she said.

"Here in Bardsville," Specter said.

"It's a border town. We're in the army. Is that such a mystery?"

"No," Specter said. "You're Dragon's Teeth."

The man's face blanched, whiter than it already was. He chewed on his cheek. He didn't know what to say. Clearly, they weren't supposed to be there. Or, people weren't supposed to know they were there.

Specter grew bored quickly. The curly-haired man began to rouse again. He let the man get to his knees and stand. As the Durathnan turned to face the room, Specter stabbed him with his spear. The soldier jerked backward, foaming at the mouth and convulsing. His poison worked quickly.

When Specter retracted his weapon, he ran his finger along the bony blade, scooping up what blood he could, and then licked it. It was sour, but it was blood. The man fell to his knees, and Specter attacked, jerking his head to the side and plunging his teeth into the soft part of his neck. In moments, the man's skin turned gray, and he looked a ragged husk of a person.

Specter stood and closed his eyes for a moment. He could feel the magic working. The small creases around his eyes disappeared. The minor aches in his joints faded. The few wrinkles on the back of his hands vanished again. His skin was new and soft. His muscles strong. His mind sharp. And after so many years, he enjoyed draining a person as much as the first one.

The blond-haired man looked on in horror. The girl looked on with a mixture of awe and delight. She squinted, a malicious look on her face, and glared at her one, living attacker.

"You were saying," Specter said.

"We're a small unit," the blond man said. "Please ... don't hurt me."

"Go on," Specter said.

"We are accompanying a unit of Atrimus."

"The Shadow Men?" Specter asked, more to himself than the man in front of him.

"Aye," the man said, his voice shaking uncontrollably. "They're following a man, some westerner. They have orders to kill him."

"Erik Eleodum," Specter muttered.

"I don't know," the man said. "Please. Please."

"Stop whining," Specter said, almost disappointed. Cowardly behavior always soured their blood even more.

"They have spies in the dwarvish lands, in Wyrma and Ghrâg."

"The righteous King Agempi has spies?" Specter said facetiously. "How dare he being such an upright man. What did these spies say?"

"Supposedly, word reached Ghrâg that the westerner we are seeking is in Stangar," the soldier replied. "I don't even know what Stangar is. I just overheard them saying it."

"It's a dwarvish outpost," Specter said, "in the Gray Mountains, at least a fortnight north of Wyrma."

He watched the man for a moment.

"Is that all?" Specter asked.

The man nodded.

"Thank you," Specter said.

The man seemed to relax at that. He sighed deeply, and his shoulders slumped with relief. That's when Specter attacked. It was so much easier to drain a person right after they died. Their blood had lost some of its vigor, some of its warmth, but they didn't struggle. But this man was northern scum. He deserved the pain he received. And he was unsuspecting.

Specter felt the artery open up in his mouth, like popping a berry. The blood was warm and squirted with each beat of the man's heart. He drank and drank until the Durathnan's skin was a sickly gray, his body rigid and stiff and brittle. He dropped him and stood, closing his eyes and relishing the new life he had just received.

Opening his eyes, he looked at the Isutan girl sitting on the bed, legs curled up underneath her, and her clothing rearranged. She looked a little scared, but when she looked at the two men, she smiled.

"Thank ..." she began to say.

Specter was quick, quicker than he had been, new blood coursing through his veins. He grabbed the girl by the throat. He barely squeezed, but it was enough to make her choke and gasp for air. She didn't struggle, but she looked at him with wild eyes. She was frightened now.

Looming over her, Specter turned her face to the side, staring at her neck. He could see the artery thumping against her soft, young skin. Thump. Thump. Thump. He felt his own heart quicken with each thump, became aroused by it. He heard it. Felt it. Smelled it.

Specter let her go.

"Go back to Isuta," he said with sudden lazy eyes.

"But my father ..." the girl began and then faltered.

"What about him?"

"He's here," she said. "He'll die if I don't ..."

"He's not Isutan is he?"

The girl shook her head.

"You'll die if you stay," Specter said. "Isutan women are strong, powerful, independent."

Specter turned to the dead men, opening his arms as if to present them.

"Look at them," he said. "Is this what you want?"

She shook her head.

"Go back to Isuta," he replied. "Let your father die. Join your *own* people and live."

Specter wasn't a compassionate man. Truth be told, if this girl hadn't been Isutan—even if she was only partly—he would have drained her too. Her blood alone would give him a year, maybe more. The younger, the stronger, the younger, the sweeter.

That was his payment, after all. He would do this thing for the Lord of the East—he smiled at himself thinking of the title and not the man's name—and he would give him blood ... young blood. Orphaned children. The babes of homeless or slave women. He would kill them first, of course. Specter wasn't that cruel. And their death would be quick and painless. He couldn't use poison, it always soured the blood, made it almost unpalatable, but he had ways to make their passing quick and painless.

"Leave," Specter said.

The girl nodded, gathered a heavy animal skin coat, and left. As soon as she was gone, he lifted his hands, an ancient incantation running through his mind. The two drained bodies levitated and caught fire. Within moments, they were nothing but ash to merge with dust and dirt on the upswept wooden floor. No trace. Stangar was a long way away for a normal man, weeks, months even, but he was no normal man. A shadow traveled faster, much faster. He pushed his hands forward, slipping through the cracks of the window as if smoke, and then he was gone, traveling in the shadows ... towards Stangar.

29

"To Erik Dragon Fire," Turk said, lifting a mug of ale.

Everyone at the table—his companions and some of the dwarves who had helped save them—lifted their mugs and took a hearty drink of either strong, dwarvish ale or spiced wine.

"So," Erik said, "what should I expect from this baptism?"

"We do not speak of it," Yolli said.

"A warrior is sworn to silence," Yora added, patting the place on her breast where her brand sat, "but know this, it is a great honor and if you survive ..."

"Survive?" Bryon asked, cutting Yora off.

"Not everyone who goes through the initiation process lives," Yolli said in all seriousness.

Erik took another drink of his ale, thinking of the dead, grassy plain and the red sky and the black mountain range.

"How did you do it?" Nafer whispered to Erik. It was perhaps the twentieth time. "Look Erik, they are saying my arm wasn't actually broken, but you and I both know it was. And I could feel the ártocothe poison coursing through my veins, burning me from the inside out. There is no simple cure for that."

Erik wondered if he should finally tell. It was not as if he could not trust Nafer. Even when it wasn't invading his thoughts, he could feel his dagger's presence, like a fellow traveler, always next to you even in moments of silence. But he couldn't feel it now, beyond hanging from his belt. The normal glow that seemed to surround the weapon was gone as well. Erik looked at Nafer, and he knew his face looked sad.

"It wasn't me," Erik finally replied. "I placed my dagger on your chest. That's it."

"It needed you to take action, and so I still owe you my life," Nafer said. "I am always indebted to you."

"And I owe you my life," Erik replied. "It is what friends ... brothers do for one another."

"Truly," Nafer said.

Erik took another drink of ale and then met his dwarvish friend's eyes.

"Demik said something to me before he died," Erik said. "He said to me, *there is no greater love than for someone to lay his life down for a friend.* I think, at the time, I didn't quite understand it, but those words were not only meant for Demik and me, in that moment. I think he said them to explain Befel's death, and Drake's death, and Samus' death, Mortin's, Threhof's, and Thormok's deaths, and any one of our other friends who had died on our journey. When I saw you lying there, saw Bryon lying there, I thought of my unborn child and my wife, my parents and sisters. What Demik said finally made true sense. To truly honor life, and to truly honor the Creator, you must be willing to give your life. So, I don't know what happened. All I know is that we are family, and, as much as you would give your life for me, I would give my life for you."

He had meant those words for Nafer, but what he didn't realize was that by the time he finished speaking, everyone was listening to what he said. Bryon and his long-time dwarf friends stared at Erik.

"Well said, Erik," Turk said, lifting his mug. "To those who gave their lives so others might live."

The others lifted their mugs, toasted, and drank.

Erik stood at the edge of an underground lake, torches on poles illuminating the area where he, Captain Khâmuth, Lieutenant Güthrik, his two guards, his friends, and a few other dwarves stood. The water rose just above his knees, and it was cold and dark. He felt goose pimples all over his body and, even though he tried to stop it, he shivered. Captain Khâmuth stood next to him, the water rising above the dwarf's waist, wearing a red robe, his hair and beard unbraided and falling freely.

"A warrior must first be cleansed with water," Captain Khâmuth said, lifting his hands to the air, "Then, a warrior must be cleansed by fire."

Erik looked over to a tall barrel. Steam rose from the top, and he knew that a bed of red-hot coals sat in that steel container. The handle of a brand rested against the edge, the other end shaped in the dwarvish rune for *Dragon Fire* and turning a golden reddish color. Despite the cold water, he sweated.

"Are you ready?" Captain Khâmuth asked.

Erik swallowed hard and nodded. Firmly but not squeezing, the dwarvish leader reached up and grabbed Erik by the neck and, pulling him backward until he could push on his forehead, the freezing water rushing over his face. Erik tried to keep his eyes closed, but the cold forced them open. Staring up, he only saw black. The dwarf's strong hands held him there, even as his air began to run out. As the last bubble escaped his mouth, in the darkness of a cavern lake, Erik wondered if he would drown, he opened his mouth— knowing he shouldn't—to scream and water rushed in and into his lungs.

Erik emerged from the water just as consciousness began to wane. As soon as his face hit the air, he expelled what water had filled his lungs in three, large, heaving retches. He wrapped his arms around his body, shivering violently. He felt disoriented as the strong hands of Captain Khâmuth led him to the shore.

"As a warrior," Captain Khâmuth said, "we must be accustomed to fear and death," he added, and Erik signaled his understanding with a look.

If you only knew.

"We must embrace the chill of death and the searing, burning fire of pain," Captain Khâmuth continued, "so that when our time comes, we welcome it with open arms, like a long lost friend, and we are prepared to meet An when our time in this world is done."

Captain Khâmuth nodded to the two attendants watching the barrel full of red-hot coals. One of them extracted the brand. The iron glowed white; it was so hot. Erik felt his pulse quicken.

"You will receive no medical attention," Captain Khâmuth said. "This is the test, and, if you survive, you will be a true warrior. When the fever comes, you will take a journey. Survive the journey and rejoin your brothers. Fail on your journey and meet An tonight. Are you ready?"

Erik nodded, still shivering. The attendant with the brand stepped forward, took careful aim, and pressed the white-hot iron against Erik's left breast. He was told not to scream, and he obeyed. He clenched his teeth and embraced the pain. As he felt his skin melt and smelled burning hair and flesh, he fell to one knee.

He knew the brand had been removed, but he still felt the pain of fire.

"It is done," Captain Khâmuth said. "By this time tomorrow, we will know if An has selected you to be a warrior."

Erik looked up to see everyone in attendance. He felt proud and smiled, but then everything went black as he passed out.

30

$\mathcal{E}$rik opened his eyes and stared at a red sky. He couldn't tell if the orb hanging there was a sun or a moon, but either way, it glared down at him. Sweat collected around the collar of his shirt in the hot air as a wind fluttered through the tall, brown grass around him; it felt like the heat from a blacksmith's furnace. He breathed fire, the searing air burning his lungs. He sat up, looking around. He stood. He knew this place. He recognized the distant range of black mountains, the black clouds and the purple lightning dancing over the rocky peaks.

He looked behind him. The hill with its weeping willow tree was not there, and that made him shiver. Ilken's Blade lay on the ground, unsheathed, and he picked it up. His shield lay there as well, his new one with the name *Dragon Fire* inscribed on the front in dwarvish runes. He picked that up as well, and immediately the sky began to darken. Purple lightning now streaked across the sky, above him even though the clouds remained over the mountains, and the low rumble of thunder, even from the great distance of the plains, shook the earth.

A flock of thousands of blackbirds, moving together like a giant bed sheet in the wind, flew by, further blanketing the red, dull glow of the land. Erik thought at first that the birds were a simple flock of ravens, but as he squinted and watched them move and flow together, he saw that was a false presumption. Their heads gleamed in the dull light, and he saw there was no flesh, nor feathers, just black, shining bone. Their feathered wings stretched out in tatters, ripped and shredded, and their talons hung slackly below their bodies, long, black claws also glinting in the fiery light. Instead of a tail of feathers trailing their bodies, a tuft of black hair, coarse and stiff, fluttered haphazardly behind them.

As the flock of bird-like creatures passed, Erik stepped forward, in the direction of the luminous thunderclouds. As he stepped, the dead earth below his boots cracked, and suddenly, a great din of buzzing, like the green summer beetles that escaped from the sun in his mother's rose bushes, rose up and filled the air. Erik dropped his sword and shield and put his hands to his ears as the sound, the chorus of dissonance, grew. He closed his eyes, bowed his head and screamed, but could not hear his own voice. Out of instinct, Erik picked up Ilken's Blade and swung. At what, he didn't know—the sound, the red sky, the air, the black clouds. As he swung, he chopped down the tops of the grass all around him. The grass bled, reddish-orange liquid oozing out of the tops he had cut like old milk, plopping to the ground. Where the blood fell, the earth burned black.

The sound stopped, and as a quiet hush settled over the dead plain of grass, a great fluttering echoed and beetles the size of a man's closed fist shot into the air, their wings quivering, again creating that buzzing, chattering sound. It was a plague of insects like Erik had never seen before. Their heads were those of vultures, with curved beaks of a gleaming black and yellow eyes looking wildly in every direction. Their six legs all ended in talons, and the hairy bristles looked hard as iron. Some fluttered towards Erik, and he instinctively put his shield up and swung Ilken's Blade again. The bugs he made contact with split in two, sending green puss splashing across his face before the bodies dissipated into black smoke, blown away by thousands of buzzing wings.

In time, the mass of insects simply looked like a spiral of smoke, floating aimlessly in the red sky. In the east, the black clouds of thunder and lightning remained, and Erik saw the veil of distant rain. It had never rained here before.

Time didn't matter in this place. It never did. It always seemed to just stand still. But he would eventually wake, the dream world around him would grow faint and hazy as his real world came back into view. As Erik marched towards the mountain range, never seeming to get any closer, he didn't get the sense that he was about to wake up. Another flock of bird-like creatures flew overhead. Maybe this wasn't a dream ... at least, not like any one he had ever experienced before.

A swirl of wind blew dust in his eyes, and after he'd blinked it away, a man wearing a black robe stood in front of him. He knew this man. The black-robed man turned towards Erik, the space underneath his cowl dark and invisible. Erik heard laughing. Carriages. Fire. A forest. That was where he had seen him before. A golden carriage appeared next to him.

"You escort the fallen even in this place?" Erik asked.

"Is there a place I should not?" the figure replied.

"This doesn't seem like a place where the heaven-bound fallen would reside," Erik said.

"Sometimes, they lose their way," the man said.

Erik looked to his left and gripped the handle of Ilken's Blade.

He recognized the tall, bald-headed, broad-shouldered man who now approached him. He was as he was in life, unmarked by wounds and fire, flesh free from decay. He was the Durathnan who had stolen the Dragon Scroll from Erik. His companion, the frog man, was the one who had killed Demik. Erik felt a lurch in his stomach, a surge of hatred in his heart.

"Not in this place," the robed figure said. "A hateful heart, and you will never leave."

"You've been here before?" the Durathnan asked, his eyes flitting from the robed man to the carriage.

"Every night," Erik replied, "in my dreams."

The man smiled.

"This is an evil place," he said.

"It can be," Erik said. "It can be beautiful also."

"Not with them running about," the man replied.

"You've seen them, then?" Erik asked. "The dead?"

"I have," the man said. "A lovely bunch of … whatever they are."

"You are not like them?" Erik asked.

"No," he replied. "Am I supposed to be?"

"Most everyone I see here is decaying and rotten," Erik said. "What was … is your name?"

"Cliens," the man replied.

"And the froksman?"

"Ranus," Cliens replied. "He was my best friend."

"You shouldn't have stolen the Dragon Scroll," Erik said.

"We did what we were ordered to do," Cliens said. "We did what we thought was right. And now, here I am. I will never see my wife or children again. I'm doomed to wander this place, forever. Every time I close my eyes, I see fire, feel fire, hear the thundering sound of it."

"You'll see your wife and children again," Erik said. "That's why he is here."

Erik pointed to the robed man.

"I'm not supposed to be here," Cliens said, "that much I know. The train of carriages came for me. But I was so angry I refused to get on board. Ranus did and others who were waiting, but I turned my back on them and walked away into the forest, vowing to seek my revenge."

"Revenge?" Erik asked.

"Revenge on you. Revenge on dwarves. Revenge on the dragon, the east, anyone. But then they came."

"The dead," Erik muttered. "The cursed."

"You stole my family from me," Cliens said. "I will never feel the warmth of my wife's skin, the gentleness of her kisses, the sweetness of her breath."

Erik thought of Simone.

"And now my family becomes a shadow, memories that fade away with each passing minute like the glow of a hot coal cooling through the night."

He is the reason Demik is dead. He attacked us.

But he didn't deserve to die, burned by dragon fire. Was he any different than Erik, doing what he was commanded to do?

"I'm ..." Erik stared at Cliens. "We were both doing our duties, what we felt was right at the time, but I'm sorry."

"I'm scared," Cliens said.

"Don't be," Erik said with a smile. "I watched my brother get onto that carriage. I've watched countless friends get on that carriage. You will see your family again."

Cliens looked at Erik and nodded. The cloaked figure presented the carriage to the man, the door open and ready, and Cliens walked to it. He looked back at Erik and nodded once more before he stepped inside. The robed man closed the door, and the carriage rolled away, quickly fading in the distance.

"What is this place?" Erik asked, facing the cloaked figure.

"You know what this place is," the cloaked man replied.

"The edge of the Shadow's realm."

The cloaked head nodded.

"The Shadow distorts," the figure said. "The Shadow feeds on despair, anger, hatred, hopelessness, and those emotions will ensure you never leave. Clear your mind, Erik, if you wish to pass this trial. You will see things, evil things, but always follow your heart."

Erik nodded and looked at the black range of mountains. They looked closer than they were before. He turned back to the cloaked man.

"Is it you?" Erik asked.

"Me?"

"Are you the one I always find under the willow tree?" Erik asked.

The cloaked figure laughed, a sound so loud that for a moment it drowned out the distant thunder. And then he was gone.

As Erik walked on, it now seemed that he made progress and, eventually, the grass stopped, giving way to a wide space of sand, dotted with a mixture of brown and black pebbles. The mountains now loomed overhead, and he saw they were comprised of a myriad of peaks of jagged rock, each ready and willing to pierce flesh. Erik strapped his shield to his back and began to climb; he didn't get very far when his hands began to bleed. Holes appeared in his pants at his knees, and they bled as well. The slope was steep, and when he looked down, it looked like the world below was already leagues away. Too far away to turn back.

The lightning had stopped for a time, but then it started up again. Erik felt the hair on his arms and legs and back of his neck stand on end just before a flash, and then immediately after, a thunderous boom rattled the mountainside, bringing debris down upon him. A large rock hit the top of his head as he pressed himself closer to the jagged side, and he felt blood trickling down the side of his face while the jagged protrusions dug into his legs and arms and chest.

The sickening red pallid color of this place seemed eternal. There was no day or night, and Erik soon became disorientated and thought he might have been in this place for days. The air had become so hot his skin blistered and peeled, and the cuts on his body so numerous, blood soaked every part of his clothing. The lightning was so close it blinded him and the thunder so loud, it deafened him. When it started rain, it burned, like boiling water from a kettle.

The ground below had disappeared, and while he hadn't thought the mountains were that big, he could see nothing else except black rock and distant red sky. As when he walked and got nowhere, the same happened now, and no matter how high he climbed, the sky never seemed any closer.

I could just fall back and let myself go.

No! You must not give in.

He reached up, blindly gripping at one jagged edge after the other. On and on, he forced himself, and his determination seemed to have created a change. Now he made progress, and when he pulled himself up a large piece of rock, he saw the flat top of a tall plateau. He thanked the Creator silently, used what little strength he had left to pull the rest of his body up, and lay there for a long time, eyes closed, and face pressed against the rock, ignoring the searing heat, burning rain, and deafening thunder.

With no sense of how long he had laid there, he finally pushed himself up and stood. The ground underneath his feet shook, and the sky overhead flashed. As the rain intensified, another cloaked figure appeared in front of him, but this one's robes were tattered and torn. He turned and spoke with another man who appeared at his side, this one armored from head to toe in plate mail. The steel of his armor was as black as the mountains and his helm in the shape of a gaping dragon mouth, the teeth replacing the visor crossbars.

They both turned to face Erik. Erik pulled his shield from his back and drew his sword. He heard laughter. The armored man extended his right hand and a long sword, the blade flamberged and burning with white flame, appeared in it. He extended his left hand and a flail appeared there, three iron balls in the shape of skulls at the end of three chains. The cloaked man lifted his hands, their skin pale and sickly looking, his fingers long and bony, and the earth rumbled even more. Fire and molten rock erupted from the mountains on either side of Erik and ran down its steep slope.

Another figure appeared in between the two men, a man on his knees, shackles around his wrists, ankles, and neck. When he looked up, he had piercing blue eyes, long blond hair, and long, pointed ears.

"An elf?" Erik muttered in disbelief.

Both the cloaked man and the armored man laughed. Erik knew he had to fight them.

"Carefully now," a dwarvish voice said.

He looked to his right, and there was King Fire Beard, the ruler of

Orvencrest when the fabled dwarvish city fell. Most had believed it was lost to time, perhaps even a myth, but Erik had found it and discovered the true reason for the city's demise: the dwomanni—fallen, evil dwarves—and the dragon. They had only found the skeletal remains of Fire Beard, his son, his queen, and his daughters, but Erik saw the dwarf in a vision, he knew what he had looked like. And this was him, standing next to him with his fiery red hair and beard.

"They will try to lure you in," the dwarvish king said. "That is how evil works. It plays on your emotions. It makes you feel weaker or more powerful than you really are. It will make you act out of fear."

Erik nodded.

The way the elf looked up at him, his eyes sad and defeated. There was recognition in those eyes. The elf knew him, but Erik couldn't guess from where. He felt like he needed to free the elf, break his chains.

The cloaked man lifted a hand, and the chains around the elf's neck, wrists, and ankles burst into flames. The elf screamed out, and Erik rushed in.

The cloaked man threw several balls of fire at him, but he blocked them with his shield. He rolled underneath a heavy swing from the burning flamberge of the black knight. Standing and turning, Erik gave his own strike, but the armored man blocked the attack sending flames into Erik's face.

Erik smelled burning hair, felt his skin burning, but he fought on. The wizard shouted something in what Erik knew to be the Shadow Tongue, and a green fog rose from the ground. Erik coughed and wretched, and the armored man took the opportunity to attack. The sword slammed into Erik's shield, and he flew backward. He rolled away as the tip of the flamberge jammed into the ground and kicked out, his heel slamming into the knight's knee. There was an audible crunch, but it didn't seem to faze the knight. All the while, the elf's screams rose, and his pain seemed to urge Erik's opponents on.

The wizard shouted again, and the clouds overhead swirled about and brightened with purple lightning, the bolts of energy striking the ground all around Erik. He continued to fight on, blocking strikes from the flaming sword while dodging magical fireball attacks from the black wizard. Then, Erik heard more laughter, laughter he recognized.

Erik turned around and saw her looming over him. Her golden-green scales shimmered with a sickening glow under the reddish sky and the purple lightning. Then, as if her shadow came alive, another dragon appeared next to her, its scales black with streaks of red, and Erik knew it was her mate, father to the young dragon that had injured Bryon so badly. The she-dragon hissed, her scales rattling as she shook her head. Her mate roared and blew fire into the sky, the clouds opening up in burning rain as a response.

I have no time left.

No! Think!

Erik turned to look at the elf, his skin turning black and cracking under the fire, and he understood the purpose of the elf's presence, his place in Erik's battle to avoid being taken by the Shadow. Erik lifted his sword and struck at the shackles that bound the elf. They fell away and disappeared as they hit the ground and the elf stood, his burns gone. He was an imposing figure, slender at the waist, but his chest and shoulders showed his strength. He was as tall as Erik and the muscles in his arms knotted as he lifted them and flexed. His blue eyes glowed, and the elf spoke in a language Erik was unfamiliar with, but the words caused the ground to shake even more.

Erik heard the sucking of air, and all sound disappeared as the ground opened up and consumed both the black wizard and the black knight. And then the fire came.

Wind washed over him and Erik opened his eyes. The mountain range was gone. The hill was still gone. The dragons, the dark knight, the black wizard, and the elf—all gone. The sky was a pallid gray.

"Was that the test?" Erik asked himself, looking around. He looked down at himself and his body was intact.

"Yes, it was," a voice said.

Erik turned to see another figure, cloaked in black, cowl pulled over his face. He had seen this figure here before, the last time he dreamed.

"You passed," the figure croaked, "the first man in a thousand years to be given a clan."

The figure cackled an evil laugh.

"Are you the Shadow?" Erik asked.

The laughter intensified.

"You defeated the Shadow," the figure said.

Erik cocked an eyebrow. Defeating the Shadow wasn't, couldn't have been, shouldn't have been that easy.

"You fear the Shadow?" the figure asked.

Erik wanted to say no, but he nodded.

"Your fear is misplaced," the figure said. "There is one you should fear more."

Erik looked to the east and the west, the north and the south, and saw giant shadowy figures on the horizon. He looked up and black wings spread across the sky. His first thought went to the dragons, but then he remembered the dream of his farm, and the ghostly thing in that dream. This reminded him of that creature, whatever it was.

"Who are you?" Erik asked.

"All in due time," the figure laughed, and then he was gone and the world around him faded as Erik's consciousness came back.

$\mathcal{E}$rik lay in his bed. As soon as the fever had set in, Captain Khâmuth had given him his own room, which was sparse in the outpost. It was like no fever Erik had ever experienced before. His body ached, his skin burned, and his hands and feet were freezing, no matter how many blankets he lay under. His head felt like someone had repeatedly slammed a hammer into it. And the dwarves would give him nothing—no dream milk, no sweet wine, no food, only water; he couldn't even keep that down.

"Did you see ..." Erik began to say as he woke up from his dream.

"Everyone's vision is different," Turk replied, "and it is yours, yours to remember, yours to keep until your final day."

That was the last time Erik spoke of the dream that played over and over in his head. Always the same, but he only remembered how it ended when he slipped back into unconsciousness. It meant something important. That much he had gathered, but he could not fathom what it meant beyond his normal dreams. And each night since—how many he couldn't remember—the scene and outcome were the same, some mysterious, hooded man and a vast shadow that seemed to consume the world, but wasn't *the* Shadow.

Erik closed his eyes and traced his fingers over the brand on his left breast. It was healing but still painful. Erik didn't care. He continued to trace the circle—symbol of the Creator and eternity—and then the runes in the middle of the circle—Dragon Fire. The small outline of a sword sat above the circle, and the outline of a dragon's head sat below it. Each brand was made specifically to the one being baptized. This was Erik's brand. No one else in the world would ever have one like it. It made those dwarves who mutilated their brands that much more nefarious.

Erik closed his eyes, welcoming and dreading sleep all at the same time. He heard the door open and guessed it would be Bryon who had come to see him multiple times every day. He was worried, and Erik appreciated it, but he just wanted to rest now. If the fever took him, so be it, but he just wanted to sleep through the rest of it and wake up renewed and well.

"Bryon, please, I'm tired," Erik said, rubbing his temples with his thumb and forefinger.

His cousin didn't reply.

"Bryon," Erik said.

Still no reply.

"Bryon?"

Erik opened his eyes and turned his head. A dwarf stood in the doorway, and he looked like Hragram who had been holding Erik's shield at his baptism. Behind him in the doorway was what looked like one of Lieutenant Güthrik's personal guards. A helm hid all of his face save for a bit of beard that escaped through the bottom.

"Hragram isn't it?" Erik asked, lifting his head and looking at the dwarf with a cocked eyebrow. "What do you want?"

As the guard closed the door and Erik heard the lock click, Hragram stepped forward.

"Lord Fréden Fréwin sends his regards," Hragram said with a malicious smile on his face.

Erik's face paled, and his heart quickened as the dwarf produced a long-bladed knife that glimmered in the candlelight of the room.

32

Bryon walked towards Erik's room. He knew his cousin didn't want any visitors or company, but he was by Bryon's bedside almost the whole time he was infirmed. How would it look if he didn't do the same?

Bryon stood in front of Erik's door when he heard a loud crash coming from within the room. He grabbed the handle and tried to turn it, but it was locked. There was another crash and a quick shout. Bryon couldn't understand the voice, and it wasn't Erik's. He tried the handle again, but it wouldn't move. He shouldered the door, but it was too sturdy.

"Damn dwarvish construction," Bryon said, withdrawing his sword.

Bryon stabbed the door handle with his elvish blade. The magic flared to life, increasingly brightening as the iron of the door warped and drooped. As the molten metal pooled on the floor in front of the door, Bryon kicked it open and stepped into the room to see Hragram and another dwarf standing over his cousin. The mattress from Erik's bed lay halfway off the frame, and Erik, his face red and sweaty, crouched between the bed and the wall. He was reaching for his own sword as Hragram held a long-bladed knife in his hand.

"Hragram, what's going on?" Bryon asked.

He looked from the dwarf to his cousin. He was familiar with the look on Erik's face. It was a look that used to irritate him, one his younger cousin used to give all the time, one of fear and worry. It was a look Erik rarely wore anymore.

Bryon lunged at Hragram. The dwarf backed away, just in time, grabbing a pillow and throwing it at Bryon. Little feathers floated through the air as Bryon backhanded the bedding away, a tear in its cover already present from where, apparently, Hragram tried to murder Erik.

"Bryon, watch out!" Erik shouted.

Bryon jumped out of the way as the other dwarf swung his double-handed, broad sword. Hragram attacked, knife held over his head, blade pointing downward. Bryon swung with his off hand—soft knuckles as Wrothgard had taught him. His fist thudded against Hragram's jaw, and an audible crunch echoed through the room. The dwarf dropped the dagger, bounced off the wall, and fell to his knees, spitting out a broken tooth as he tried to regain his wits.

The other dwarf came fast. His swings with his broad sword put Bryon on his heels, but he eventually blocked one strike, his magical blade notching a melted nick in the sword, and cut a neat line of burned steel and blood along the dwarf's arm. A scream erupted from underneath the dwarf's helmet.

"By the Creator, you stink," Bryon said, wrinkling his nose.

Bryon recognized that smell, even if he had a hard time putting his finger on it. He had smelled it in Orvencrest, in the darkness of that lost city. It was the smell of death, but not rot or decaying flesh. It was almost like a body odor, pungent, and stinging to the nose.

Bryon kicked the inside of the armored dwarf's knee. The warrior grunted and went down, but before Bryon could deliver a killing blow, he lurched forward when a body rammed into the middle of his back. He landed, face down, his sword sliding away along the floor.

Bryon turned quickly as Hragram's rescued knife thunked against the floor where his head was just moments before. The tip of the blade broke off, but the dwarf slashed again at Bryon.

"Bryon!" Erik shouted again, and when he looked over, his cousin had his sheathed sword in hand. He threw it to him and, just as Hragram jabbed with his broken knife, Bryon caught the weapon, unsheathed Ilken's Blade, and blocked the attack.

Holding Ilken's Blade in his left hand, he swiped up with the sword, and the tip of the blade caught Hragram's wrist, drawing blood and causing the dwarf to drop his knife again. He retrieved his axe from his belt, and Bryon crouched, reaching for his elvish blade.

The blade of the axe came down, Hragram swinging it with both hands, so Bryon crossed the steel of his elvish sword with Ilken's Blade, blocking the attack and catching the axe's wooden handle between the two blades. The axe handle began to smoke, a black, charred line forming where the elvish magic burned. Hragram cursed in Dwarvish, retracted his weapon, and swung it again. Bryon swung upwards with the elvish sword, the blade flaring and burning, slicing through the wood of the axe easily. The half-moon blade bounced away harmlessly, and Hragram cursed again, swinging at Bryon with gauntleted fists.

Bryon looked beyond Hragram and saw the other dwarf glaring at Erik. Dragging his injured leg, he moved towards his cousin, but Erik pushed out against his bed and that knocked the warrior off balance. As Hragram came at Bryon again, he kicked the dwarf in the chest, launching him into the stumbling armored dwarf. They crashed into each other, falling in a heap. Bryon closed the distance on the two dwarves as they struggled to get up.

Hragram looked surprised and tried to swing at Bryon with a sloppy fist, but Bryon kicked the outside of his leg then punched his elvish blade into the dwarf's belly, hilt deep. Hragram looked at him with wide, angry eyes, blood pouring from his mouth. The smell of burning flesh hit Bryon's nose and, even though it normally made him gag a little, he breathed it in unfazed.

"Give my regards to the Shadow," Bryon hissed, spitting in the dwarf's face and retrieving his sword.

As Hragram dropped, face-down on the floor, the other dwarf rose, his helmet crooked, and staggered to his feet again. He tried to grab his sword, but Bryon easily hooked his foot around the back of the dwarf's uninjured leg, and the warrior crashed into the wall. As his head smacked against the stone, his helmet flew off, and Bryon gasped.

White eyes stared at him. The dwarf's skin was pale and sickly, paper-thin. His hair hung in clumps from a mostly bald scalp. Scabs oozed with pus and blood, all over the dwarf's face.

"By the Creator," Bryon said, backing up, putting an arm to his nose, and giving the dwarf space.

"Dwomanni," Erik gasped.

The dwomanni swung on Bryon, and it was all he could do just to keep his footing. As the sickly-looking dwarf attacked, he spoke in a language Bryon didn't understand, but as he did, the candles in the room flickered.

"What magic is this?" Bryon muttered as he found his back almost against a wall.

"The strongest," the dwarf hissed, revealing yellow teeth that had been filed to sharp points.

As the dwomanni spoke, Bryon's sword dimmed, and he felt less heat from the blade. Struggling at keeping the dwarf at bay, he saw Erik crawl over his bed to stand behind the attacker. He stood, his legs shaky, his eyes half-closed, and sweat beading down his face. He was in no condition to fight, but he might have been Bryon's only chance. Bryon kicked out at the dwomanni's injured knee, tossing Ilken's Blade to Erik at the same time. Erik caught the sword gingerly, almost dropping it before he gripped it with both hands and brought the Dwarf's Iron across the dwomanni's back. He was so weak with fever that his attack probably didn't even cause a scratch on their assailant's armor, but it distracted the dwarf enough. As he barely turned to look at Erik over his shoulder, Bryon drove his sword through his ribs.

The blade caught, at first, but then the dwarf gasped, sucking in as much air as he could, as the purple blade flared and Bryon thrust, driving the sword deep. The dwomanni's smell was even stronger now, as his blood seeped from his wound and boiled around magical steel. With a grunt, Bryon removed his blade, and the dwarf collapsed on the floor, dead.

"Erik," Bryon said, going to his cousin as he began to falter on his feet and catching him before he could fall. "Are you all right?"

Erik was about to reply when Hragram let out a loud gasp. He rolled over onto his back and stared at Bryon and Erik.

"Let me go," Erik said, and Bryon complied.

Erik walked slowly to the dwarf, kneeling next to him and putting Ilken's Blade next to his throat. He grabbed Hragram's shirt and pulled at it.

"What are you doing?" Bryon asked as Erik sought to tear buttons from the cloth.

"You do it," Erik said, breathing heavily. He was so weak, the stitching of the cloth barely moved as he tugged at the piece of clothing.

Bryon grabbed the bottom of the shirt and sliced the front open with his sword. He flipped it open and exposed the dwarf's chest, a hairy mass of muscle, and, on his left breast, a scabbed and bloody mark. Something had once been there—a tattoo or brand—and the dwarf had tried to remove it.

"You mutilated your mark," Erik said.

Hragram didn't say anything.

"You said Fréden Fréwin sent you, but he didn't, did he?" Erik asked. "At least, not really?"

"That piece of troll dung sent this dwarf?" Bryon asked, but Erik put up a hand.

"Why?" Erik asked.

"Strength," Hragram replied.

"You sold your soul to the Shadow," Erik hissed.

"Power," Hragram said.

"Death," Erik said.

Hragram locked eyes with him.

"Yes," he said with a smile.

"You brought a dwomanni into Stangar," Erik accused.

"Not full dwomanni," Hragram replied through belabored breaths. "Not yet."

"You are trying to infiltrate Stangar," Erik said.

The dwarf laughed. Bryon stepped on the wound in his stomach. Hragram groaned.

"Not so funny now, is it?" Bryon said.

A look of realization came over Erik's face as Hragram gave a mixture of laughter, groaning, and cursing.

"You're not infiltrating Stangar," Erik said, more to himself than to Bryon or Hragram. "No. You are infiltrating the Wicked Spire. You're using Fréden Fréwin, aren't you? He's the perfect, idealistic fool, isn't he, for the dwomanni to gain a foothold in the world once again?"

Hragram didn't answer. Bryon pushed on his wound harder. The dwarf groaned. The look on his face told Bryon that Erik was right.

"How many are here?" Erik asked, reaching down to Hragram's collar and pulling him up. He could barely lift the dwarf, but he did. "How many at the Wicked Spire? Where else are you? Tell me."

Hragram stopped breathing for a moment, a look of lunacy creeping into his wide eyes, and looked at Erik with an insane smile.

"We ... are ... everywhere," Hragram said, and then he slumped back, dead.

"What, by the Shadow, does that mean?" Bryon asked.

"We need to get out of here," Erik said, holding on to Bryon so he could stand.

"You can barely move," Bryon said.

"It doesn't matter," Erik said. There was that look again, the look of worry and fear. "We need to leave. Now. Help me with my armor."

"With your armor?" Bryon asked. "How do you plan on walking, even with dwarvish armor? Do you expect me to carry you? Because I can tell you right now, that isn't happening."

"Please, Bryon," Erik said, looking up with hard, serious eyes.

"Fine," Bryon said, sheathing his sword and throwing his hands up in defeat.

Bryon dressed Erik and his cousin could barely stand, seemingly in and out of consciousness as he struggled to stand up straight. He handed Bryon his sword again.

"Remove the dwomanni's head," Erik said, his voice quiet and shaky.

"What?" Bryon asked.

"Just do it," Erik replied. "Please."

Bryon did as he was told, and then bundled the head up in Erik's bed sheets.

They gathered Erik's other things into his haversack and walked down a hallway that led to one of the barracks, hoping no one noticed the bundle of bloody sheets Bryon held under his right arm while Erik leaned against him. Bryon wrapped his left arm around his cousin, propping him up and eventually just dragging him along.

"How do I get wrapped up in this nonsense?" Bryon muttered, more to himself. He looked down at his cousin. "I told you I'm not carrying you and here I am, dragging you through a dwarvish outpost."

Turk and Nafer were in the barracks, along with a room of sleeping, dwarvish warriors. Bryon could see they were still awake, whispering to one another.

"Where are the others?" Bryon asked, kneeling next to Turk's cot.

The dwarf looked startled at first.

"What are you doing?" Turk asked, sitting up. "Why are you dragging your cousin out of bed? Don't you know he is still sick with fever and ...?"

"*Listen!*" Bryon hissed in interruption. "The last thing I want to be doing is carrying this sick idiot all over Stangar, but he insisted we come here. He's lucky to be alive."

"I don't understand," Turk said.

Erik reached up, regaining a moment of consciousness, and grabbed Turk's hand.

"Come with us to the latrine," Erik said, his voice barely a whisper.

The latrine was little more than an open room with long troughs set into the stone floor.

"Show them," Erik said to Bryon.

Bryon dragged Erik to the back of the room, not even looking to see that their friends were following him. He turned and they were there, looking on with confusion.

"Alright. What is going on?" Turk asked.

"This," Bryon said, lifting the bloody bed coverings.

Both Nafer and Turk looked at Bryon and Erik as if they were going crazy, and, for a moment, Bryon felt like he was. He opened the bedding, and the head of the dwomanni plopped onto the floor.

"By An's beard!" Nafer yelled.

"Hush," Bryon said, putting a forefinger to his own mouth.

"What is that?" Turk asked.

"The head of one of the two dwarves who attacked me only moments ago," Erik replied, trying to lift his head up to make eye contact with Turk.

Both dwarves stared at him.

"They claimed to be attacking me on orders of Fréden Fréwin," Erik said.

"That snake," Turk hissed.

"But," Erik said, putting up a finger, "Bryon smelled the stink on them."

"The stink?" Nafer asked.

Erik looked around and ducked his head as if that would help keep his voice down.

"Dwomanni," Erik whispered. "Look closely."

"Not in my life," Nafer said, bending down to look at the head and then backing away. "It can't be."

"Hragram said ..."

"Hragram?" Turk asked. "He was at the ..."

"Yes," Bryon interrupted again. "More importantly, he was one of the two dwarves that attacked Erik. This little shite is lucky I'm a caring cousin and was coming to check up on him. Hragram said this dwarf wasn't a full dwomanni yet, as if they could turn into one."

"Is that possible?" Erik asked.

"I don't know," Turk replied. "I suppose anything is possible with black magic."

"We need to tell Lieutenant Güthrik and Captain Khâmuth," Nafer said.

"No," Erik replied. "But I'm sure this one was one of the lieutenant's guards."

"You don't think the lieutenant ..." Turk began to say.

"No," Erik replied, "but we need to leave. Now. Where are the others?"

"You're in no condition to travel," Nafer said.

"I'll be alright," Erik replied.

"Of course you will because I'll just end up carrying you," Bryon said, rolling his eyes. Then he added more quietly, "Like you did for me."

"We need to get out of here," Erik said, ignoring Bryon. "We can leave a note for Captain Khâmuth, but I fear there will be more assassination attempts. Hragram said they are everywhere."

"Well, we know they are in El'Beth-Tordûn, whether Fréden Fréwin knows it or not," Nafer said.

"It's doubtful he does," Turk added.

"We need to leave," Erik said. "We need to find Fealmynster before it is too late. It seems everyone wants us dead."

"Where are Bofim and Beldar?" Bryon asked.

"The dining hall, I think," Turk replied.

He looked down at his cousin. Erik looked up at him as much as he could and nodded. Bryon turned to Turk and Nafer.

"One of you go and get them, while the other gathers their things and yours," Bryon said.

The two dwarves muttered to each other before Nafer headed out of the room and Turk set about filling haversacks. While Bryon gathered his own things, Erik took a piece of parchment and stick of charcoal from his own haversack and began to write.

33

______

*B*ryon dragged Erik and led the four dwarves towards the rear entrance of Stangar. The main entrance faced south, but they didn't want to go that way. The outpost wasn't that big, but they moved slowly, slinking in the shadows. Who knew if there was another assassin waiting for them? Finally, they came to the rear entrance. It had a pair of large double doors like any other dwarvish entrance, but a smaller door stood within one of the main ones.

When they got to the final corner, they peeped around and saw a sole dwarf on nighttime guard duty; it was Yora. Erik eased around the corner while he retrieved the piece of parchment.

"Yora," Erik whispered.

The female warrior spun around and immediately dropped her spear into a fighting stance.

"What are you doing here?" she demanded. "Get back to the barracks."

"Yora," Erik said, holding up a hand, "we need to leave."

Erik looked at Bryon and jerked his head sideways. Bryon nodded, inching closer to Yora. She looked at them with suspicious eyes, a white knuckled grip on her spear.

"Yora, we mean no harm," Erik said, "but we have to leave."

"No one leaves at night," Yora said, "captain's orders."

"Yora, give this letter to Captain Khâmuth," Erik said. "It will explain everything. We can't stay in Stanger. Our being here puts you and the rest of the dwarves in grave danger."

Yora laughed.

"You expect me to believe that?" she asked, but all six warriors looked at her with serious eyes. "You have no idea how much trouble I'll be in if you're just feeding me bear scat."

"Yora, please," Erik said.

Bryon watched her. He was within striking distance. He could drop Erik, unsheathe his sword, and have her pinned against the floor before she knew it ... maybe.

"Please," Erik pleaded, "give this letter to Captain Khâmuth and let us leave."

Yora looked at them for a moment longer before lifting her spear.

"Don't make me regret this," she said as she pushed open the smaller door, large enough for Erik and Bryon to pass through if they ducked their heads. "You'll see a ladder in just a few paces. It leads to the surface."

Before she closed the door behind them, Erik turned and smiled.

"Thank you," he said.

She nodded, her returning smile looking more like a grimace. She was watching to make sure they all got on the ladder.

They walked a few steps before Erik stopped, pulling on Bryon.

"What?" Bryon asked.

"The ice bridge," Erik said.

"The what?" Bryon asked.

"We have seen everything the old man in Eldmanor said except for the ice bridge," Erik explained, but Bryon hadn't a clue what he was talking about.

"Ice bridge ..." Bryon began to say, but Erik cut him off.

"Yora," Erik said, turning around, "there is a place I need to go, somewhere in these mountains I need help finding."

Yora gave a short, quiet laugh.

"Where, in these mountains, could you possibly want to go?"

"Do you know of an ice bridge?" Erik asked.

Yora's smile faded.

"You don't want to go there," she said.

"I must," Erik replied.

"It's cursed," she said, "and guarded by more giants."

"Yora," Erik said, "please."

She seemed to think for a moment and then gave a quick huff.

"Follow the green light in the sky," she explained. "You'll only see it at night. It will eventually take you to the ice bridge ... and beyond. But those are forbidden lands and you won't see any dwarves or receive their help—no matter how special you are—once you cross that bridge."

They heard footsteps, other guards coming.

"You must go," Yora said. "An be with you."

And before Erik could thank her again, Yora closed the door behind them, and they were plunged into darkness. Bryon drew his sword, but it didn't shed enough light.

"Your dagger," Bryon said.

"I can't," Erik said.

"Why not?" Bryon asked.

"I just can't," Erik replied.

"Your circlet, then," Bryon said. "I can't carry my sword while I'm pushing your hairy ass."

Erik retrieved the circlet, and, when he placed it on his head, the sapphire began to glow.

Ahead was a long dark tunnel, but to their left, they glimpsed the first iron rungs of a ladder, fixed to the rock face.

"That way," said Erik, his circlet pointing towards the ladder. "Look here. There's the ladder Yora told me about. It leads to the surface."

The ladder led the way upwards through a small hole cut in the roof of the tunnel, and awkwardly, Bryon led his cousin upwards, one hand grasping Erik's belt beside his dagger, and the other holding on to the side of the ladder. Occasionally, Erik missed his footing and they were lucky he didn't send them all falling back down. It wasn't long before Bryon's left arm and shoulder burned with the exertion. In a way, he was glad because it distracted him from thinking about his claustrophobia.

"Cousin, are you alright?" Bryon gasped as he gave another upwards shove.

"I'll be fine," Erik replied. "How much farther?"

It was dark, and Bryon couldn't see the top.

"Turk?" Bryon asked.

"I don't know," Turk replied. "Who knows how deep into the earth Stangar is?"

They kept on climbing, and just at the time when Bryon was ready to call for a rest, the circlet picked out a round, wooden door with a handle built in it. It looked thick and when Erik pushed on it, it didn't budge. Erik moved to one side so Bryon could pass, and after Turk had climbed up to make sure Erik was steady, Bryon tried to open the door. It moved a little but no more.

"You'll have to push harder," Turk said. "It probably has years of dirt and roots and creepers on top of it, as well as something hiding it from plain view."

"Thanks," Bryon replied sarcastically. "Give me your sword Erik, mine will only burn the door and have it fall on top of us."

Erik drew his sword passed it up, and Bryon worked it around the edge of the door, pushing through roots and rocks until he worked out where the hinge was. The door moved more than before, and with more cutting and shoving, he finally managed to get it open, with rocks and soil cascading down on them. Bryon couldn't free himself from the tunnel fast enough, but when he emerged from the hole leading to the surface, he found himself in another narrow, dark space. He drew his sword, and looking around, saw what looked like bark. He looked down at the hole, Erik halfway through the opening and staring up at him as Turk struggled to help.

"I think we're inside a tree," Bryon said, reaching down to grasp Erik's arm and help lift him out.

Once Erik was clear and the others were joining him, Bryon looked around some more, and in the dim light, his hand brushed against what felt like a handle. He pushed and a low door opened up into the mountain at night. Ducking through the doorway, the briskness of a never-ending winter in the Gray Mountains struck Bryon in the face like a fist. He felt and heard the crunch of snow beneath his boots, and he looked around. He had hoped they might emerge close to the site of the avalanche and they could just continue as they had, but he knew that was highly unlikely.

Bofim emerged behind him and then, one by one, the other dwarves until Erik appeared, his face ashen in the dull moonlight.

"Well," Bryon said, "which way?"

Erik looked north. They were off their original path, and Bryon knew they could probably wander the Gray Mountains their whole lives and not find a large city, let alone a keep guarded by a wizard that had been purposely hidden. Then he saw a faint glow to the northeast. It was greenish and reflected off the bottoms of distant clouds.

"Is that the glow Yora spoke of?" Bryon asked.

"Aye," Erik said. "I think so."

"Lead on," Bryon added.

They hadn't gone very far when Erik collapsed in the snow, and Bryon knelt by his side, a hand on his cousin's forehead.

"It's his fever," Bryon said, looking up at Turk. "Fool."

"We have to find shelter," he heard Turk say.

"Can you heal him?" Bryon asked.

"No," Turk replied.

Bryon stood, puffing his chest out and staring at the dwarf angrily.

"Why not?" Bryon asked.

"His baptism," Turk explained. "The fever is from his baptism. I am not allowed to heal him. It is his passage. The test. He must survive the fever on his own."

"To the Shadow with his passage," Bryon said, pointing at Erik lying in the snow. "He'll be dead if you don't help him."

"Perhaps," Turk replied.

Bryon wanted to punch the dwarf in the face but knew it wouldn't do any good. He looked down at Erik again.

"Fool," Bryon hissed.

He bent down and lifted his cousin up, throwing him over his shoulder.

"Fine then, dwarf," Bryon said, "lead us to shelter."

34

He wasn't in a field of grass. He was home, staring at his father's farm. It was night, and he heard the galloping of hooves before he watched as an army of knights rode through the farm. They held torches and tossed them into the fields, the barn, the pigpens, the house. Everything caught fire. A horse, its tail burning, galloped by. His sisters ran from the house, led by their father. An arrow thudded into Rikard Eleodum's chest. He went down. Two more arrows thudded into Beth and Tia.

"No!" Erik shouted as his mother emerged, crying hysterically.

One of the knights dismounted, grabbed his mother by the throat and pushed her into the house. The din of a roaring fire eventually drowned out her screams, and Erik unsheathed Ilken's Blade and ran. A horse stopped him, blocking his path, and he looked up to see a gaunt face, green and black with rot, eye sockets vacant, looking down at him. The dead knight smiled, and a millipede crawled from his mouth, up his cheek, and then into one of his eyeholes.

"Come to join in the fun?" the dead knight asked.

Erik brought his sword across the horse, also a creature that was rotting, its hair barely clinging to sagging skin. The creature collapsed on top of the knight. Erik stepped over the dead man, who simply laughed.

"We will have fun tonight," the dead knight said. "Your sweet wife ... we will have fun."

As he laughed, Erik screamed and brought his blade across the dead man's throat. Both he and his horse exploded into a million specks of light.

His father's farm was gone, his home a pile of ash. The bodies of his family were gone, and when Erik thought he was alone, he heard a distant scream.

Simone!

He ran as fast as he could, passing burning buildings, burning fields, and burning animals, but he didn't care. All that mattered was Simone. He knew it was his dream, and he knew that what happened here wouldn't happen in the real world—probably—but he couldn't help it. He saw his own home, surrounded by an army of the undead. He heard another scream and began cleaving his way through the army, each undead soldier exploding into pinpoints of light as he struck them down with Ilken's Blade. He felt blood flow from his body as they scratched and clawed and bit at him. He didn't care.

He made it to the front of the crowd, and the soldiers stopped fighting him. Simone emerged, walking slowly, painfully. Her face was covered in blood, her eyes wild, her nightgown torn and all but useless. A gaping wound consumed her belly, exposing ribs and internal organs. Their baby. Blood ran down her legs. She saw Erik but didn't recognize him. She fell to her knees.

Erik ran to Simone, cradling her head in his lap.

"No," he cried, nothing more than a croaking, weeping whisper.

"You think this is pain?" a voice croaked. He had expected Sorben Phurnan, but it was the cloaked man from his baptismal dream.

Erik ignored him.

"They can't hurt you in this place," Erik whispered. "Do not worry. You will wake, and you will be all right. Our baby will be all right."

"Are you so sure of that?" the cloaked man asked. "I am not some rotting corpse you killed in life. I am not some pawn the Shadow toys with and sends to haunt you in your dreams. So much more pain. So much more."

The figure laughed with malicious glee.

"You will be all right," Erik whispered, over and over again. "You will be all right. You will be all right. You will be all right."

Erik lifted his head and screamed. He heard more croaking laughter, and he wept, and then he felt steel pierce his chest.

35

"A third of the Dragon's Teeth have been stationed along the southern border, Your Majesty," Darius, General Lord Marshal of Gol-Durathna's armies said, "along with another twenty thousand regular troops."

"We are on the brink of war, Darius," King Agempi said. "Two hundred years, and I will be the king to break the peace."

"You're not breaking anything, Your Majesty," Darius replied. "The Lord of the East thinks he can do what he wants. By the gods, he thinks his dung doesn't stink."

"He grows more and more powerful, Darius," the king said.

"We are stronger," Darius replied. "Our people love you, and they follow you out of respect, not fear. Like before, the other nations will rally around us, and we will shatter the east. Only, this time, we will break them forever, scattering their ruling families, and forcing their cities into submission."

"And then what, Darius?" the king asked, his face a look of sadness and concern. "Do we then rule the east as well as the north?"

"We could," Darius replied.

The king shook his head, lifting his cup to his mouth, pausing for a moment, and then taking a hearty draught of mead.

"Then we would be no different than the east," the king said. "I fear, if Syzbalo gets his hand on something powerful enough to control a dragon ..."

"We will stop him," Darius replied, but he didn't quite believe his own words.

He watched the king. He was a man in his middle years, about the same age as Darius. They trained together and, unlike many rulers, Agempi was an adept soldier. It was the pride of the northern kingdom that their king rode into battle with his troops. But that hadn't happened in over two hundred years, not since Justus Guerus signed a treaty of peace with Rimrûk Aztûk at the Battle of Bethulium and became King Agempi the First.

The present King Agempi was always a lively man and looked young for his age. With a few gray whiskers, his beard still held vibrant browns with streaks of blond and red, and his body was fit and well-muscled. But lately, he seemed to have more gray in his hair, and his shoulders seemed to slump more. His age was beginning to show. Or perhaps it was the stress and worry.

Darius knew anything that might suggest war would weigh on a king's mind and shoulders; at least, on a king that cared. Darius knew the Lord of the East could care less. He would send tens of thousands of fools into battle and watch them die with a smile on his face. He had been doing it across the Giant's Vein—in Mek-Ba'Dune—for years.

"What of the Atrimus?" Agempi asked, speaking of the secret army of assassins Gol-Durathna employed.

"Our agent in Eldmanor is dead," Darius replied. He had gotten word of the man's death only a few days before. He was one of his best. He had underestimated this Erik Eleodum.

"Call them what they are, Darius," King Agempi replied. "Assassins."

"Very well, Your Majesty," Darius said. "Shall I send more … assassins?"

"They must be stopped because the Lord of the East must be stopped. Yes, send more assassins. And instruct them … they cannot simply kill this Erik Eleodum and his companions."

"Your Majesty?" Darius asked.

"They must recover the Dragon Sword," the King replied. "That is of the utmost importance. They will recover the sword and bring it to me."

"To what end?" Darius asked.

For a moment, he watched Agempi's eyes. He was not a power-hungry man. He was a fair ruler. He was a man who enjoyed sharing his wealth. But, for a moment, a flash of something Darius had never seen in the king flickered in his eyes. A small smile touched his lips. The king gave the slightest of shakes of his head and looked at Darius.

"We will take the sword to our smelters," Agempi replied. "We will have it melted in the hottest furnaces as if breathed on by the very dragons it was meant to control and destroy."

"What of its magic, Your Majesty?" Darius asked.

"We will hire the most powerful wizards," the king replied, "if we must. We will find them from the Isutan Isles, the Feran Archipelagos, and Wüsten Sahil if need be. But we will destroy this weapon so that men like the Lord of the East may never use it."

"As you command," Darius said, standing up from the table in the middle of King Agempi's personal quarters and bowing.

The king cleared his throat as Darius was leaving the room. He turned.

"We cannot fail, Darius," the king said, his face looking drawn and tired. "We cannot fail."

"Did you really find it necessary to send for Specter?" Andragos asked.

He and the Lord of the East sat on the raised dais in the hall of Fen-Stévock's keep, facing one another. The Black Mage rarely found the Lord of the East alone, without his witches or Isutan advisor, so he took the opportunity to ask some awkward questions.

"Are you questioning my judgment?" the Lord of the East asked.

"He is dangerous," Andragos replied, "and his magic is something I wouldn't even touch, not in all of my years."

"Erik Eleodum murdered my agents," the Lord of the East said. "He was simply supposed to meet them, travel with them, and deliver the sword."

"You truly believe Erik murdered them?" Andragos asked.

"They are dead by his hand," the Lord of the East said. "I have seen it in my visions."

"I have a hard time believing Erik murdered them," Andragos said.

"You have a soft spot for the boy," the Lord of the East said. "It is your weakness."

"Perhaps," Andragos replied.

"He has learned the secret of his dagger," the Lord of the East said.

"How?" Andragos asked. "You took the scroll from him. He cannot, and could not, read it."

"And yet he subdued the dragon," the Lord of the East said. "He wants the sword for himself."

Andragos said nothing. He just sat and shook his head.

"I must have the Dragon Sword," the Lord of the East said. "And the Dragon Crown. Whatever the cost. Our people deserve it. Our country deserves it."

"Be that as it may, Syzbalo," Andragos said, shaking his head, "but we need to speak frankly about this Specter business."

"You dare speak my name," the Lord of the East said, leaning forward and pointing an accusatory finger at Andragos.

"Please," Andragos said, opening his hands, "I watched you being born. I tutored you from the time you could crawl. When you fell and cried, who was there to pick you up?"

The Lord of the East's face changed a little. It softened, and he looked down at the floor for a moment. His eyes, outlined in black paint, usually looked harsh and fierce, but they looked like the eyes of a child at that moment. He sat back, almost slumped in his chair, like he did when he was a child, when he was confused or didn't know what the answer to something was.

He was a kind boy, attentive to his studies, but not very bright. His father would rage when he didn't pick things up quickly, whether it was arithmetic, history, writing, or magic, but Andragos knew he would eventually learn, and he was patient with him. Syzbalo was always afraid when he couldn't figure something out, and Andragos would comfort him and do some simple magical trick for him to cheer him up. Then he would sit him up straight and get him to work a little harder, eventually learning whatever the Black Mage was trying to teach him.

Andragos saw that boy, for a moment, a thin lad with messy, black hair, a little gangly at times, with a snorting laugh and an affinity to animals and, oddly enough, flowers. He had gotten that from his mother, and when his father—Mörken Stévock—found that out, Syzbalo wasn't allowed around his mother.

Perhaps that was what eventually changed him, the lack of a mother's love. Perhaps it was watching his father—idolizing a man who was always hungry for more power. The boy that was Syzbalo hated his father for the things he did, the way he shunned his son, and the amount of time he spent trying to become a mighty ruler, but no matter how innocent a boy is, he can only watch a father torture so many people, suck their souls from their bodies using black magic, and be beaten down so many times until he becomes just as corrupt.

Syzbalo sat up and looked at Andragos, who was smiling. He smiled himself, a small, smirking smile and then furled his eyebrows and pursed his lips.

"You forget yourself," the Lord of the East said. "I am no longer a boy, and you are no longer my teacher. And one day, soon, my powers will be greater than yours. So, watch your tongue."

"Very well," Andragos said with a quick nod of his head. For a moment, his heart ached. "My concern is only for you, Your Excellency. There are few in this world that could actually harm you, but Specter is one of them. And his price ..."

Andragos shuddered. Who knew how old Bone Spear was; his price was never gold. No, his price was blood, and the younger, the better. Through whatever Isutan magic he wielded, he sucked the life from people to rejuvenate his, and he didn't care who it was—children, young mothers, nursing babes.

"It doesn't matter," the Lord of the East replied. "The Dragon Sword and Dragon Crown are paramount."

"For the good of the Empire?" Andragos asked.

"Of course," the Lord of the East replied.

Andragos knew otherwise but worked to block his thoughts from his leader.

Be it on your own head Syzbalo.

"I will continue to follow Erik Eleodum," Andragos said, "and keep you informed."

Andragos stood.

"You do like him, don't you?" the Lord of the East said, looking up at Andragos from his seat. This time his voice showed interest rather than anger.

"I do," Andragos replied. He knew he answered too quickly. He had to cover for himself. "Under different circumstances, he would make a good pupil. It is a pity he must die."

"If we are speaking frankly, I always suspected you had a fondness for young men," the Lord of the East said with a malicious smirk.

Andragos gave a courteous laugh.

"He reminds me of you."

The Lord of the East's smile faded. Andragos walked down the steps of the dais. He was halfway through the hall when the Lord of the East called to him again.

"I sent my men to retrieve Ja Sin's family," the Lord of the East said. "A traitor's family should face the same fate as the traitor, don't you think?"

"Of course," Andragos said without turning around.

"We couldn't find them," the Lord of the East added. "None of them. Nieces and nephews. Even some of his close friends. Strange, don't you think?"

"These are strange times," Andragos replied. "But I suspect they fled the moment you arrested Ja Sin. The citizens of Fen-Stévock know the price of treachery. Surely, they feared what would happen and left."

"Yes, indeed. Well, keep your eyes out for them, as well. They must be brought to justice."

Andragos turned, faced the Lord of the East as he watched him, and bowed.

36

Syzbalo sat on the chair on top of his dais, hunched over, hands clasped together, seething. Andragos increasingly irritated him. The man wielded power—more power than any other man in all of Háthgolthane. But he held back his teachings. And the Lord of the East couldn't help but think the Black Mage scorned him for his harsh tactics, whether it be with traitors, enemies, or the other families of Golgolithul. How could that wizard deride such actions? He had done far worse. One did not earn the names Harbinger of Death and Terror of the East by being peaceful and loving. Andragos was fooling only himself.

Syzbalo stood. He dismissed his soldiers, even his personal guard. He felt like being alone. But as they left, he wasn't alone. He felt a presence, someone standing behind him. Perhaps the witches? They had a particular smell to them—sweet and musky. It wasn't them. Melanius? He smelled old. It wasn't him either.

Syzbalo turned quickly, his hands clenched, green electricity flowing through them and around them. A cloaked figure stood in front of him.

"Before I disintegrate you, tell me how you got in here," Syzbalo hissed.

A croaking laugh echoed from underneath the low hood of this mysterious figure. Syzbalo growled and threw both hands towards the hooded being, the green electricity buzzing and snapping, but it passed right through the intruder and struck the large, purple curtain that separated the front of the throne room from the forbidden back.

Syzbalo straightened.

"Who are you?"

"You desire power?" the hooded figure asked. "You desire strength? Magic? Authority?"

Syzbalo cocked an eyebrow.

"What ruler doesn't?" he asked.

"You desire the Dragon Sword and the Dragon Crown?" the figure asked, to which Syzbalo tensed.

"What is this?" he asked. "Whatever magic you are using, mine is stronger."

More laughter.

"Insolent fool," the figure said. "You were always so brash and egotistical, weren't you?"

Syzbalo's eyes narrowed and his lips flattened.

"How can you give me these things?" Syzbalo asked.

"Not I," the cloaked figure said, "but my master. He can give you the sword and the crown. He can give you power unlimited."

"The power to control a dragon?"

"Bah," the cloaked man said with a wave of a pale, bony-fingered hand. He scoffed. "Dragons. Pittance."

"Pittance?" Syzbalo asked. "Have you seen what one dragon did to my city?"

"My master will give you greater power," the cloaked figure said. "All he asks in return is your allegiance."

"Even if I did believe you, I am beholden to no man," Syzbalo said with a laugh. He thought this figure was a simple vision, perhaps, not truly there but transmuted there by some powerful magic. Such a thing wasn't beyond Syzbalo's capabilities. He turned to walk away.

"My master is no man," the cloaked figure said.

Syzbalo turned back to the figure, slowly.

"Pledge your allegiance," the cloaked figure said. "Help with his return to this world. And you will know no end to the power you will wield."

"Who are you?" Syzbalo asked. "Who is your master?"

The cloaked figure reached up, gripping the edges of the robe's cowl with his long, pale fingers, and pulled it back. Syzbalo's eyes went wide.

Specter watched from the shadow of a tree. Two dwarves stood there, ostensibly next to another tree, but the entrance was hidden by the tree trunk. Most would have missed it, but Specter was not one of them.

The guards talked about nothing. Specter had never taken the time to learn to speak their primitive language, but with his powers, he understood them nonetheless. Specter was growing bored, picking at a fingernail and staring at the sky, when one of the dwarves mentioned a man. His ears perked up. He had vanished, along with another man and several dwarves. They were curious. Confused. What were dwarves doing traveling with men? One of the guards scoffed, saying they were southern dwarves so what would you expect?

You should expect death.

Specter's thrown Bone Spear punched through one guard's chest, and all the dwarf could do was stare at Specter in confusion. The other one turned just as Specter came up behind him and slashed his throat with a knife also made of bone. Blood sprayed in unison with the dwarf's heartbeat as he slid to his knees and then slumped over, dead. Specter wouldn't drain these dwarves, not if he didn't need to.

Their blood tasted awful; it was dirty and thick, just like them. He was about to leave the bodies there but then changed his mind.

He retrieved his spear from the dwarf's chest and held it upright in both hands, his body still, as he incanted several words quietly. When he'd finished, he nodded to himself and then pushed the tip of the spear into the ground and began to walk backward; as he did so, the furrow he made opened up to a depth and width for a body. He rolled the dwarves into their resting place, head to head, and then reversed his walk with the spear and the soil and dead leaves returned to as before as if never disturbed.

"You love the earth and the underground so much," Specter said, almost laughing, "you can join it and miss out on your dwarvish death rituals."

Now he was a shadow, slipping through the hidden door in the tree trunk, and down the ladder leading into the main tunnel of Stangar, before materializing in front of the outpost's main entrance. He made quick work of the two guards standing there. They didn't see him until it was too late, but he let them see him. If he couldn't ... wouldn't drain them, he wanted the last thing they saw to be his white eyes, his white hair.

Then he slipped under the main entrance. It was hard to find a crack. These doors were sturdy and well made. *Dwarves.* The space he eventually found was the smallest of cracks in a littler door set within the main, larger ones.

A single dwarf stood guard. A woman? Interesting. He materialized beside her, and she must have felt his presence, for she turned hard, spear ready. Her eyes widened when she saw him—shock—but then they squinted, and she crouched into her fighting stance, barely peering over the top of her shield.

"Ayndling!" she yelled.

Intruder. Cute.

She was an adept fighter, blocking the Bone Spear with well-trained precision. But he was Specter. As he was about to become shadow, a spear flew past his face and thudded into the outpost's main gate. Another one struck him in the shoulder. He felt it break skin; he felt blood underneath his thick, leather armor even if the weapon bounced away.

"Yora!" one of the dwarves cried.

Specter retrieved his large, leather, oval shield from his back and assumed his own fighting stance. Two dwarves charged him, both with broadswords ready. Another dozen followed them.

Two more spears flew towards Specter, but he was ready for them. He ignored the woman dwarf and engaged the coming onslaught of dwarvish guards. He floated past the first two, partially in ethereal form.

"Shadow demon!" one dwarf shouted.

That made Specter laugh aloud.

Two dwarves fell before they could unsheathe their swords, but they were a well-trained lot, and the fight became more difficult. He blocked one broadsword only to feel a bruise rising along his ribs where another one struck true. That dwarf lost his arm before he lost his life. Specter kicked out and up at another, catching the guard's throat with his boot. He fell to the ground, choking, his windpipe crushed. He would be dead soon.

A dozen dwarves became three—the woman dwarf and the two who had actually surprised him. As one fought ferociously, actually pushing Specter back, he considered becoming a shadow and materializing behind him.

"Yora! Go alert Captain Khâmuth!"

As this dwarf commanded this Yora, he turned his head, exposing just a bit of his neck. The bone-blade of Bone Spear slashed along that spot. Specter's poison worked quickly. The dwarf dropped his sword and pressed his hand to his wound. It was painful. He groaned, gritted his teeth, and fell to his knees.

"Yolli!" Yora yelled.

"Go!" the other dwarf yelled.

This Yolli—he and Yora must have been friends, perhaps brother and sister—foamed at the mouth, his skin turning green before he fell back.

"Tu ... Tu ...Tûkgad," was the last thing the dwarf said as he breathed his last.

"You coward," the last dwarf—Tûkgad—said. "Using poison. Typical Isutan."

Specter would have been lying if he said the insult didn't sting, just a little. But he smiled, laughed even. He liked this dwarf, these dwarves. He knew he was dead, but he stood there anyway. He had to respect that. He wasn't going to drain him. Maybe he would let him live. What did he care?

The butt of Bone Spear swept the dwarf off his feet. As he stood again, the butt crashed into the inside of his knee. Specter heard the crunch of bone breaking. The dwarf screamed out, trying to slash at the Isutan even as he fell to the ground. Specter kicked upward, catching the dwarf in the chest. He gasped, dropping his sword and clutching at the spot of the kick. Another kick, this one to the face, and the dwarf was unconscious.

"You're welcome," Specter said, staring down at this dwarf called Tûkgad with lazy eyes.

This fight was taking a lot of energy, more than he thought it would. He briefly considered draining a few of the dwarves, but then he spat. No. Instead, he quickly followed Yora as a shadow as she burst through a door. Five distinguished looking dwarves stood around a table, all of them clad in plate mail. One of them, a dwarf with more gray than black hair and beard, wearing a long red cape, looked up, staring with one good eye and one, white, dead eye that might have matched Specter's eyes.

"Captain!" Yora said, but as she was about to explain what was happening, Specter materialized next to her and threw her into a wall. She slumped to the ground.

The other four dwarves drew swords, readied axes, or picked up hammers. The fifth dwarf squinted with his good eye, hands still clasped behind his back.

"Bone Spear," he said, almost calmly.

"Protect the captain!" another dwarf said, with wild red hair also mixed with white and gray. He moved to stand next to the captain, the last line of defense.

The other three dwarves came at Specter. He kicked one in the groin before stabbing him in the face. Another one caught the butt of Bone Spear to the face while the third flew back when Specter punched him with his shield. The last defender was about to move in front of the table, sword ready, when the captain's hand shot out with speed the Isutan didn't expect to see from a dwarf.

"Lieutenant," the captain said, "stand down."

"But Khâmuth ..." the lieutenant began.

"Peace, Güthrik," Captain Khâmuth said.

Interesting. Specter waited.

"What do you want here, Specter?" Khâmuth asked.

"Do we know each other?" Specter asked, standing straight.

Khâmuth shook his head.

"No. We've never had the pleasure of meeting." Then, the dwarf did something interesting and began speaking in Isutan. "But I know of you."

Specter laughed.

"Dwarvish trickery never ceases to amaze me," Specter said, "especially for little, backward tunnel dwellers."

"That doesn't mean much coming from a man—if that truly is what you are—who drinks blood to stay young and practices black magic," Khâmuth said.

"Fair enough," Specter said with a shrug.

"What do you want?" Khâmuth asked.

"You don't want to fight?" Specter asked.

"I'm sure you have already killed more of my warriors than I can afford to lose," Khâmuth said. "I believe in my abilities as a fighter, but I am a realist. And besides, I have more pressing issues at hand than dealing with you. If you are going to kill us, then kill us, but it is rather unlike an assassin to kill more than needed, especially when you have no intention of draining us."

This dwarf was clever, worldly. Specter liked him.

"Erik Eleodum," Specter said.

"What about him?"

"Come now," Specter asked. "Are we going to play this game?"

"Erik Dragon Fire is ..." Khâmuth began, but Specter cut him off.

"Dragon Fire?" Specter asked.

"He's been given his own clan," Khâmuth explained.

Specter laughed.

"You dwarves," he muttered, shaking his head.

"You know where he is going," Khâmuth said.

"Fealmynster," Specter said.

Khâmuth nodded.

"Do you know how to get there?" Specter asked.

Khâmuth shook his head, slowly.

"I will slaughter every dwarf in this outpost," Specter said calmly, and Khâmuth nodded his acceptance of this as the truth.

"They went northeast," Khâmuth said, "intending to cross the ice bridge. That is all I know."

Specter heard footsteps, cries, horns, and bells. He smiled and gave the captain a slight bow before becoming a shadow and disappearing from sight.

37

"How are you feeling?" Turk asked.

Erik began to feel better. They hadn't moved for two days, but on that third morning, his fever broke.

"Fine," he replied. "We should get moving."

"Are you sure you're ready?" Turk asked.

"I'm ready enough," Erik replied. "We need to follow the green glow in the sky."

"We can't see it during the day," Bryon said.

"Do you remember the direction?" Erik asked.

"Enough, I think," Turk replied.

As dusk fell, the green glow off in this distance appeared again, and Erik was relieved that they had been walking in the right direction.

"Are you sure that is Fealmynster?" Bryon asked.

"No," Erik replied. He saw his cousin's shoulders slump. "And yes. We need to cross an ice bridge, and Yora said following that green light would lead us to the ice bridge."

"And this ice bridge will lead us to Fealmynster?" Bryon asked.

"I hope so," Erik replied.

"That doesn't give me much confidence," Bryon said.

It was cold where they were, freezing, and no matter how tightly Erik pulled his bearskin, the temperature bit at him like a ravenous wolf. But there was no snowfall, no freezing rain, and the ground turned from hard-packed snow to frozen lichen and grass and pine needles. They hiked mostly at night, so they could follow the green aura in the distance, and it looked like it was getting closer and closer. One night it was brighter than another, and then the next, it had dimmed to almost nothing.

"Now what?" Bryon asked the next night, throwing his hands up and sighing with frustration.

The green glow had disappeared, and there was no moon this night. The forest was dark, and Erik noticed the trees started to thin, growing farther apart and allowing more of the freezing wind to howl through the forest. He ignored his cousin and pressed forward, at least a hundred paces when the tree line stopped and opened to a wide, icy ledge.

Erik saw the reason for the disappearing green light as he stared across a wide ravine lined with tall, black peaks, rising into the night sky and blotting out everything from his vision. A gigantic bridge extended from the side on which Erik stood to the other side, attaching, seemingly, straight into the wall of the gargantuan mountain peaks. He couldn't tell if it was an ice bridge, and he really didn't know what that meant. Was it a bridge that was icy, or one made of ice? Or, perhaps, it was simply a bridge named the ice bridge due to its location in the cold wilds of the Gray Mountains.

As they neared the bridge, Erik heard a loud screech. It pierced his ears, and he couldn't help but cover them with his hands.

"What was that?" Bryon asked.

"Whatever it is, it doesn't sound friendly," Erik replied.

Erik readied his shield and drew Ilken's Blade.

The ground in front of the ice bridge moved and shifted, rising as if water was bubbling up. Snow flung about as something shook itself, much like a wet dog trying to dry itself. Erik's feet felt unsteady as a shadow rose in front of him. All he could see were two, blue, cat-like eyes. He heard another screech.

"It can't be," Nafer whispered in disbelief.

"What?" Bryon asked.

"A drake," Beldar replied.

As the snow settled, a reptilian creature stepped forward, its blue eyes piercing and angry. It had a long body, longer than a horse's, and, walking on four legs, its shoulders were a head taller than most oxen.

"A damned dragon?" Bryon gasped.

"No," Beldar said, and then repeated, "a drake."

The creature's white scales glimmered, as the moon broke overhead. Blue, icy plates ran along its spine, ending in a tail tipped with icy looking spikes. As the animal snarled, it revealed fangs, through which a blue snake-like tongue flickered. Protrusions that looked like icicles projected from its joints at the shoulders, hips, and knees. It opened its mouth again, and Erik thought it was going to let out another, ear-piercing screech, but, rather, what looked like blue fire erupted from its mouth. It didn't melt the snow away, however; it instead froze the ground in front of the creature, turning the snow into a thick layer of ice.

"An ice drake," Beldar said as the creature eyed them warily, pacing back and forth in front of the bridge.

It didn't screech again, nor did it belch any more icy fire, and Erik wondered if it was all simply a show of force.

"I didn't think they actually existed," Beldar added.

"Like dragons?" Bryon asked.

"What's the difference between a drake and a dragon?" Erik asked, pointing Ilken's Blade at the creature.

As Erik pointed his weapon at the drake, it bristled, the icy plates running down its spine rattling. It pranced in place for a moment before crouching, like a cat ready to pounce on a mouse. A cold mist spewed from the creature's nose, and, when it touched the air, icicles fell to the ground.

"I would put down your weapon," Bofim said, and Erik complied with a quick nod.

"A drake is simply an animal," Beldar said, "unlike dragons, which have an intelligence like dwarves and men. They have no wings, either, and can be subdued and used as mounts and guards."

"Is that why this drake is here?" Turk asked. "Is it guarding something?"

"The bridge?" Erik added.

As if in response to Erik's question, the drake screeched again, and the ground around it shifted once more. Four forms rose from the ground—men made of ice. They were featureless, save for two arms, two legs, a torso, and a head void of a face. Each extended its right arm, and a spear made of ice materialized. They extended their left arms, and icy shields appeared. The drake spewed ice from its mouth, towards the sky, snow raining down around the companions, and the ice golems charged.

Each of them threw their spears. One struck Erik's shield, and as soon as it touched the steel, it splashed away as water. Nafer cried out as another grazed his arm, cutting a neat line into his flesh and then turning to its liquid form, just like the one that had struck Erik's shield. The other two disappeared into the forest behind them. The icy figures extended their hands again, more spears appearing.

One of them reached Erik first. It moved with precision and speed and staring at the thing's vacant face disoriented Erik, as his reflection in the ice stared back at him. It ducked one attack from Erik, kicked out and tried to sweep his legs, and then jabbed its spear at him.

"These are two precise to be simple golems," Turk said as another of the ice figures attacked him.

Erik blocked another attack with his shield, the spear turning to water, and as the golem held out its hand to form yet another weapon, Erik brought his steel down on its shoulder. The appendage fell away, turning to water, which froze again on the ground. It held its shield up, but Erik swiped at its hip instead, cutting away its leg. Leg and arm gone, the thing toppled over, seemingly staring up at him with its featureless head. He brought Ilken's Blade down on that head, and the whole golem turned to water. The same happened when Turk cleaved his attacker in two with his battle-axe and when Nafer's four-spiked mace crashed into the head of another. Bofim and Beldar had the last one firm to the ground with the spears while Bryon punched his sword through its chest, the ice turning to steam rather than water.

"That was easy enough," Bryon said with a deep sigh.

The drake screeched again, crouching and blowing ice at the companions. They all ducked or rolled out of the way, and when Erik looked behind them, he saw five of the trees at the edge of the forest frozen. The ground shifted in front of the drake again; this time, eight golems rose up.

"Is this the doing of the wizard of Fealmynster?" Erik asked.

"I don't know," Turk replied, the blade of his axe crushing the head of an icy attacker. "But I've never heard of men using drakes as guards."

"Dwarves then?" Bryon asked, his elvish sword flaring as it melted away another golem.

"Elves," Beldar replied, throwing his spear into the chest of yet another ice figure and then drawing his sword. "And goblins in the Shadow Marshes."

"Are there elves in the Gray Mountains?" Erik asked. He twirled past one golem only to find another coming at him. This one actually pushed him back, but Bofim's spear sailed overhead, and when Erik looked up, there was nothing but a puddle of freezing water at his feet.

"They detest the cold," Beldar replied, stabbing another golem. "It's why they live in the forests of Ul'Erel, where it is warm and temperate year-round."

The eight new golems were gone. The drake shook and screamed again, this time sixteen figures rising from the snow around it.

"Why doesn't it just attack us?" Nafer asked.

"We're going to be here all night fighting these *golems*," Bryon said.

"Maybe we need to kill the drake," Erik said.

"Might as well kill a dragon," Bryon said.

"No," Turk replied. "They are very mortal. We just need to get close. Erik, we will draw the attention of these golems. You get close to the drake."

"Great," Bryon said. "When I die, Erik, skin me and tan my hide to stretch over your shield. It seems that's all I'm good for."

The dwarves and Bryon tried to consume the attention of the ice golems, but each wave that came at them seemed tougher than the one before. These ones were bigger and faster and stronger. They wielded icy swords rather than spears, and iced spikes protruded from their shields. Erik found himself dodging and rolling out of the way, away from the drake. When he tried to rush the drake, three of the golems blocked his path, and he felt as if he had to use all his energy to destroy just one of them.

He watched as the dwarves and Bryon did all they could do to stay alive. For the first time, the drake joined the fight, breathing ice in front of Turk, and, even though it struck one of the golems, destroying the thing, the dwarf's boots looked frozen to the ground. The drake turned, whipping its tail outward. Beldar ducked out of the way, but as the tail came down to the ground, it swept Bofim's feet from underneath him and as soon as he crashed to the ground, two more golems were on him.

"This is ridiculous!" Bryon shouted. Whenever his elvish blade struck a golem, it flared brightly, and the animated ice formed to look like a man melted away. He was the only one that seemed to have any luck in fighting the things.

But before Erik could cheer for his cousin, one golem shouldered Bryon in the ribs, sending him staggering backward until he finally lost his balance and landed at the drake's feet. The creature turned hard, Bryon coming up to his feet with his elvish blade held firmly in both hands. He looked ready to fight, and when the drake reared up and opened its mouth, ready to breathe ice again, Erik could tell his cousin was about to lunge forward. His elvish blade flared to a brilliant purple, and Erik could feel the heat from the weapon even several paces away. But the drake stopped. It glared at Bryon with those crystalline, blue eyes and then screeched. The golems turned into snow.

"What's going on?" Bryon yelled as the drake poked its snout close to him and began to sniff him, his hair swirling about as the creature smelled and snorted.

But before any of the dwarves could say anything, the drake sniffed at Bryon's sword. It backed away from Bryon and seemingly bowed and then lay down in front of Bryon, as a cat might lay at the feet of its owner.

"Something about your sword?" Turk asked.

"It's elvish," Beldar said. "Maybe the elves built this bridge and put the drake here to guard it."

"Here north of the Gray Mountains?" Nafer asked, and Beldar just shrugged.

"Will it let me pass?" Bryon asked, still holding his sword in both hands, ready to fight if he needed to.

"I don't know," Beldar replied. "Try."

"Oh sure," Bryon said, "it's not your ass that gets frozen or eaten."

But Bryon sidestepped around the drake, and the creature just watched him with its blue eyes. He stopped once when mist rose from the drake's nostrils, but when it rested its head on its front feet, Bryon started up again. He looked to Erik and shrugged.

"Let's go," Bryon said.

They all gathered at the bridge, watching the drake cautiously.

"Is it truly made of ice?" Bryon asked. "The bridge?"

"I think so," Erik replied.

"It feels as cold as ice," Turk said, "and looks like ice."

"It can't be safe," Bryon added.

"It looks sturdy enough," Erik said.

The bridge was wide enough for a horse-drawn carriage to

comfortably cross. Looking over the side, Erik saw a solid ice abutment, holding the bridge firmly to the wall of the dark ravine. A large arch extended from the abutment to another abutment on the other side of the chasm, and it looked as if it were reinforced with beams crossing over to the arch on the other side of the bridge. Guardrails and barriers lined the bridge to either side, the topmost guardrail arching up to a tall point roughly halfway across the bridge, and then arching downwards to the other side. More beams extended from the tall guardrail, seemingly adding even more support to the bridge.

"It could have been made from stone or iron or wood," Erik said, stepping out onto the bridge. "It's just made of ice, but this bridge marks the edge of dwarvish lands."

"How do you know that?" Nafer asked.

"Something Yora said," Erik replied. "She said as soon as we cross the ice bridge, we will not receive dwarvish help."

He looked over his shoulder at the drake as it watched them.

The bridge was at least three hundred paces long, but as they walked its length, it didn't move, sway, or give any hint of instability. An extra chill emanated from the bridge, mixing with the howling wind funneled into the chasm, and Erik not only felt his teeth chatter, the rattling sound echoing through his skull, but heard his companions' teeth chatter as well.

"So is this dwarvish?" Erik asked.

"No, this is no dwarvish bridge," Turk said as they crossed the halfway point on the bridge.

"How do you know?" Bryon asked.

"It is too intricate," Turk said, stopping and inspecting one of the support beams rising up from one of the guardrails. "These designs show an artist's embellishments. Dwarves wouldn't have taken the time to bother with something as simple as elaborate, and if it is the edge of our territory, why build access to land beyond?"

"Who built it then?" Erik asked.

"Elves," Turk replied.

They had walked halfway over the bridge when Erik felt a flutter in his stomach. The air around him swirled, and it felt warm when it was icy cold only a moment before. He took another step forward and looked down. The bridge was no longer white ice, but black and made of iron and wood. He turned. The whole of the bridge was black, and the drake that lay at the entrance to the bridge was now green, with emerald eyes.

"Do you see this?" Erik said, his mouth open in wonderment.

"See what?" Bryon asked, rolling his eyes and shaking his head, but when he took one more step, his eyes widened. "By the Creator's Beard."

Erik looked all around them. The mountain was still there, as was the tunnel that the bridge led to, but shrubs and creepers clung to the side of the mountain, green and lush. Looking back, the once icy forest was green, but not with tall pines but a canopy of wide, broad-leafed trees. The air was warm and humid.

"It is a jungle," Turk said.

"A jungle?" Erik asked.

"Aye," Turk replied. "The humid forests of the Feran Archipelagos and Wüsten Sahil. It is even suspected that some of the forests of Ul'Erel look like this."

"What magic is this?" Erik asked.

"Elvish magic," Beldar said. "Truly, this is elvish magic."

"Look at Bryon's sword," Nafer said.

The sword didn't glow as it had before, but rather, a purple light shimmered along the blade, like waves lapping up on the seashore.

"It's never felt like this," Bryon said.

"How does it feel?" Erik asked.

"Powerful," Bryon replied. "Like I can feel its magic running through my veins."

Erik felt a small tingle at his hip and looked down at his golden-hilted dagger. It didn't enter his thoughts, but for a moment, he could feel its presence.

"Could you be ..." Erik whispered, but then shook his head.

38

---

he bridge led them through a small tunnel in the adjacent peak, a solid slab of vertical rock that looked icy and black before, but now looked green with shrubs growing from little crevices and creepers crawling all along the side. The tunnel was short, and when they stepped out on the other side, they found a small clearing where they all quickly shed their bear skins; cold was far from being an issue now.

Bryon looked down at his elvish sword and smiled. For once, he was the savior and, even though he hated himself for it, it felt good.

"Do you see that?" Erik asked.

He looked at his cousin, to see what it was that had caught his attention. A white tower, once tall and imposing, now nothing but ruins, rose from the middle of the small clearing. White stone littered the ground, some of it nothing more than rubble, but in other places, large slabs piled against one another. They walked over to the tower.

A thick forest, or jungle as the dwarves referred to it, surrounded a wide glade, presumably cleared for the tower, even though there was no evidence of anyone living in this place. Small animals like rabbits and squirrels, scurried about, and Bryon heard the call of quail and saw the topnotch of a male bouncing through the tall grass of the meadow in which they stood. A blue-collared lizard stood atop one such pile, basking in the warmth of the sunlight. Bryon looked up at the sun.

"Isn't it night?" Bryon asked. "What sort of enchanted place is this?"

He looked up at the ruins of the building. Gaping holes pot marked what remained standing of the structure.

"Elves," Turk said, standing at a door that now seemed useless, but stood intact. The dwarf traced his hand over runes in and around the door. "I can't read them, but I know these are elvish runes."

"What are, or were, elves doing in the Gray Mountains?" Beldar asked.

"I don't think we are in the Gray Mountains anymore," Turk replied.

"I don't understand," Erik said.

"I don't know if we have been transported to some other place in the world," Turk said, "or if the elvish magic keeps this place green and warm. It is powerful magic indeed."

Despite the dilapidation of the white-stone tower, the door was locked. Turk pushed and pulled, but it didn't budge.

"Help me," Turk said, and all six of the companions pushed on the door until Bryon heard something snap on the other side and the door swung open.

Birds flew through the opening, a few feathers floating gently to the ground as they scattered. Bryon expected the smell of rotting wood and mold, but the sweet scent of mint and lavender and, perhaps, honey hit his nose. Stepping into the tower, Bryon looked up. The wood of the floors above them was gone, as was the ceiling, so he stared up at the sky.

"What is this place?" Bryon asked, more to himself than anyone else.

"It was definitely built by elves," Beldar said. "Look at the etchings along the walls."

Engravings of trees and leaves and nature scenes covered the walls. Giant marble planters sat along the walls as well, clearly void of any foliage but big enough to hold even the grandest of trees. A stone altar sat in the middle of the room, wide and square vines etched into its sides. The light spilling through the open ceiling illuminated the altar as if it was meant to, and Bryon cocked an eyebrow, walking around the thing and brushing a hand along its surface. His sword pulsated with its purple light as he stood there.

"More runes?" Erik asked.

"Aye," Beldar replied, standing next to Bryon and inspecting the altar. "The elves have a special affinity for nature."

"All of nature?" Bryon asked.

"Yes," Beldar replied, "all of nature."

"Even the cold reaches of the northern Gray Mountains?" Bryon asked.

"Aye," Beldar replied. "Although they don't like the cold so much."

Both Beldar and Bryon continued to look at the altar, covered in runes and carvings when Turk shouted.

"Come look at this!"

He pushed broken furniture and rubble aside and lifted up a large book. He carried it to the altar and set it down. Bryon couldn't help but think the cover of the book, a thick, tan leather-bound thing, glowed slightly when Turk set it down. He opened the book.

"There are names," Bryon said.

"How can you read them?" Erik asked.

"They are written in Westernese," Bryon replied.

"Your eyes are tricking you," Beldar said with a laugh. "These names are written in Dwarvish."

Erik stood next to Bryon.

"No, Beldar," he said, pointing to a name—Sarah. "It is clearly written in Westernese."

"I see Dwarvish as well," Nafer said.

"Elvish magic," Turk said.

"Just like the Dragon Scroll," Erik said to himself.

"What?" Bryon asked.

"When I read from the Dragon Scroll," Erik explained, "the words on the parchment shifted until they formed the spelling in Westernese, and I could read it."

"But none of these names are elvish names," Beldar added. "They are all women ... human women."

"Is that all that is in this book?" Bryon asked. "Women's names?"

"Aye," Beldar replied. "Their names and their lineage."

"There are blank pages, though," Bofim added. "Only half the book has been used."

"Names yet to be written, maybe?" Erik asked.

"Names never to be written, more like," Bryon said, looking around the broken-down tower.

Inspecting more of the tower, Bryon found broken statues, tapestries, and rugs that were almost mere dust and splintered furniture. He knelt down, picking up the head of a white statue. It was a woman, her features perfect, and he rubbed a thumb tenderly along her cheek and over her lips. He wondered if she was once real ... as crazy as that sounded. He could envision her, pink flesh, hair blonde and blue eyes, her lips red and sensuous. He picked up a piece of another statue—another woman, one of her cheeks, eyes, and half her lips gone. Her eyes were brown, her hair almost black. The piece of statue in his hands was alabaster white, but he could see the woman the figurine represented. Another broken piece, just the torso of a woman with no arms below the elbows and wide shoulders filled his mind. Her skin was dark—a deep brown—and her eyes were almost black, matching her hair that was wound in neat braids, falling to the bottom of her backside.

Bryon shook his head, standing and brushing dust off his hands. He stared at the broken statues. He drew his sword, and the purple glow brightened. He felt pain and sadness as his stomach knotted and his chest felt tight. His hands were shaking as he stepped back.

What was the purpose of this place?

39

"Why did you send us here, old man?" Erik mused as he walked about the first level of the white tower.

Despite the intricate engravings on the walls, the oddly placed altar, and the thick book filled with women's names, this place felt wrong, tainted, and cursed. He had seen his cousin looking at a pile of broken statues, fragments of ancient figurines. He wondered what curiosity Bryon could possibly have with them, but when he saw that most of the statues were of women, he figured it had just been so long since Bryon had been with a woman, broken statues started to look pretty. But when his cousin walked away, he looked upset, perhaps even worried.

Erik walked over to the pile of broken figurines. Blank, alabaster eyes stared up at him. They were fake images of some make-believe women, but they looked sad and lonely. One of the faces caught Erik's attention, a soft face with a pointed chin staring up from the pile, seemingly at him. He knelt down and touched the cheek, pushing other pieces of stone aside. This statue was almost completely intact, and when the whole head was visible, Erik could see it had pointed ears.

"An elf," Erik whispered.

The elf statue had a stern jaw, and, among all the broken statues of women, Erik could tell it was an elf man. As he looked at it, the vision of an elf popped into his head. He was tall and slender, but with strong arms and shoulders. His eyes were a piercing blue, and his hair was long, held off his face by a leather thong, and blond if not almost silver as the light hit it just right. As the elf stared at Erik, his eyes seemed to recognize him, and Erik remembered the dream he had after his baptism. This elf reminded him of the one in his dream once he had broken the chains. An elf who looked powerful and strong...a leader.

Erik felt a tickle at his hip. He immediately touched his golden hilted dagger, his heart racing, but then he felt nothing. Even though the conscience of his weapon was seemingly gone, something about this place, about this elf, made him feel he longed to hear the voice in his head again. He lifted up the statue, inspecting it.

"Who are you?" Erik asked.

It was as if a bee had stung his hand as he flinched and pulled away his hand, the statue slipping in his grip. It was a sturdy thing, heavy and thick, but when it struck the ground, the head of the elf statue shattered.

"Damn," Erik said, rubbing his hands together.

A shocking sensation ran up his arms to his shoulders for a moment, and then it was gone. He shook his hand a looked at it but could see no sign of a sting and looked down again at the shattered head, annoyed at his clumsiness.

What's that?

Something in the rubble around the elf statue glimmered. Erik squinted and then crouched down, moving some of the broken stone aside with his finger until something sparkled when struck by the sunlight gleaming through the tower's open roof. Erik picked up a smooth stone, perfectly round and white, and when the light struck it, it seemed to soak it up as if it might give it energy. It reminded Erik of two stones a gypsy named Mardirru had given him, once belonging to the gypsy's father—Marcus—a man Erik remembered fondly. He was a man who, up to the moment he died at the hands of Samanian slavers, had an optimistic view on life despite having lost his first wife and children, being chastised for being a gypsy, and having endured hardships beyond what any man should.

The stones Mardirru gave Erik were red, but they were also perfectly round, and as the light hit them, they seemed to drink it up. He had one left. The other he had used against the dragon in Orvencrest. He had thrown that stone—after his golden-hilted dagger had told him to use it—into a river of molten lava, which then consumed the dragon. He thought the beast dead, but dragons are made of fire, so fire cannot kill them.

Erik held the stone in the palm of his hand. If he stared intently, peering deeply into the oddity, he could almost see a pinpoint of light, but otherwise, it looked dull. He removed his haversack and retrieved a coin pouch, slipping the new stone in beside the ruby-like stone Mardirru had given him.

"Erik, come here," Turk said.

Erik put away his coin pouch and turned to see the dwarf standing in the doorway of the broken tower.

"Come see this," the dwarf added.

Erik followed Turk outside, and they walked to the other side of the tower. He followed the dwarf's gaze upwards and stared at a flock of a dozen birds simply floating overhead. Their feathers looked like a rainbow, and their tails spread out like some fancy lady's fan, fluttering in a small breeze. Their wingspan was wide, wider than Erik had ever seen, and their yellow legs just dangled underneath their bodies. Their beaks were equally as yellow as their legs and long. When one of the birds turned its head and made eye contact with Erik, he could see a flamboyant, crown-like, colorful topnotch. The animal squawked, and the flock flew away, high up into the sky until they disappeared.

Bearded lizards scurried in front of Erik, chasing each other. Ground squirrels poked their heads out of holes and, when they saw the men and dwarves, ducked back into their shelters. Erik heard a bleating sound and turned to see a giant ram, his wool fluffy and white, standing atop some of the ruined stones of the tower. He eyed the men and dwarves warily, making sure to puff out his massive chest and stamp his sharp hooves against the rock. He brandished his large, curled horns, black and a stark contrast to the brilliance of his coat. Half a dozen sheep milled about, in front of the ram, grazing off the lush grass growing in the meadow. Quail milled about, calling to one another, and Erik saw the shadowy silhouette of a deer, brown speckled with a white tail, at the very edge of the glade, shrouded by low hanging, dark green, broad-leafed trees. That was when something else caught Erik's eye as Bryon came to stand by his side.

"Is that ..." Erik said, leaning forward and squinting.

"A wall," Bryon said, finishing what Erik was about to say.

As Erik looked closer, he saw a high wall, made of the same white stone that made up the tower, surrounding the meadow. In certain places, thick vines and creepers covered the wall, or leaves and branches hung over the walls, but where the jungle and foliage allowed for it, the wall stood tall and strong. A wide, wooden double door sat in the middle of the wall, more of a gate than anything else, towering statues of mailed warriors standing on either side.

"Were those there before?" Erik said, pointing to the statues.

"I don't know," Bryon replied. "I guess so. I didn't see them, though."

The statues were tall, rising above the wall, and reminded Erik of the stone images of dwarvish warriors that filled the courtyard of the castle of Thorakest.

"You'd think we would have seen something that large right away," Erik added.

"Elvish trickery," Nafer said.

"Is that anything like dwarvish trickery?" Bryon asked.

Nafer narrowed his eyes and furrowed his brows, but then smiled and gave a quick laugh.

"No," he replied. "It's worse. But that's just a wall."

Erik walked to the wall while his companions wandered off in different directions, each with his mind on something that interested him that warranted further investigation. As he walked closer to the gate, he felt his stomach turn. His chest tightened, and he felt the artery in his neck thump against the collar of mail shirt. Large, iron rings hung from each door, so big it might take three or four people to pull them. Besides the latched lock in the door, three thick iron bars also crossed the space where the gate met, holding it closed.

The locks and the gate and the wall looked as if they were meant to keep out a military force, not simple intruders or trespassers. Erik's stomach sunk even lower. What could possibly need such reinforcement?

That was when he heard them, on the other side of the gate and the wall. The chorus of laughing and cursing. He smelled them and the rot of death. They were there, on the other side.

"I know you're there," Erik said, and they laughed, and a voice hushed, and the sound of their shuffling feet stopped.

"Is that you Sorben Phurnan?" Erik asked. "I wondered when you would show up.

No one answered.

"You're not being sneaky," Erik added. "I wonder what you look like now? Certainly uglier than before. Has your member fallen off yet?"

Still no response.

"I'm here now," Erik said. "Come in and get me."

"Open the gate," a voice said. "Come see us."

"You can't pass through it, can you?" Erik asked. "The elves enchanted this place, didn't they?"

He laughed.

"You think you are so clever, Sorben, don't you?"

"Are you so worried about that worm, Sorben?" the voice asked, and it was clearly not the voice of the dead lieutenant.

Erik didn't smell the typical dead, rotting smell of the undead. He smelled fire and burnt wood, the smell of charred flesh like Aga Kona and the memory twisted his stomach. He felt sweat trickle down the side of his face as the temperature rose.

"Who are you?" Erik asked, leaning forward, placing a hand on one of the iron rungs of the doors. It was warm—almost hot.

"All in due time, Erik," the voice said, just on the other side of the door. "Although, you could come out right now. Find out who I am. Open the door, Erik."

Erik gripped the handle, gently tugging on the iron. The heat intensified, the smell of coal filling his nose, and his hand dropped.

An audible hiss filled the air.

"Who are you talking to?" Bryon asked.

Erik turned. He didn't realize his cousin was there.

"No one."

"What do you want to do?" Bryon asked.

"What do you mean?" Erik replied.

"Are we leaving?"

Erik shook his head.

"I don't know," he replied, and when Turk walked up to them, he added, "I say we stay here the night. This seems like a safe place."

"As safe as any place can be north of the Gray Mountains," Bryon added.

Erik looked up to the sky again. There, amidst the welcomed sunlight, he saw green waves in the sky, faint and almost invisible. But if he squinted, they were there, the green glow they had seen at night. Turk joined them as they walked back towards the tower.

"Erik?" Turk asked.

"I believe it will darken soon so we'll find something to eat—there are plenty of animals around here—and sleep for a few hours. Then we follow the green light; we continue north."

The others nodded and he looked over his shoulder, at the doors in the wall. The air had cooled and the sweet smells of grass and flowers filled the air once again, but whoever the voice belonged to was still there and the slightest hint of burning wood touched his nostrils.

40

─────────

Specter stared at the long bridge supposedly made of ice. He could see the magical aura emanating from it. It was strong, almost blinding in the darkness of the tall mountain peak and the clouded night, a white and bluish hue.

"Elves," Specter grumbled.

He saw the creature as well. Drakes were common on the Isutan Isles. Some even viewed them as pets, but they disgusted Specter, dragon kin that were about as intelligent as a dog. They took up too much space, ate too much, smelled worse than dogs, and had bad tempers. This one cleverly disguised itself as a mound of snow. Specter laughed, but then his jollity disappeared.

"How did Erik Eleodum make it past you," he whispered.

This man he was supposed to follow, rob, and then kill was becoming more than just a simple job.

Specter had no doubt his target and his companions passed this way. He had no doubt they somehow made it past the ice drake and then over the bridge. The tracks, the residue of their essence told him that much. As stupid as drakes were, they were formidable fighters. That was the reason elves trained them. They hadn't the will or intelligence, dragons had but possessed the same ferocity.

Specter, despite feeling tired and drained from the fight with the dwarves, turned himself ethereal and floated close to the ice drake. The creature lifted its reptilian head and sniffed, icy mist puffing up from its nostrils. It shook the snow from its head the way a dog shakes water from its fur and looked about, its eyes cold and blue. The animal must have smelled him, as it rose from its slumbering position to all fours, its white scales and ice-like protrusions along its spine and at its joints shaking as it growled.

The drake walked around in a circle, sniffing and nudging its snout against the ground. It looked in every direction, but as Specter floated down to the beginning of the bridge, his ethereal form touching the ice as a feather might touch the ground, the drake turned hard and breathed flame-like ice specifically in his direction. It knew he was there.

Specter threw up his hands, and when the stream of ice struck the invisible shield in front of him, it splashed away. The cold from the drake's attack bit at Specter's face, and he quickly changed into his physical form. The drake growled again and gave an ear-piercing shriek. The ground before the creature shook, and figures arose—ice golems.

"Damn the gods," Specter hissed.

He produced the Bone Spear. Dodging two long shards of sharp ice, he thrust the bony blade of his weapon against the blank, smoothed, icy face of one of the golems. The animated soldier exploded and became snow. Another one, attacking from Specter's side, almost surprised him, but he put a hand out and an unseen force pushed the ice golem into the ravine over which the bridge crossed.

There were now four ice golems, and Specter made quick work of them. The drake screeched and, before Specter could rush the animal and drive the Bone Spear between its ugly, blue eyes, eight more golems rose from the snow. When he dispatched them, sixteen golems rose.

"What? Is this a fight of mathematics," Specter hissed, spitting a bit of blood on the otherwise pale snow. "Leave it to the elves to devise such a trap. This whole place bears their stink."

He slammed Bone Spear's butt into the head of one golem and then pierced another where its heart would have been if it were a real man. Specter looked to the clouded sky.

"Elves!" he shouted. "Elenderel! I hate you! I know you are watching this from somewhere in your cursed forests! Get ready to watch me shove the Bone Spear up your pet's ass!"

Just then, the earth shook, and Specter had to put out a hand to steady himself. He heard cracking and, looking over his shoulder, saw a piece of the mountain falling away into the void of the ravine.

Maybe I went too far.

As more forms rose from the snow, Specter turned and looked to the bridge.

"To the nine hells with this," he said.

Specter tried turning himself ethereal, but couldn't. It felt as if someone bound his magic, holding it, chaining it, almost like an invisible force holding his arms to his side. He felt empty, a feeling he hadn't felt in hundreds of years. He ran. The golems didn't follow him. As he reached the halfway point of this ice bridge—clearly an elvish construction— he thought he was free, staring at a small tunnel at the other end of the bridge. But then he lurched backward, his back hitting the icy floor hard and the breath rushing from his lungs.

Specter stood, legs wobbly, vision blurry, and head hurting. He tried to step forward, but something pushed him back. He put his hands out, and a shock ran from his hands to his shoulders.

"Elves," Specter said and then spat, spitting at the force field. Even that was expelled.

He leaned forward as much as he could and squinted, trying to peer past the invisible barrier holding him back. The other side of the bridge was hazy, distant and shadowed, a silhouette more than anything, but what he saw, on the other side of the unseen obstruction, wasn't a nighttime, icy, mountain bridge. It was green and bright and warm.

Specter turned. More golems than he could count ran towards him, followed by the ice drake.

"I guess I really pissed them off," Specter said with an insincere smile.

He tried again to change into his ethereal form, but his magic still wouldn't work. He was feeling tired and, even with Bone Spear, without his magic, he would be no match for countless golems and a drake. He looked to the side of the bridge. The magic of this place, restricted him, but what if ...

As the first golem reached him, Specter ran to the edge of the bridge and jumped. As he fell, the wind whipped past his face, stinging his eyes. All around him was dark, a black abyss. He still felt his magic restricted, even though, as he looked up, the bridge became smaller and smaller. He had no idea how deep this ravine was, but this was a chance he had to take. Death was certain on the ice bridge.

He tried his magic again and felt a tingle in his fingers and toes. His head hurt a little less, and his magical vision, that allowed him to see even in the darkest of places, began to illuminate mountainous features around him. It was working. The farther he was from the bridge, the less restricted he became. His enhanced hearing heard water and rocks breaking from the mountain wall as he saw the valley floor—a mixture of craggy protrusions and a winding river—coming up to meet him quickly. He closed his eyes and concentrated. He felt his stomach flutter, his heart race, the wind ... and then he was shadow.

41

They had expected the sun overhead to have faded, but it blazed down all the while they established a camp, cooked and ate, and settled down to get some sleep. Restless, Erik leaned against a wall in the broken white tower of this strange, clearly magical glade. Bryon lay next to him, trying to sleep, eventually covering his head with his haversack while Turk continued to explore the ruins of the circular keep. Bofim and Beldar sat cross-legged near Erik, whispering to each other; Nafer was the only one who had actually fallen asleep.

Erik reached into his haversack and retrieved his wooden flute, the one Mardirru had given him when the gypsies left Erik, Befel, and Bryon in Finlo. It was an odd gift at first and, truth be told, Erik was never very good with music. Bryon was the one that seemed more musically inclined. But whenever Erik would put this flute to his lips, he would imagine something, a scene, and that was what he would play. How could someone play an image, a vision from their imagination? Erik didn't know, but if someone could turn nature into a song, that is what he did.

Erik closed his eyes. He stood in a wide, green meadow, a tower in its center, and surrounded by a wall, both made of alabaster stone. Women sat and worked and talked inside the tower; all ages and from all corners of the world, but they were all human. Some had pale skin and almost white hair while others had very dark skin with black hair that fell in ringlets to their waists. Some girls were barely five summers old while others were grandmothers. The girls that looked to be adolescent and younger had their heads shaved, while the older girls and women wore their hair in whatever fashion they wished. Some girls read and studied; others washed and cleaned. A few trained in combative arts in the meadow with wooden staffs or with their hands.

All around the busy women and girls, the sounds of a peaceful glade filled the air with blue jays and robins offering up joyful songs to the sun. Squirrels and rabbits scurried about, chattering at one another while they looked for food. Erik couldn't help but smile. The temperature was perfect, the grass soft under his bare feet, and he felt as if he could simply lay down and rest wherever he pleased. The scent of lavender and summer flowers filled the air, along with the familiar buzz of honeybees, collecting their treasure for their queen, hidden away in their hive somewhere. But then the ground shook, and Erik looked north.

The horizon was dark until it flashed with purple lightning. The darkness was far away, but it felt constricting, and there was a pervading sense of evil. He looked to his left and saw a woman standing there, her dark, brunette hair falling past her knees, streaked with gray and white. Her jaw was stern and strong, belying her obvious age, and she wore a thick, white robe. She watched the growing darkness. He looked to his left, and there stood the elf from his baptismal vision. He didn't wear armor, just a white robe as well, the golden hilt of a sword poking through the opening in the front. He watched the north as well. Hesitant joy mixed with worry, that's what Erik felt ... and that's what he played.

The sun was out when Erik opened his eyes.

"Is it always day in this place?" Bryon asked, grumbling.

"It would seem that way," Erik replied, sitting up, yawning, and stretching.

"Elves," Beldar said.

"We need to leave," Erik overheard Bofim say.

"I think I wish I could stay here a little longer," Erik said, more to himself than anyone else.

"Truly?" Bryon said. He looked down at Erik with a raised eyebrow.

"This place is safe," Erik replied.

"Safe?" Bryon said. "This place is a ruin. It is broken and dead."

"It is broken," Erik said, "but it isn't dead. No. It's very much alive. Death lies outside those gates on the far side of the meadows. That is what we must face, that is where we need to go first, through those gates before we move further north."

"You speak in riddles, cousin," Bryon said, walking away towards the trees to take a pee.

"That's because my dreams speak in riddles," Erik whispered.

Erik stood, readied Ilken's Blade, and patted his golden-hilted dagger, wishing he could feel its presence once more. He put his haversack on his back and strapped his shield over the top. He had the sense he'd need the shield before the haversack.

"Are you ready?" Turk asked.

Erik nodded and led the way over to the double-doored gate in the wall surrounding the meadow.

"What's on the other side?" Bryon asked.

"I don't think I want to know," Bofim replied.

Erik grabbed a large circular handle on one of the doors. He looked at Bryon over his shoulder.

"I told you," Erik said, and then pulled on the handle. "Death."

42

The cold came as a shock. When Erik opened the gate door, the jungle outside the wall looked normal—a thick, dense forest of vines and creepers and tall, wide-trunked trees with broad leaves. Moisture and heat hung in the air like a heavy blanket. But as soon as they passed through the gate and stepped into the jungle, the world around Bryon shimmered and twisted, and his next step gave off the loud, audible crunch of snow. He immediately started shivering and retrieved the bearskin his father had given him and pulled it tight around his shoulders.

Despite his thick animal fur, the cold still bit Bryon all the way to the bone.

"What, by the Creator, happened to the nice, warm, elvish meadow?" Bryon said through chattering teeth.

They all looked behind them, and all they saw was a thick, mountain forest covered in a blanket of snow.

"Elves," Beldar grumbled.

"What was the purpose of that?" Bryon asked, looking at his cousin.

Erik just shrugged.

"That old man in Eldmanor is crazy," Bryon added.

"I don't disagree with you on that point," Erik replied. "But my gut tells me there was a reason for us finding the white tower, as broken as it was."

Where it was daytime in the elvish meadow, here, it was night again. Despite the snow and the cold, when Bryon looked to the sky, it was clear, the moon and stars brilliant and bright and closer than when they were on their farm. And he saw the green glow they had been following.

As they walked the whole night, the green light changed its position in the sky, almost fading until it looked as if it actually glowed in front of them, the light snaking through the trees. They rested for a moment in the morning when watery sunlight first broke through the cloud cover, but after what Bryon supposed was noon, they started off again. As dusk settled, the greenish glow remained in front of them, emerald, ghostly shadows seeping through the trunks of tall, wide pines.

"Carefully," Turk muttered.

They crept closer to the green light, now glowing bright and brilliant. As they neared it, they heard voices—deep, booming voices— and the clanging of metal and what sounded like the crushing of rock. The trees stopped at a ledge, and the green light was even brighter as Bryon leaned against a tree trunk to peer into the canyon below.

There were open fissures, smoke or gas escaping the cracks in the earth. Bryon squinted as a bright white light illuminated the whole area, coming from tall poles. The light hissed and sizzled but looked more like a beacon than a fire. As the smoke rose from the crevices— already a pallid green in color—it merged with the light from the torches, casting the green glow into the sky.

The sound of two male voices yelling at one another erupted, even though Bryon didn't understand the language he sensed cursing and scolding. He looked to the origin of the commotion and saw two etenweird, one with a large axe and the other with a large pick. Another three stood on either side of one of the fissures, striking the ground hard with their tools.

"It's a mine," Turk said.

"A giants' mine?" Erik asked.

"Aye," Nafer replied. "They're quite good at it too."

"What are those torches?" Bryon said. "Why do they burn white?"

"Firestone," Bofim explained. "Rock that catches fire burns brighter than any fire and doesn't emanate as much heat as wood. Some of the gas that comes through the earth can easily catch fire with a regular torch, causing devastation. But the firestone is less likely to ignite it."

"What are they mining, do you think?" Bryon asked.

"They could be mining more firestones," Bofim replied, "or obsidian. Coal. The etenweird have little use for gold or silver, but iron perhaps."

The two giants who had been arguing started fighting, punching each other with heavy fists. As the fight went to the ground, they wrestled around, crushing smaller rocks and overturning trees as if they were nothing. When they rolled into the cavern wall of the ledge on which Bryon stood, the ground shook. Another giant, an even bigger one, emerged from one of the fissures, his face gray and dirty. He coughed and then yelled.

Pushing himself out of the crack and to his feet, he rushed over to the two fighting giants, kicked one in the ribs, and punched the other one in the face. He grabbed them both by the backs of their necks and stood them up, scolding them and then throwing them towards the mining site. He pointed to the fissure from which he had just emerged, and the shoulders of the two fighters slumped. The huge brute began barking orders, and the other giants, six in all, visibly increased their efforts.

"Do you understand what they're saying?" Erik asked.

"Their language is primitive," Turk replied, "but he said something about magic or wizard."

"Do you think they're working for the wizard of Fealmynster?" Bryon asked.

"It's possible," Turk replied. "Either that or they're speaking about some etenweird shaman."

"Maybe they can lead us to Fealmynster," Erik said.

"Oh, right, cousin," Bryon said, throwing his hands up. "Are you just going to walk down there and ask half a dozen giants to show you the way to their boss, who just happens to be a powerful and crazy black mage?"

Erik just shook his head and continued to watch the giants. He could be so frustrating. As much as he had grown over the last three years, he was still the idealistic Erik Bryon had always known.

The wide canyon in which they worked was definitely giant made, and Bryon scanned the fissures that made up the mine. There were tents and mining tools, implements for crushing rock and sifting and melting ore. There was a large crack on the other side of the camp, opposite of where they spied on the giants, and another giant emerged from that one. He looked smaller, weaker.

"We should lure one of them up here," Erik said. "That smaller one."

"Oh, just like that, eh?" Bryon replied, his voice dripping with sarcasm.

As Erik turned on Bryon, his face turning red, Turk cleared his throat.

"That is a tall task," Turk said. "Firstly, how do we lure a giant up here? Secondly, do you think it would be so easy to subdue a giant? You saw what just one did, how violent and aggressive and powerful they are. Even a juvenile such as that one is a dangerous foe."

Erik took in a deep breath and then sighed deeply.

"What should we do then?" Erik asked.

"Firstly, it is a big assumption that these giants work for the wizard of Fealmynster," Turk said.

"You heard them," Erik said. "They spoke of a wizard."

"But how do we know which one? It could as easily be one of their shamans," Nafer added. "They're little more than novice necromancers, but they practice the dark arts mixed with nature magic."

"I say we just pass them by," Bryon side. "It's not worth the fight."

Turk put up his hand, silencing everyone. He nodded towards the giant that had broken up the fight, listening as the etenweird spoke to one of the others.

"I just heard him mention Fealmynster," Turk said.

"So, what do we do if luring one of them up here isn't a good idea?" Erik asked.

"Your idea to get one of them to lead us to Fealmynster is a good one, but we should wait," Turk said. "One of them will eventually need to relieve himself. As uncouth as giants are, I doubt they piss down there. Wait until one of them goes into the woods, and by that time, we should have a good plan devised as to how we can subdue him."

Bryon watched the giants while Erik and Turk devised a plan to ambush one of the brutes when they walked into the forest to relieve themselves. It didn't take very long for the juvenile to eye the forest above him, and despite his previous doubts over the plan, Bryon grinned to himself. The youngster looked to the giant Bryon assumed to be their leader and said something. The leader looked irritated and curtly replied. The young giant jumped up, grabbed the ledge of the circular pit, and pulled himself up, disappearing into the nearby forest.

"There's our chance," Bryon said.

Erik led Bryon and the dwarves around that wide canyon, making sure to stay well behind the trees that lined the ledge. They could see the giant, his large back turned to them.

Erik put his circlet on; the sapphire in the center glowed as soon as it fitted snuggly on his head. He poked his head out from behind a tree and bobbed his head up and down, back and forth. To anyone looking up into the darkness, it would have looked like some dancing light, a will-o-wisp or one-eyed animal spying on them. If this giant was young and curious, he might be tempted to investigate.

The giant turned, letting his tunic made of skin fall to his knees and wiping his hands off on the front of it. He must have seen the bouncing light as the juvenile scrunched his eyebrows and peered forward, squinting. He stepped forward, peering even closer.

"Here he comes," Erik said.

Erik backed away from the tree behind which he hid, Beldar and Bofim standing each beside another tree, and tied a length of hemp rope between the two of them. Turk waited with Bryon, each a balled-up bearskin in their arms, and Nafer stood behind them, an axe held tightly in both hands.

"Careful with that," Erik said. "We don't want to kill him."

Nafer nodded.

The giant followed the light into the forest, and Bryon grinned again.

Curiosity skinned the gnome.

The giant stepped farther into the forest, somewhat cautiously, and Beldar and Bofim pulled tight on the rope. As the giant stepped into the rope, he stumbled and, even though he snapped the rope with his girth and strength, he tripped and crashed to the ground.

The giant landed on his face but rolled over. He was three times as tall as the dwarves and almost a body length taller than Bryon, but Bofim and Beldar were on him with their rope, nonetheless, trying to hold him down. As he opened his mouth to scream, Bryon and Turk stuffed their bearskins in, stifling any sound, and Nafer was quick with three heavy strikes to the back of the head with the flat side of the axe. One such strike to the side of a man's head would have crushed his skull, but the giant simply slumped a bit, losing the desire to struggle, and then his eyes rolled to the back of his head as blood seeped from the spot where Nafer attacked him.

"We need to tie him up," Erik said.

"What will hold him?" Bofim asked. "Surely, not the rope."

"He won't be unconscious for long," Nafer said. "His skull is thick. He is already starting to come to."

"Stand over him," Erik said to Nafer. "Bryon, you point your blade at his eye."

Bryon unsheathed his elvish sword and pointed it at the giant's eyelid, fluttering as he regained consciousness. He looked at his bearskin stuffed in the giant's mouth.

My bearskin is ruined, and if this doesn't work, it will be all for naught.

Bofim and Beldar attempted to hold him down with rope. Erik stepped on the giant's chest, unsheathing Ilken's Blade and pointing it at the etenweird's throat. Nafer swapped Turk's axe for his own spiked mace.

The giant began to struggle as he rolled his head side to side, and when he first opened his eyes, he looked furious, lifting his arms and easily flinging Bofim and Beldar aside. But then, he saw a glowing, purple blade at his eye, a dwarf with a mean-looking mace overhead, and another man with a sword to his throat, so he rested his head back and waited.

"You may be able to stop one of us," Erik said in Dwarvish, "but you can't stop all three; one of us will kill you."

The giant understood enough to keep still, and his only movement was to slightly grimace.

"Ask him, Turk," Erik said.

Turk nodded.

"I will have them remove your gag," Turk said, "but the moment you breathe too deeply, this man here with the magical sword will pluck your eye out with his sword, and the dwarf with the mace will crush your other eye. Do you understand?"

The giant nodded, slowly. Turk looked at Bofim and Beldar, and the dwarves removed the bearskins from the giant's mouth.

"What do you want?" the giant asked, and even being young, his voice was deep and reverberating.

"What are you mining?" Turk asked.

"Iron ore," the giant replied. His Dwarvish was rough, but he spoke it well enough for them all to understand. "And firestone and some other rock that is brittle and smells terrible. The others simply call it black rock. I don't know its real name."

The giant looked around. Bryon knew he was surveying, planning.

"He's wondering how he can get out of this, Erik," Bryon said in Westernese. "Be careful."

Erik looked at Bryon and nodded slowly.

"Why is a man speaking Dwarvish?" the giant asked.

"Why are you mining here?" Turk asked. "Why are you mining black rock?"

Bryon and Erik both knew what black rock was, and, like the giant, Bryon didn't know its real name, but he knew it was flammable and volatile. Some of the farmers would crush and sow it with their soil, supposedly helping produce better crops.

"I do what I am told," the giant said with a shrug. "That's all. Boss says mine, so I mine."

"You know what Fealmynster is, don't you?" Turk asked.

The giant squinted and lifted his head, then smiled. He chuckled.

"You seek Fealmynster?" the giant asked with a weird hint of mirth in his voice. "To the Shadow Lord with you."

"You will take us there," Turk commanded.

The giant shook his head and spat through broken teeth at the dwarf. Most of the spittle landed on the giant's chest, but it reeked of black root and bad breath.

"Bofim. Beldar," Erik said.

The two dwarves stuffed the bearskins back into the giant's mouth, and before he could reach up to pull them out, Bryon traced a neat burn line along the giant's cheek, just under his eye. The hair of his patchy beard burned away, and the wound immediately began to blister. The giant screamed against the bearskin and reached up to remove the gag when Bryon pointed his sword so close to the giant's eye he shied away, clearly feeling the intense heat from the blade. Erik nodded to Beldar.

"I'll die," the giant said after Beldar slowly removed the gag. "The wizard will kill me."

"What do you think is about to happen?" Erik asked.

"We will burn your eyes out first and then kill you very slowly," Turk added. "Lead us to Fealmynster, and we will let you go. No one will ever know it was you."

The giant stood, Nafer and Bryon behind him, weapons trained on hamstrings. Bofim and Beldar held their spears, pointed at the giant's balls.

"Lead on," Turk said.

The giant grunted, looked over his shoulder at the mine, seemingly contemplating whether he should cry out. He seemed to accept it would be to his death, and he simply stood waiting to see what they wanted to do next.

Even though the rope was broken, Bofim and Beldar tied the giant's hands behind his back and put another rope around his neck, roughly tightened. Bryon didn't think they could actually hold the giant, but as long as he thought his life was in danger, he would be obedient.

With a prod in its butt with Bryon's sword, the juvenile lumbered forward through the mountain forest, each one of his steps was three or four of the dwarves'. When he moved too fast, Bofim would tug hard on the rope around the giant's neck and the giant relented and slowed down. They marched through the whole night, and around noon the next, the men and the dwarves were getting in need of a rest, but the giant moved as easily as he did at the start.

"By the Creator," Bryon said, "does he not tire?"

"Men," the giant grunted with a disapproving stare. "Weak."

"Strong enough to subdue you," Erik replied.

The giant just growled quietly.

They continued on until the sky darkened again and even in that dim light, Bryon felt everything looked the same.

Are we going in circles?

Bryon looked up and saw a green glow in the near distance; it was ahead of them and not behind them. He looked up at the giant and then grabbed Turk's arm.

"We're going in a circle," he said in Westernese.

"I think you're right," Turk said.

"What?" Erik asked.

"He's been leading us in circles, now we're going backward," Bryon reiterated. "He's leading us back to the mine. I'm guessing he knew the others would come looking when he went missing."

Without a word, Erik drew his sword and jammed it into the back of the giant's leg. The giant howled, turning and swiping at Erik with the back of his hand. Erik rolled out of the way just as Bryon also brought his sword across the back of the giant's leg. Nafer thumped his mace against his knee, and the giant stumbled, the leg they'd injured giving way. Beldar and Bofim stabbed each one of the beast's shoulders with their spears.

Turk was about to strike the giant in the back of the head with his battle-axe—with the edge—when a deafening roar stopped him. Turning, at least half a dozen giants burst through the trees, crudely made axes and clubs and maces in their hands.

"Run!" Erik cried.

They raced towards the mine, the only way to go. The thundering footsteps of six large and angry giants echoed behind them. The giants were easily gaining on them, and Bryon saw the tree line stop, knowing the ledge was close. He didn't know what to do. One, adolescent giant was hard enough to subdue, but six fully-grown, very angry giants would be impossible, and they were close to becoming simple meaty smears on the bottoms of these monsters' feet.

The edge of the mining chasm was only five steps away ... four ... three ... two ... Bryon leapt. His stomach fluttered, his breath caught, and the ground came up fast. Instinctively, he tucked his knees to his chest and bowed his head. As he struck the ground, he rolled, tumbling head over heels, finally coming to rest on one knee. He would be lying if he said it didn't hurt, but he knew his movement avoided broken legs or other broken bones.

Erik bounced off his ass as he reached the ledge, turned, grasped the ledge with both hands, pushed away against the chasm wall with his feet, and landed. The dwarves did the same, all but Nafer, who slipped and fell, crashing into Turk.

Bryon looked around, sheer walls surrounding them and a dozen cracks in the earth. They were trapped. It's what the giants wanted. He heard laughter as the giants approached the ledge. They weren't running anymore. They didn't have to.

"Man flesh," Bryon heard one of the giants say; their language that was almost a copy of Dwarvish.

"You get the dwarves," another said. "Boss gets the men."

"This was a bad idea," Erik said, and as if to prove his statement, another dozen giants emerged from the cracks in the ground.

"By the Creator," Bryon said, moving shoulder to shoulder with his cousin, "how deep and wide do these cracks have to be to hold a dozen of these brutes?"

Bryon looked over the edge of one of the fissures as his companions came close to him, and the giants began to surround them, eyeing them greedily. He looked into the crack. It was certainly a mine of sorts, and deep, with scaffolding and piles of iron ore and black rock and firestone here and there. But it wasn't big enough to hold a dozen giants. It was barely big enough to hold one, maybe two. A green light emanated from the bottom of the mining hole, the gas and steam that escaped these fractures, undoubtedly. But Bryon didn't see any gas escaping.

He moved closer, accidentally kicking a rock into the fissure. It fell into the crack, and as it hit the green aura, the light flashed a little brighter, and the rock disappeared.

"What the ..." Bryon gasped.

He watched the giants move closer, saw a few more emerge from other mining holes, and looked back into this one.

"It's a doorway," Bryon said.

"What?" Erik asked.

"These cracks aren't just mines," Bryon said. "They're doorways. Magical doorways."

"You're making no sense," Erik said.

"A doorway to where?" Turk asked.

"More giants if that's how they're coming here," Nafer added.

"Well, do you want to stay here and become giant dung," Bryon asked, "or give this potential portal a chance?"

Turk looked at him and nodded. Bryon jumped in the darkness of a mountain hole. The misty, shimmering green aura of magic raced up towards him. As he hit the light, the world around him began to twist and distort, just like it did when they had crossed the ice bridge. He felt himself falling, but into nothing. There was no sound or smell, and, soon, the world around him was black. And then the space around him swirled and twisted and distorted again, and he fell on his face. Before he could push himself up, someone landed on top of him. And then another, and then another until he had five bodies piled above him.

"By the Creator!" Bryon grunted. "Get off!"

He felt bodies rolling off of him, and as soon as the last did, he pushed himself up and breathed deeply.

"Where are we?" Bryon asked.

"Judging by the wind I can hear, in a cave," Beldar replied.

"Where are the giants?" Turk asked.

"I don't see any," Bofim replied.

"I'll take a look outside," Bryon said.

With help from the light of his sword, he moved over the mouth of the cave and peered outside. As Beldar suggested, a strong wind howled outside, but there were no trees to flutter and bend; there was only unending, bright white snow. Bryon stepped to the edge of the opening, and his nose immediately turned red from a deep, chilling, biting cold. His hair whipped around his face, slashing at his cheeks, and he knew no amount of bearskins would stop this cold as he involuntarily shivered like he never had before.

As he looked out on the vast plain, the first light of dawn appeared, and a shape emerged on the horizon. As the others joined him, the sky brightened some more against the frozen tundra and in the distance, rising up from the flat land like a dark, menacing beacon for weary, unsuspecting travels, a tall, black keep appeared.

43

───────

Fréden Fréwin crumpled the letter and let it fall from his hand. More disappointment. His agents had failed in their attempt to stop Eleodum. This Mungrun Flint Toe failed. The letter used his real name—Hragram. Clearly, he wasn't as great a warrior as Fréden had thought. The letter, sent by another spy, used the term *assassin,* but Fréden thought of them as freedom fighters, trying to stop the expansion of power that men constantly sought. Assassins were evil, but these dwarves were heroes, killed by this Erik Dragon Slayer.

Fréden seethed and wanted to hit somebody. King Stone Axe, that fool king of Thrak Baldüukr, had given this man a dwarvish name; a dwarvish clan even! The gall. The nerve. The impudence. Further proof that his people were in dire need of a true leader, a dwarf who respected other races but recognized the superiority of the dwarvish kind. The world was calling this Erik a Friend of Dwarves. Fréden shook his head. No. He was an enemy of dwarves. He needed to die.

Fréden sensed his seneschal standing there, just behind his throne.

"What is it Nalbin?" Fréden Fréwin asked.

"The numbers are in, my lord," his seneschal replied.

They kept track of the number of dwarves flocking to their cause every week. When they first left Thorakest, they must have had five hundred dwarves go with them. It was nothing compared to the five hundred thousand that lived in Thorakest, but those that went with Fréden were only the necessary pieces—soldiers, architects, commanders, civil planners, laborers. The rest, the women and children, would come later. Another five hundred would come each week after. They even had two weeks where over a thousand dwarves heeded his call and joined the cause—what he was now calling *The Movement*. Just under five thousand dwarves had joined them in El-Beth Tordun, but he knew his support was far-reaching.

Recently, however, less and less had been coming. The previous week a paltry eighty-four dwarves with various useful skills showed up. More had come, but what good were artists and musicians and writers and holy men and entrepreneurs when they were concentrating on building a new nation, a new world? Support had slowed.

"Tell me," Fréden commanded.

"Fifty-three," Nalbin replied.

Fréden Fréwin slammed a fist against the armrest of his throne. It was audible enough that the military commanders and politicians in the room turned to look at him.

"It is better than nothing, my lord," Nalbin said.

"*Better than nothing?*" Fréden roared. He turned to face his seneschal, his vision growing red. "If we wish to build a nation, an empire, a new world, we must recruit ten times that a week, until we are strong enough to first retake lands once held by dwarves."

He turned to look at the dwarves in his hall.

"General Kizmit," Fréden said, and his commander of his army, armored from shoulders to toes, snapped to attention and bowed. "How many regular soldiers in our army?"

"Two thousand, my lord," Kizmit replied. "But we have another five hundred that can fight if the need is pressing."

"We need more," Fréden said, pushing himself to a standing position. "We need to expand our recruiting efforts."

"Might I suggest, my lord ..." Kizmit began with another bow.

"Go on," Fréden said.

"If I could train all able-bodied dwarves," Kizmit said, "we would have a standing force of five thousand."

"Are we truly having this conversation again? What would you have me do," Fréden asked, his voice rich with sarcasm, "train our doctors and engineers?"

"Yes, my lord," General Kizmit replied. "It is what we have always done. Everyone is a warrior, and then they specialize in other areas."

"Have you not listened when I've told you we are creating a new world, Kizmit?" Fréden said, "You need to expand your efforts in recruiting able-bodied warriors or I need to find a new commander of our army."

"Your will be done," Kizmit said with a bow.

"How are the repairs to the castle going, Bilkath?" Fréden asked his Commander of all engineers.

"With only five hundred engineers, it is slow," Bilkath replied. "If some of the soldiers could help in the efforts..."

Fréden put up a hand.

"Not you too. It will not happen," Fréden replied. "They need time to train and prepare. Each dwarf will serve his purpose. A single purpose only."

His advisors were constantly trying to get him to let the dwarves that had answered his call help in several ways, but he wouldn't have it. They were going to do things differently.

"Leave me," Fréden said, waving his hand. "Kizmit, send for Long Spear."

The general bowed as those who were in the hall left. Only a moment later, Belvengar Long Spear walked in. He was one of the first to hear Fréden's call, disenchanted with the dwarves' acceptance of man encroaching into their lands and stealing from their people. He was as trustworthy and loyal as they came.

"My lord," Belvengar said with a bow.

"I need you again, Long Spear," Fréden said.

"Anything, my lord."

"Erik, Enemy of Dwarves must die," Fréden said, "as do the dwarves that have aided him. They are traitors to their people."

"My lord," Belvengar said with another bow.

"Will this be a problem?" Fréden Fréwin asked.

"No, my lord. Like you said, they are traitors to their people ... Skull Crusher worst of all."

44

———

Bu stared at the black structure that dominated the horizon, sensing the evil that resided within. He shuddered, wishing he didn't have to go there, and then glared over his shoulder. Andu's short beard had frozen, turning a bright shade of white, and he shivered uncontrollably, as did the remaining four knights. One of them, Sir Reginald, leaned against another, Sir Caleb. They were both cowardly men, and Bu suspected they enjoyed each other's company a little too much at night. The other two knights, Sir Garrett and Sir Alster, had proven themselves a little more worthy, and Garrett had actually started to show he recognized Bu as his king and assisted with leading the Hámonians. In fact, the fat lip Sir Caleb wore came from Sir Garrett, the back of his hand in response to the knight's disrespectful response to the King of Hámon. Still, they, along with Andu, shivered, shielding themselves as best they could, the cold freezing the iron of their hauberks.

Bao Zi stood next to Bu, motionless. Bu wondered if the old, grizzled soldier had frozen to death and become a statue, but the steam coming from his nose said otherwise. He simply dared the cold, challenged the weather to do its worst, and he would stand there and take whatever the environment had to offer.

Finally, the old soldier turned to Bu, slowly.

"Your orders?" he asked in his croaking voice. Bu sometimes wondered if Bao Zi's voice had been gruff when he was a child.

"We move," Bu said.

"You heard your king," Bao Zi commanded, "move."

They walked down to the bottom of the small hill on which they had stood and began to cross the vast expanse of ice and snow. Bu had never seen a place like this—tundra was what Bao Zi referred to it as. He looked down at his feet and, at times, saw frozen grass or dirt and, at times, saw nothing but ice. The idea of walking on frozen water unnerved him, but he would not show it or let his step falter.

"By the gods," Reginald said, having slipped yet again. "What are we doing in this place?"

"Shut your mouth!" Garrett yelled, lifting his hand like a father ready to discipline a petulant child.

"But it's *so* cold," Reginald whined, tears freezing on his cheeks. "I'm chilled to the bone."

"If you keep talking," Bao Zi said, turning hard, "I'll flay you alive and use your damn skin as a coat. Then you'll truly be chilled to the bone."

Garrett put up a hand.

"My lord," Sir Garrett said, "let me handle this."

Bao Zi looked like he was going to draw his sword, but Bu caught his hand.

"Let's see what he does," Bu whispered in Shengu.

"We're going to die out here," Sir Reginald said, fear in his voice as he cried as well.

"Perhaps," Garrett said. "Regardless, your composure as a knight of Hámon is pathetic and without honor. And the way you speak to your king should warrant your immediate death."

Bu saw the look that Reginald gave Garrett. Just a week ago,

Garrett argued with Bu any chance he had. It was a look of pure confusion.

"Why don't you remember the vows you took as a knight and," Garrett said, "if you die out here, die with honor so the gods might bless your family."

Reginald hung his head, and Caleb gave the knight a disgusted look.

"Did you see that?" Sir Alster asked.

"What?" Bao Zi snapped, his irritation and anger evident.

"Over there," Alster added.

Bu looked in the direction of where Alster was pointing. There was a short mountain range some distance away, but that wasn't what caught Alster's attention. It looked at first like the snow was moving, but then they could see the color was slightly darker.

"What is that?" Bu muttered.

"Bear," Bao Zi simply replied. "Snow bear."

Bu's question was also answered by a deep and reverberating roar, carried to them on the strong, icy wind. He had never heard a roar like that; it could only be described as being full of hatred.

"We need to move," Bu said.

As they started to run, they heard more roaring. Closer now.

"Wait!" Sir Reginald cried. "I can't keep up."

Bu looked back over his shoulder. It seemed the wind was howling all around them, and he saw a shadow behind them. It lumbered forward with a long, loping gait as it got closer, and grew bigger.

"Faster!" Bu cried.

"I can't," Sir Reginald said again.

"We must wait for him!" Sir Caleb called.

"Then stay and die with your lover," Garrett said as the distance between him and the two other knights grew. "At least die fighting. Die with honor."

Sir Reginald fell to his knees and cried. Caleb stood over him, a look of genuine worry on his face.

"Stay with me," Bu heard Reginald say. He looked over his shoulder again and saw Reginald reach up and grasp Caleb's hand. "Please."

The snow bear was closer, and it roared again. Caleb looked up and pulled his hand away, turned and ran. Reginald cried after the other knight, but Sir Caleb didn't look back.

"He'll slow down the bear," Bao Zi said.

The other three knights and Andu caught up to Bu and Bao Zi. Sir Caleb had tears in his eyes, all of them freezing on his cheeks and in his beard.

"We're running out of men," Bu said as a long scream almost drowned out the bear's roar.

"Reginald was a poor excuse for a knight, Your Majesty," Garrett said.

"We'll need as many men as we can when we get to Fealmynster," Bu said.

"Understood," Garrett said.

Bu stopped.

"We can rest for a moment," he said.

As the others took a breath, Bu grabbed Garrett's arm and pulled him close.

"What are you about?" Bu asked.

"Your Majesty?" Garrett asked, his brow furrowed, and his lips pursed.

"Don't play with me," Bu said, pulling him even closer. "A week ago, you fought me at any chance, and now, you serve me like a lap dog."

"You are my king," Garrett said with a shrug.

"Lies," Bu said. "What's changed?"

Garrett looked over Bu's shoulder. Then he stared at Bu, his mouth flat, his eyes emotionless.

"I am starting to realize you are a strong warrior," Garrett said. "Clearly, stronger than any of these other knights. I am an opportunist. Firstly, I will not survive this mission if I continue to oppose you. Secondly, I can see that you are loyal to those who serve you. When we return to Hámon, I would expect you might bless me with more land and titles as I have served you loyally. I am a vassal to Count Alger. I wish to be free of him and have vassals of my own."

"I see," Bu said, releasing his grip a bit. He remembered having almost the same conversation with his seneschal, Li, when Patûk was still alive. Li knew he would be a powerful man one day. And rather than hate the man for his opportunistic tendencies, Bu actually respected it. "And your feelings on having an easterner as your king?"

"Do you want my honest reply?" Garrett asked.

Bu nodded.

"It disgusts me," Garrett replied.

Bu expected as much. At first, he felt a tinge of anger in his gut, but he pushed it away. He wanted this knight to be honest. Garrett thought that Hámonians were superior to all others, much in the same way most easterners believed they were better than anyone else.

"But your wife is Hámonian," Garrett added, "and of noble blood, which means your children, as long as the gods see fit to give you offspring, will have Hámonian blood coursing through their veins. Over time, your eastern blood will slowly fade away."

Garrett gave a quick shrug. He was haughty but confident, and Bu was starting to like him.

"Besides, you will have to learn our ways—become Hámonian—if you wish to earn the favor and loyalty of the nobles and rule my people," Garrett replied.

Anger flashed across Bu's face. He stepped closer to Garrett.

"I appreciate your honesty, Sir Garrett," Bu said, "but let's understand one thing ... they are *my* people. And unless they wish to find their roads decorated with the crucified, they will obey. I will learn the ways of Hámon, but you had better hope the nobles support me. Otherwise, I will simply find new nobles."

Garrett nodded.

"Your Majesty," he said, bowing quickly.

When Bu turned, Bao Zi was there. He bade his lord to come close to him.

"Your life matters the most, my lord," Bao Zi said. "Your life; then mine. Be careful of this two-faced western knight. He is false."

"That he is," Bu replied, "but we do need the support of the nobles."

"My lord," Bao Zi said with a bow. "We should get moving again."

Bu nodded.

It felt like they hurried across the snow and ice for hours, the black keep slowly getting closer and closer, until the landscape changed from flat, icy plains to jagged, icy rock and they had to slow and move more carefully. The rock jutted up from the ground in all different directions as if the earth had given Fealmynster natural defenses. Bu knew it was black magic.

The keep was even larger than Bu had expected. Once they passed the icy crags—Caleb and Alster falling at least once and opening old wounds or cutting a new gash on their forehead or cheek —they came to a wide, circular slope, almost like a reverse palisade. It must have slowly and gently dropped a hundred paces when it finally ended in a collection of buildings—homes perhaps or more likely, barracks. The keep itself stood at the center of the round, flat area, not only rising the hundred paces to where Bu stood, but another fifty more.

The keep was a circular building made of black stone that seemed to drink up all the light and reflect nothing back. As far as he could tell, there were no windows, and the top did not have the crenels like other castles or keeps but was rather flat. A walkway surrounded the keep halfway up, but other than that, it was one huge wall of solid black stone.

Bu saw men down below, in the town of Fealmynster, if one could call it that. The sun was setting, and he couldn't see them well, but they all looked like men, and they all looked armored, taking up defensive positions all around the reversed circular palisade.

"That's a hard fight, Bao Zi," Bu said.

"Aye," Bao Zi croaked. "Just remember what you said. We get the sword and get out of there. Pay no concern for these bastards."

Bu heard something from behind them. Another roar. Another snow bear? The same one? No. He now recognized that sound; men screaming.

45

———

*E*rik could tell by the scattered tools and the cracks and open pot marks in the walls that most of the mining took place in the cave. Tall baskets of rock and ore leaned against the walls.

"Where are the giants?" Bryon asked.

As if in response, they heard the sucking of air, looked behind them, saw a bright flash of green light, and a giant fell from the cave ceiling, landing on his feet and crouching low, hand on the ground to steady himself. The giant looked up, saw them, and roared.

"Run!" Erik yelled, and they rushed out of the cave, setting out over the icy plains of this new place.

The wind whipped at them, and every step felt unsure and unstable, but Erik knew death lay behind them. Where were they going? To the keep. He saw green flashes to his right and left in other caves, other portals to the mine, and more giants emerged and joined the chase.

They ran as fast as they could, but the ground beneath their feet was slippery. The space between them and the giants was clouded with wind-blown dust, but they could still make out the shape of the giants in pursuit. Every once in a while, one of them would yell or roar, but they didn't seem as fast in this place as they were in the mountain forest. Erik looked to his left and saw one giant catching up with Nafer but then the huge creature stumbled. Erik heard a loud crack, something breaking, and the giant screamed, not in anger but terror. He threw his hands up and disappeared with a great splash.

"We're on a frozen lake!" Erik shouted.

The beasts chasing them were so heavy, they had to be careful not to crack the ice and fall in, but Erik and the others never slowed as the distant sun, a veiled yellowish-white orb hanging gingerly in the sky behind a myriad of wispy clouds, began to sink below the western horizon. The winds died down a little with the advent of dusk, and the reflections of the sun along the icy ground was something Erik had never seen before. The sun itself was a hazy blurry ball of light, but the ice reflected deep oranges and yellows and brilliant purples in long, gentle streaks. It was as if the Creator had simply brushed the color along the ground.

Even though the sun was distant and blurry behind clouds and snow, it cast a rare warmth on Erik's face in this frigid wasteland as day slipped into night. For a moment, Erik slowed, wanting to take in the vision of sun and its reflections, and the warmth on his skin was refreshing, like the scent of mint on a cool spring morning. He wondered if that was what the sun looked like when someone first opened their eyes in the afterlife.

"Erik! Keep going!" Bryon said.

"Don't ... slow ... down," Turk panted.

Erik looked behind them. The giants were gone.

"They're not following us anymore," Erik said and drew to a halt. He looked at his feet. Frozen grass. "And no more lake."

"There may be ... no need to run," Turk said, as he bent over with his hands on his knees as he caught his breath, "but I wouldn't ... trust this place to just stand here."

"Do you think the ice on that lake ever melts?" Erik asked.

"Once, maybe," Turk replied. "Maybe once there were hot summers here. But I am sure it has been ice for many years."

For all the horrible things about this place, it seemed to truly sit closer to heaven. Night fell and the clouds washed away, leaving a black sky teeming with stars that were not only white, but red, yellow, green, and blue. They were so close, and Erik thought he could reach out and touch them. He poked at one, bringing back a distant childhood memory. The bright moon reflected off the ice that covered the ground, just as the sun had at dusk, casting long purplish-white fingers over the ground, and not only stars filled the night sky. Mesmerizing lights—green and purple, yellow and red, violet and blue—danced and flowed like water, undulating back and forth.

"I always wondered what those lights were," Erik said, looking over his shoulder, checking the giants had still given up the chase.

"The sun," Turk replied.

"How?" Bryon asked. "It's night."

"I hadn't noticed," Nafer replied with a quick, forced laugh.

"Truly," Turk said. "The sun reflects through the heavens as it reaches into our world and something about our sky what is up there causes these lights."

Erik remembered a moment when he was in the treasure room of Orvencrest. His dagger had given him a vision, a picture in his mind of the space beyond their world, of stars and suns and even other planets. The cosmos, his dagger had called it, and Erik understood.

At first, it was distant, but as they moved on again, a tall tower-like structure, black in the tundra night, rose up, looming over them even from so far away. As they grew closer, the structure seemed the very antithesis of the white, broken, elvish tower, and Erik could see how truly large it was.

"Do you think the elvish tower looked like this?" Bryon asked, voicing Erik's thoughts.

"Perhaps," Beldar replied, "Who knows?"

As they neared the tower, they could see it was made of black stone that darkened all around it as if it sucked up any ambient light. The icy plains before the building turned into rocky crags, white and jutting upwards from the earth at all angles. They did their best to watch their steps, but it was difficult as they tried to circumvent these dangerous rocks. One slip and a fall could be their last. Erik looked back again. Still no giants.

"This doesn't seem natural," Bryon said.

"No, it certainly doesn't," Nafer replied.

The jagged rocks stopped just before the earth gave way to a vast, round bowl in the earth, and the icy ground sloped gently downwards until it leveled off into a town with mostly dark buildings. Armored men stood shoulder to shoulder and surrounded the whole of the town, seemingly all the way around the vast gorge. They clearly guarded the tower, and it looked as if they knew someone was coming as they stood at attention, waiting.

The town looked barren and, in a way, fake. It reminded Erik of Orvencrest, where everything was dead or stale. The buildings all looked the same and were spaced evenly, allowing roads of slabs of stone to easily crisscross the whole valley. There were carts and wagons sitting next to roads and structures, but they seemed out of place, stuck in time, almost. Erik didn't see any citizens, men and women who had nothing to do with combat or the protection of the keep. He saw no children and no animals. The place was silent.

Erik could now see the tower was a castle keep that rose up in the middle of the bowl, taller than Erik had expected when viewed from a distance. In the moonlight, the black stone walls reflected none of the pallid light, and the only thing that broke up the smooth sides of the cylindrical building was a circular walkway that sat halfway up. Erik saw a figure standing there, black robes fluttering gently in the nighttime breeze, a hood pulled over the face. He remembered the faceless man from his dreams and his vision from his baptism.

"Welcome to Fealmynster," Turk whispered.

"I don't think I'm very happy to have finally found it," Erik added.

Erik looked to his left and saw six men. He could barely see their faces in the darkness and distance, but he knew they stared back at him. Three of them looked like knights ... Hámonian knights.

"By the Creator," Erik murmured, "How on earth did they make it all the way up here?"

But then he thought they might be asking themselves the same question.

He drew his sword and pulled his shield off his back.

"What is it?" Bryon asked. He'd been keeping an eye on the men down below.

"Hámonians," Erik replied. "To our left."

He strained, squinting, and then his eyes went wide. He knew that man who stood slightly apart from the others. He had seen him once before, in the Southern Mountains, when he had killed Patûk Al'Banan. He didn't know his name then, but now, he did.

"Bu Al'Banan."

"The one who supposedly calls himself the new King of Hámon?" Bryon asked.

But they didn't have time to talk anymore about it. Erik heard crashing behind him, and then something struck him in the back, launching him forward to tumble down the slope of the round valley and towards the town, the soldiers, and the keep. Shards of rock and ice showered the ground around him as he slid. He heard shouting—his friends—and more shouting, this time in Shengu. Someone had pushed him, perhaps the defenders of Fealmynster, sneaking behind them. Whatever it was, Erik slid down the slope to certain death.

46

———

As he slid down the slope, Erik's body spun around, and at the right moment, he could see the ledge above. The men who had pushed them were giants, but instead of wearing simple vests and tunics made from fur, they wore plates of iron armor pieced together, covering their stomach, throat, and chest. One of the giants screamed as he bashed away the jagged rocks of ice with a massive mace, one that made Nafer's weapon look like a child's toy.

Erik's friends slid after him. It looked as if Bu and his men were given the same treatment, but a giant picked up the last knight left at the top and threw him down the slope as if he were one of Beth's dolls. The knight flew through the air and landed right next to Erik with an audible crunch. His armor scraped against the ice and caught in such a way that the knight, presumably dead, spun around and around as they continued their descent.

The armored men below took notice of the commotion—it would have been hard not too—and all snapped to attention. They looked the same, round shields, long spears, tight leather armor that covered their whole body, and leather, conical helms. As Erik neared the bottom of the valley, he lifted his feet so that he might come quickly to stand when he landed. The armored men all lowered their spears in unison and crouched into a fighting stance.

Will they attack as soon as I hit the ground?

He came to a stop and was quickly back on his feet, shield and sword ready. The armored men in front of him didn't move. The dead knight haphazardly sliding down the slope slid past Erik, skidded along the icy ground—which was made of slabs of stone—and stopped just in front of the line of defenders. In unison, the five closest to the dead knight pointed their spears at the deceased man and stabbed. The body flopped about under the attack. If any breath remained in the man's lungs, it was gone now. The leather armored men then moved back into their fighting stance.

The dwarves and Bryon joined Erik, all readying themselves to fight, but none of the spearmen moved. Bu and his remaining men landed in the same fashion and, in the same way, the spearmen nearest to Bu's group waited. Erik looked up, over his shoulder. The giants glared down at them but didn't give chase. One of them grunted and, looking as if he was their leader with more armor than the others and a large, double-headed battle-axe, growled and gave a quick shout Erik didn't understand.

Suddenly, Erik heard a low buzzing murmur, and he felt his hair stand on end. The keep, looming over them like a giant, black fang, began to glow with a faint bluish-white light. It looked as if lightning pulsed up and down the structure until the lightning rose up from the top of the tower into the sky, snapping and popping and dancing haphazardly.

The lightning, crackling like fire, formed a ball of blue light that hovered just above the tower. It hissed, like damp wood burning, and flashed brightly. In harmony, the spearmen took one step forward, staying in their fighting stance. The ball of light crackled again, and a low hum reverberated through the valley of Fealmynster, and, again, the spearmen stepped forward one step. It was as if the light was directing the soldiers.

As they neared, Erik could see the spearmen's faces. Their skin was a pale green, their cheeks sunken and drawn. Their mouths were flat and emotionless. Their armor was all the same, with no markings or standards, as were their shields. They looked like specters. As eerie as these soldiers looked, the most unnerving thing about their appearance was their eyes. Their eyes were black orbs, small round pools of emptiness. Their eyes said nothing. They were like the dead, and they all looked the same. There was no diversity in these soldiers.

Erik glanced up and saw again the robed figure, standing on the circular walkway of the keep. The figure moved a hand, lifting it up, and the light crackled again before the town's defenders all took another step. He thought he heard shouting and wondered if it was this mysterious person. He then looked to Bu Al'Banan standing with his remaining men.

"We can't fight them and each other at the same time!" Erik yelled, keeping his eyes trained forward.

"Are you Erik Eleodum?" Bu asked, shouting. He must have remembered seeing him as well.

"I am," Erik called back.

"When this is over," Bu said, "you will be the Dragon Sword's first victim. Call it revenge for killing my father."

"We both know he wasn't your father," Erik replied.

He saw Bu shrug out of the corner of his eye.

The blue ball of light that hovered above the keep pulsated, its circumference growing and shrinking, hissed, and then popped. The robed figure then clapped and the ball exploded, spreading its light out like the canopy of a tent, shedding an eerie glow over the whole of the town. The spearmen attacked.

"*Do we fight together?*" Erik shouted to Bu.

Bu didn't answer, even though the spearmen were almost upon them.

"*Yes!*" Bu finally replied. "*We fight together!*"

Erik ran the first ghostly soldier through with Ilken's Blade. It was as if the spearman felt nothing. There was no cry of pain when Erik withdrew his blade, and the spearman tried to fight on but faltered. Erik lopped his head off.

"They're already dead," Bryon said after he'd also removed a head.

But these men didn't look like the dead in Erik's dream. They weren't rotting. They bled. They breathed.

"No," Erik said. "They're possessed."

The spearmen fought with expertise and precision, but they fought without emotion. They were programmed, moving in predictable patterns. And when singled out, they were almost useless.

The first to die was one of the Hámonian knights. Another one of the knights tried to run to the man, lying face down, when Bu yelled.

"*Garrett, leave him!*" Bu yelled. "*Stay in rank.*"

Another one of Bu's men was the next to go down. He looked like he was from Golgolithul, like Bu and the old, grizzled soldier fighting next to him. One of the ghostly soldiers stabbed the man in the leg. Another spear punched through his shoulder, breaking through the other side.

"*Together!*" Erik cried. "*Bu! Together!*"

Bu and his two other men seemed to understand. They ran to Erik as Bryon and the dwarves stood shoulder to shoulder with each other. Bu pressed hard against Erik, groaning angrily as he did, and the old soldier stepped to the other side, next to Bryon. They stepped forward, slowly, methodically. Beldar and Bofim jabbed out with their spears. Any of the possessed who got by the ranged weapons met dwarvish and elvish steel. The smell of searing meat filled the air with each man Bryon killed. Every once in a while, the older soldier seemed to get bored. He would break rank, kill four or five of the spearmen, and then step back in line with Bryon. Erik remembered him as well, especially his scar. He had cut the man with Bryon's sword and expected him to be dead. He was a true fighter.

Erik heard a cry from their ranks and saw blood running from

Nafer's forehead. The tip of a spear blade poked out of Bofim's chest, and even Bryon's face was covered in blood, a mixture of his and his victims'. The other Hámonian knight, Garrett, faltered and went to one knee, but then fought back to his feet with a loud, angry grunt. The three dozen that had stood in front of Erik were dead, only to be replaced by more possessed soldiers coming to fill their ranks. And still Erik and Bu and the others fought on.

Eventually, Erik stared at a dozen men, faces drawn and gaunt, and eyes blank and black. Another blue ball appeared above the keep, and when it flashed, the spearmen stopped and stood at attention.

"You have failed me!" said a voice in Westernese that reverberated through the valley. It was an angry voice, deep and malicious. It reminded Erik of the Lord of the East.

The robed man threw his hands to the sky and streams of lightning erupted from the ball of light, enough to strike each of the possessed spearmen. They shook and convulsed, their faces still and emotionless, until they fell to the ground, bodies smoking and dead.

"You as well!" the voice shouted, causing the ground to shake.

Another bolt of lightning struck the giant leader, still standing up on the ledge. The giant's hair caught fire, followed by his beard until his while head was a ball of flame. He screamed as he shook, not the deep roar that the giants normally emitted, but a frightened, dying scream. The giant slumped forward and slid down the valley slope. The other giants ran.

The black keep glowed a faint blue before turning green, then yellow, then blue again. It hummed as the colors pulsed, dimming and brightening as if with a heartbeat. The light began to travel up and down the keep, from the top to the bottom and then to the top again. The ground shook, and Erik lost his footing, going to one knee. What rubble and dirt and snow that was on the ground began to levitate, floating chest high. It all gathered to the keep and all sound disappeared. It reminded Erik of the dragon, just before she unleashed her fiery breath. He knew an attack was coming, a powerful attack.

Erik cried out in surprise, but his voice might as well have been a whisper as he felt himself lift off the ground and float like a feather on the wind. The same happened to his companions and Bu and his remaining man. There was a crack of thunder as the ground lifted and visibly rolled towards Erik. Everything went dark before an explosion emitted the brightest of lights that burned his eyes as debris was sent everywhere. The force struck Erik like a battering ram and he, his friends, and Bu and his men flew backward. Purple lightning began to strike the ground, causing instant fires, and as cries of pain filled the air, Erik hit the ground, and everything went black.

Specter knew he should have felt cold. The wind howled, snow seemed to fall horizontally, and the ground was hard with ice. He could see minor tufts of grass in places, and in others, he knew he was walking over frozen water, but he was warm, his skin almost hot to the touch as new life, new power coursed through his veins like lava from a volcano. He was untouchable.

The blizzard meant he could only see clearly a few paces in front of him, but as he squinted through the white world around him, he could see red specks in the distance as his magical vision picked up on the heat living bodies emanated. He had found one body, its heat slowly dissipating, mauled and opened, half-eaten by some creature. In the distance, moving towards the mountains, he saw something shaped like a bear. Ahead, where the huge black structure dominated the skyline, he saw larger figures, probably more giants, and the smaller shapes of men and dwarfs. He followed.

As the day waned, and dusk gave way to the night, Specter felt the unmistakable zing of magic, mighty, powerful magic, as it disturbed the air all around. Again, on the horizon, he saw it, flashes of blue and purple and white. Then, in one blinding moment, the intensity grew and grew into a magical explosion that shook the ground and rushed through the air at incredible speed. For a moment, until his own magic righted himself, it tossed Specter around like a fallen leaf. As he regained his footing, he nodded his head in acknowledgment of the awe he felt for such power.

"Fealmynster," he muttered.

47

———

*E*rik surveyed the valley where the battle took place. Dead littered the field. The buildings were nothing but dust. All that stood there was Erik and the black keep, looming over him.

He saw his companions. The others who fought with them and yet, opposed them. Bu was dead. So were the old, grizzled soldier, and the Hámonian knight. Bofim and Beldar were crumpled together, the shafts of their spears shattered as if they were made from kindling wood. Nafer lay face down, but Erik couldn't see his back moving with breath. Turk's head rested on Bryon's chest as if he had crawled to his cousin, but he too was still.

Erik walked to Turk and his cousin, and his hands shook, his nerves getting the better of him. The dwarf didn't move. Bryon didn't move. Erik rubbed his face angrily as if he could scrub away what he saw.

"Wake up," he told himself.

He crouched next to Turk, placing two fingers to the side of the dwarf's neck. He felt no pulse. Something caught in his throat as his stomach churned. He looked at his cousin. Bryon was looking away, and when Erik leaned over him, Bryon's eyes were open. His chest wasn't moving. Erik reached to him, but then drew his hand back quickly as if the body would burn. He wanted to check his pulse, make sure, but he couldn't.

"Wake up, damn you," he said again.

He felt tears collecting at the corners of his eyes.

"Not again," Erik muttered. "No ... no ... no ..."

He closed his eyes, sitting back on his heels and rubbing his temples with his thumb and forefinger. He opened his eyes. They were still there.

"*No!*" he screamed, his head flung back.

He stood, his fists clenching so hard his fingernails dug into his palms, drawing blood. He didn't know what to do. He paced back and forth, breathing quickly, clenching his teeth so hard, his jaws hurt. He rubbed his hands through his hair.

"It's just a dream," Erik said. "Wake up. Wake up. Wake up!"

But where were the dead? Where was Sorben Phurnan? Where was the laughing and the scuttling and the smell of decay? Where were the mysterious cloaked figure and the shadow that had been in his dreams recently? Someone would pay for this. Pay with their life.

I need my sword.

He couldn't find Ilken's Blade, but his golden handled dagger was still on his hip. His dagger was never in his dreams. It couldn't be a dream.

Why won't you talk to me?

Nothing. Silence. Emptiness. Death.

What will happen if I use you?

Erik put his hand on the handle, drawing the blade halfway before he stopped. The dagger explicitly told him not to use it. It would be to the destruction of both of them.

"Use it," a voice said. "Find out."

Erik turned to see a man standing in front of the keep. A cowl covered most of his face, although Erik could see the outline of a chin. As he walked, the black robe lined with silver thread that covered his body dragged along the ground.

"Who are you?" Erik asked.

"Your dagger is powerful," the robed man said. "Use it. Bring your friends back to life. Destroy the keep. Kill Sustenon the Damned."

"Can it do that?" Erik asked. "Can it bring a man back to life?"

"You have seen its power," the robed man said, stopping only a few paces from Erik. "Do you know what that dagger is? Do you truly know what it can do?"

Erik didn't say anything. He heard a distant roar, the flapping of wings, and the rushing of hurricane-like winds. With a great crash, the dragon—his dragon—landed atop the keep, turned her head to the sky, and belched a column of fire that drowned out the twinkling of the stars.

She looked down at him.

Pathetic.

He growled as her voice rang inside his head.

"You saw what it did to her," the robed man said. "It can do it again."

Erik drew the dagger.

"Listen to your heart, Dream Walker," another voice said. This one croaked with age and sounded familiar.

He looked around and saw no one else. Turning back, he saw the robed man pull his hood back, revealing a young face, one not much older than Erik, with long, wavy brown hair and big, brown eyes. His face was smooth and didn't look like he could grow any form of beard.

"Do it," the robed man said. His voice turned hard and angry. "Kill the dragon."

You can try.

Her voice was deep and menacing and condescending.

"Listen to your heart, Dream Walker," the old man's voice said, and Erik knew who it was.

Go away old man. You sent us on the wrong path. You sent me on a road of destruction.

"I sent you on the road you needed to take, Dream Walker."

"Kill her," the robed man said, the volume of his voice elevating. "Ignore that old man and kill the dragon."

She spat another column of fire again. Erik could feel the heat, the devastating intensity of her breath.

"Kill her," the robed man said again, this time his voice harder and deeper.

Dream Walker.

Erik looked about, confused. His heart raced. He looked up to the dragon, and he could hear her laughing. He looked at the robed man. He looked to his dead friends. He breathed faster and faster and faster and ...

48

ℰrik opened his eyes. He thought at first he was floating, then realized he was being carried. He watched the ceiling pass by, a solid piece of black stone. He tried moving his arms, but they were stuck to his sides. He looked down. There were no chains, no rope, no bindings of any sort. He looked to his left and right. Black walls with torches at regular intervals. He was on a litter carried by four men, their faces pale green, their eyes soulless pools of black. The possessed. The ghost men.

"Where are you taking me?" Erik asked. He struggled to move his arms and legs, but still couldn't.

The ghost men wouldn't look at him. It was as if they weren't even aware he was there. When he tried to raise his head, a green hand pushed him back down. The man whose hand it was didn't look at him when he pushed him back, but he was far stronger than he looked. There was the hint of magic in his touch.

It seemed like they had been walking for hours, and they finally stopped and set Erik down on the ground. He still couldn't move.

"Erik Eleodum," said a familiar voice, the one Erik heard outside the keep.

Erik felt himself lift—he was floating this time—then his feet turned to the ground, and he stood, his arms and legs still immobile. The man wearing the silver and black robe stood in front of him. He looked young, barely ten summers older than Erik. Clearly, this wasn't a wizard who was a hundred years old. Then again, how old was Andragos?

The man smiled. It was a kind smile. The way his wavy, brown hair silhouetted his face made him look almost ethereal, angelic even. His skin looked soft, almost like a young girl's and seemed to glow, his jawline more round than sharp. And his brown eyes were large and wide and welcoming.

The man stepped to Erik, unfolding his hands underneath the sleeves of his robe, now palms up.

"Where are my friends?"

"You know where they are," the man said. "You saw them."

"It was a dream."

The man shook his head, stepping closer.

"No. It was no dream, Erik Eleodum," the man said. "Your friends are gone."

Erik's stomach twisted. His chest hurt. His breathing became sporadic, and he tried to hold back his tears, but he felt them escape and roll down his cheek into his beard.

"No," Erik muttered.

"Yes," the man whispered. He stood right in front of Erik. His eyes inspected him. "I'm afraid so."

Erik looked away and swallowed hard. He would be sad some other time. He would grieve later. He remembered when he wanted to find Ilken's blade and gathered himself, steeled himself, and looked back at the man.

"You killed my friends," Erik said. "That was a mistake."

The man clapped his hands and laughed, revealing perfectly straight and brilliant white teeth. This man was not real. He was an image created by magic.

"You personally killed many of my men," the man said. His smile was gone, and where he appeared pleasant and welcoming, he now looked menacing. He lifted a hand, forefinger extended threatingly. "That was the mistake."

"You killed them," Erik retorted. "You could have killed us from the very beginning. Why didn't you?"

The man shrugged and dropped his hand as if his anger was a pretence.

"I wanted to watch you," he said. "See what you could do."

"You're the wizard of Fealmynster," Erik accused.

"Sustenon, at your service," the man said, extending a hand. Erik still couldn't move. "Oh, my apologies."

Erik's right hand lifted without him wanting it to, and Sustenon took it and shook it. The skin felt cold, like the flesh of a dead animal, handled before it is cooked. Erik's arm moved back down and was stuck back next to his body.

"Yes, I am Sustenon of Fealmynster," he said. "Some call me Sustenon the Damned, but I don't feel damned. I feel great."

Sustenon twirled around, arms lifted up like one of his sisters showing off a new dress. There was something effeminate about the man, but Erik knew he was powerful and his demeanor false.

As Sustenon did his display of vitality, Erik finally looked around the room. It was circular, and like the halls, torches were placed at regular intervals on the wall, which was also made of black stone. A round, single-stepped dais stood in the center of the room. An altar, a singular, square piece of white marble stood in the middle of the dais, a blue light emanated from the top and extended upward to the ceiling, which must have been twenty paces tall.

"Your men are possessed," Erik said.

"Only because they want to be," Sustenon said, standing still again.

"You killed them," Erik added.

Sustenon's smile was gone again. He straightened both his arms next to his body, clenching his fists. He looked very different, and his youthful appearance could not mask the true person beneath the façade.

"*Failure!*" Sustenon shouted, his voice a deafening roar shaking the room and cracking the floor under Erik's feet.

As quickly as the anger arose, Sustenon relaxed again and noticed the damage to the floor. He tutted, and he snapped a finger. The cracks were gone.

"I don't like failure," Sustenon said, but it was as if he said he didn't like a particular color.

Erik said nothing.

"You failed, didn't you," Sustenon went on, smile still on his face. He leaned in close to Erik. "You failed your mission, didn't you?"

"What I did ..." Erik began, but Sustenon held up a finger and shook his head with a muttered, "Tsk, tsk, tsk."

"You shouldn't interupt," Sustenon said. "It's not polite. The Lord of the East is not as powerful as he thinks. But you failed him, didn't you?"

Erik looked away, looked at his feet. He didn't care about failing the Lord of the East. That was the least of his worries

"You failed King Skella, too," Sustenon said. "He trusted you, didn't he? He let you give the Lord of the East the Dragon Scroll because he believed in you. He thought you could save his people ... maybe even the world."

"He knew the risks," Erik said, tilting his head back and looking at Sustenon, trying not to reveal the immediate pangs of regret.

"Yes, he did," Sustenon replied. He folded his hands behind his back and smiled, took in a deep breath, and sighed slowly. "But did Befel? Did your brother truly know what dangers lay before him when he left home? And when you went with him ... well, you just saw it as confirmation that he was doing what was right. You failed your *brother*."

Sustenon leaned forward, hanging on the final word before he shrugged and turned around, facing the altar at the center of the room.

"But, of course, it wasn't just him you failed," Sustenon continued. "You failed Drake and Vander Bim, Mortin, Threhof, Thormok and Demik. All dead … because of you."

Sustenon turned back around.

"So you see, my dear Erik Eleodum, I know more than you think," Sustenon said. "I know that you've now failed your cousin and your friends. All so willing to give their lives for you. And you let them, didn't you? They pledged themselves to you. You were their leader, Erik, and you returned their loyalty by leading them where?"

Sustenon shrugged his shoulders again, closed his eyes, and shook his head, a look of disappointment spreading across his face.

"To … their … deaths," Sustenon added. "And let's not forget your parents. All they ever wanted was a son who would love and obey them. Have you done that, with your adventures, letting your brother die, ignoring your duties on your father's farm?"

Sustenon waited as if expecting a reply.

"Did you, Erik?"

Erik did want to, but he slowly shook his head.

"No," he said, his voice a whisper.

Sustenon then unfolded his hands and steepled his fingers in front of his face, pressing his index fingers against pursed lips. He breathed deliberately, thinking, contemplating. He dropped his hands.

"Simone."

Erik looked up at the mention of his wife's name.

"Now there's the biggest failure of them all," Sustenon said. "You left her. She could have had a life, a family, and you left. And because she is a loyal and good person, what did she do, Erik? She waited for you."

Sustenon turned and started walking the circumference of the room.

"She is the most beautiful woman in the free farms of Hathgolthane, and she waited … for you."

Sustenon was on the other side of the altar. He looked at Erik, the blue light casting odd shadows across his face, and pointed at him as he spoke.

"She waited, and you show up, asking her to marry you, and, of course, she accepts, thinking this man who she had been loyal to would return the favor. But were you? Are you?"

Sustenon completed the circle of the room, walking quickly and deliberately, meeting Erik face to face, so close Erik could feel his breath.

"No," he said. "You put a baby in her belly, and then you left. And now, because you have now failed the Lord of the East for a second time, she will die. Your baby will die. Your family—mother, father, sisters—they will all die."

Erik cried out as if he stood over their bodies. He didn't try to hold the tears back anymore. Sustenon was right. Erik had failed everyone he loved and, because of him, they had already, or would all lose their lives. And here he was, still very much alive.

"What did they ever see in you, Erik?"

"I don't know," Erik replied amidst sobs. "I never wanted this. I never wanted to be a leader, or a fighter, or anything."

"*No, no, no!*" Sustenon yelled. "Don't make excuses. I hate excuses. You say you never wanted any of this, but how do you feel when people call you Dragon Slayer? Troll Hammer? Wolf's Bane? Hero? You delight in it, don't you? You say you never wanted any of this, *but you welcome it with open arms!*"

Sustenon stepped back, opening his arms with a sarcastic smile on his face.

"What could they have seen in you?"

Erik closed his eyes, the vision of Simone in his mind's eye. She looked beautiful. But then he remembered the way she looked in his dream. Bloody. Her belly open. His baby gone. Bruised. Beaten. Raped.

"You, the leader, son, husband, cousin, brother," Sustenon continued, "you're nothing but a coward. Your family will die, Erik, because ... of ... you."

"I would do anything to save them," Erik muttered, more to himself than anyone else.

"What could you do?" Sustenon said, exasperated. Then he gripped his chin gently with his thumb and index finger as if thinking. "What could you do? You are such a failure and a coward. Perhaps the Lord of the East would forgive you, perhaps he would at least spare your wife and your baby if your final act was one of bravery. Maybe ..."

Sustenon stopped, crossing one arm along his belly and resting his other elbow on his hand.

"Maybe, he would forget your failure if he knew that you recognized your immense shortcomings, and acted to save your family," Sustenon suggested.

"What could I do?" Erik said.

He couldn't stand to look at his accuser because he spoke the truth. Erik's shame weighed on him like a boulder, and he cried and shook his head in despair.

"You could redeem yourself Erik by taking your own life," Sustenon said quietly as if coaxing a reluctant child. "End it. End the pain. End the misery. Be brave, just once, and own up to your biggest failure ... your life."

Sustenon snapped his fingers, and Erik collapsed to his knees. When he raised his head, Sustenon had something in his hands, and he extended it to Erik. His golden-handled dagger.

"Take it, Erik," Sustenon said. "End it all."

Erik's arms became free, and he grabbed the dagger. He looked at it with tired, worn eyes. Then, he looked at his hands. The dagger fell from his hands, clanking on the floor.

"I didn't think so," Sustenon said, shaking his head before he looked up to his men, waiting by the entrance to the room. "Take him away."

49

———

*E*rik sat on his hill. The branches of the willow tree seemed to droop lower than usual, and the night sky was starless. He stared out over the grassy plains, a gentle wind causing the tops of the grass to flutter. There were no dead. The mountain range in the distance, the black and ominous clouds that sprouted purple lightning, they weren't there either. The man was gone too, the one he knew but, then again, didn't. Erik was alone, and that's how it should have been. He didn't deserve anyone.

Erik stared down at his dagger. It was odd that it was in his dreams. It never had been before. A part of him thought it couldn't be in his dreams, but here it was, in this place he had visited so often. Even his dagger didn't want to have anything to do with him. When he was lonely, he could count on his dagger, but he hadn't heard from it since it saved Nafer. What a waste? Nafer still died.

You're a fool. People called you a hero, and you started believing them. You're no hero.

He wondered what would happen after he died. Had he actually passed away? Would he now spend all eternity in this place alone? Maybe if he wasn't yet dead, when that happened, would he wander with the rest of the dead, those who lived wretched and meaningless lives? Would a golden carriage come to get him? Would he join his brother? He doubted it very much. He wasn't worthy of joining his brother. Befel was the true hero.

Erik hadn't really thought about how many had lost their lives because of him. It wasn't just the dwarves that had died on their first journey or men like Vander Bim and Drake. It wasn't just Befel or Bryon. No. It was thousands; the people of South Gate. He was to blame for every single life lost to dragon fire. And since he released the dragon, how many more should blame him for their deaths in the future? Tens of thousands? Hundreds of thousands? The dragon would eventually kill everyone in the world, and it would all be because of him.

Sustenon's words rang through his head. Do something brave. He wasn't brave. He was a coward, the worst kind of coward who pretended to be brave. What did anyone ever see in him? What did his parents see in him? He was a terrible son, nothing compared to his older brother. He couldn't run a farm. He couldn't carry on the Eleodum name. And because of him, the Eleodum name would cease to exist. His sisters? How could they look up to him? He only hoped and wished they would marry men that were the opposite of him.

He thought of Turk and the other dwarves. Demik had given his life, specifically for Erik. He was a warrior, and Erik was nothing. His stomach twisted when he remembered the dying look in Demik's eyes. And poor Turk ... he had put so much trust in Erik, in men, in Erik as a representative of men. Better he would have left with the zealot mayor Fréden.

Finally, he thought of Simone, his wonderful wife. She was far too beautiful for him, and yet he was the one she waited for; the one who married him. He buried his face in his hands. She had wasted so much of her life on him. His child would be better off without him. His father, Rikard would help raise the child, and his father-in-law, Brok. His child would be better off because of his death. In fact, it wouldn't even be his child. Some other man, a real man, would come along and raise the baby. Thank the Creator.

Erik looked to the sky. The Creator. He must be looking down on him with utter disgust. Maybe this last act of bravery would please him. Maybe.

Dream Walker.

The voice was a whisper on the wind, and Erik looked out over the field of grass.

Dream Walker. Why do you let a deceitful man sway you so?

I am nothing.

"The Friend of Dwarves, a coward?" said the voice, and now it was no longer in his head.

Erik looked up and saw a cloaked man standing amongst the grass. He lifted the cowl, and it was the old man from Eldmanor.

"I am a coward. I am no friend of dwarves," Erik said. "If anything, I am an enemy of dwarves."

"Wolf's Bane? Troll Hammer? These names are given to cowards?"

"The deeds of other people that I have taken credit for," Erik replied.

"Dragon Slayer?"

"The dragon wouldn't even be awake if it wasn't for me," Erik said.

The old man laughed.

"If you believe that, you truly are a fool, Dream Walker," he said. "You are a faithful son, husband, and father. Does that make you a coward?"

"They're better off without me," Erik replied.

The old man laughed again, but there was a hint of sadness, even pity in the sound. Erik didn't want pity, so he shook his head before he looked down at the ground.

"Dream Walker."

Erik lifted the golden-handled dagger and gripped it, blade pointed at his chest, with both hands.

"No more talk," Erik said. He could feel the tears in his eyes. "No more."

He plunged the blade into his chest. His whole body felt on fire and then nothing.

Erik woke. A single candle sitting on a small table at the end of his bed was the only light in the room, and it glowed with an eerie green flame. He sat up. There was nothing else in the room—just the bed, the table, and the candle. No. There was something else next to the candle. He squinted his eyes and saw his dagger, the handle glinting in the flickering flame. Everything else was gone—Ilken's Blade, his shield, his armor, his haversack—but his dagger was there. How?

He stood and crossed the room and grabbed his dagger.

"Speak to me," he said, sitting back down on the edge of the bed.

Nothing.

"Why would you speak to me?" Erik asked. "I'm not worthy."

He stared at the ground for a long time and then looked at the dagger again.

"One last act of bravery," he said, gripping the handle of the dagger with both hands and pointing the blade towards his chest. "One last act of bravery to compensate for a life of cowardice."

50

———————

Bu awoke to find Bao Zi, staring down at him. Sitting up, he looked about and discovered he was in a prison cell. Sir Garrett was there, leaning against a wall, unconscious. His face was badly bruised and his breathing shallow. Blood caked his beard, long and unkempt from lack of grooming and shaving. There were other men in the same cell. It was large enough for several dozen men. There was no door in the prison bars and no lock.

"Where are we?" Bu asked.

"Dungeons," Bao Zi croaked.

"Is it just you, Garret, and me?"

"No," Bao Zi replied. "Andu survived. He's in the cell across from us."

Bu stared over and saw his sergeant, still and lying on the floor. The dwarves were over there, as well as the other man Erik Eleodum was with. But he didn't see Erik.

Bu's head hurt, and his vision was blurry. He tried rubbing the heels of his hands against his eyes, but that only made the pain worse.

"What happened?"

"Magic," Bao Zi replied. "This is a cursed place."

He nodded to another cell, one cattycorner to theirs. Bu stood, shaky at first, and, when he finally regained his balance, walked to the bars. He stared in the direction that Bao Zi had indicated and then took an involuntary step back. A spider ... a giant spider was locked behind those bars, and when Bu looked at it, it hissed and spines along its legs rattled. Saliva dripped from its mouth, and Bu could see its fangs protruding as its two feelers fiercely rubbed together.

"Something's excited it," Bu said, and then he saw why.

Two creatures—that's all Bu could call them—walked down the hall. They were large, lumbering bipedal things. Their skin was all gray and ashen. One had four arms, two sets on top of one another, while the other had three, its third arm sticking out of its chest. Their faces remotely resembled a man's, although the one with four arms had no nose, no ears, a bald head that looked like lumpy dough, one eye half a hand's span lower than the other, and a mouth that was entirely too big for its head. The other had wild hair that hung in long, dirty clumps. Its nose looked more like a pig's snout, and its mouth was too small for its face, with cat-like eyes and pointed fox ears, complete with black tufts of hair. Two people followed them, both men, naked, and their skin was the pallid green color similar to the soldiers they fought outside the keep of Fealmynster. Erik had called them possessed ... and that was how they walked.

The two lumbering creatures held no weapons, but when they stood in front of the cell containing the giant spider, the eight-legged creature backed away, apparently afraid. The four-armed beast produced a key from its pocket and a door formed in the bars, bearing a large lock. It opened the door. It looked at the two possessed men. They didn't say anything. They simply walked through the open door, at which time, the four-armed monster shut the door with a loud bang. The door disappeared, as did the lock.

A line of silvery spider silk struck the first possessed man in the chest, throwing him against the bars of the cell, but the man didn't seem to notice. He just stood there, arms by his side, and let the spider stand over him and spin him into a cocoon of webbing. It dragged him into the darkness of the cell and did the same thing to the second man.

"Damn the gods," Bu cursed.

As the lumbering, multi-armed creatures walked by, they looked at him and laughed.

"An ártocothe," one of the dwarves said. Bu was surprised he spoke Shengu.

"What is that?" Bu asked.

"The spider," the dwarf said. "It's an ártocothe. You have seen them before, yes?"

"Yes," Bu replied. "In the mountain. They attacked our camp."

The dwarf nodded.

"We found their lair," the dwarf said, his voice carrying a hint of pride. "We burned their nest."

"How is he?" Bu said, nodding to Andu. He didn't really care, but making small talk helped time pass.

"Not good," the dwarf said. "He is near death. In here," the dwarf shook his head, "he won't last much longer."

"He's a fool," Bu said, albeit a loyal fool. Bu still didn't like the man. He remembered him as a sniveling, pompous prick captured when Patûk had Aga Min destroyed. Any man worth the title of nobility, as Andu was—even if he was from a small house in Golgolithul—would have died before letting himself be put in chains.

"We are all fools," the dwarf said.

"He deserves to die," Bu added.

"Most of us deserve to die," the dwarf replied.

Bu shook his head. This dwarf thought he was some sort of philosopher.

"Where is Erik Eleodum?" Bu asked.

"How do you know his name?" the dwarf asked.

"It's hard not to," Bu replied. "Dragon Slayer. Troll Hammer. Friend of Dwarves."

"I suppose," the dwarf said.

"He killed Patûk Al'Banan," Bu said.

"You were there," the dwarf said, "weren't you? When we stole back the scroll?"

Bu nodded.

"You were too, then?"

The dwarf nodded.

"I don't recognize you," Bu said. "All you dwarves look the same to me. I was surprised Erik Eleodum killed Patûk. I thought that man would live forever. It seemed even death was afraid of him."

Bu gave a quick laugh.

"If any man could have killed him," the dwarf said, "it would be Erik."

"Is he dead?" Bu asked.

The dwarf shook his head.

"Where is he?" Bu asked.

The dwarf looked upwards.

"Up there. The wizard took him. I saw them carrying him into the keep as I was waking up from whatever magical force knocked us out."

"What do they want with him?" Bu asked.

"I don't know," the dwarf said with a shrug. "He's a remarkable man. He's the one that wounded a dragon."

"He killed my father," Bu said.

"Come now," the dwarf retorted, "we both know Patûk Al'Banan wasn't your father. There's little point in pretending in here."

"Nonetheless," Bu said, "he was a mentor. He was like a father."

"He was a brutal man," the dwarf replied, "a cruel man."

"Still," Bu added, "I plan on killing Erik Eleodum. And his family."

"Good luck with that," the dwarf said. He muttered something in Dwarvish to someone else in his cell. A tall man stood up and came to the bars. He was muscular but lean with long, brownish-blond hair. His eyes squinted as he stared at Bu.

"If you plan on killing Erik," the man said in Westernese, "you'll have to kill me first."

"My pleasure," Bu replied, also speaking Westernese. "Can I have your name before I kill you?"

"Bryon. Bryon Eleodum."

"His brother?" Bu asked.

"Cousin."

"I must say, you'll have to kill me as well," the dwarf said.

"And your name, master dwarf?"

"Turk Skull Crusher."

The three other dwarves in the cell also stood.

"I suppose I would have to kill them also," Bu said.

The man—Bryon—nodded with a smile.

"It seems Erik would be a hard man to kill," Bu said.

"It seems that way," Bryon replied.

He watched as the lumbering monsters walked back between the cells. He heard some creature whining, and then it banged on iron bars, its voice changing to a deep, reverberating roar.

"Sounds like a snow bear," Turk said.

"Why would a snow bear be trapped down here?" Bu asked.

"Why would an ártocothe be trapped down here?" Turk said. When Bu didn't say anything, the dwarf added, "The wizard who controls this place was banished from Gol-Durathna for performing magical experiments on people. I am sure they are here for that purpose. We are most likely here for that purpose. The possessed soldiers, those hulking deformed things that serve as prison guards, I am sure they are all the results of his experiments."

"I'd rather die," Bu said.

"Aye," Turk replied.

"If I only had my sword," Bryon muttered.

"Your sword is so special it would help you now?" asked Bu, his tone clearly mocking. "Nonsense."

"It's elvish."

"Elvish? As in magical?"

"Aye," Bryon replied.

"Magic or not," Bu said, "what good would it do you here?"

"The blade burns," Bryon replied, "with a purple heat. It can melt flesh and bone alike … iron too."

"I remember your cousin wielding a magical sword like that when he killed Patûk."

"That was mine."

"Good for you," Bu replied. "Too bad you'll never see it again."

"We'll see," Bryon said.

One of the man creatures—the four-armed one—walked by and slammed a wooden baton against the iron bars of Bu's cell.

"Shut your mouth!" the beast said in Shengu, spittle flying through the space of the bars and striking Bu in the face.

"You'll pay for that," Bu said defiantly.

The creature laughed. He said something to the other one in a language Bu didn't understand. The other creature joined in the laughter.

"How?" the four-armed creature asked, speaking Shengu again.

"Come in here and find out," Bu said.

More laughter.

"You'll be a fun one to break," the man-beast said. "The boss will turn you into something interesting … and I'll enjoy watching you be fed to one of his pets."

The guard walked away, and Bu shrugged as if he didn't care, but now felt a little less brazen. He could no longer see the spider—an ártocothe the dwarf had called it—but he could hear the sounds of the arachnid draining its victims of their bodily fluids; they just stood there and let it happen. He heard the roar of a snow bear again, which caused more howling to echo through the dungeon; imprisoned wolves he presumed.

"This place is cursed, Bao Zi," Bu said, leaning against one of the cell walls and sliding to his behind.

"Truly," Bao Zi croaked.

"We need to get out of here," Bu added.

"How?"

"I don't know," Bu said, "but a fate worse than death awaits us in here."

"What about the Dragon Sword?"

"What good will it do me if I am dead?" Bu replied.

"What about this Erik Eleodum?" Bao Zi tilted his head towards the man's cousin and dwarvish friends. "What about them?"

"Right now, I don't care about them," Bu replied. "In truth, if I get out of here, I may never care about them. If Eleodum is up there, I pray to every god that is out there that he can somehow set us free."

51

———

*E*rik stared at the steel of his dagger.

"I'm sorry, Mother. I'm sorry, Father."

He gathered his courage, closed his eyes, took a deep breath in, and ...

Dream Walker.

The voice was a whisper in his head.

Erik.

He wasn't dreaming. When he heard his name, he suddenly remembered his mother's parting words to him. They came to him as did the old man's words.

I can't lose another son.

He remembered what his father had told him.

You're a good man. I am proud of you. Proud of the man you have become, the leader, the friend, the brother ... the husband.

Those weren't words of derision and disappointment. Those were words of pride. He remembered looking down at Demik, as the dwarf's life slipped away. Saw the dwarf's face in his mind as he spoke.

There's no greater sacrifice than a friend to give his life for another friend.

Would he have done that for a coward?

Erik

Why would the old man start to use his name?

Erik

Now he recognized the voice and looked down at his dagger in his hands. It glowed, faintly, every gem in the handle giving off the faintest light. Erik closed his eyes, and in his mind, he saw a woman. She was tall and lean, muscular yet beautiful. A slight breeze blew aside her golden hair revealing her pointed ears. An elf. She wore a long, blue gown and a steel breastplate over the gown. She held a long sword in her right hand. The weapon could have been his dagger, only larger. An elfling clung to her left leg, a little boy, but Erik could tell what the child would look like when he was grown. It was the elf from his vision after his baptism.

A shadow blotted out the sun, dark and looming and moving quickly, too fast to be a cloud. In his vision, Erik looked up. The wings were unmistakable. The shape of the body. The tail. A dragon.

Erik's heart quickened, and he felt his hands shake. But the elf maiden and her boy were unmoved. It was as if they recognized this dragon and, to confirm Erik's suspicion, the dragon landed, softly, behind the she-elf. It nuzzled her hand as if it was a dog. The elfling boy ran to the beast and hugged its nose.

The world around Erik shimmered and disappeared. It reappeared as the same place only the elf maiden was gone. The elf that stood before him was the elf from his dwarvish baptismal vision. He wore a suit of plate armor adorned with ornate embellishments. He now carried the sword his mother had held. His shield was shaped like a dragon wing, and what looked like two dragon horns extended from his helm. Stones of all different colors of gems—red, green, blue, white, black—but perfectly round, floated about the elf's helmet, spinning about his head and moving with him. They reminded Erik of the stones that Mardirru had given him and the white stone he had found in the white, broken tower. The elf warrior stepped up onto the dragon's foot, pulled himself up its leg using its scales and sat in a high saddle. He looked at Erik and nodded. Then he heeled the dragon. The beast roared, spit fire, and then leapt into the sky, flying high and away.

"A dragon rider?" Erik muttered.

Yes,

Erik opened his eyes and was back in his room. His dagger had replied.

The elf from my baptismal vision?

Yes.

Why do I keep seeing him? Why here? The tower? My baptism?

The dagger made no reply. Erik thought of the sword the elvish warrior carried and how similar it looked to his dagger. He again saw the stones floating around the elf's head and then looked at the stones in the handle of his dagger. This warrior had looked powerful, a mighty warrior, maybe a wizard even. Erik remembered the elf maiden and the young elfling that ran to her; her son. Then, he remembered something his dagger had said to him a long time ago, something about a mother's voice. Erik's eyes went wide, and then he nodded in understanding.

You were an elf, once. That was you in my vision.

Yes, I was the Commander of the Dragon Riders, a most honored position among my people.

So, there are good dragons and evil dragons?

Yes.

I see. But where have you been?

It took all of my energy to save your friend. I risk much by speaking to you now.

Then why do it? Why save Nafer? Why talk to me now?

I sensed how much you cared about your friend. I remembered caring for someone as you do. You are no coward, Erik. For you to take your own life, especially using me, has more ramifications than you could possibly know.

Eric could tell the dagger's strength was waning again, but he had to know more.

The sword you wielded. The sword your mother had. That was the Dragon Sword.

Yes.

I thought it was a weapon possessed by the dwarves.

They created it and gave it to the elves...as a gift.

The sword, Erik thought, *looked so much like...*

Erik looked at the dagger. He remembered how it transformed when he fought the dragon. His eyes went wide, and he almost dropped the weapon.

You ...

Yes. You have had the Dragon Sword all along.

Why not tell me?

I am bound, Erik. I could not.

Then why have I traveled all this way?

I will explain in due time. For now, before I cannot communicate with you anymore, you must take me to the altar of Fealmynster. You saw it, didn't you?

Yes.

You will place your sword, Ilken's Blade, next to me, on the altar, along with the dragon tooth you cut from the dragon's—Black Wing's —mouth.

They're gone.

No. They are hidden away. You will find them in the dungeon. Your friends are there too.

My friends! My cousin! They aren't dead?

No. They are imprisoned in the dungeons, with others. You can still save them.

I have no weapon.

You have me.

That was all Erik needed, but when he moved to the door, it was locked. How could he go about this? Sustenon wanted him to kill himself for some reason, and if he did, Sustenon would know, and his possessed soldiers would come to his room. Sustenon was a powerful wizard, and, as the old man in Eldmanor said, he was a Dream Walker too. He would know if Erik was pretending. He would know what Erik was doing.

Dream Walker.

The whisper again. It was the voice of the old man from Eldmanor.

I know what you need. I will cloud his vision as he walks through the land of dreams. Wait behind the door. They will come.

Erik waited behind the door of his small room. He heard footsteps and someone standing on the other side. A key turned, and the door opened slowly as a commanding voice said something in a language Erik didn't understand. The door opened fully, and when they must have seen the room looked empty, there were shouts and men marched in. He could see the backs of two possessed soldiers, but there was someone else with them. He sounded angry. He pushed passed the possessed soldiers and into the room. He was some odd combination of mountain troll, an ogre and a man. Maybe some animals too. He had heard Sustenon performed experiments.

The thing was large, half a man taller than Erik, with a sloping brow, a flat nose, little horns growing through thick, black, knotted hair, an under bite exposing small fangs, and three, cat-like eyes. It didn't wear a shirt, and its skin was gray and scaly and covered in warts. Bony protrusions ran the length of its spine. Its knuckles almost dragged along the ground—the arms were so long, and its legs were so short and bowed it walked with a wobble.

It said something again. Its voice was angry. It pushed one of the possessed men out of its way and punched another. They ignored the assault and simply continued to stand at attention. Then, the beast put its nose to the air and sniffed. It smelled him. Erik gripped the dagger in his right hand.

The man-like creature reached out to slam the door shut and as it did so, Erik lunged and thrust the dagger upwards into the meaty part of its arm and twisted. Blood exploded from the wound, and the creature howled. One of the possessed soldiers thrust his spear at Erik, but he easily dodged the predictable attack and stepped on the spear shaft, knocking it out of the soldier's hands. As the soldier drew his sword, Erik dropped his dagger back on the table and picked up the fallen spear and thrust it into the large beast's armpit. It howled again, flailing about and knocking the bed over, in turn, knocking over the soldier who had drawn his sword. The soldier's head hit the wall with a thump, and he went still, lying across the mutant.

The other soldier attacked with his sword, and Erik rolled underneath the attack, coming up right in front of the possessed man and jamming his dagger into the underbelly of his jaw. The man's black eyes rolled back, and he fell to the ground dead. Erik hoped he had released the man from a tortured life of servitude.

As the mutant struggled to its feet again, Erik grabbed the spear once more and thrust it into the inside of the giant creature's leg. Again, it howled, ripping the spear from its body, bringing flesh and blood with it, but it squared up to Erik.

"Fool," Erik muttered with a mirthless smile.

"I'll feast on your bones," the creatures said, speaking Westernese.

"You speak," Erik said. "You looked too stupid to form words."

The beast roared and charged Erik, who dove to one side and watched it run headfirst into the door, pulling it off its hinges and smashing it open into the corridor outside. With a grunt, it staggered to its feet, only for Erik to thrust one of the soldier's swords through an eye into its head. The creature's mouth opened, and it crashed to the floor, taking the sword with it.

Gasping slightly to get his breath back, Erik returned his dagger to his belt, pushed a sword through his belt as well, and grabbed a spear, holding it in his left hand. He clambered over the broken door and looked left and right. Both directions looked the same. Left. He knew to go left. He didn't know if it was his dagger or the old man from Eldmanor, but the inclination was unmistakable. He ran. The walls were black stone, and all looked the same. Everywhere was so similar, Erik even wondered if he was running in place. But he eventually came to the end of the tunnel and a stairwell that wound both up and down. Down. He would free his friends first, and retrieve his sword and the dragon tooth, as his dagger had instructed him.

Erik ran down the stairs. Just like the hallway, it looked the same. At regular intervals, he saw a new hallway, and then the winding staircase continued downward. He heard footsteps. He stopped. The tips of spears came into view, followed by two possessed men, their faces green and their eyes black and emotionless. He kicked out at one. The man fell backward and tumbled down the stairs. The other pointed his spear tip at Erik, but he kicked it out of the way and jabbed with his own spear. The blade easily slid into the soldier's neck.

Erik grabbed the dead soldier's oval, leather shield, holding it high to his face in his left hand and his spear over the top of the shield with his right hand. He slowly descended and saw the first soldier crumpled in a broken heap at the well of another hallway, his neck at a peculiar angle. Erik stopped for a moment to peer down the hallway. No one, nothing, was there. He continued down the stairs, eventually coming to the bottom.

For the first time, this section of the keep was different. The stones that made the wall were large and gray, stained with green moss and crawling with creepers and fungus that didn't need the sun. The hallway he stared down was short, and he could see bars at its end, dividing the corridor. Two possessed soldiers guarded the door in the bars. They stared, blankly.

Erik moved quickly, keeping his shield and spear high. When the possessed soldiers saw him, they immediately dropped their spears to fighting positions.

The soldiers were strong and well trained, but they were robotic in their movements, lacking the tactical ingenuity a normal soldier might have. Their attacks were precise but predictable. As one stabbed at Erik, he twirled, swinging his spear behind his head and then towards the soldier, slamming the shaft into his face. Blood exploded from the soldier's nose, knocking him back, but he seemed unfazed. It didn't matter. Erik had opened him up enough to expose the man's neck, and he attacked, killing the soldier with one quick strike. He stuck the spear between the legs of the other soldier, tripping him, and when he looked up, Erik slid the blade of his spear into his eye.

Erik stood in front of the bars. There was no door, no hinges, no lock.

Use me. Point me at the iron bars.

Erik did as his dagger told him, and the bars shimmered, and the outline of a door appeared. A large lock materialized as well, and Erik jammed the dagger blade into the lock. The latch shook, and, with an audible clicking sound, the door opened.

Erik walked into an enormous room of cells on two sides, all consisting of three stone walls and bars on the front with no doors. It looked like there were more cells around the corners at the end of this first group. He didn't have time to see who or what was in the cells, as the sound of the door opening attracted two more possessed soldiers. They marched towards Erik, crouched, in their fighting stances, shields up to their eyes. Erik deflected one strike, returning with a strike to the inside of the leg and then an exposed eye. He swatted away another, punching out with his shield, pushing the man back and then skewering his belly as he tried to regain his footing. As he heard the loud smack of a head against stone, a mighty roar came from somewhere in the dungeon.

Erik looked to his left and saw an open door, weapons lining the walls. He ran to the room and found it was the place where the jail keepers kept the weapons of those who were imprisoned in this horrid place. Scanning the room, he saw Ilken's Blade, Bryon's elvish blade resting against the wall next to it. Then he saw Turk's half-moon bladed battle-axe. He saw the scabbard with iron embroidery made to look like vines and thorns, the broadsword once wielded by Demik Iron Thorn and now carried by Nafer. Nafer's four-spiked mace rested next to the broadsword.

Erik grabbed his sword and Bryon's as well as his shield, slinging it across his back. As he exited the room, he came face to face—rather, face to chest—with another grotesque monster that remotely looked like a man. The thing had three arms, one of them springing from its chest, and the middle hand reached for Erik and he instinctively swung upwards with Bryon's elvish sword. The blade flared and the man-creature roared as black blood spewed from the severed arm. The monster punched at Erik, but he easily dodged the attack, the large mallet-like fist slamming into the stone wall. Erik heard the crunching of bone as the stone cracked, and the beast pulled its hand away, bloodied and deformed.

Two down, one to go.

Erik stabbed upwards with Ilken's Blade into the creature's upper ribs, slashing the elvish blade across its belly at the same time. The beast howled, turning on Erik, but as he removed his sword from the monster's ribs, exposing bone, he slashed it across the creature's knee. It went down, now eye level with Erik, and he punched the elvish blade into one, large, oversized, bulbous eye, and it exploded in a white and yellow filmy mess. Ilken's Blade slashed across the beast's neck, and black ichor spewed from a severed artery. Bringing the elvish blade to the other side of the monster's neck brought it down. Face down it scratched at the ground as its life drained away in a black sticky mess, its final breath a gasping gurgle.

52

---

ndragos had followed Erik as long as he could. He watched him pass the ice bridge, marveling that they had solved the riddle of its elvish magic. How? His cousin's sword maybe? As they walked along the ice bridge, magic—he presumed it was Elvish—began to cloud his vision, but what was the purpose? The memory of a white tower passed through Andragos' mind, followed by a huge gate in a wall. If Erik made it through there, he would be closer to Fealmynster.

He knew Specter, the Isutan assassin was close, and he knew a hard fight awaited the young man and his friends, but he didn't know exactly when the two would come across each other. Maybe Erik would have to deal with Sustenon first? Apart from the dragon, that would probably be Erik's hardest challenge. It would certainly be the most complex.

As mad as Sustenon the Damned was, he had grown even more powerful in the last few years. He was always a strong mage, even when Andragos had tutored him, but he reveled in his power and thought himself more than he was. He wanted to be a god—and that was his undoing—but Erik would have to be at his best to win this battle. But what about the comment Syzbalo had made?

There was something the Lord of the East had said that had struck Andragos as worthy of considered thought, something about a mistranslation of the Dragon Scroll. He had made sure to make a copy—unbeknownst to Syzbalo—before handing the scroll over to the Lord of the East and had found some inconsistencies in the text as well. It was something about a key, but not a key, a golden dagger. Erik had the key. No, that wasn't it either. He tried again to bring up a vision of Erik and his companions but to no avail.

Andragos sat in his favorite chair and closed his eyes to think. Images and ideas flashed across his mind and then he smiled and opened his eyes again. Now he understood, The Lord of the East thought himself so brilliant, with his Isutan mage and his witches and his growing knowledge of the dark arts, but the dagger Erik carried with him was not just a key. No. It was the Dragon Sword.

Tread lightly, Erik.

A knock came at the wizard's door. He thought it might be more inquisitors from Fen-Stévock. For a while, it seemed as if they came every day. The Lord of the East had become bold in his mistrust of Andragos, sending such men to his door, looking for a traitor's family and friends, as if he would know where they were. Andragos soon sent them back on their way to Fen-Stévock.

Andragos knew they would come. He saw it on Syzbalo's face when they spoke of the traitor, Ja Sin. He knew the Lord of the East didn't believe him. But there was no one to seek out; Ja Sin's family was no longer at Andragos' cottage.

The Black Mage had foreseen, long ago, that times like this might arise. He knew that his position would put him at odds with the leaders of Golgolithul, and so he created a portal in each of his dwellings. They led to various places, most of them pleasant and hospitable. The portal underneath his cottage led to a forest meadow on the other side of the world, a place no man had discovered yet, a place once inhabited by elves. He had taken care of the elves and much of his magic he gathered from the ruins they left behind. His thoughts of the white tower made him believe Erik had discovered a similar place—a meadow much like the one to which he had sent Ja Sin's family. Of course, Fealmynster was once such a meadow as well.

It was just happenstance that Andragos had discovered it, and, as the years passed by, he learned the elves had many such meadows around the world. It was cool in his meadow, but not too cold. As far as he could tell, there weren't any real predators of note, save for the occasional cat, but the magical wall Andragos had built around the enchanted meadow kept them away. That's where Ja Sin's family was.

Another knock came.

"Imperial Inquisitor!" the harsh, almost metallic voice said on the other side of the door. "Open, Mage!"

Andragos had had enough. He felt his face grow hot as he stood and faced the door. How dare these men, these insects not worth the dirt on the bottom of his boots, speak to him in such a manner? He lifted a hand, and when he blinked his eyes, he was behind the inquisitor and his two thugs.

The inquisitor was a stout man with short-cropped black hair and a blue cape that fell from two large pauldrons. He wore a long-handled sword at his side, and his plate mail, as he turned to face Andragos, was all black, the breastplate embossed with the Lord of the East's symbol. His two guards wore similar mail with blue capes as well. They wore helmets with pointed visors and carried kite-shaped shields and spears in addition to their swords.

"What do you want?" Andragos asked.

"Open your door," the inquisitor commanded, again, his voice metallic and hard.

"You may want to think twice about the manner in which you speak to me, insect," the Messenger replied. "I could kill you in the most horrible way, bring you back to life, and then kill you again ... over and over and over. I am tired of your bothersome inquisitions. I am done with you. Go away."

He had thought, once, the Lord of the East didn't know about this cottage, away in a remote forest of Northern Golgolithul. He would have to be more careful in the future.

The inquisitor looked flustered and scared, eyes wide, and face red. He didn't quite know whether he believed the Black Mage, especially after Andragos flashed the man an insincere smile. Part of him wanted to kill this man. He wanted to turn him inside out, remove his intestines through his ass and show them to the insolent bastard before crushing every organ in his body ... slowly.

"Orders of the Emperor of Golgolithul," the inquisitor said. "Open your doors and let the inspection happen."

"Emperor?" Andragos asked with raised brows, and then simply said, "no."

The two guards stepped towards the mage.

"You don't want to do that," Andragos said.

They didn't listen and lowered their spears to point at him. Enough was enough. He lifted a hand, and the black mail of one of the guards began to glow red, then white. He heard a scream emanate from the visored helm, but as the guard dropped his shield and spear and tried to remove the helmet, he found it was sealed and locked into place. He fell to his knees, his screams muffled by the visor, but Andragos could smell burning hair and flesh. Smoke spilled from the crevices in the armor, and, within moments, the guard fell forward. The iron of the mail began to melt and pool on the ground, the grass underneath catching fire until there was nothing left but a black spot.

Andragos looked to the other guard, who took a step back. He lifted his other hand and made a fist. The guard's armor began to twist and crumple until it folded in on itself as if it were made of paper the Messenger had simply crushed in his hand. As the iron folded in, stabbing flesh, blood spilled from every joint and crevice in the armor. The man in the armor screamed, dropping to his knees. The sound of skin ripping, flesh tearing, and bones breaking filled the air until only a ball of iron remained.

The mage looked at the inquisitor.

"I am not scared ..." the inquisitor began to say, but something stopped his voice.

Andragos held up a hand.

"Yes, you are. You are trying to hide your fear, but I can smell it, see it, feel it."

Andragos closed his eyes and took in a deep breath. He could feel the souls of the two dead men floating about, hovering just above their bodies. The Black Mage smiled and opened his mouth. He sucked in the air and felt the souls drift towards his mouth. They tried to resist, but there was no resisting the Harbinger of Death when he was driven to the point of rage. He sucked the souls into his mouth and felt their essence. Immediately, he felt stronger.

"You are stupid," Andragos said. "Syzbalo is stupid. The Lord of the East thinks I am weak. My thousand years in this world have made me more powerful than any other wizard in the world."

A ball of fire, small and compact, appeared in Andragos' other hand, and he pushed it towards the inquisitor. It floated through the air slowly, and the inquisitor was unable to move. The ball of fire was close to the man, and it simply touched a bit of his cape when the fabric burst into flames. The man screamed as fire consumed his hair, the skin on his face melting away. As Andragos stared into the dying man's eyes—the inquisitor falling to his knees, screaming and begging for mercy—the wizard wondered if the Lord of the East, or the witches or the Isutan mage were watching him; he suspected one of them was.

"Do not send another inquisitor," Andragos said to whoever may have been listening. "I will not be as merciful to the next one."

Andragos turned to see Terradyn and Raktas dragging a man roughly between the two of them, his hands bound behind his back, his face puffy and bruised.

"This is the traitor," Terradyn said as he pushed the man to his knees.

Andragos looked at the man. He remembered selecting him after Patûk Al'Banan had foolishly attacked his caravan. Several of his

Soldiers of the Eye had died in that attack while four hundred of the general's perished, but that was his plan. He only needed to have killed one Soldier of the Eye. Undoubtedly taught by Patûk, Andragos had selected the man because of his prowess, his strength, and his skill.

"You were a spy for Patûk?" Andragos asked.

The man didn't answer, and Raktas struck him across the face with the back of his hand.

"Were you?" Andragos asked.

The man nodded.

"He attacked me," Andragos said, "and wasted four hundred lives just to implant a spy into my ranks. That has never happened before. Quite a sophisticated ruse, wouldn't you say?"

The man didn't reply.

"Patûk is dead, you know," Andragos said.

"I know," the man said flatly.

"So, do you now serve this Bu?" he asked.

The man just shrugged.

"You have caused Fen-Stévock quite a bit of trouble," Andragos said, crossing his hands behind his back and walking around the man.

The traitor tried not to make eye contact with the mage, but Andragos caught the traitor looking at him through the corner of his eye. He also saw the man looking at the crumpled ball of iron that was once an armored man and the remains of the burning inquisitor.

"Fen-Aztûk is the true capital," the man said.

Andragos laughed.

"Of course, it is," Andragos said. "Because of you, ten thousand or more people died."

Andragos stood behind the man, and the traitor looked at the mage over his shoulder.

"Traitors," the man said, "all of them."

"Even the women and children?" Andragos asked.

"Yes," the man said, and then looked forward.

"You know, when I first came to Golgolithul, it didn't exist. It was a collection of small city-states, each city its own government, vying for control of the east. A bunch of backwards men, awkward and clumsy all chasing a single whore. It was I, the Black Mage, who helped unite these city-states into what is now Golgolithul. Did you know that?"

"No," the man said with a shrug of his shoulders.

"The Aztûkians, Stévockians, and any other family have no claim on the east," Andragos added, his voice an iron-hard hiss. "I am Golgolithul. Not Patûk or Syzbalo. Not the Aztûkians. Bu or Pavin...me."

He realized he was talking to himself and he turned back to the man kneeling before him.

"I had thought about asking you to spy for me," Andragos said, and he didn't miss the disapproving looks both Raktas and Terradyn gave him. "I need a spy in this Bu Al'Banan's court."

"Never," the traitor said.

"I figured as much," Andragos said.

He waited a while, letting the man kneel there, probably wondering what was going to happen next.

"The Lord of the East found a spy in his court, you know," Andragos said.

"I didn't know of him," the traitor replied.

"He wasn't one of Patûk's," Andragos said. "No. He was from Gol-Durathna. The Lord of the East had him flayed alive."

"Sounds about right," the traitor said.

"Shall I do the same with you?" Andragos asked.

"Do as... do as you wish," the traitor said, trying to sound resolute and tough even though something caught in his throat.

"I am sure you would be a strong and brave man," Andragos said, "up until I cut away that first piece of flesh, and you saw it fall to the ground. Maybe I would cook it in front of you, maybe eat it. It has been a long time since I have tortured a man in such a way. How would that make you feel, watching me eat your flesh as your life slowly slipped away?"

He walked around the man so he could face him. The traitor didn't look tough anymore. He tried not meeting the mage's gaze, but Andragos jabbed a finger hard under the man's chin and made him look at him. Blood oozed where the fingernail had cut flesh.

"Once, I would have done it," Andragos said. "I would have flayed you, healed you, flayed you again, healed you, and then flayed you a third time, just because I could. But not today."

Andragos nodded to Terradyn, who held up a giant, two-handed sword. He brought it swiftly down against the traitor's neck and, with a single swipe, severed the head. He did it so quickly the head stayed in place for a moment, and then toppled to the ground. Andragos looked up.

"Find this man's battle brother," he said, "Execute him in the same way."

Andragos commanded one hundred Soldiers of the Eye, his personal guards, loyal only to him. They trained in twos. Each soldier had a battle brother, and they were responsible for one another—their training, clothing, food, guard duties. If one made a mistake, both were punished. If one was valiant in battle, both were rewarded.

When Raktas and Terradyn gave him a hard look, suggesting they disapproved of his leniency with both men, he added, "I will not torture a man like the Lord of the East, and I will not kill his family and friends; nor will I burn his whole company, but the men must know that a failure of their battle brother is failure for both."

Raktas and Terradyn bowed, but they weren't appeased. He knew it. He had softened lately—saving Ja Sin's family was proof of that—but when the need arose, Andragos the Black Mage, The Messenger of the East, the Herald of Golgolithul, the Dealer of Death, could be just as terrifying as the Lord of the East.

53

*E*rik ran down one aisle of cells. It was clear that this place was old, ancient even. The stone of the cells was covered with years of muck and dirt and moss. He stepped gingerly, the floor slick with lichen and moisture. Without visible doors, the thick, iron bars of the cells rose all the way to the ceiling and seemed to be a part of the structure, as there were no holes from which they originated or in which they inserted.

Men and women of all shapes and sizes and colors filled the prison, but the dungeon didn't just house humans. He saw a cell filled with white-haired wolves twice the size of a normal wolf, a cell with ogres—the giant man-like humanoids that he had seen in Finlo— antegants, dwarves, a creature with the torso of a man and coppery skin and the body of a scorpion, and another creature with the body of a man and the head of a wooly bull or bison. The prisoners clamored when they saw Erik. They yelled and cried and screamed and reached through the bars at him. The scorpion man clicked and hissed, the wolves barked and howled, and the man with the head of a bison snorted and grunted. They all looked lost and tortured, shadows of what they would have looked like outside this hell.

Erik understood some of them, pleading for him to set them free, and he wanted to. He presumed his dagger would help again, but he needed to see if he could find the others first.

"I will free you," he said, standing in front of a cell containing several people—far too many for the size of the prison—and staring at the mournful, brown eyes of a woman who once had pale skin, now caked with dirt, and wild, brown, curly hair that stuck out in all directions and clumping together. Her dress was so torn and tattered, she might as well have been naked, and Erik's stomach knotted as he considered what horrors must have befallen her in this place as she sat in a cell with mostly other men.

At the end, as he suspected, he turned the corner and ran into another hallway.

"Erik!"

He turned to see Turk, clinging to the bars of a cell.

"Turk!" Erik yelled, almost in tears.

"Cousin, get us out of this hell!" Bryon yelled, pressing his face between the iron bars.

"I will, let me just get my dagger and ...."

"Watch out Erik!" Turk yelled, but it was too late.

Erik felt something slam into him, and he flew through the air, landing with a thump on the stone floor, expelling the air from his lungs. As he regained his vision, albeit a little blurry, he saw a cell—rather, a cage—with an ártocothe in it. The giant spider hissed, and the bristles on its legs rattled. The arachnid tucked its abdomen under itself and spewed silky web at Erik. As the webbing shot towards him, he rolled to the side and jumped to his feet, the spider's attack barely missing him. To his right, he saw another cage with a huge, white bear—entirely too large for the cell—with three little cubs. It roared and butted its head against the iron, shaking the space around them.

As he struggled to his feet, Erik saw the thing that had struck him —another magical experiment mutant that was, Erik suspected, once a man. Before he could really see the creature, it barreled into him again, lowering its shoulder into Erik's chest and sending him backward, this time against a wall. The ártocothe hissed and the snow bear roared as Erik slid to the ground and fought the unconsciousness that tried to take him.

His vision blurry and his legs wobbly, Erik pushed himself to his feet. The beast standing in front of him had four arms and a rotund belly that sagged over its belt. Its mouth consumed half its face, and its eyes were lopsided, one half a hand lower than the other. It yelled a cry of victory and came at Erik. He moved out of the way just as the monster slammed its shoulder into the wall, cracking stone, shaking the foundation, and bringing bits of rubble down on Erik's head.

Erik swung the elvish blade at the lower of the creature's left arms. The magic in the sword flared to life and burned through flesh, removing the arm. The creature didn't even seem to notice. In fact, it laughed. Where the wound glared at Erik, red and raw and smoking, two more appendages grew, tendons and arteries knitting together as new arms erupted from the injury with the sickening sound of tearing meat.

The monster—now with five arms—swung both of its right arms at Erik. He caught the lower arm with Ilken's Blade, removing it, while catching the upper arm with Bryon's sword, removing that one. Just like the other arm, two more arms grew where there had been one.

"By the Creator's Beard!" Erik exclaimed. "If I cut your head off, will you grow two more?"

Erik ducked and rolled underneath the monstrous jailor. An errant back hand caught Erik on the shoulder, throwing him into the iron bars of another cell. He jerked away quickly as a gigantic cat, its fur as white as snow, leaped at the bars and growled angrily. The hair on the beast's back stood on end, and it swiped at Erik through the bars, its claws huge and sharp. He saw the jailor remove a large key from a pocket in his tattered pants. The monster said something to the key, and as Erik had done with his dagger, a door with a lock appeared in the bars of the cell of the large cat. Erik heard the latch of the lock turn and saw the door begin to open. He pushed the door closed as the cat leaped again, but there was no use trying to keep it closed. The animal was so powerful, Erik found himself flying backwards.

The snow cat crouched and growled at Erik, ready to pounce. It was a magnificent animal, far too lean for its size. It was hungry. Its claws scratched against the stone floor, and its canines were like daggers. It leaped at Erik and he rolled under the great cat, coming up in front of the jailor. As the grotesque creature swung down at Erik, he slashed a hand away, producing two more hands. He cut away a foot, and two more feet grew. Erik raised an eyebrow as the magical abomination stumbled, two feet emerging from the same ankle was awkward and difficult to manage.

Your magic is flawed.

Erik swung Bryon's elvish blade at the monster's knee, removing the leg from the knee down. It fell with a thundering crash, two lower limbs growing just below its knee. The jailor struggled to get up as it tried to balance on two feet coming from the same ankle and then on its other leg—one part of it sticking out to the side while the other twisted inward.

Erik heard a growl, turned, and dove away just as the cat leaped at him again. It skidded across the floor, crashing into the jailor just as it regained its footing, taking him to the ground again. The monster yelled and cursed and swatted the cat away in anger, sending the beast into the wall with a hiss and a pitiful growl.

As the cat shook itself, clearly stunned by the attack, and as the jailor tried pushing himself back up to his feet, Erik prepared for another assault, but the cat looked to him and then the monster. It growled low and deep and, instead of attacking Erik, who had done nothing to it, lunged at the jailor, who had swatted it into the wall. The cat's powerful jaws latched onto the throat of the grotesque mutant and, even though the jailor squeezed the cat with all its might, black, sticky blood began to spill to the ground.

Erik rushed next to the cat. He could see blood coming from the animal's nose as the jailor squeezed it with all its might, so he dropped the elvish blade, gripped Ilken's Blade with both hands, spied a spot on the side of the mutant's head, and stabbed. The magical abomination's eyes went wide, and then it stilled, black blood gurgling from its mouth. When Erik retrieved his sword, the thing went still, and the cat limped away, purring and licking at its feet.

Erik stabbed again, Ilken's Blade going cross guard deep just to make sure. When he removed the sword, the jailor fell forward. Erik heard a low growl and looked to the cat. It had crouched again, ready to strike.

"No," Erik said. He dropped his sword and kneeled, lowering his head into a subservient position. He slowly extended a hand. "I won't hurt you."

The cat crouched lower, shifting back and forth on its haunches, its tail up and flicking to the left and right. Erik suddenly regretted dropping his sword, and eyed Ilken's Blade and the elvish blade and wondered if he had enough time to get to either one. However, the cat stopped growling and slowly limped towards Erik, sniffed at his extended hand, and licked it, its tongue rough. Erik dared himself to be courageous, and, as the animal licked his hand, he cupped its chin with his other hand, scratching the cat. It purred, and Erik transitioned to its ear. It rubbed up against Erik and, even in its weakened state, almost knocked him over.

"It seems I've made a new friend," Erik said. "Now, what do you say we release all these poor prisoners?"

The cat purred and moved out of the way as Erik stood. He was about to retrieve his dagger, and then remembered the key in the monster's pocket. He retrieved it and held it up in the dim, greenish torchlight of the dungeon.

"You don't know the words?" someone said in Westernese.

Erik turned to see a man—at least the remnants of a man, emaciated with black eyes like the possessed—staring at him from a barred unit at the end of one of the many rows of cells. He didn't have the green, pallid skin like the possessed soldiers, and he pressed his face hard against the bars. He looked sick, his ribs poking through stretched skin, his hip bones clear and pointed, barely holding up his tattered pants. His cheeks were sunken, jawbones and cheekbones visible, and his hair was thin and hung from his scalp in splotches.

"Clearly," Erik said, and he heard a low, almost inaudible growl, rumble from the snow cat's throat.

"I've listened to that thing say the incantation every day for the last ... well ... I'm not sure how many years," the man said. "I can help."

"Your eyes," Erik said.

"Yeah," the man said. "I was once one of those green freaks, but my will was too strong."

The man smiled, revealing a mouth with half its teeth missing and the other half rotting.

"You are so special you get your own cell?" Erik asked.

The man kept smiling.

"I wasn't always alone," the man said, "but all my cellmates left me."

"Left you?"

"Food, torture," the man said with a quick shrug.

"Will the incantation let everyone out?" Erik asked as screams and yells for help echoed through the dungeon.

"I only know mine," the man replied, "and the one for the cell next to me and across from me. But I know of a way you can release everyone."

"Tell me," Erik said.

"Let me out first."

"No," Erik replied.

The prisoner laughed. It was the laughter of a madman, a wheezing, sporadic laugh.

"I have seen death," the man said. "What can you do to me? I have seen the void of magical enslavement, years of nothing but nightmares. Leave me here. Fine. Then you will die down here too. You will know what death looks like."

"I know what death looks like," Erik said.

The prisoner stepped back, away from the bars, and just stared at Erik with his black, blank eyes.

"Release the prisoners next to you and across from you," Erik said, looking at the adjacent cell, filled with a dozen men, all similar looking to this fellow, and the one across from him, filled with a mixture of men and women. "Then, I will let you free yourself."

The man seemed to think for a moment and then nodded. Erik lifted the key in front of the men's cell. The prisoner leaned forward, the stink coming from him almost unbearable—a mixture of dirt and body odor and fecal matter. When he spoke, his breath was equally as horrid, the smell of rot. As the imprisoned man spoke, the bars in the cell next to him shimmered, a door appearing with its lock.

"Use the key," the man said, and Erik obeyed.

The lock clicked, and the door opened. The men just stood there for a moment.

"Go," Erik said. "You are free."

No one moved.

"They don't know what to do," the once possessed soldier said, laughing. "They are broken, little more than animals."

Erik remembered the cannibals that had attacked them in the Gray Mountains. He remembered the destitute that called the streets of Finlo their home and the homeless prostitutes that hung around *The Lady's Inn.* He remembered the slavers that had attacked Marcus' gypsy caravan. Were they little more than animals?

"They're scared," Erik said. "That is all. Open the other one."

The same thing happened. The man spoke an incantation. A door and lock appeared. Erik opened the door. And the cell's inhabitants just stood there.

"Now me. Now me. Now me," the man said, jumping up and down as much as he could and pestering Erik like a petulant child.

"First," Erik said, "how do I release everyone else?"

The prisoner looked at him, furrowed eyebrows and face growing red.

"That wasn't the deal."

"I'm changing the deal," Erik replied.

"I don't know," the man replied.

"You lie," Erik said.

The prisoner screamed, clutching his hands into fists, holding them to his face, and falling to his knees. He began to weep and pull out clumps of his remaining hair.

"Please!" he shouted. "I don't know!"

"Hush," Erik hissed.

"I don't know," he said through tearless sobs. "I only know mine."

Erik looked at the man warily. Emaciated, broken, insane. He was wasting time. He thought to try his dagger in the cells here, but maybe the door it opened before did not have the incantation spell. He tried it, and it didn't work.

"You can open the cells all at once," said a gruff voice, coming from behind Erik.

He turned to see a dwarf. His head had been shaved and not kindly. His scalp was scarred and scabbed and patches of reddish-brown hair hung in dirty clumps. Like all the others, he looked like he hadn't eaten a real meal in some time.

"How?" Erik asked, and the dwarf looked surprised the man could speak Dwarvish. "Do you know the incantation?"

"At the end of this hall, there is a door," the dwarf said. "It won't be there now, but after speaking a spell over the key, it will appear. In that room, there is a lever that will release all the prisoners."

"Do you know the spell?" Erik asked.

"I do," the dwarf replied.

"By listening to the jailors like this broken fellow?" Erik asked, pointing to the other prisoner, now lying on the floor and crying.

"No," the dwarf croaked. "I used to be a jailor."

Erik glared at the dwarf.

"Be disgusted all you want," the dwarf said, his eyes without emotion. "I am disgusted with myself. But, when presented with the option of becoming bear or cat scat, or working for a madman, I chose the latter. Besides, I rescinded my position, and this is what it got me."

"Alright then," Erik said to the prisoner curled up on the cell floor, "speak your incantation."

The man hurried to his feet and spoke the spell over the key. His door and lock appeared, and Erik freed him. At first, the man didn't know what to do, then he cheered. He limped to the cell next to him, grabbing one man by the shoulders.

"You are free, you fool!" he shouted, pulling on the man as much as he could in his weakened state.

When the other prisoner stumbled out of the cell, the snow cat growled, and Erik patted the animal on the neck. The freed prisoner looked around as if he couldn't believe what had happened. Finally, he fell to his knees and cried, lifting his hands up and then covering his face. The others finally spilled out of the cells. The broken man, the one who was once possessed, clasped Erik's arm, to which the snow cat growled again and he let go, backing away slowly.

"Thank you," he said, clasping his hands together.

Erik just nodded, and the man limped away.

"It warms my heart to see such kindness," the dwarf croaked sarcastically.

"Speak your spell, dwarf," Erik said, lifting the key to the dwarf's cell.

The dwarf did as he said he would, and, also as he suggested, a door appeared at the end of the hallway.

"The key will open it," the dwarf said.

"Erik!" Turk's voice was unmistakable. He called from the next hallway over. "Are you alright?"

"Fine!" Erik called back and then unlocked the door and went inside. He quickly stepped out of the room and slammed the door shut.

"What tricks are you playing, dwarf?" Erik asked. The room was filled with several dozen possessed men and women, all naked and all with green-pallid skin and black, blank eyes.

"They won't attack," the dwarf said, pressing his face into the bars of his cell. "They are food for the animals. They have been commanded to just stand there. The lever just inside the room will make all the locks appear."

"How?" Erik asked.

"By the gods, how should I know?" the dwarf replied, his voice dripping with irritation. "It's magic. I just know that it works."

Erik opened the door again. The snow cat growled and hissed as it stared at the pale-green possessed. He looked to his right and saw a lever. He pulled it. A loud click echoed through the dungeon. He turned and saw locks in all of the doors within his vision.

"There should be another lever next to it," the dwarf said. "That one will open the doors. Hurry. Sustenon will know you are down here if he didn't already. It is his magic."

Erik moved to pull the second lever, but then he spotted one cell that held a mountain troll. It was still big, as big as Erik remembered the ones from the Southern Mountains, but it was a shadow of its former self. It looked scared and beaten and broken.

Erik didn't want to set it free. He remembered what mountain trolls had done to Drake and Samus. He remembered what mountain trolls had done to Aga Kona. Those poor people. He looked down at the snow cat by his side. It looked up at him, and Erik was sure it understood him.

"No one deserves to be imprisoned like this," Erik said.

He pulled the lever. Another audible click echoed through the dungeon as hundreds of doors opened. The troll slowly left the cell, walking on all fours. It stared at Erik for a moment. Erik gripped Ilken's Blade, ready. The troll snorted, said something in its archaic language, turned, and ran from the dungeon. So many others did the same, from animals to people, all running, all blundering about, and all—undoubtedly—raising the alarm.

Erik ran back to the hallway in which his friends were imprisoned. The lever had unlocked all the doors ... all the doors. The snow bear opened its cell door with its head, its three cubs following it. It looked at

Erik. The snow cat grumbled, and the snow bear grunted. It looked from the cat to the man, back to the cat, and then over to its cubs. It plodded by Erik, its massive paws smacking hard on the floor. She watched Erik, over her shoulder, as her cubs passed him, making sure he, nor the cat, did nothing untoward. Another door slammed open and the unmistakable hiss and chitter of an ártocothe came from the darkness of the cell.

The ártocothe walked from its cell, looking every which way it could. Then, it locked its eight eyes on Erik. It hissed again, venom dripping from its feelers and fangs under its body. Erik sheathed Bryon's sword and retrieved his shield, crouching in his fighting stance. The spider took a few steps backward, ready to strike, and then it turned and ran, as fast as it could and paid no heed to other creatures, man or beast. It wanted to escape this place as badly as anyone else.

As Turk and Bryon and the other dwarves emerged from their cells, Erik ran to his cousin, wrapping his arms around the man and squeezing as hard as he could.

"By the Creator's Beard!" Bryon exclaimed. "What is that?"

Erik turned and saw what Bryon was referring to.

"A friend," Erik said, looking down at the snow cat.

"You are alright?" Turk asked.

"I am now," Erik replied.

"What a lovely reunion," someone said, and Erik turned to see the man who called himself the son of Patûk Al'Banan.

"You're welcome," Erik said.

"For what?" Bu asked.

"For rescuing you," Erik replied.

"Do you want your man?" Turk asked, pointing to one of Bu's soldiers lying on the floor of the cell. He didn't look well.

Bu shook his head.

"He is as good as dead and will only slow me down if I expect to escape this place," Bu replied.

"Well," Erik said.

"Well what?" Bu asked, his old, grizzled soldier stepping up next to him, the arm of one of the Hámonian knights draped over his shoulder.

"Are we done?" Erik asked.

Bu seemed to think for a while.

"For now," Bu replied. "I had every intention of killing you and taking the Dragon Sword, but the Lord of the East could send his whole army up here and still wouldn't succeed. I am going to go home to my kingdom and my wife."

Bu looked to his old soldier and then back to Erik.

"You saved my life," Bu said. "I think, for now, that deserves a truce."

"Perhaps. I could kill you instead, but maybe another time. Your weapons are in a room just around the corner," Erik said.

Bu gave him a curt bow, and the old soldier just grumbled. He turned and walked away, slowly, looking over his shoulder every once in a while.

"How do we get out of here?" Bryon asked.

"We don't," Erik replied. "At least, not yet."

"I don't understand," Bryon said.

"The Dragon Sword," Erik replied.

"To the Shadow with the Dragon Sword," Bryon said. "Haven't you had enough of this place?"

"More than you could imagine," Erik replied, "but we have to retrieve it. And we have to defeat Sustenon."

"Why?" Turk asked.

"All these people," Erik said, "all these creatures. They've been possessed, experimented on, terrorized, and tortured by this wizard. We owe it to them."

"Very well then," Turk said.

Bryon grumbled.

"Where do we find the wizard and the Dragon Sword?" Nafer asked.

"Up," Erik replied, pointing to the ceiling. "I was in the room where it was kept."

"You saw it?" Beldar asked.

"No," Erik said, "but there was an altar, and something tells me that's where we could find the sword."

"What do we do with him?" Bryon asked, pointing to the who once served Bu, lying on the floor of the cell.

"We can't leave him here," Erik said.

"I will carry him," Turk offered. "His master has cast him aside, and he will only end up as food for one of the many creatures in here if we leave him."

Erik nodded.

"And what about her?" Bofim asked, pointing to the snow cat.

"What about her?" Erik asked.

"Do you intend to keep her?" Bofim asked.

"I'll just see if she follows me," Erik said with a smile. "If she does, consider her an ally."

"That's a good ally to have," Turk said. "Lead on, Friend of Cats."

Erik obliged with a small smile on his face.

54

___

*E*rik and his companions passed a pack of white-furred wolves as they made their way to the depot of stored, confiscated weapons.

"Are they winter wolves?" Erik asked, speaking of the wolves he had encountered in the Southern Mountains that had a higher than animal intelligence and willingly served evil—in his case, the dragon from Orvencrest.

"No," Bofim replied, "simply wolves with fur to match their environment. I would imagine winter wolves might align themselves with a man like this wizard."

The wolves growled as they passed, staring intently at the snow cat, and the snow cat replied with a hiss of its own.

As they ascended the stairway to the upper levels of Fealmynster, Erik saw the signs of fighting and battle. Blood. Body parts. He saw the mountain troll, lying face down and headfirst on the third flight of stairs. At least half a dozen dead green-skinned, possessed soldiers lay around the beast, as well as another mutant. A part of him actually felt sorry for the troll.

At least it died free.

They had climbed another five flights of stairs when they found the dwarf Erik had freed, once a grotesque monster in servitude to Sustenon the Damned. He had killed even more possessed soldiers than the troll and two of the man-like monsters, but his fate was much worse than the troll, which had been simply too many spear and sword wounds. The dwarf looked burnt, the skin around his chest, legs, and arms peeled back as if it were simply the skin of some fruit. A look of terror was tattooed on the dwarf's face. Payback, perhaps, for betraying the wizard.

"Every damn level looks the same," Bryon grumbled as they passed yet another stair landing and hallway, only to continue to climb the seemingly endless stairs.

"That is one of the many maddening things about this place," Erik replied.

They came to another landing. Erik stopped. He felt the artery in his neck thump hard against the collar of his mail shirt and coif. His stomach twisted, and gooseflesh rose along his arms. He had been here before. As much as each hallway looked the same, he recognized this one. He readied his shield and gripped Ilken's Blade tightly.

"This is it," he said.

"How can you be sure?" Turk asked.

"I just am," Erik replied, and as if they needed some sort of confirmation, the snow cat growled, and the hair on the back of her neck stood on end. "Follow me," said Erik.

He didn't wait to see if they followed, but he knew his friends would. They walked slowly for a while, the sound of their feet echoing off the walls. The hallways curved with the curvature of the keep, so they couldn't see nor hear the coming troops, but Erik knew they were there.

The first possessed soldiers came into view. A spear flew over Erik's shoulder and thudded into the chest of the first soldier. Another one struck the man next to that soldier and both fell, dead. A hand axe thunked into the face of a third man, right between his eyes.

There must have been a dozen soldiers in all, marching through the hallway and led by a grossly fat mutant with two heads, four legs, and four arms. Its two heads looked different, one with long, matted hair and a messy beard, while the other one was bald with a droopy, oily mustache. Its skin was almost black and saggy, folds upon folds of fat layering its body, and the stink that came from the thing made Erik gag. He wondered if it was two men that the wizard had combined, melding their bodies together as another one of his experiments.

As large and powerful looking as the grotesque creature was, it was awkward and unwieldy in the hall. As it moved towards Erik, it squashed two possessed soldiers between its massive girth and the wall. Erik charged the thing, and as it swung at him with two of its arms, he rolled underneath it. He heard his friends engage the creature, unable to turn in the hallway with any sort of ease, as he fought with the remaining half dozen soldiers.

Their movements, as before, were so predictable and uniform, they weren't much of a challenge for the well-trained warrior. An army of these possessed soldiers would be a force to be reckoned with, especially against a nation such as Hámon, who used men-at-arms and peasant conscripts to fill the majority of its armies, but one on one—or six on one—against a fighter such as Erik Eleodum made them easy work.

Erik punched one soldier with his shield, breaking the man's nose, while slashing at the shins of another, bringing him to his knees. With one soldier blinded by blood and another on his knees, two more stumbled over the disabled men. A blade to the throat killed one and then across the chest incapacitated another. He kicked out at a knee and heard cracking. The soldier dropped, and he brought a knee into the possessed man's face. Ilken's Blade to the back of a leg hamstrung the last soldier.

Erik looked over his shoulder. The fat creature was on one knee, black blood covering its whole body. He saw the flash of a bright purple light, and one of the black-skinned arms fell to the ground, the wound crackling with red burn marks. The snow cat leapt onto one of the heads, biting at the bald scalp and clawing at its eyes, but still the mutant fought on.

"*Go, Erik!*" Turk shouted. "We will meet up with you!"

Erik ran. The hallway, like all the other ones, seemed never-ending, but he eventually came to a door he recognized. No one guarded it, and when Erik touched the brass handle, it opened without any effort.

He's expecting me.

A short hallway led to the circular room. Stepping into the hallway, Erik didn't see anyone, but someone—or something—could easily be hiding.

Careful, Dream Walker.

"Do shut up, Dewin," came an actual voice, the sound echoing a little in the high-ceilinged room.

Erik recognized the softness of Sustenon's voice, one that indicated a formal education, someone who knew people and could easily influence them. He almost convinced Erik to kill himself.

Dewin. So that was the name of the old man from Eldmanor.

"Yes, Dewin," Sustenon said, reading Erik's thoughts again. "Believe it or not, we were classmates."

"Classmates?" Erik said.

"We were apprentices together," Sustenon said. "Obviously, the practice of magic has not been as kind to Dewin's body as it has on mine."

"And for whom were we apprentices?" Sustenon asked. It sounded as if he was actually asking Erik if he knew.

Erik crouched, raising his shield to just under his eyes, and didn't move. He just shrugged, and though he didn't verbally reply to Sustenon, he knew the wizard would know his response.

"But it was Andragos, of course," Sustenon said, laughing.

He was a liar, this Sustenon. He was a deceiver, a manipulator, a crafter of honeyed words. He used words to sway people, hypnotize people.

"It's no lie," Sustenon added. "Andragos, the Black Mage, used to train wizards. We were two of his greatest students. I am a product of your beloved Andragos."

How did Sustenon know Erik had anything to do with Andragos? Beloved? What an odd word to use for the Messenger of the East. As if Erik and the Black Mage were friends.

"Of course," Sustenon continued, "Andragos has done far worse than I have; than I ever will. Thousands upon thousands of deaths are the fault of the Black Mage. I was persecuted for trying to perfect the race of men, for trying to make society better through my experimentation, and he is lauded for destruction and death. Fools."

Sustenon was nothing more than a whining child at that moment, and he sounded ... mad. Crazy was the only other word Erik could think of. He kept quiet, waiting for the tirade to continue.

"I am ostracized for trying to help my fellow man and yet Andragos is lifted up and given more power for destroying lives!" Sustenon complained, as his perfect skin got redder and redder. *"Why oh why can't I be heard? Why am I so misunderstood?"*

Sustenon had worked himself up into a temper tantrum, and as he yelled, the room shook, dust and rubble shaking loose from the ceiling. Erik now worried that the wizard would do something terrible again to appease his anger. From the short hallway, Erik could see the room brightening, and he felt the hair on his arms and neck stand on end. Something akin to lightning filled the room, zapping the ground and walls and leaving burn marks where they touched. Fire flashed in front of Erik as two pillars of flame struck the entrance but missed him as he was protected by the narrow hall. Then Erik heard a heavy breath and a deep sigh.

"I apologize, Erik," Sustenon said, still out of sight. "I am not being a very gracious host. I did, however, see that you did not have the courage to take your own life. Pity. You are truly a disappointment to the people around you."

Erik remembered his grandfather at that moment. He was a smart man, the smartest Erik had ever met. He told Erik a number of ideas and sayings to cling to in times of trouble, and one had encouraged him a lot in recent times.

The Creator is with you Erik, even in the deepest, darkest places.

But that wasn't the one that crossed his mind at this moment. It was something his grandfather had told him when he was a little boy, a time of tragedy in the free farms of Háthgolthane. A young man who lived several farms over from theirs—a man who was at that time perhaps as old as Erik was now—had left, the only heir to his father's farm, to serve as a deckhand in Finlo and make some extra money before returning home and taking over his father's farm. While out at sea, pirates had attacked the ship on which he worked, and he lost his life. When his body returned to Northwest Háthgolthane, the men who escorted the young man told tales of his legendary courage in battle, that they were still alive because of him. The very next day, the young man's father took his own life, so struck with grief.

"Why, Grandpa?" Erik had asked.

It was a double question. Why had a young man, knowing he would one day run a profitable farm, been so willing to die, and why would his father take his own life. His grandfather's response was the words Erik said to Sustenon now.

"Most men have the courage to die," Erik said, his voice stern and loud and sure, "but few have the courage to live."

There was a slight pause, broken only by Sustenon's deep and reverberating laughter.

"Spoken like a true coward," he said, but Erik knew the laugh was false and the wizard knew the truth.

Erik inched forward, still in his fighting stance, and as he came into the room, he could see Sustenon on the other side of the illuminated altar. The wizard clapped his hands, and lightning exploded from his palms. Erik thought it might be futile, but he raised his shield anyways and, to his surprise, the electricity splashed off the dwarvish shield.

"Tricky boy," Sustenon said through clenched teeth.

"Where are your minions?" Erik asked. "The men you have

possessed and changed for your supposed experiments that better mankind?"

"They are perfect, are they not?" Sustenon said, raising his hands up. "Do you not see? They feel no pain. They don't get tired. They don't age. What were they before me? Simple peasants. Lowly and unequal. Destined to suffer the pains of life—poverty, sorrow, sadness, age."

"And the grotesque mutants that were clearly once men?" Erik asked.

"You may say grotesque," Sustenon replied, "I say beautiful. They are built to protect the herd. They have kept their ability to think so they might serve me better."

"They are monsters," Erik said.

"They are my children!" Sustenon yelled, clenching his fists as spittle flew from his mouth, and the room shook again.

"You are mad," Erik said with a slight smile, knowing the response he would invoke.

The wizard lifted his hands and sharp spikes of rock exploded from the ground. Erik jumped to the side again and again as pointed shards of stone stabbed upwards. Sustenon waved his hands and a tornado rolled around the room, picking up stone and tossing it about. Erik hid behind one of the pillars of rock until the whirlwinds subsided, managing to avoid the projectiles the winds threw about. Sustenon clapped again and, where there was empty space in the floor, creepers with thick, dark green vines riddled with long spines broke through the stone and spread faster than any plant should ever move. Erik cut at several vines deliberately growing in his direction, but where he cut, two vines grew.

Sustenon's laughter was maddening as Erik fretted over what he could do. He looked to one of the sconces on the wall, glowing with a white light, and he knew it was firestone. It didn't burn like a wood torch, but the sizzling flare might be enough to ignite pitch. He jumped over vines as they lurched up at him, the thorns scratching his face. Wherever they touched, his skin burned. Poison. Reaching one of the sconces, Erik sheathed Ilken's Blade and retrieved a pitch-smeared torch from his haversack, putting the black tar to the fire-stone. He held it there, waiting, as creepers wrapped around his ankles and clawed up his legs.

Finally, the pitch caught fire, and the torch flared to life. Just as a thorny creeper was about to make for his crotch, he put the fire to it, and it recoiled like a wounded snake. He thought he even heard a distance screech. Touching the creeper fully with the torch, the green vine flared with flame and burned away.

Erik ran about the room, touching the torch to the green vine and watching it burn away, all the while dodging fireballs Sustenon threw at him. It was too late when the wizard realized he was actually helping Erik's cause, as the sparks from the fireballs also caught the green creepers aflame. He yelled and, when the wizard opened his mouth, thousands of bees flew from it, all buzzing directly towards Erik. He hid behind one of the rocky pillars and his shield as much as he could, but still felt the slight pinch of bee sting after bee sting on his neck and face.

Erik threw his torch at Sustenon and drew Ilken's Blade.

"Enough!" Erik said. "I've had enough of you. Your time has come to an end. Your curse on this place is over. And the Dragon Sword will be mine."

Sustenon began to laugh, almost uncontrollably.

"You still don't know, do you?" The wizard laughed. "You have had ..."

"The sword all along," Erik said, "yes, I know."

What Erik said had truly shocked the wizard, and he stopped laughing.

"Then why come back?" he asked, almost looking like a child who has understanding of a complex matter.

"Because that is my mission," Erik said. "Because that is what I was told to do. And the reason is because I am freeing the people and this land from your slavery and evil ways."

Place me on the altar.

The voice was faint and weak, its power—or the elf's—waning more than ever, so Erik hurried to take his dagger from his belt as he ran from rocky pillar to rocky pillar, dodging lightning strikes and fireballs hurled once more by Sustenon.

Whatever happens, thank you.

He felt the slightest of tingles in his hand by way of response as he raced towards the altar. An errant fireball splashed against a rocky protrusion next to him, some of the flame scorching his beard and hair on one side. He felt the sting of burning on his cheek but pushed aside the pain. Reaching the altar, he placed the dagger within the light that seemed to have no source.

Upon seeing the weapon lying there, Sustenon stopped all his attacks, and his face filled with panic. He pushed his hands out towards Erik, who felt a wind strike him in the chest and he fell backward. The wizard ran to the altar, but before he could reach it, something pushed him back, throwing him to the floor more forcibly than Erik, who was already staggering to his feet.

Place your sword next to me.

The voice was even softer than before, and Erik didn't hesitate, his trust in the dagger unswerving. He drew Ilken's Blade, hastened back to the altar, and placed his blade next to the golden-handled dagger. Before he could see what happened, he heard the commotion and yelling of fighting, and looked over his shoulder to see his companions rushing into the room, battling with possessed soldiers and another mutant.

"Erik! Behind you!" Beldar yelled.

Erik turned to see Sustenon standing again, and as he chanted something inaudible, a purple light appeared between the wizard's hands, flowing from palm to palm like electricity. A crystal appeared there and flew through the air, aimed straight for Erik's heart. Erik felt something, a shoulder, ramming into his side, and fell into the altar, purple light exploding where he stood only a moment before. Beldar flew backward, crashing through one of the rocky protrusions, his chest black and charred where the purple crystal had struck him.

"Beldar!" Erik yelled.

The snow cat ran to the fallen dwarf, standing over him and growling, its jowls pulled back and revealing dagger-like teeth. Erik was about to attend Beldar alongside the cat when the voice of his dagger stopped him.

Erik! The dragon tooth!

The dagger's urgent call was barely audible, and Erik looked to his friend, his breathing shallow, for a final moment before he did as he was told. Retrieving the shard of dragon tooth, cut from the dragon of Orvencrest, from his haversack, he unwrapped the cloth he kept it in and it glowed and burned his hand when he touched it. Erik ignored the pain of the dragon's poison and placed the tooth on the altar, next to the dagger and Ilken's Blade before Sustenon could stop him.

The altar lit up, almost blinding Erik, and he found himself shielding his eyes.

"The Dragon Sword is mine!" Sustenon cried.

Erik couldn't see the wizard now, so bright was the light, and could only make out his silhouette and hear the shuffling of his feet as he moved towards the altar. When the light subsided, the elf from his baptismal vision stood there on the top of the altar. He wore a mail hauberk and held a longbow that was as tall as Bryon. He looked to Erik first, smiled, and nodded. Then, he looked to Sustenon.

A frown touched his brow, and his mouth turned down as the elf shook his head, drawing back a red fletched arrow. As soon as he saw it, Erik knew it resembled an arrow Erik's dagger became the first time he used it in battle. The elf fired, and the arrow struck Sustenon in the breast. The wizard stumbled backward and began chanting something. Another arrow struck his chest, and then another, and another. As the wizard fell backward and lay still, the sconces filled with firestone flared, and all that had erupted from the floor disappeared, and the floor was smooth stone once more.

Erik stared up at the elf, his piercing blue eyes meeting Erik's before the elf jumped down from the altar to stand face to face with Erik.

"You are the elf from my vision," Erik said, "and from the dagger. You are the first dragon rider."

The elf bowed, and now Erik could tell this was not a true living being, the elf's body translucent.

"Rako Rokhev," the elf said with a slight bow.

By way of habit, Erik extended his hand, but the elf shook his head.

"I am only here in spirit," Rako replied. "This is the punishment for my pride. But before we speak, you must look to your friend. I fear the worst for him."

In the moments of the elf revealing himself, Erik had forgotten about Beldar, and now he cursed himself.

"Excuse me," said Erik and he hastened over to where the others had gathered.

The snow cat purred softly and rested its large head on Beldar's legs. Bofim gently placed Beldar's head on the ground and stood, his eyes red-rimmed and wet.

"He gave his life for you, Erik," Bofim said.

He looked angry, at first, his eyes slightly squinted, and his lips pursed.

"Too many good people have given their lives for me," Erik said.

Bofim shook his head.

"He willingly gave his life for you," the dwarf said. "It was a commitment he made the moment he decided to follow you. I would have given my life for you, too."

"We all would have," Bryon added.

"But ..." began Erik, but his cousin interrupted him.

"There is nothing any of us could do to change what has happened, and now, I believe you have some unfinished business with your friend over there."

Erik looked to his cousin and then the dwarves in turn before he wiped the tears from his eyes and turned to see Rako standing behind him.

"I don't have long, Erik," the elf said.

"I am ready now, to learn," said Erik, and the elf nodded his head.

"My pride killed many people, Erik. I hope I am a lesson to others. The Dragon Sword is a powerful weapon, one that must be wielded with care and conviction."

"I can't return it to the Lord of the East, can I?" Erik asked.

"No," Rako replied.

"What about my family?"

"We all must make hard choices," Rako replied, "especially when the Shadow offers us easy ones."

"I don't understand why Sustenon just didn't take you if I had the Dragon Sword all along," Erik said.

"I don't have much time here," Rako said, "but this much I will explain to you. The Dragon Sword must be freely given in order to do what it is supposed to do. It is why it never worked for Marcus. He bought it, and before that, it had been stolen, and before that hidden by the dwarves, but because his heart was righteous, Marcus passed it to his son, who then freely gave it to you, thinking it was nothing more than a fancy dagger. The magic within the blade worked for you; your heart is good and pure. Sustenon could not simply take it from you, not without magic that would have even been beyond him. However, he knew that if the wielder takes his own life with the blade, then the next person to hold the sword becomes its owner."

"But why me?" Erik asked.

"I don't know," Rako replied with a shrug. "I only know what it does and how it is passed from one generation to the next. Originally, it was meant to be passed to my first-born, just as my mother passed it on to me. It was the great gift given to the elvish Dragon Riders by the dwarves when our peoples were still friends."

Erik looked to the altar. His dagger was gone, and so was the dragon tooth. Only Ilken's Blade lay there.

"Take it," Rako said. "It is now the Dragon Sword, reforged by magic."

The elf began to fade, his body becoming even more translucent, wavering as if he was a specter about to disappear.

"It almost looks like it did before," Erik said, noticing that the handle looked to now be golden and there was greenish hew to the blade.

"It is not the same blade," Rako said. "But it is a blade crafted by the dwarves—your dwarvish friend Ilken Copper Head—as the original Dragon Sword was so many years ago. When they forged the original, it contained a piece of a dragon—a scale from the ancestor of the dragon both my mother and I rode. The dragon tooth was part of the key to reforging it."

"How was the original Dragon Sword destroyed?" Erik asked.

"It was a powerful weapon, but it had its limits," Rako explained. "I overexerted the magic in the blade. In my pride, I destroyed it...and all that I held dear."

Erik picked up the blade. It felt like it had before. No. It felt better, even more suited to him, if that was possible.

"Dragon Tooth" murmured Erik.

"That is a good name," Rako said, and Erik looked up to see the elf smiling.

Erik looked at the blade. Ilken Copper Head's inscriptions were still there—his name and the etching of a raven. But there was a new set of etchings, just next to the raven. They were the same runes as Erik's shield.

"Dragon Fire," Erik muttered.

"My gift to you, Erik," Rako said. "Whoever the sword passes to, for all eternity, your name will be etched into the blade as the first wielder of Dragon Tooth, the Dragon Sword reforged."

"And will you be with me as well," Erik asked, "like before? Or have you been released from your bondage to the blade?"

The elf smiled. It was a sad smile.

"I am not actually bound to the blade," the elf replied. "I am bound to something else, and after exerting what little power I once had, I don't think I can ever extend myself beyond my bonds, ever again. This is farewell."

Erik considered this, and another tear touched the corner of his eye. His dagger, this elf, had become as good a friend as any flesh and blood person could.

"What if I released you from your bonds? How could I do that?"

"You cannot," the elf said, his spectral body fading more quickly. "It is too dangerous."

"People have told me that before," Erik said, "and I didn't listen."

The elf smiled momentarily and then looked serious, his body mostly gone.

"There is a shadow growing across our lands," Rako said. "You have seen it in your dreams."

"The Shadow," Erik said, but Rako shook his head.

"No. Something different."

"Something more dangerous?" Erik asked.

"In a way, yes. So, I give you this task, not so that you can free me from my prison, but so you can save us from the growing evil lurking in the darkness."

"Tell me," Erik said, insistent. "I will do it for you."

"Then listen to this: Find the Dragon Stone. It has many names, but for now, we will call it the Dragon Stone. It is hidden away, in a village in Hargoleth," Rako's voice said, a distant whisper that came out of the air. "Find it and take it to the Lady El'Beth El'Kash in the Forests of Ul'Erel. She can release me as well as help stop the spread of this darkness. Do this, and not only will I be free, not only will we cause this new evil to stumble, but you will be one step closer to solving the riddle of the Dragon Scroll."

With that, the voice was gone. Erik looked at the Dragon Sword ... no, Dragon Tooth, and the green hew that consumed the blade deepened, and it was as if green flames engulfed the steel. He heard a rustling behind him. Sustenon sat up, gingerly, the red fletched arrows still protruding from his chest. The wizard looked haggard and much older than before, his magic fleeting with the blood that ran from his wound.

"The Dragon Sword is mine," Sustenon croaked, and he began to incant something under his breath.

"No," Erik said, stepping to the wizard, "it is no longer the Dragon Sword, it is Dragon Tooth, and it will never be yours, just as it will never be the Lord of the East's."

Erik raised the sword over his head. The blade flared to a green brilliance and flashed as he brought it down on the wizard. Sustenon screamed, and when the blade struck him, he disappeared as if a puff of smoke through an open window.

Erik looked back at the altar, the place where his sword—Ilken's Blade—became Dragon Tooth. The place where an elf who had possessed his golden-handled dagger—Rako Rokhev—once stood and explained the consequences of his pride. A low, reverberating sound echoed through the circular room, and the altar cracked, the light that once illuminated it disappearing. And Erik wondered if he would ever hear Rako's voice again. Then he remembered he would never hear Beldar's.

55

Bryon stared at the broken altar. The stone hadn't turned the same gray as the keep but remained an alabaster white. It reminded him of the white altar they had found in the tower in the meadow, another magical place. The altar held runes, even though they were hard to see because of the broken stone, but they resembled the runes he saw on the white tower's altar. He wondered now if, over time, the gray of this place would slowly become white again.

A doorway had appeared in the wall of the altar room and Bryon passed through it, walking out onto a balcony that surrounded the tower. He looked out at the surrounding tundra and the valley in which Fealmynster rested. As people gathered together below, what was once a stale looking town was now a myriad of different buildings and homes and shops. Many of them were broken and run down, but nonetheless, they no longer had the uniformed look they once had.

Looking back out to the surrounding frozen plain, even the land looked different. The craggy, icy protrusions that rose from the ground just before they reached the edge of the slope that led down into the town were gone. And the plains, still white and covered in snow and ice, seemed brighter and less threatening. Even from the circular platform, Bryon could see the green of grass poking through an icy covering.

"Erik," Bryon called, "come look at this."

It took a moment, but his cousin had finally joined him on the platform.

"Look," Bryon said, "it's as if the wizard's magic had cursed this whole land."

"It's amazing," Erik said. As he stared out, he was surprised that a smile grew on his face.

"Does this place remind you of anything?" Bryon asked.

Erik just shrugged.

"The white tower," Bryon said. "It's as if this place was its opposite."

Erik looked around, even looked back into the altar room, and his eyebrows raised.

"You're right," he said.

Bryon walked back into the room, and, as the magic of Sustenon faded away, he found another pile of broken statues, just like the white tower, but all of these statues were of men, and they were made of some black stone. He crouched down and picked up the head of one, half its face gone.

"This was an elvish tower once, too," Bryon said.

"You think?" Erik asked.

"It has to be," Bryon replied.

He heard Erik walk away, but he continued to look through the broken statues. He found one with pointed ears—an elf. He picked it up, inspecting it. It was a female elf, and, even though the head of the statue held pot marks and chips, Bryon imagined that she would have been beautiful. As he held the black visage of an elvish woman, something stung his hands, a wave of pain traveling up into his shoulders. He dropped the effigy with a yelp, and it broke.

"Are you alright?" Erik asked.

Bryon stared at the rubble that was the elvish head. It shouldn't have broken so easily, and not into as many pieces. He looked at his cousin over his shoulder.

"Yeah," he replied. "Fine."

Turning back to the rubble, something caught his eye. Something, among the broken stone glimmered, something polished and black. Bryon pushed the broken statue aside and saw a perfectly round rock sitting there, underneath all the shards. It sparkled at first, a shimmering black—the antithesis to a white star in a dark, nighttime sky—and then it turned dull, drinking up any light that hit it. Bryon picked it up and, squinting and peering closely at the thing, he saw the faintest glimpse of a light, deep inside of it.

What are you?

It reminded Bryon of the red stone Erik had. He had two of them, once, but he used one to defeat the dragon, in the mountain just outside of Orvencrest. They were clearly powerful magic, and, as Bryon stared at this one, he felt a flutter in his stomach. He put the rock in a pouch hanging from his belt.

Bryon watched as Bofim cried over Beldar, silently, stoically. Erik put his hand on Bofim's shoulder and knelt next to him. He saw tears form at the corner of his cousin's eyes. He was sad too, but the burden that Erik carried—Beldar had given his life for him. Bryon didn't quite know how he would handle such a load. He had moments when he wasn't sure his life was worth much, let alone the life of another. When the other two dwarves joined them, along with the emaciated snow cat who had befriended them in their fight against the wizard, they hoisted the dead dwarf's body up and left the room.

As they carried Beldar's body through the hallways and down the stairs of the keep they met no resistance. With the passing of Sustenon, the possessed soldiers they had been fighting no longer had a greenish, pallid tint to their skin, nor were their eyes black anymore. They looked like normal men and women. They were all different skin colors and sizes, seemingly from every corner of Háthgolthane. The last mutant they had been fighting when Beldar died had been injured, and as they had made a litter for their friend's body, the monster regained consciousness. As it did so, this one with yellow plate-like scales, two sets of horns on its head, and two sets of tusks in its mouth, melted away into a rather small man with beady little eyes and a bald head. The scales fell all around him, like a snake shedding its skin. The man screamed and curled up into a ball, obviously afraid of what fate might now face him. When nothing happened, he got up and ran away.

The men and women, no longer possessed, looked about in a daze. They seemed to have no clue where they were or what had happened. Through his sadness at another death, Erik tried to smile as he looked to each one of them, free from their mental bondage.

"I don't always know why you do what you do, but look at these people. Look at this place," said Bryon, walking up to Erik and putting a hand on his cousin's shoulder.

Indeed, those who were once possessed began to recognize others. They embraced and laughed and cried. Even those who had died had reverted to their original form, and though they became a source of sorrow, Erik could sense relief as their loved ones cried over them. They were free as well. Even the keep began to change. The blackness of the stone washed away, leaving the bright gray of freshly shorn rock. There had been no windows in the tower, and now many openings, allowing in cool air and sunlight, appeared in the walls.

Once he stepped foot onto the ice-cold tundra, Specter could feel this place was full of magic. Even the natural, mystical essence of enchantment, something that reminded the assassin of the elves and made him think of the ice bridge, had been infected and twisted by something dark, the mad wizard no doubt. Specter didn't care, but it changed the feel of the magic, the taste even. As Specter made his way towards the keep of Fealmynster, he could feel it in his skin and bones. He didn't need a map.

This wizard, Sustenon, was truly a powerful mage to be able to infect a place so significantly. He wasn't some simple mad experimenter. Specter didn't know much about the man, but to infect the land and curse the natural magic of a place—especially if that originated from the elves—took strength and much experience in the dark arts. No simple mage at all. This man was a mighty necromancer, but he had been trained by an even mightier one.

As evening fell, he felt a surge of magic. It might have been the same way an animal could sense when the weather was changing, or a storm was coming. If it was possible, the necromancer of Fealmynster's magic had grown even stronger, spreading out over the land like a wave. It washed over the Isutan assassin, and he felt stronger as the black magic hit him, but then something strange happened. His strength waned, and he became dizzy. His thoughts were jumbled and, even though his own power was still there, he couldn't access it. His feet were unsure, and he had to hold out his hands to steady himself.

What, by the gods?

He blinked, his vision blurry, and he tried to breathe deep even though he couldn't. It wasn't like the ice bridge, where the elvish magic literally stole his power away. No. His power was still there; he just couldn't summon it. The cold bit at his skin, where it had not affected him before. He felt the aches and pains of life, of an old worn-out body, and then ... it was gone.

Specter turned his hand ethereal, just to make sure he could still access his power; it worked although he felt drained and tired, so he materialized his flesh quickly. He needed to rest. He needed to feed.

He saw the keep ahead, its shape more distinct as it glowed in blue magic. Something was happening. Should he go ahead and investigate? He'd maybe find some sustenance, but Specter decided to wait. He let the night pass him by, moving more slowly towards Fealmynster, careful to feel the ebbs and flows of necromantic magic around him. Then, as the new day took hold with a rising sun that brought an almost inaccessible warmth, there was another surge of magic. It washed over Specter like before, but this time he lost none of his power.

Looking up, Fealmynster looked the same and yet different. The magical glow that Specter could see before was gone; something had happened. The natural magic of the tundra didn't feel tainted anymore; the dark curse and enchantments of this land were gone. There was only one reason, one answer ... Sustenon was dead. But how? Surely this Erik could not have killed such a mighty necromancer? Specter watched and waited.

Erik stepped out into the sunlight. He closed his eyes as the sun hit his face, relishing in the warmth despite the cold air. The air smelled cleaned as he breathed deep, and, despite his mourning Beldar, he couldn't help the smile that crossed his face.

This place north of the Gray Mountains remained cold, but it didn't seem as cold as before. He didn't know what its name was before it was Fealmynster—if it had a different name—and he didn't know what it would be called after, but people bustled about, greeting one another and mourning over their own dead. Life had to go on. Both they and he knew that.

The town was a beautiful sight, even in its disarray, once lifted of the wizard's curse. Each home and shop, the ones that still stood, had their own personality. As the black of the tower was gone, each home stood with different colors of paint, artistry, and architectural nuances in their construction. Small gardens contained by waist-high fences, were already being worked, and he saw men, women, and children praising their gods for the deliverance from evil.

As he watched the town's population go about their newly-restored lives, Erik realized some of the people who had been part of Sustenon's army of possessed were maybe a hundred years old or more, like the mad wizard. Perhaps the original inhabitants of the town were the first to be enslaved. Even though they had been robbed of normal lives, they still went about their day with smiles on their faces; the new mood was distinctly infectious, and Erik understood why Bryon had pointed this out as being part of Erik's purpose. Rescuing people like this was what Erik did, Bryon had suggested, and it felt good to give life as opposed to take it away.

Erik looked down at the snow cat that stood by his side, purring and stretching and sniffing at the air for the first time in who knew how long. As the farm cats reached his ankles, this one's back almost reached Erik's hip.

"Do you plan on keeping her?" Bryon said, standing next to Erik and tilting his head upward, sniffing at the air much like the cat.

"I don't think she is something that is to be kept," Erik replied.

"What are you going to do with her then?" Bryon asked.

"Let her follow me as long as she wishes," Erik replied, "and then when she chooses to leave, let her leave."

"She might turn on you, you know," Bryon said. "She's a wild animal."

Erik looked down at the snow cat, and she ignored him but continued to purr deeply.

"I don't think so," he said.

"Suit yourself," Bryon said, a wry smile touching his lips, "but don't say I didn't warn you when you wind up as cat droppings."

Erik laughed and scratched the cat behind her ear. He heard a commotion as he was reveling in the new day and the smell of untainted air and saw a crowd gathering around the foundation of what looked to once be a very large building. He and Bryon walked to the gathering and saw that nine men, most of them scared, had been herded into the center of the ever-growing mass of people.

"What's going on here?" Erik asked. All of the town spoke in Westernese, but with an accent Erik had never heard before.

"They served the mage," a man standing next to him said.

"You all did," Erik replied.

"No," the man said, his eyes meeting Erik. He could tell those eyes—a deep brown—were old eyes filled with fear and sadness and worry. "They willingly served him."

"What should we do with them?" another man asked.

"Burn them," one woman shouted, to which the small, bald man began to cry.

"No!" one of the culprits shouted. He looked to someone in the crowd, and his eyes said he knew the person he saw. "Samson, we grew up together."

"Long ago," Samson replied, "and before you betrayed your people."

The people began to shout out whatever methods of execution they could think of, most of them terrible and slow and painful. A man taller than Bryon walked up to Erik, his skin as dark as midnight. His arms and legs teemed with muscle, and his chest was naked despite the cold, showing several scars.

"What do you think we should do with them?" he asked. The accented way he spoke Westernese reminded Erik of the Samanian slavers. He must have originally been from Wüsten Sahil.

"What would you do with them?" Erik asked.

"Where I come from," the dark-skinned man said, "we would castrate and enslave them, but after the hell I have been through, I would not enslave my worst enemy."

"Death is a kinder fate, then," Erik said.

"Death is too good for these traitors!" another man yelled.

"Please," the bald-headed man cried, "mercy."

"The same mercy you had on our people," another screamed, "the same mercy you gave Meredith?"

"I suggest you banish them," Erik said, stepping into the clearing where the nine traitors stood and facing the crowd. "Send them away, to survive on their own. Give them each a water skin and a loaf of bread."

"But we'll die," the small, bald man said, tears streaming down his cheeks.

"Would you rather burn at the stake?" Erik asked, his voice hard and flat and unremorseful.

That only caused the man to cry more. They had all willingly served the wizard Sustenon. One might ask what choice they had, willing service or mindless enslavement, but still, they chose.

A murmur spread through the crowd.

"They were once your people," Erik said, "and certainly you have experienced enough horror for a thousand lifetimes. Why not start fresh and relish the joy of freedom. Send them away and forget about them. Start anew."

Erik saw the dark-skinned man nod. He stepped into the clearing, standing next to Erik, as the commotion in the crowd began to build.

"I agree," he said, his voice loud and reverberating. "We will banish them. Give each one of these men a water skin and a loaf of bread and send them on their way."

"Who made you the boss?" someone from the growing crowd asked.

"No one," the large, dark-skinned man said, "but I agree with this man, the one who gave us our freedom. Our new life should start with life, not death."

"Are we to listen to a man from another continent?" another questioned.

That caused the large man from Wüsten Sahil to grumble. Men were always stupidly suspicious of those that didn't look like them.

"Are you truly that bigoted?" Erik asked. "Is this man any different than you? He has suffered the same horror you have. And from the way he conducts himself, he is the best candidate to lead you people."

Erik looked at the man and smiled.

"Then I suggest we take a vote," the dark-skinned man said.

With some murmurs of discord, perhaps more about the dark man than the suggested punishment, agreement flowed through the crowd, and when they were done, banishment was the answer.

"It looks like you have made yourself the boss," Erik said with a smile when they were done with the vote and getting ready to send the exiles on their way.

"I do not wish to be boss," the man replied.

"That is probably what will make you a good leader," Erik said, realizing he could have been talking about himself. "But don't you wish to go back home?"

"I have no home," the man replied, and when Erik gave him a questioning look, added, "I left Nai Na'Kinasa almost seventy summers ago, as I have just recently found out. My wife is probably dead. My children are now old men and women. Who am I to try and return to their lives? No, I will stay here and build a new life."

"It seems many have the same idea," Erik said, looking around as most of the people who were once possessed, a mishmash of men and women, dwarves, ogres, goblins, antegants, and even giants and another troll, went about repairing old and broken homes.

"How did you survive here, in this cold tundra?" Erik asked.

"It wasn't always so desolate and frozen," the man replied. "We traded with other towns, most of which were only a week or so away. They're all gone now. It's interesting..."

"What's interesting?" Erik asked as the man trailed off in his thoughts.

"Everything that I have done, for all those years," the man said, "I can remember it all like some distant nightmare. Some of it is hazy and incomplete, but I remember. I remember destroying towns and enslaving people. I remember watching as the once temperate summers—warm enough to grow greens and tubers—grew colder and colder. I remember the animals, so bountiful that we never went hungry, disappearing."

"Sustenon enslaved all these different towns?" Erik asked.

The man nodded.

"So, you once farmed?" Erik asked.

"A little," the man replied. "We mostly hunted and mined, trading with the other towns. Those that traded with the dwarves and plains would bring us the foods we couldn't grow here, and we would trade firestone and black rock and iron with them."

Erik put a hand on the man's bare shoulder. It was still warm to the touch.

"Time will create new memories, you will see to that," he said.

"I hope so," the man replied. "I truly hope so."

Erik saw the dwarves with another group of people. He walked to them and saw that they stared down at the body of Beldar. Bofim knelt at the dwarf's head, crying and praying. The easterner that had traveled with Bu leaned against Turk, looking half-conscious with lazy eyes.

"What will you do with Beldar?" Erik asked.

"We will bury him here," Bofim said through sobs. "We will honor the place where he made his greatest sacrifice."

"I am sorry," Erik said.

"I told you before," Bofim said, standing, "it was his sacrifice to make ... and it is a sacrifice that all of us would have made. Honor it by simply accepting what he has done. Do not pity him, rejoice in his life."

Erik nodded his understanding. There was nothing more to be said. He felt an elbow in his side and turned to Nafer.

"Who would have thought?" Nafer asked, staring at a dwarf and a goblin lifting a piece of rubble together. "An alfingas and dwarf working together."

"Maybe this is the beginning of a new world?" Turk said.

"Maybe," Erik replied. He touched the now golden handle of his sword—Dragon Tooth. "This will be a hard life, up here in the north."

"We will manage," the large dark-skinned man said. Erik was startled as the large man had snuck up behind them. "Of that, I am sure."

"You are sneaky for such a large man," Erik said, to which the man laughed.

"Will you stay with us?" the man asked.

"For a day," Erik replied, "maybe two. But we must return home.

"

"I am glad you have a home in which to return," the man replied.

"Hopefully," Erik muttered to himself. He looked at the large man. "What should we tell people this place is called? Is it still called Fealmynster?"

"No," the man said quickly, shaking his head with a frown. "It will never be called that again."

"Then what?" Erik asked.

"If I am to be their leader, I will suggest Mayisha Maythia," the man replied with a smile.

"And what does that mean?" Erik asked.

"In my language, it means *New Life*," he replied. "This place is our new life."

"Well, there won't be another northern town with such a name," Erik replied with a short laugh. Erik extended his hand, and the big man took his whole forearm. "What is your name?"

"Shu'ja'a," the man replied.

"Well, Shu'ja'a," Erik said, "I wish you and your people good fortune. May the Creator smile on you."

56

———

*A*fter burying Beldar, Erik and his companions stayed in Mayisha Maythia for another two days. Scouting parties had confirmed that four of the nine men they had banished were already dead—one mauled by a snow bear, another eaten by a pack of wolves, one wrapped in the silk of an ártocothe and drained, and the last simply frozen to death, although the reports said he looked drained as well. The scouting parties also found the freed ártocothe, dead and frozen, surrounded by half a dozen giants, also dead and frozen, presumably poisoned by the giant spider. Erik had asked about three men—two easterners and a Hámonian—but the scouts knew nothing of them.

"I wonder if he will honor his word," Erik muttered.

"Who's that?" Bryon asked.

"Bu," Erik said. "He said our feud was done ... for now. He was going home, and he would leave us and our families be."

"He's an easterner," Bryon said. "Can he really be trusted?"

At that moment, Erik watched a mountain troll holding up the frame of the front of a house by itself while men busied themselves with securing it to the rest of the home.

"Two days ago," Erik said, "I would have never thought a troll would be helping men build homes."

"So, are you ready to move on?" Turk asked.

"I am," Erik replied.

"Where are we going?" Turk asked.

"Home," Erik replied.

"You are not taking the sword to Fen-Stévock," Turk said, and it was more of a statement than a question.

"No."

"The Lord of the East will not be happy," Turk said. "He will send assassins after you ... after us."

"Would you have me take the sword to him?" Erik asked.

Turk thought for a moment and then shook his head.

"No."

"What about our families?" Bryon asked.

"I don't know," Erik replied.

"We will be watching our backs for the rest of our lives," Bryon added.

Erik just nodded. Then, he smiled and gave a short laugh.

"We could move them to Thorakest," Erik said.

"King Skella would welcome you," Turk said.

"We will see," Erik said, "but I fear moving them to Thorakest would do little good against the type of assassins an enraged Lord of the East would employ."

"If this is An's will," Turk said, "he will protect us."

"I hope," Erik muttered.

Erik told the people of Mayisha Maythia that anyone wishing to travel with them was welcome, and as he and his companions readied themselves to leave, twenty people joined them. Some of them were recently imprisoned by Sustenon and hoping their families would still be waiting for them, and some of them simply wanted to distance themselves from a nightmare.

"What now, for you?" Erik asked Andu.

The man shrugged. He cradled one arm close to his body and still walked with a limp.

"I cannot go home," Andu replied. "My father has probably already disowned me for serving Patûk, and then Bu, even if I had no choice. And I doubt Bu will take me back. He cared little that I was dying."

"You can go with us," Erik said.

"What?" Bryon asked, grabbing his cousin's arm and pulling him to him.

"This is a time of redemption," Erik said. "Look around you. Look at the brokenness that is being repaired."

"I would like that," Andu said. "I will serve you in whatever capacity you need. I am not worth much."

"Why don't you go with us as a free man," Erik said, "to make your own choices."

Andu nodded, tears welling up in his eyes.

"It is settled," Erik said. "You will go with us and start a new life in the free farmlands of northwestern Háthgolthane."

"I don't know how you got here," one man said, a gray-haired fellow with deep crow's feet at his eyes, "but I know the way to Green Tree—assuming it's still there—a trading town north of The Fangs. From there, several roads lead to at least a half dozen towns along the feet of the Gray Mountains ... at least they did a hundred years ago."

Erik thought of the portals that had brought them to Fealmynster. He guessed they would be quicker, but he wasn't sure if they would still find giants waiting to make them a meal. He nodded.

"Do any of the roads lead to Eldmanor?" Erik asked.

"Aye," the man said, and then he shrugged and added, "at least, it used to."

"Then lead on," Erik said.

As they left, climbing a newly fashioned stairway carved into the icy slope that led down to the town of Mayisha Maythia, the people cheered them and applauded. When they reached the top of the inverted palisade, the jagged ice boulders were gone, giving way to a vast plain of white that seemed to have melted away enough to reveal some green grass. White-haired rabbits poked their heads from several holes and watched them, and then hurried back into their homes as a white-feathered hawk screeched overhead. Shu'ja'a met them there, his chest still bare and daring the cold to afflict him, even though he wore a cloak made of some heavy hide and thick leggings of the same animal.

"I don't suspect you will ever come this way again," Shu'ja'a said, "but if you do, know you are welcomed as family."

"You never know," Erik said. "I thank you. I would encourage you to reach out to the northern dwarves. They are friends. Mention my name—Erik Dragon Fire—and they will know you are friends too."

Shu'ja'a bowed.

The windswept, icy plains of the lands north of the Gray Mountains wore on Erik, even if some of the ice melted away revealing the tundra plains and lakes, including some that had meager trees for wood for nighttime fires. The land seemed tamer than before when they first came to this place through the mine portal, but the cold was unceasing and still bit to the bone regardless of how many layers of fur and clothing they wore, or how close they got to a fire before sleep. Erik wondered how it was Shu'ja'a could simply walk around bare-chested.

Of the twenty people who decided to follow Erik and his companions, most were single men or women, former travelers hoping their families were still waiting for them back home or desiring to simply leave a place that held so many horrible memories. Only four of the travelers were a family—a father and his three daughters—and of all of the people, they seemed the hardiest, the girls going out and hunting rabbits and even a white-haired fox one time, but they always had the snow cat's protection.

Erik thought they would soon lose one of the men that traveled with them. He had come down with a fever, and the biting cold didn't help, but he got better after a few days, and the group remained intact.

The old man whom they followed—Dego Valens from as far away as Finlo— had been making regular journeys up the Giant's Vein from Finlo and Crom for many years before his capture, and he insisted the lands north of the Gray Mountains were always cold. But never this cold. The one beautiful thing Erik found about this icy place was the sky at night. Lights—Turk said they were reflections from the sun as its light passed through the world's atmosphere—danced through the sky, and the stars seemed so close.

"How much longer?" Bryon asked one night.

"We've only been traveling a fortnight," Dego said, lifting his hand to the sky and looking at the stars with one, squinted eye.

For a moment, Dego reminded Erik of Vander Bim, his old sailor friend who had originally hired him and his brother and cousin on as porters. He was a good man, even though he liked his homemade apple rum a little too much, and Erik felt a knot in his stomach as he thought of him. He deserved better, certainly better than a knife in the back in a dwarvish alleyway.

"But I would say we have no more than another week," Dego added.

"Thank the Creator," Bryon said.

"That is until we reach the road leading to Green Tree," Dego added. "From there, I would say another fortnight, maybe more, before we reach Eldmanor."

Bryon groaned.

"Will you dwarves be leaving us at Green Tree?" Dego asked Turk as the dwarf stared up at the sky.

"No," Turk replied. "We travel with Erik. Where he goes, we go."

"Truly?" Dego asked. "What does a man have to do to earn such loyalty from dwarves?"

"Be extraordinary," Turk said.

Erik pretended he wasn't listening to their conversation, but he couldn't help smiling.

"What's wrong?" Erik said, kneeling next to the snow cat after he heard a low growl rumble through the cat's throat. She crouched on her haunches, the hair on her back straight and her ears flat against her head.

"Careful, Erik," Turk said, but Erik knew the growl wasn't aimed at him.

The snow cat stared out at the plain behind them. Erik couldn't see anything but a wide, flat, icy expanse, but something had spooked his companion. It couldn't have been food. Over the last two weeks, the thin, almost emaciated cat had found plenty of animals to hunt, and she was now developing, thick with muscle and much needed fat to fight the cold of the northern region. At first, she would pounce at anything she could, from the small, white-haired field mice that somehow made their homes in little holes in the ice, to the occasional, white-tailed deer, but now, she was picky about her food. No, something was out there, even if Erik couldn't see it.

They had found the road leading to Green Tree, lined with flat flagstone and marked with a tall, man-made pole every league or so.

"Come on," Erik said, standing and tugging gently on the snow cat's fur.

She didn't respond. She continued to stare out at the wide plains and growl.

"Come on," Erik insisted, pulling on the fur at the scruff of her neck a little harder.

The snow cat wheeled on Erik, growling, and he thought that, perhaps, he had gone too far. She was, after all, still a wild animal. But she quickly began to purr, licking Erik's hand and rubbing her massive body up against his leg, almost knocking him over.

"What has gotten into you?" Erik asked.

"She is a wild creature of these northern lands, Erik," Turk said. "Do not be surprised if we wake one day soon, and she is gone."

"I know," Erik replied, his heart sinking just a little, "but I would be lying if I said a little part of me didn't wish she would travel with us the whole way home."

"She would be a formidable ally," Bofim added.

They camped alongside the road that night, and when they woke in the morning, the snow cat was gone.

Be well, my friend. I pray the Creator protects you and makes your hunts bountiful.

57

———

*S*pecter's magic to render himself undetectable worked on men and the like, but animals always seemed to have a different sense. He had drained dogs and cats, cougars and wolves, bears, birds, reptilian predators of the swamp, and sharks even, in an attempt to learn or absorb their almost magical ability to sense his presence when no one else could. On a number of occasions, a barking dog or chirping bird had alerted a target and made his assassinations more trouble than they needed to be. It was about to happen again.

He had been watched as this Erik and his dwarvish companions and these twenty some odd fools camped along a road with which he wasn't too familiar. It was dark, and their campfire was small because of the lack of wood. Without alerting anyone, he materialized several dozen paces away and checked all was still quiet. He became ethereal again, but when he materialized a second time, his view of the camp was blocked by the huge mass that descended on him.

The snow cat pushed Specter to the ground, its foreclaws digging into the flesh on his shoulders. It had been a long time since anyone, or anything, had caused him pain and made him bleed, and he had forgotten the sensation. As a fang-filled jaw snapped at his face and claws dug deeper, pain coursed through his body, he became smoke, floating away from the cat and the party of men and dwarves. Only the giant animal pursued.

Specter materialized a hundred paces away, only to find the cat chasing after him. He became smoke and floated another hundred paces away. The cat was still there, hissing and growling and running faster than even a large cat should run. In fact, it reminded him of the lean, spotted great cats of the plains of Wüsten Sahil that could chase down anything, they were so fast.

"Fine," Specter huffed, "have it your way."

Specter produced the Bone Spear. It seemed a pity to kill such a magnificent creature, but he had a job to do. While the Isutan assassin circled with the snow cat, both eyeing one another suspiciously, wondering who was going to strike first, he had another thought: why was this creature attacking him? It was a wild cat and, yet, it was almost as if it was protecting this Erik Eleodum, like some trained dog.

You're better than that.

The cat growled as if it could read his thoughts, and its ears flattened even more before it lunged at Specter. He could feel its strength and power as its claws barely missed his face, digging again into his already hurt shoulders. The attack was so swift, he barely had time to get his head out of the way, but as soon as the cat hit the ground, he jabbed at it with his poisoned blade. It spun on Specter and swiped at his legs, first with one front paw and then with the other. He had never seen a creature of its size move so quickly.

Before he could gather himself, it leaped again. Specter summersaulted backward, coming to a crouched position with his spear ready, but the cat snapped at his ankle with his fangs. Again, it was too quick, and it bit into his flesh. Specter screamed and jabbed at the cat's shoulder with his spear, but the animal jerked away. It leaped yet again, and this time, Specter became smoke. He swirled around the cat as it passed through him, and he materialized behind the cat, the bone blade of his spear cutting the cat's flank, and blood soon stained its otherwise white coat. The animal turned and hissed, its eyes so full of anger they looked like fire.

Specter's poison worked quickly ... at least, it should have. The great cat stumbled as it took a step forward and looked confused for a moment, but then it hissed again as it regained its composure. It crouched.

"By the Shadow," Specter muttered, drawing his bone bladed knife, which he held in his other hand.

The snow cat came again. Specter missed with the blade of his spear but struck the animal in the ribs with the shaft. It knocked the cat to the side but did little more than to anger it some more. It lunged, and its claws ripped the leather of the armor that protected the Isutan's legs, and he felt blood trickle down his knee. He had tried becoming smoke and sneaking behind the animal, but it always knew where he would be and didn't bother leaping anymore.

Specter looked in the direction of the small campfire. Erik was there, his quarry, and this encounter was sapping his energy and time. The cat gave a low growl as Specter looked in the Dragon Slayer's direction and jumped in front of the assassin.

"Oh," Specter said with a smile, "you truly are protecting him, aren't you? That will be to your undoing."

Specter began to turn ethereal. It was taking a lot of his energy, but he had a plan. The cat crouched and turned, thinking the man would materialize behind it, but Specter stayed where he was, becoming whole again as the cat looked the other way. He jammed the blade of his spear into the cat's ribs and it yowled and spat. Hissing, it leaped, taking Specter by surprise as he thought, surely, the cat would have succumbed to his second successful attack. It landed squarely on his chest and shoulders, claws digging into his flesh again. He flung his face away from the snapping teeth and he raked his dagger across the animal's chest and ribs.

The snow cat jumped off Specter, now clearly hurt as it wobbled, staring at the assassin. But Specter was hurt too. He had used much of his energy fighting this animal of the north, and blood poured over tattered leather armor. He looked over his shoulder, at the campfire, and the cat hissed. He would have to heal his wounds and find blood to replenish lost energy.

"Perhaps another time," Specter said, nodding at the cat, still surprised and wondering how the animal wasn't dead yet.

In his current state, he was still confident that he could kill this Erik, but to attempt it when he was surrounded by several dwarves and twenty other men? That would be folly, and he was all about self-preservation. Specter became smoke and floated away, and as he did, he watched the snow cat limp off into the cold darkness of the northern reaches of the world. They would both retreat to fight another day.

58

———

Green Tree was a small town of some two hundred citizens as well as a trading post, complete with its own guards, comprised of some men and dwarves as well as several resident ogre families. A supply depot was run by a pair of goblin brothers, and alongside a few stores, a longhouse had been converted into an alehouse and brothel. Tucked away in the forests of the Gray Mountains, but just off the main road leading from the icy northern tundra, it was a place of ingenuity and adaptation. The trees were so plentiful and thick in these parts of the mountains that the people of Green Tree used them however they could. Some people had built their homes around a tall gray-barked or red-barked pine, while others simply built their homes in the trees, and as Erik looked up, he saw a network of bridges and ladders leading from one tree house to another.

"Where's the damn brothel?" Bryon asked, pushing past Erik.

"We've almost died, once again, this time at the hands of a mad wizard before we lifted a hundred-year-old curse, and all you can think about is sticking some whore?" Erik asked.

Bryon turned hard on his heels, glaring at Erik, and it had been a long time since his cousin had given him that angry, steeled look.

"Yeah, it is," Bryon said. "You have Simone to go back to. Your own little family. Your farm. I just want to feel needed just for a short while."

Before Erik could say anything else, Bryon turned back around and walked away, towards the brothel. Erik just shook his head.

"What's wrong?" Turk asked.

"My cousin is a fool," Erik replied.

"We all are from time to time," Turk said.

They hadn't been in Green Tree more than an hour before the place buzzed with gossip and talk of the curse of Fealmynster being lifted. As Erik and his dwarvish friends sat in the alehouse, eating breakfast and drinking spiced wine, they could hear snatches of several different conversations as the townsfolk sneaked glances in their directions.

"Elk's piss," one man said.

"No, it's true," another replied. "We have men and women from Fealmynster in the town right now."

"It's true," Erik said, not taking his eyes off his plate of bacon and eggs.

"I'll believe it when I see it," another naysayer said.

"You should establish trade with Mayisha Maythia—that's the town's new name—it would be good for you and them. They'll have furs and possibly black rock and firestone."

"How would you know this?" the naysayer asked.

"Because we are the ones who lifted the curse and killed the wizard, Sustenon," Erik replied, looking at the man and smiling.

A murmur of awe spread through the alehouse, and soon, Erik found his breakfast and drinks paid for.

"Please tell me you didn't do that for free food and drink," Nafer said, his face flat and disapproving.

"No," Erik replied with a short smile. "I did it for the looks on their faces."

"Our travel home should be as unassuming as possible, Erik," Nafer said.

"Too late for that," Bofim added, pointing to a group of people huddled together and just staring at them.

They returned to their food, and Erik eventually looked up and saw Turk staring at him.

"Erik, are you alright?" Turk asked. "You have a troubled expression on your face."

"I don't know," Erik said and, then, shaking his head added, "No."

"You can tell us," Turk said.

"I haven't dreamt in days," Erik replied, and even though his friends knew he had fevered dreams almost every night, they didn't know he now welcomed his dreams. He thought he might see Beldar, one last time, in his dreams and have a chance to thank him for his sacrifice. He relished the time he spent under his tree with the man he knew but didn't know. "I can't stop thinking about Beldar."

"There's more," Nafer said. "I can tell."

Erik smiled. His friends knew him too well.

"True," he replied. "I worry about my family. What will happen now I have disobeyed the Lord of the East?" Erik rubbed the scabbard of Dragon Tooth, resting his hand on the pommel of the golden handle. "And then there's ..."

"What, Erik?" Bofim asked when Erik didn't finish.

Erik just shook his head. They wouldn't understand. His dagger. Its presence. Its voice. The elf in his dagger, now the Dragon Tooth, was gone. They certainly didn't speak regularly, only when necessary, yet Erik always felt its presence. It was comforting, coveted even. He remembered speaking with Ilken Copper Head when he confessed to the blacksmith about the weapon's conscience. The dwarf had warned him to be careful. He had said that others, in the past, had become *addicted* to their weapons, forgoing daily duties, friends and family to simply converse with their sentient weapon. Was that it? Had he become addicted to his dagger's presence?

Erik shook his head again. No. It was a friend, as close a friend as the dwarves and his cousin. And like so many of his other friends, it ... he had given his life for Erik.

"Nothing really," Erik finally said. "I just want to get home."

When he'd finished eating, Erik said he wanted to go for a walk, and the others knew he wanted to be alone. He wandered the streets, stopping here and there, and he bought a thick, leather coat lined with bear fur. Eventually, he found himself standing next to an ogre's cart, full of fine and exotic cloths and leathers, along with a few other intricacies like gold flatware. The ogre was a massive creature, almost twice as tall as Erik with broad shoulders and a thick jaw and arms and legs knotted with thick muscle. The ogre's hair was gray and long, although his bald face showed youth.

"Would you like something?" the ogre asked, his voice deep and slow.

Erik would have suspected the ogre of being stupid, his speech so slow, but through stories and tales of the creatures, he knew better.

"No, thank you," Erik replied. "Just people watching."

The ogre nodded slowly as a man handed him several coins and retrieved a belt from several hooks drilled into one of the cart's tall poles.

"People are interesting, aren't they?" the ogre said, and Erik was a little surprised the ogre could speak Westernese that well. And, as if the ogre knew what Erik was thinking, he added, "We ogres must know many languages in order to sell our wares everywhere we do."

"Makes sense," Erik replied.

"You seem troubled," the ogre said, handing a woman some fabric she had apparently paid for earlier in the day.

"No," Erik said with a shake of his head, and the ogre stared at him with dull, gray eyes that seemed to bore into him.

"You do not lie well," the ogre said, turning slightly towards Erik.

"I'm not ..." Erik began to say, but the ogre pursed its lips and squinted its eyes. "I miss several friends."

"To lay down a life for a friend," the ogre said in his slow, methodical way, "is the greatest sacrifice ... the greatest gift."

How did he?

Erik cut the thought off. Perhaps this ogre had heard of his exploits in Golgolithul, and the many who had sacrificed their lives fighting a dragon?

"I am worried about going home," Erik added.

"Does home hold so many bad memories?" the ogre asked.

"No," Erik replied. "I am worried about what I have done to my family. I feel I have made a mistake."

"What do your dreams tell you?" the ogre asked, turning more to face Erik.

Erik's mouth dropped, and he stared up at the ogre, those gray eyes still inspecting him.

"My dreams?" Erik asked.

"Yes, Erik Eleodum," the ogre said, and then repeated, "your dreams."

"How ..." Erik didn't know what to say as the ogre just stood and waited, face flat and emotionless. "I haven't dreamt in weeks."

The ogre nodded, slowly.

"Sometimes we rely on the dream world too much," the ogre said. "Sometimes, we never want to leave the dream world. Reality becomes distorted. The Creator has, perhaps, given you a reprieve from the dream world."

"You know of the dream world well?" Erik asked.

The ogre nodded.

"The Creator has given we ogres special access to the dream world," the ogre said. "We watch and move through it, but rarely intervene. We have watched you for a while now, Erik Eleodum."

"What do you mean *move*?" Erik asked.

The ogre actually cracked the slightest hint of a smile.

"Tread carefully, Erik," the ogre said. "Leave this place tomorrow. Hurry home. And then wait. Your dreams will come ... and they will lead you."

Erik sat on the wheel of the ogre's cart while he sold several yards of fabric to another woman, a hunting knife to a hard-looking adventurer, and a large cup to a gray-haired dwarf.

"Have you ever been to Hargoleth?" the ogre asked, keeping his eyes on the people who bustled by, mostly going to and from the alehouse.

"No," Erik replied, "although, I have heard of it. Only recently, though."

"It is a beautiful place," the ogre said, "although it has seen hard and terrible times."

"Beautiful and terrible?" Erik asked.

"Yes," the ogre replied. "Most things that are beautiful can be terrible as well. I ask if you have ever been because you have the look of the Hargolethians."

"I do?"

"Yes," the ogre replied. "Hargoleth is a relatively new nation, settled by men and women just after the end of the Great War. They are mostly like those living in northern Háthgolthane and from Gongoreth."

"The same people as those who settled the free farms," Erik muttered to himself.

"Yes," the ogre said as if Erik had asked a question. "If you go, remember your name ... your given name."

"Eleodum?" Erik seemed to have so many names these days.

"Yes," the ogre replied. "It is an old name; a noble name."

"I'll remember to do that," said Erik standing again. He now wondered where the others were and felt an urgent need for their company and security.

"Go, Erik Eleodum, and find your friends," the ogre said. "I will see you in your dreams."

Erik nodded to the ogre and soon found his cousin sitting against a tree just outside the brothel.

"Do you feel better now?" Erik asked.

His cousin looked up at him with red-rimmed eyes. He was

drunk.

"Nope," Bryon replied. He reached between his legs, grabbed a bottle, and tipped the rest of its contents into his mouth. "I should have listened to you. You're the wise Erik Eleodum, and I'm the dumb troll shit of a cousin. Don't feel any better. Feel worse, in fact."

"Come on," Erik said, reaching down, grabbing Bryon by the collar of his mail shirt, and pulling him to his feet. "Let's find the dwarves, get some rest, and get home."

But before Erik could lead his cousin to one of the small tents the goblin brothers rented out as rooms, Bryon grabbed Erik's arm.

"Why do you put up with me, cousin?" Bryon asked. "Look at me. Look at you. I'm nothing like you. I'm a failure. I've let everyone I love down, including your brother."

Erik remembered the words Sustenon spoke to him. They had the same flavor.

"You're not a failure," Erik said with a smile. "There're not many people who could do what you do, fight the way you fight and are willing to stand up to bullies. And it's a good thing you're not like me. I don't think I would like you much if you were. As to why I put up with you ... it's because I love you, and I see the good in you, something you ought to see in yourself. Now let's find the dwarves, you can sleep off the ale, and we'll get ready to go home."

After another dreamless sleep, Erik stepped out into the forest morning. A thick mist hung just above the ground, and it reminded him of the mornings along the Blue Forest when he, his brother, and his cousin first left Waterton. It was on a morning like this that he took his first life when slavers attacked the gypsy caravan in which they traveled. He shivered and pulled his new coat tight around his mail. Through the flap to the tent, he could hear his cousin and dwarvish friends stirring and getting their things ready. Nothing stirred in the outpost, and only two guards stood at the road leading into Green

Tree. Erik saw two more guards meandering about, but they seemed more interested in talking than checking for mischief.

It was in the early morning mist that Erik saw something that gave him pause. The mist swirled about, in the distance near a tree. It seemed to dissipate for a moment, twirl about, and almost take the shape of a man, his features ghostly. But when Erik blinked and rubbed the sleep from his eyes, the figure was gone. A year ago, he would have passed such a sight off as happenstance, early morning sleep playing tricks on his eyes, but the world wasn't so simple, especially in far away, isolated places like Green Tree.

He pulled the flap open.

"We need to go," Erik said.

"Hold on," Bryon said, "I have a raging hang ..."

But Erik let go of the flap before Bryon could finish.

Only four of the people who had traveled with Erik from Fealmynster decided to stay in Green Tree, the rest following him, his cousin, and the dwarves out of the outpost and back onto the road. Bryon couldn't stop staring at a young woman with long, red hair and a button, freckled nose, and Nafer wouldn't stop grumbling about the slow pace because of all the people, but Erik was glad for the company. He didn't talk to many of them, but he enjoyed overhearing their conversations. It made time pass by quickly.

"How much longer, Dego?" Erik asked the older man who had led them to the road several nights after they had left Green Tree.

"You can see The Fangs are close," the man said, pointing a finger at the two gigantic shadows rising up from the Gray Mountains and disappearing into the clouded, night sky. "Shouldn't be too long. Seven days maybe."

Erik looked over his shoulder, into the darkness behind them. He saw a shadow move among the darkness, a mist barely visible in the intermittent glow of the moon and stars, mostly clouded.

Seven days may be too long.

59

——————

*E*rik opened his eyes. Stars twinkled overhead, but the air was comfortably warm. He felt something brush against his cheek, and he jerked back, but it was only a stem of grass, stirred by the breeze. He sat up and stared at the vast plain of grass, with the large, black mountain range beyond, with its usual black clouds and purple lightning. He looked over his shoulder to see the hill and willow tree. He saw a shadow under the tree and hoped it was the man.

Still in his armor, Erik stood and felt his shield on his back. He looked down and saw Dragon Tooth. He set off to walk towards the hill but felt something behind him. He stopped and turned to see smoke swirl about the air, taking the form of a person until a man stood in front of him. Erik recoiled at his appearance.

"I get that a lot," the man, if that was what he was, said.

His skin was tan like he spent most of his time in the sun, but his hair was a pale white as were his eyes, even his pupils. The leather armor he wore hugged his body, tightly, accentuating his muscles even though he was lean.

"You've been following us," Erik said.

"I've been following you," the specter of a man said.

"Me?"

"Is that so hard to believe, Dragon Slayer," the white-eyed man said, and then he gave a short, scoffing laugh.

"Why?"

"Why do you think?" the man asked.

He stared at Dragon Tooth.

"The Lord of the East sent you?"

"He knew you wouldn't return the sword," the man said.

The pale-eyed man held out his hand, and a spear appeared in it. It was a long spear, white with a white blade. When Erik looked closer, he saw the weapon was made of vertebrae and the blade was also bone. The man held a dagger, also made of bone, in the other hand.

"You can't kill me in the real world, so you mean to try and kill me here," Erik said, drawing Dragon Tooth and watching its green luminescence reflect off the man's pale eyes.

The man laughed loudly as if he had been told the greatest joke ever.

"Don't be a fool," the man said. "No man is a match for Bone Spear."

It was Erik's turn to laugh.

"That isn't seriously your name is it?" Erik asked, and the man looked offended. "Let me guess. Is it because your spear is made of bone?"

"I also go by the name of Specter, of Isuta," Bone Spear said, standing tall and puffing out his chest, one fist resting resolutely on his hip.

"You can't be serious," Erik said, laughing again, but Bone Spear became mist again, flowing through the grass.

Erik crouched into his fighting stance, Dragon Tooth held in both hands. The man materialized just paces away from him, and Erik didn't wait. While he was still translucent, a mist coalescing into a man, Erik stabbed, the blade of Dragon Tooth glowing brighter. Bone

Spear screamed as he fully became flesh, dropping his dagger and pressing a hand to his ribs. Blood seeped through his fingers.

"How?" Bone Spear asked, seething before he disappeared again.

Erik felt a boot to his back, and he reeled forward as the tip of the spear grazed his shoulder, scratching along the steel of his pauldrons, leaving a streak of smoking green liquid.

Poison.

Specter jabbed with his Bone Spear. Erik parried, and the bone blade struck wider than intended, skidding off the mail on Erik's arm. He could see the trail of poison the blade left and could smell its stink, but it didn't penetrate. The man looked frustrated, and Erik wondered if his quarry was normally much easier, but dwarvish steel was strong, and Erik was even stronger.

The Isutan pressed harder, jabbing and kicking and punching. He became mist, and Erik turned, only to sense the man materializing behind him and turning just to catch a fist to the face. Specter became ethereal again, but this time Erik didn't move. He felt a boot to the back of his shoulder as he lurched forward.

"Not so smug now, are we?" Specter asked.

"Stand still and see what happens," Erik said.

Erik could feel himself becoming frustrated. He breathed to calm himself and pulled his shield off his back.

"A dwarvish shield isn't going to help you," the Isutan said.

They continued to battle, Specter becoming ethereal and reappearing wherever he fancied and Erik trying to guess where he would materialize. Erik's blade struck several times, and the Bone Spear scratched along Erik's armor, but nothing fatal.

The dream world was different than the real world, and Erik always had more energy and strength in this place. It was as if he could will himself to keep going, fighting, walking, running, whatever he was doing, but they had been fighting for so long, he felt fatigued, even in this place. He looked up to his hill. The man still sat there as if nothing was happening.

"You're getting tired," Specter said, "I can tell."

"I don't tire in the dream world," Erik lied.

"You're a bad liar," Specter said.

Wake up, you fool, or this magician-assassin is going to kill you.

A thought, a familiar voice, passed through his mind.

Your sword is just as magical, the old man, Dewin, from Eldmanor said.

Erik held his sword in front of him, not sure what to do, just knowing he wished to stop this Isutan from disappearing and then reappearing wherever he wished. Dragon Tooth flashed with a brilliant green light and, as Specter tried to dematerialize, he couldn't, looking frustrated and cursing in his native language. Erik laughed.

"You won't be laughing when my poison courses through your veins," Specter said. "I will poison you and then drain you, but before you die, I will let you watch as I drain every single person you love. And then I will finish you."

"Drain?" Erik questioned.

Specter just threw his head back and laughed. Erik lost his concentration and the Isutan became transparent. This time he didn't return.

The sun in the dream world rose in the east, and Erik saw a cloaked figure, his black robes tattered and old.

"Be careful, Dream Walker," the old man from Eldmanor said.

"Tread carefully, Erik," the man on the hill added.

And then Erik woke to a chilled morning, the sky clouded and partially blocked by tall reaching pine trees.

60

$\mathcal{E}$rik began to recognize this part of the mountains. They had been here before. They passed by the petrified tree, and a knot formed in his stomach. Within a few days, the road sloped downward steeply, and, as they walked past a tall peak, the small town of Eldmanor came into vision, the homes simple specks from where they were at that moment.

"I never thought I would be so overjoyed to see this little dung heap of a town," Bryon muttered.

When they stepped onto level ground at the feet of the Gray Mountains, each of the people that had traveled with Erik and his companions thanked them. Erik gave each one of them several coins —he had more than enough to spare—and bid them farewell.

"Dego," Erik said, "thank you for leading us."

"Thank you for freeing us," Dego replied.

"Andu," Erik said, "will you continue to travel with us?"

"I don't know," Andu replied, a perplexed look on his face. "If you'll have me."

"As I said before," Erik said, "you are welcome in our company. You may travel to our farmlands and live there as long as you like."

Andu looked like he was going to cry.

"Bryon, take everyone to Hagmer's alehouse," Erik said. "I have something I need to do, and then I'll meet you there."

"The goat herder?" Bryon asked. "That weird hut?"

"Yes," Erik replied.

"Let me go with you," Bryon said.

"There's no need," Erik said with a sincere smile. "I will be fine. I'll meet you at Hagmer's, and then we'll go home."

"Just as long as there isn't another assassin awaiting us there," Bryon said.

"I think you will be safe," Erik said, this time his smile insincere. He looked over his shoulder, up towards the mountain road, and saw a light mist swirl around a tree, and then it was gone.

Erik stood at the entrance to the small hut on the outskirts of Eldmanor. He stepped into the darkness, and it took his eyes a moment to adjust to the smokiness and the faint light a single cook fire produced in the middle of the meager dwelling.

"Dream Walker," the old man croaked, sitting cross-legged at the fire, stoking it with a stick and not bothering to turn around.

"Dewin," Erik said with a slight bow.

He saw the old man's hooded head turn just slightly.

"To call a man by his real name," the old man said, his voice almost an inaudible whisper. "There is power in a man's name."

There was a moment of silence as the old man breathed heavy and just sat.

"Why has the Slayer of Dragons returned to my hut?" the old man asked.

"You knew I would come?" Erik said.

"Yes," the old man croaked.

"So, you know why I came," Erik said.

"Perhaps," the old man replied. "Why do you think you have come?"

"I can't return the sword to the Lord of the East, can I?" Erik asked.

The old man sat for a moment.

"No, you cannot," he finally said.

"But if I don't, my family will die," Erik said.

"Many have sacrificed themselves for you," Dewin said. "Many more will do the same. You wield the Dragon Sword reforged. You uncovered the mystery of your dagger. You know of the dragon rider, Rako. And you have seen a new shadow spreading across the land. It is not just the Lord of the East who will seek your life, Erik Dragon Fire."

"Specter?" Erik asked.

"The Isutan, yes," Dewin replied, "but he is working for the Lord of the East. Many people are beginning to love you. Many people are beginning to hate you."

"I don't care about myself," Erik replied.

"I know," Dewin said. "But you do care about those you love."

"How do I save them?" Erik asked.

"You cannot," Dewin replied.

"I don't believe you," Erik said.

"Believe or don't believe," Dewin said. "It doesn't matter. But you cannot save them. Only they can save themselves."

"Whatever comes next," Erik said, "I must do it alone."

"Yes," the old man croaked.

"And what comes next?" Erik asked. "Rako said something about a stone. Elves."

"The Dragon Stone," Dewin croaked, "but called many other names. The Ruling Stone. The Stone of Chaos. Prison."

"Yes," Erik said.

"There is more to the Dragon Stone than Rako," Dewin said. "An ancient evil has surfaced. A new shadow is rising."

"I don't understand," Erik said.

"You will know soon enough," the old man replied. "For now, go home. Be with those you love. Your dreams will speak. The wind will tell you what to do."

Erik turned to leave but then turned towards Dewin again.

"You helped me," Erik said. "You saved me ... from myself. Thank you."

Dewin laughed that same croaking laugh.

"I helped you, Dream Walker," Dewin said, "but it isn't about you. It never was. It never will be. This battle between good and evil is eternal. Some battles we win and some battles we lose."

"You are on the side of good, then?" Erik asked.

The old man didn't answer.

"You were a student of Andragos," Erik said. "You were a pupil with Sustenon. Neither one of them are good. What happened?"

The old man still didn't answer. He just sat and stoked his fire. Erik turned to leave.

"Wait," the man said, only, it wasn't the voice of an old man.

Erik turned to see a man barely older than he standing where Dewin had been. He had long, blond hair and broad shoulders. He wasn't very tall, but he was muscular, Erik could tell even through his robes. What struck Erik the most were his eyes. They were the blue of the sky just after a thunderstorm, clear and sharp.

"Magic ... black magic ... it takes a toll on a person," the man said.

"Dewin?" Erik asked.

The man nodded.

"Long ago, I chose to throw off the chains of black magic, and this is what it did to my body," Dewin said, and he snapped his finger, returning to the visage of an old, broken, blind man. His voice was croaking and frail once again. "But do not give up hope on my old teacher."

"I don't understand," Erik said.

"The winds of change are moving swiftly these days," Dewin said, "and this new shadow will change many things."

"So, what do I do now?" Erik asked.

"Wait," Dewin said, "and go when you are called."

"My family?"

"Save the world, you'll save your family," Dewin replied. "Save your family, the world dies."

It was like Dewin had put the weight of the world on his shoulders, but all Erik did was nod.

"There is power in a name, Dragon Fire," Dewin said. "Know the Lord of the East's name ... Syzbalo of House Stévock."

Erik bowed.

"I'll see you in my dreams," Erik said.

"I will be there, Dream Walker," Dewin said as Erik exited the hut.

As he walked towards Hagmer's alehouse to gather his friends and return home, he saw a horse, off in the distance. It was a giant of an animal, gray with just the hint of white around its nose and mouth, reminding Erik of the draft horses back home that pulled heavy wagons and plows. It had a saddle on its back, one that would be used for battle, but Erik didn't see anyone around.

Erik walked towards the animal, and the horse noticed him as it turned and snorted heavily. It was scared. No. It looked angry. Erik stopped. He looked at its feathered hooves. Each one of those could easily kill a man, crush his skull.

"You are wandering about, alone," Erik said to the horse, "with cougars and wolves around."

The horse snorted.

"Yes, of course," Erik said with a smile. "They are too afraid to attack you, aren't they?"

Erik thought that he recognized the horse from somewhere, as if he had seen it before. Was it Finlo?

"Are you going to stay out here alone?" Erik asked.

The horse snorted again and took a couple of steps forward, bobbing its head once or twice. Erik stepped forward, but then the animal snorted again, gave an angry whinny, and stomped its front hooves.

"Fine," Erik said, throwing up his hands, "you want to wander out here alone, be my guest. Eventually, the wolves and cougars will get hungry enough that they'll take a chance on you. Remember, there's always someone out there bigger, stronger, and meaner than you."

Erik turned away, but as he walked towards the center of Eldmanor, he heard hooves behind him. When he looked over his shoulder, the great, gray horse apparently saw Erik looking, because it stopped and nibbled at a bit of grass.

"Stubborn," Erik muttered with a smile, "and playing hard to get."

Erik walked through the door of the alehouse to find his companions, Andu, and several of the others who had traveled with them eating and drinking.

"It is good to see you again," Hagmer said, the fat man walking up to Erik and bowing.

"I see you have put my money to good use," Erik said with a smile, looking around and seeing more patrons, new benches and tables, a larger bar where the bucket of ale used to be, and a few men with large cudgels standing about the alehouse and just watching.

"Yes, sir," Hagmer replied. "Can I get you anything? Roasted goat. Ale. It is on the house."

Erik looked at Hagmer. The fat man smiled, but there was fear in his eyes. He saw the red-haired girl running about, delivering food and drink.

"No," Erik said. "We are leaving, Bryon."

Erik's cousin nodded, and his companions rose and walked to the door.

"I bid you good fortune, Hagmer," Erik said. He retrieved five gold coins from a pouch in his haversack and placed them in Hagmer's hand. "Once again, we were never here."

The owner of the alehouse nodded, and Erik saw Dego, sitting at one of the tables. "Dego. Farewell and thanks."

Dego looked at Erik and smiled.

"If you are ever in Finlo," the man said.

"I will find you," Erik replied.

"We need horses," Byron said as they stepped outside.

Erik saw the gray horse standing there, just away from the hitching posts outside the alehouse.

"I don't," Erik said with a smile, walking to the animal and rubbing its nose.

"Where did you find him?" Bryon asked. "And fully bridled?"

"He found me," Erik replied.

"You don't think his owner is going to come looking for him?" Bryon asked.

"I don't think he has an owner," Erik replied, then he heard a gasp and turned to see Andu, standing there and staring at the horse with wide eyes. "What?"

"This is Warrior, my lord," Andu said.

"Who is Warrior?" Erik asked. "And don't call me lord."

"Yes, my ... yes, sir," Andu replied. "This is the destrier of the former Patûk Al'Banan. Now the horse of Bu Al'Banan."

"Are you sure?" Turk asked.

"This warhorse is unmistakable," Andu replied, "I would know it anywhere."

"But why is Bu Al'Banan's warhorse wandering about Eldmanor, ownerless?" Erik asked.

"Bu let him go," Andu replied, "when we were attacked by giant spiders. I don't know if it was out of love for the horse, or self-preservation, but he saw that everyone who rode were easier targets for the spiders. I should be surprised that this horse survived, but I am not."

"Why?" Erik asked.

"I have never met a hardier, stronger, or more cantankerous creature, other than Patûk Al'Banan, in my life," Andu replied.

Erik grabbed the horse's reins, hanging from its bridle.

"Will you let me ride you home?" Erik whispered to the horse, to Warrior.

Warrior didn't do anything. He just stood there, seemingly waiting. Erik shrugged, put a boot in one of the stirrups and hoisted himself into the saddle. The horse didn't move.

"Shall we?" Erik said.

The horse still didn't move.

"He probably understands Shengu," Turk said.

"Tell him, *Ban Ko*," Andu said.

Erik nodded.

"Ban Ko."

And with that, Warrior started walking.

Having found riding horses for everyone, they left Eldmanor and reached the northern outskirts of the free farmlands of Háthgolthane in two days. It was barely dusk when Erik heard the familiar sound of his father scolding a stubborn cow and his mother chastising him for his foul language. It wasn't that foul compared to some of the men Erik had been around.

It was late fall, almost three months from the time they left, and the harvest was almost over. Rikard Eleodum and his farmhands were going through the land and picking what stubborn stalks of wheat and ears of corn and pods of beans decided to come up late.

His father didn't see him as he rode up to the edge of the field on which they were working.

"Your cussing gets worse, Father," Erik said.

His father looked up and laughed.

"Erik, my son!"

Before his father could walk to him and offer him a hand, his mother was running from the house, pulling him from his saddle, and squeezing him so hard, he had trouble breathing.

"I knew you would come back, son," Karita Eleodum said. "I just knew it."

"Bryon," Rikard said, "I'm glad you are safe. And I see you have an extra person with you, but didn't you leave with four dwarvish companions?"

"Not everyone returns home sometimes," Turk said.

"I am sorry," Rikard said.

"His sacrifice is the reason we are here," Turk said.

"This is Andu, Father," Erik said. "He will be staying with us for a while."

"Of course," his father said. "Any friend of my son's is a friend of mine. Now, I am assuming you have seen Simone."

Erik shook his head. His mother hit him on the shoulder.

"Erik!" she gasped.

"Son," his father said when Erik gave his mother a confused look, "Simone is your wife and takes priority over all others. You should have gone to her first. Now go. We will take care of your friends."

Erik rode Warrior up to the gate of his home. Smoke escaped through the brick chimney, and it reminded him of the worst dream he had ever had, his wife dead, his baby cut from her belly, and his home on fire. His heart raced, beating against his chest with an aggressive rhythm. He tied Warrior to the fence that surrounded his home and walked up the dirt walkway, lined by tiny rose plants, gifts from his mother to Simone. He had only gotten halfway when Simone burst through the front door and ran to him, throwing herself into his arms and wrapping her arms tightly around his neck.

"I knew you would come back," she said, crying into Erik's chest.

"I promised you, didn't I?" he replied, smiling as he felt the swell of her growing stomach against his own. "Let's have a look at you."

He couldn't help the smile on his face as he inspected his wife's belly, gently touching it and putting his mouth close to it, speaking to his unborn baby.

"He knows your voice," Simone said, cupping Erik's chin in her hands.

"How do you know it's a boy?" Erik asked.

"He is stubborn and strong!"

They both laughed.

"Sounds like his mother," Erik said, dancing out of the way of his wife's striking hand. "It may very well be a girl. I would be just as happy."

"Our first child is a boy," she said, her face full of defiance. Her blonde hair silhouetted her face, and her blue eyes pierced Erik's heart. As if she couldn't get any more beautiful, here she was. "I don't care what the others will be, but this one is a boy."

"Others," Erik exclaimed with wide eyes. "We haven't had this one yet. Wait and see, wife. I may be as terrible a father as I am a husband."

"Hush," Simone said, a scowl crossing her beautiful face. "You are not a terrible husband, and you will be the best father ... a combination of yours and mine."

"I haven't been here, Simone," Erik said, looking away from her as if her eyes accused him and he couldn't face it.

"You had to," she said. "It's what you had to do to protect your family. And, besides, every night, as I fell asleep, I could feel you, sense you, almost see you in my dreams, but it was as if you were really there."

"I saw you in my dreams too, my sweet," Erik said, smiling down at his wife.

"No, my love," Simone said, shaking her head, "they were dreams, but they weren't. It was real. I watched you from a hill, amidst a field of tall grass. I could see you, but I could never call out to you, but you were there. And whenever I was worried, I would have the same dream, and I would see you, and I knew you were still alive ... that you would return to me."

Is Simone a dream walker?

Erik shook his head and hugged his wife again.

"I am home, and that is all that matters."

61

____

All of the farmsteads gathered on Peace Day, in the evening, inside the barn of Rikard Eleodum, even Jovek, and his family. There were drums and a lute, a lyre, a harp, and fiddles playing any number of songs, from fast-paced jigs to slow ballads. Everyone brought some food, more than the two hundred or so people could ever eat, even in a week, and, much to the chagrin of Erik's mother, they all brought wine and ale as well.

At first, Erik thought the celebration was for him, but when he found out it was because of the farms' survival through what was one of the worst summers and harvests they had ever had, he felt a little ashamed at his egotistic supposition. However, he was partly to be thanked for the survival of the free farms of Háthgolthane. Northern Dwarves had come down for the first time in several years, but they did not come to trade. They knew the harvest would be sparse this year, and they brought food and animals and extra hands to help.

Erik's father told him that when one farmer, who was still most thankful but rather perplexed by the gesture, asked why, one of the dwarves simply responded, "You are the people of Erik Dragon Fire, of Erik Eleodum, which means you are our people, and we always help one another."

"Men and women ... children might have died if it wasn't for you," Erik's father said, placing a hand on Erik's shoulder as they sat together and watched women dance and children play.

"But many did because of me, Father," Erik replied, looking down at the cup of spiced wine in his hands.

"Son, you must let some things go, even if you can't forget them," Rikard said. "How many more would have died if you were not there to take on that dragon?"

Erik just shrugged his shoulders. He didn't believe what Sustenon the Damned had told him, that he was a failure and a coward, but the words still remained in the back of his head.

The dwarves who had come to the farmlands to bring aid had been invited to the party, and several of them walked up to Erik and his father. One, with short, red hair and a bushy red beard, wearing a robe that covered his feet, bowed and spoke for the group.

"Erik Dragon Fire," the dwarf said in his northern dialect of Dwarvish, "it is an honor to be in your presence. Dorhûd Granite Tree at your service."

"I can't thank you enough for what you have done for my family," Erik said, extended a hand and shaking the dwarf's, "and for my people."

"You are our people," Dorhûd said, "and therefore, your people are our people, and we always take care of our own. Show someone else the kindness we have shown; that will be thanks enough."

Erik bowed, and Dorhûd and the other dwarves with him returned the gesture.

"May we see the fabled sword, Master Dragon Fire?" Dorhûd asked.

"It is not the original, you understand," Erik said.

"I do," Dorhûd replied.

"And, even though the blade is made from Dwarf's Iron and crafted by Ilken Copper Head," Erik added, "the magic is elvish."

"I think I will manage," Dorhûd replied with a short laugh and a smile.

Erik nodded and drew Dragon Tooth. The blade glowed green and, if Erik looked close enough, he could almost see the outline of flames coming off the steel.

"Magnificent," Dorhûd said with a short gasp.

"Who would have thought?" Rikard said, clapping his son on the shoulder. "My son would be speaking Dwarvish and wielding swords and slaying dragons, and who knows what else."

But before Erik could say anything, he felt a cold breeze enter the barn, and someone outside gave out a short scream. Erik saw mist move along the floor of the barn, and the several fires burning in the middle of the barn fluttered and dimmed for a moment.

"Magnificent indeed," a voice said.

Erik recognized that voice from a dream.

"I don't think I will return it to Syzbalo," the voice said. "I think I will keep it."

Erik stood. The music stopped, and everyone was still.

"He will come for you," Erik said to the mist. "He will send assassins just as he has sent you."

Laughter.

"I'm not worried," the voice said.

"Father," Erik whispered, "go to my haversack, quickly. There is a bag in it. It feels as if it is filled with sand. Get it for me urgently."

"Son, I won't ..."

Specter materialized in the middle of the barn to a combination of murmurs, gasps, and one, quick yelp. His black leather armor glistened in the firelight, and, as he produced his spear made of bone and vertebrae, the green outline of the poisoned bone blade glimmered.

"Go, Father, please," Erik whispered.

His father rushed out of the barn. Specter saw him and stepped in his direction, but Erik blocked the assassin's path.

"It's not him you want," Erik said.

"Oh, that is where you are mistaken," Specter said. "You see, our friend, the Lord of the East, doesn't just want you dead. He wants your whole family dead. He wants *all* your people dead."

One man, a tall, broad-shouldered farmer who was ten summers older than Erik stepped forward, fists clenched.

"Willis," Erik said, his voice hard, "step back."

"Oh," Specter laughed, "this is going to be fun. It never is when my victims just cower. Yes, Willis, step back and wait your turn."

"I don't see how a man, if that is what you are, can take such pleasure in killing so many people," Erik said.

"You don't know about me, do you?" Specter asked. "No, you don't. Why would you? You see, I am a man, but I am also a powerful mage. And most people find what gives me my power abhorrent, but it is also what is necessary for me to stay alive, so I revel in it. Would you like to know what it is that keeps me alive and powerful, Erik Eleodum?"

Erik just shrugged. He didn't like playing these games.

"Blood," Specter said, smiling deeply and revealing his perfectly white teeth. "The younger and more innocent, the better. I will drain every single person here; I will take that sword, and I will simply go away and hide for fifty or a hundred years; however long it takes that idiot Syzbalo to die."

"You're a monster," someone from the crowd said.

Specter just shrugged.

"Maybe," he said, smiling, "but I am a very powerful, eternal monster."

Erik heard the hiss of elvish magic and saw the purple glow of Bryon's sword. He saw Turk and Nafer and Bofim, others standing and grabbing whatever tools they could get their hands on that might be used as weapons. Even Andu drew his sword. Specter just laughed.

Erik put a hand up.

"Just you and me, Specter," Erik said. "You kill me, you'll have to contend with them. I win, well, you'll be dead."

Specter laughed harder.

"Erik, no," Simone said.

"Sure," the assassin said. "This will be fun. Your woman will watch you die, and then I will drain both her and your unborn baby."

Erik gripped Dragon Tooth with both hands, looked at his wife, nodded and smiled, and backed up, walking out of the barn.

"You wish to fight in the darkness of night," Specter said with a wide smile, although there were fires blazing outside, "and in my world. Perfect. You truly are prideful, aren't you?"

Erik wished he had his shield at that moment or his armor, but all he had was his sword, and that would have to be enough. He crouched into his fighting stance as did Specter, holding the bone spear behind his head, pointing at Erik. Erik made the first move.

He came at Specter, low and methodical, as Specter swung his spear like a stick, the assassin bringing it behind his head and then swinging it forward. Erik ducked out of the way and heard the wind whistle through the holes in the vertebrae that made up the weapon. Specter gripped the spear with both hands and jabbed at Erik. He easily dodged the attack, but then the Isutan was smoke, floating through the air. Erik watched as the smoke floated overhead, pretended to float behind them, and then back in front of Erik. He was ready for the attack, almost, and as the bone blade of the spear sliced a neat tear in Erik's shirt, a boot kicked out hard and caught Erik in the chest, sending him backward into the dirt.

Erik came up in his crouch, ready for another attack.

"You are a stubborn one, aren't you?" Specter said.

"You talk too much," Erik replied.

Specter jabbed, punched, kicked, tried to bite, jabbed again, and then swung his spear out at Erik, pushing Erik back on his heels the whole time.

"Admit it," Specter said as he pressed close to Erik, the shaft of his spear pushing against Erik's chest and a hand gripping Erik's wrist, keeping his sword at bay, "you are no match for me."

Erik brought a knee up into the assassin's crotch hard. Specter gasped and backed away, clutching his stomach.

"Cheap," Specter hissed.

"Like your magic," Erik replied.

With that, the Isutan became mist again, but instead of watching the mist float about, Erik remembered his training with the old soldier Wrothgard. He closed his eyes and felt the winds around him move, sensing his opponent. He felt the mist feign left, then right, and then coalesce behind him. He turned hard and stabbed. His blade flared green as it caught Specter's ribs, tearing leather. The assassin screamed, and, when Erik retrieved his blade, blood flowed down the man's side and onto his black, leather boots.

"You'll pay for that," Specter said.

Specter pushed out with an open hand, and Erik felt the air punch him in the chest. The Isutan then snapped a finger and a flame danced in his palm. He threw it at Erik, and, even though he dodged the ball of fire, it skidded along the ground and into the barn, igniting the old, dry timber. The assassin pointed the blade of the Bone Spear at Erik and, speaking a language Erik didn't understand, a green mist seeped from the blade. Erik began coughing as he caught a whiff of the cloud, a choking, pungent stink that stung his eyes.

Erik saw his father running towards him, the bag of fairy dust in his hand. Specter saw him too, and Erik noticed a smile forming on the assassin's face. He rushed through the choking mist, ignoring the stinging and nauseating effect it gave and, before the Isutan noticed Erik, lowered a shoulder. Specter was too nimble and making himself half-ethereal, floated out of the way, bringing the shaft of his spear across Erik's face.

Erik rolled to the ground. He could hear Simone screaming and crying. He saw the people of the farmstead and his friends close in. He saw the smile growing on Specter's face. This was what he wanted. He wanted them all to converge on him. They would be easier prey, huddled together in a mass of flesh and blood.

Specter held his spear in his right hand and drew his bone-blade dagger. He came at Erik hard, jabbing and stabbing, slashing and swinging. He turned to mist and then materialized, doing the same over and over as he continued to kick and punch, many of his strikes finding a home. He threw another fireball at Erik, produced another cloud of choking smoke, and tried to will the ground to sprout vines that might cling to Erik's legs. Erik felt spent, and Specter looked just fine. He looked over his shoulder and saw his father.

While Specter was doing his disappearing act yet again, Erik reached out as his father tossed him the bag. He thrust his hand into it and retrieved a handful of dust he blew towards Specter. The fire extinguished, and the choking cloud dissipated. When a speck of the dust touched the Isutan's ethereal form, he became whole and he screamed, a hand to his cheek. When he removed his hand, his flesh was burnt.

"Enough!" Specter yelled, finally losing his composure. "Time to die!"

He rushed Erik, jabbing high with his spear and stabbing low with the dagger. Erik brought his sword up and blocked the spear and with a speed that surprised the assassin, brought it down hard on the hand that held the short blade. He caught the Isutan's hand with the broad side of Dragon Tooth, so it didn't remove the hand, but it knocked the dagger away and burned flesh at the same time.

Erik kicked out, sending Specter on his back as the fairy dust floated about him, each speck burning him as it touched his skin. He leaped to his feet and stabbed again. Erik gripped Dragon Tooth with both hands hard and swung downwards, swatting the spear away over and over, each strike causing the Bone Spear to bend and driving the assassin lower and lower to his knees until, with the last strike and a mighty scream from Erik, Dragon Tooth shattered the shaft of Bone Spear.

Specter looked up at Erik, his eyes squinted and filled with rage. He rolled to his right and grabbed his dagger, holding it with a reverse grip. He tried bringing the blade across Erik's face, and, when he missed, he tried to stab Erik in the side of the neck, but Erik caught the man's wrist. He was stronger than he looked.

Fairy dust floated all around him, and Specter's pale eyes went wide. Smoke floated up between Erik and the assassin. They both looked down. Dragon Tooth sat, cross-handle deep in Specter's belly. The Isutan dropped the dagger.

"How?" he whispered.

"Syzbalo is going to be so disappointed," Erik said as he twisted Dragon Tooth, reveling in the sound of flesh ripping and tearing.

"Impossible," Specter said, his voice even weaker.

"And, yet, here we are," Erik replied, ignoring the welts on his face and the blood trickling from numerous wounds.

Specter's face began to wrinkle, his skin sagging. His teeth yellowed, and his muscles, normally taut against his leather armor, seemed to diminish. His white hair thinned, and his pale eyes dulled. The cost of black magic.

"How many deaths am I avenging right now?" Erik asked.

He pulled Dragon Tooth from Specter's belly, and the assassin fell to his knees. The Isutan still looked confused, bewildered.

"This is not the dream world," Erik said, "and you are no longer a powerful, eternal monster. If you are truly a dream walker, then you know what awaits you on the other side. And I will see you there. When I do ..."

Erik placed the tip of Dragon Tooth at the base of Specter's throat and winked before, with an angry grunt, he stabbed. As Specter hit the ground, his body began to shrivel and wrinkle. He became an old man, older than old, ancient, until all that was left was dust.

Simone ran to Erik.

"My love," she said, reaching up to wipe blood from his cheek.

"I'm alright," Erik said.

"Who was that?" she asked.

"That was the world around us, my sweet," Erik said as men and women rushed around to grab buckets for the burning barn, even though it was a futile act.

"I don't understand," Simone said.

"This world is an evil, cruel, and relentless place," Erik said, looking down at his wife's face, "and that is why I left. I left to keep you safe. But I can't stop my love. I can't keep you and our child safe from here. In order to save you both, I have to keep on fighting. You have to be strong; do you understand?"

"No," Simone said, weeping and burying her face into Erik's chest. "I don't understand any of this."

"Cousin," Bryon said, coming to Erik and hugging him and Simone.

"I'm alright," Erik said.

"The barn is lost," Bryon said.

"I know," Erik replied. "A small price to pay."

"Who was that?" Bryon asked.

"One of the Lord of the East's assassins," Erik replied.

"Will he send more?" Bryon asked.

"I am most certain of it," Erik replied.

He knew it wouldn't just be the Lord of the East. Gol-Durathna wanted him dead. Bu wanted him dead, regardless of what truce the man said they had. The dwomanni wanted him dead. And Fréden Fréwin wanted him dead. Probably even the Samanian slavers still wanted him dead. And this new shadow of which Dewin spoke certainly wanted him dead.

62

———

"Specter is dead, my lord," Andragos said as he sat on the Lord of the East's dais, facing Syzbalo. His two witches lounged against him, one on either shoulder.

The Lord of the East slammed a fist against the arm of his chair, and Kimber, the pale-haired witch on that side jerked away as if slapped.

"That fool," he hissed.

"He had no intention of bringing the Dragon Sword to you," Andragos added.

"How do you know?" Kimber hissed, seeking to cover up her embarrassment.

"I saw him, in my visions," Andragos replied.

"So did we," Krista hissed, the dark-skinned, dark-haired witch. "We saw nothing that indicated betrayal."

"Maybe your magic is weaker than mine," Andragos said with a smile.

Both witches hissed at that, and Andragos fought to hide his disdain.

Sycophants.

"Enough," the Lord of the East said. "Does Eleodum have any intention of bringing the sword here?"

Andragos shook his head.

"No," the Black Mage replied. "In fact, the sword has been reforged. It is now called Dragon Tooth. The dagger Erik carried was magically united on Sustenon's altar with Erik's sword and a shard of tooth from the dragon. It is, essentially, his sword now."

The Lord of the East stood, his face red. He looked at his witches.

"Send for Black Tigress," the Lord of the East commanded.

"Specter's daughter?" Andragos asked as he stood. "Haven't we learned our lesson?"

The Lord of the East turned hard on Andragos, hands lifted high, sparkling with electricity.

"You forget yourself," the Lord of the East said.

Andragos clenched his fists.

"You may very well be more powerful than me one day, Syzbalo," Andragos said, "but that day is not today. I apologize for my tone, but be careful. I have been here for much longer than you, your father, and many of your family, and I intend on being here *long* after you."

The Lord of the East dropped his hands and looked at the witches. He smiled.

"You underestimate my powers," Syzbalo said. "I am growing stronger by the day."

"Indeed," Andragos said, looking about the room with sidelong glances.

He could feel the magic in the room, but it was a different magic than what he used, what he touched. It was dark—some might call it black—like his, but very distinctive. He hadn't felt magic like it before, not since...his eyes went wide for a moment, and then they squinted. He groaned inwardly.

More powerful indeed, Andragos thought, *but at what cost?*

"Is that all?" Andragos asked.

"I have a task for you," Syzbalo said.

Andragos bowed.

"Destroy the free farms of Northwestern Háthgolthane," he said. "Kill everyone who lives there."

"That is far outside our borders, my lord," Andragos said, cocking one eyebrow. "Every nation in Háthgolthane will see it as an act of war."

"It is my desire," Syzbalo said. "My order. Are you disobeying me?"

"I will not instigate war with the west," Andragos said.

"You serve me," the Lord of the East said, pointing a finger at the Black Mage, "and I am commanding you to do this."

"I serve Golgolithul," Andragos spat back, "and my charge is to do what is in the best interest of my country."

"Even if it includes disobeying its rightful ruler?" the Lord of the East asked, straightening his back. His witches seemed to watch the exchange with increased interest, almost aroused as their master tried to exert power.

"Yes," Andragos said. "I have in the past. I will again if need be. How do you think it is that Gol-Durathna and its allies, on the verge of defeat almost three hundred years ago, pushed our forces back, forcing Rimrûk Aztûk to sign the Treaty of the Battle of Bethulium. How do you think it is, that Mörken Stévock, with very little power or influence, was able to overthrow the Aztûkians and return the rule of the east to his family."

"You speak of treason," Kimber hissed.

"You speak of treachery," Krista added, also hissing.

"I speak of loyalty," Andragos replied. "I speak of true dedication to ones country, no matter the cost."

The witches became agitated, hissing and clinging to the Lord of the East. Andragos could feel their magic rising as they touched it, ready to attack. He Melanius as well. But the Lord of the East put up a hand and looked down at Andragos lazily.

"You are dismissed, Andragos," the Lord of the East said. "I no longer need or wish you to follow Erik Eleodum with your visions."

"As you wish," Andragos said.

"And you will stay confined to your country cottage," the Lord of the East added. "How shall I advise you from my home?"

"I know longer desire your advice," Syzbalo said.

"Very well," Andragos said with a sweeping bow.

"And I expect repayment for my inquisitors," Syzbalo added.

"How would you like me to repay you for the lives of your inquisitors?"

"Lives for lives," the Lord of the East said.

"My men are the best trained in all Háthgolthane, and you would waste them on scum?" Andragos said, his voice hard.

The Lord of the East smiled.

"Of course not," he replied, and for a moment, Andragos relaxed. "I will take the lives of Raktas and Terradyn."

"You cannot," Andragos said.

"Can't I?" the Lord of the East said stepping up to Andragos so that they were face to face. "I can do whatever I want. I am the most powerful man in Háthgolthane, and soon I will be the most powerful man in the world. Terradyn and Raktas, or I start killing all the young boys in your magic academies, the young boys training to be Soldiers of the Eye, and I will seriously search out Ja Sin's family, that you think you so secretively hid from me. I will make you watch as I flay each and every one of them ... even the littlest ones that would have made Specter especially happy."

"And you think this bothers me?" Andragos asked.

"I know it does," Syzbalo hissed, leaning in closer. "You have become complacent and soft. Let me know when the Black Mage gathers his senses and returns. Let me know when the man who would have destroyed Ja Sin's whole family and executed every single Soldier of the Eye for allowing a traitor in their midst returns. I covet that man's counsel."

Andragos turned and left. He shielded his mind as best he could, but at that moment, he had no control over his emotions. It had been centuries since he had been this angry. As he walked out through the open-air colonnade that led into the black keep, the Lord of the East's guards accompanied the Black Mage.

"Get away from me," the Messenger hissed.

"Our orders," one said.

"We are to escort you," another said.

Andragos stopped. He clenched his fist and screamed, flexing the muscles in his arms. The two columns on either side of him cracked, sending dust and rubble down on the heads of the guards. He looked to one of the soldiers. The man looked scared. Good. The Messenger lifted a hand. The soldier levitated and, when Andragos closed his hand into a fist, the soldier's eyes went wide, blood streaming from his mouth and nose. The Black Mage released him, and he crumpled to the ground.

Andragos blinked. As the other guard tried to stab him with his spear, the Mage disappeared and reappeared behind the soldier and touched the back of his neck. His skin turned black, green smoke spilling from his eyes and ears until he shriveled up into nothing.

Andragos turned to face the now closed doors of the keep.

"Do not test me!"

He knew the Lord of the East heard him, even though the doors were closed.

"You do not want that man to return as your enemy!" the Black Mage added.

As half a dozen more guards rushed up the stairs leading to the colonnade, Andragos clapped, and each of the soldiers burst into flames. They screamed and flailed and fell to the ground, rolling about and trying to extinguish flames that could not be put out. Andragos opened his arms, closed his eyes, and opened his mouth, breathing in deep.

The Black Mage felt the souls of the dead enter his body and become a part of him. He felt his magic grow, and he didn't know what this meant for the future. He had fought with former rulers of Golgolithul, having to prove he was powerful in the past, but Syzbalo was going too far. Did he want all-out war with Andragos? No, he was being influenced—by the witches, by Melanius...and by something much more dangerous.

A dozen more guards rushed up the stairs.

"Is this what you want?" Andragos asked, holding his hands out like a priest towards the blackened and smoking corpses scattered on the stairs.

The guards stopped and then parted to let him walk between them.

"This changes things, Syzbalo," Andragos said loudly as if talking to the guards who stood to attention, watching him. "You have gone too far, you and your witches. Your Isutan magician. I know what influences you. I know what demon speaks to you in the darkness. This changes things indeed."

Again, he knew the Lord of the East heard him.

"I need you to travel to the northwestern part of Háthgolthane," Andragos said to his two bodyguards once they were in his carriage and headed home.

"My lord?" Raktas asked.

"Watch Erik Eleodum," Andragos said. "Protect him."

"What about you?" Terradyn asked.

"Don't worry about me," Andragos replied.

"I beg your pardon, my lord," Raktas said, "but you are our concern. Not some farm boy."

"You will do as you are told," Andragos said. Perhaps he had been too lenient on these men recently, too familiar.

"My lord ..." Terradyn began.

"*Enough!*" Andragos yelled, and the carriage went black and shook. "You will do as I command you. Either that or you stay here so the Lord of the East can execute you to teach me a lesson."

"My lord, I don't understand," Raktas said, and the Mage reached out his hands to lightly touch the arm of each man. They were beyond loyal.

"It is not for you to understand. Now is the time," Andragos said, his voice back to a much more conversational level, "to make a move, to make a stand, but in order to do so, we need Erik Eleodum alive. You will watch and protect him. Do you understand?"

"Yes, my lord," the two men said in unison.

Belvengar Long Spear watched from a distance. He saw Turk, once his friend, watching Erik Eleodum fight an opponent that was no normal man. He was a mage, and it looked as if he would do Belvengar's job for him, but then the tables turned, and Erik slew the magician. He was a strong fighter and powerful soldier. He wouldn't be so easy to kill.

Belvengar Long Spear turned to slink back into the darkness as a burning barn lit up the night sky. Before he could take a step, he flinched and gasped.

"What are you doing here?" Nafer Round Shield asked.

Belvengar stopped for a moment, surprised. He didn't know what to say.

"Looking for you, of course," he finally replied.

"You lie," Nafer said.

Belvengar looked down and saw the broad sword of Demik Iron Thorn hanging from Nafer's belt.

"Turk gave you Demik's sword," Belvengar said.

"Aye," Nafer replied.

"That man killed him," Belvengar said, pointing in the direction of the burning barn. "He should still be wearing his father's sword."

"No," Nafer replied. "I was there. Demik gave his life for that man."

"What's the difference?" Belvengar asked.

"You know the difference," Nafer replied. "The very fact that you have to ask that question proves that Fréden has poisoned your mind."

"Fréden has nothing to do with this," Belvengar said.

"More lies," Nafer said. "You, out of all of us, loathed lying, and here you are, slinking in the shadows, lying."

"Nafer, the world around us is changing," Belvengar said, "and we need to gather together to make our people strong."

"Yes, we do," Nafer said, "and Erik is one of our people. All of these men and women are our people."

"Do you even hear yourself?" Belvengar asked.

"Erik was given a clan name," Nafer explained. "Dragon Fire."

"Blasphemy," Belvengar hissed.

"But it doesn't matter," Nafer continued. "Even if he wasn't given a clan name, he is one of us, a goodly man, a follower of An, and a noble soldier."

"He is a man," Belvengar said, almost pleading with Nafer.

"Aye, that he is," Nafer said, "and a good one. I would give my life for him. Turk would too."

"You can't be serious," Belvengar said.

"I will let you leave, peacefully, just this once," Nafer said. "The next time I see you slinking in the shadows ..."

"Nafer, we were once brothers," Belvengar said.

"Once," Nafer replied. "It is not I who changed the situation."

Nafer turned and walked away, leaving Belvengar in the dark, only the distant glow of a burning barn shedding any light on the night. He would have to wait. When this Erik was alone, that was when he would strike.

63

———————

*E*rik sat under the willow tree, its branches weeping and dipping low, brushing his face gently when a gust of wind was strong enough. The sun was soft overhead, providing just enough light and heat to ward off any chills that the breeze might bring. Erik stared at the black mountains in the distance, black clouds and purple lightning endlessly raging overhead. When the thunder was especially loud and powerful—Erik could only normally hear it as a distant echo—the ground and the hill and the tree shook slightly.

"The storm over there. What does it signify?" Erik asked the man with whom he sat, a man he knew, but, then again, didn't. Every time he dreamed this dream, he would stare at the man's face. He recognized it, but couldn't place where he had seen it before. Then, just as he was about to remember who the man was, he would wake.

"You have been there," the man said, his voice calm and familiar. "You have experienced it."

"I still don't understand," Erik replied.

"Think, Dream Walker," Dewin said. The old wizard had appeared on the other side of Erik to the familiar man. He had done that in the last couple of dreams Erik had, but now he didn't appear as an old, broken man. Rather, Dewin appeared as his younger self, a handsome, blond-haired man, strong and vibrant.

"It is the Shadow?" Erik both said and asked.

Dewin shook his head with a smile.

"Am I wrong?" Erik asked.

"Yes and no," the man under the tree said. "It is an aspect of the Shadow."

"An aspect?" Erik wondered. "You too have experienced it before?"

"Oh yes, Dream Walker," Dewin said.

"The Shadow tries to infiltrate this place, influence this land of dreams," the man under the tree said, "and in doing so, the Shadow then influences people."

"I don't know if I understand," Erik replied.

"You see," the man said, "the Shadow uses others, influences them, invades their minds and hearts to do his work. He poisons relationships and corrupts leaders. He causes divisions amongst people ... hatred and bigotry and prejudice. The Shadow is not the one carrying out evil. He finds others to do it for him. He was defeated long ago, cast away in ages past into the depths of the cosmos, and so this is how he must work. And one of the easiest places to influence men and women is the world of dreams, a place that most disregard as the leftover thoughts and worries of the day, or the hopes and fears of the subconsciousness, or the conjured, deep memories that seem lost to time save for the faded glimpse one sees when they sleep."

"His strength ebbs and flows," Dewin said. "Right now, the Shadow gains strength, both in his part of this world and the world of the living. The greater the thunder over there, at the edge between this dream world and the shadow lands, the more he is succeeding."

"More and more people are serving the Shadow?" Erik asked.

"No," the man under the tree said. "At least, not purposely. But when they do wrong, when they intentionally hurt, they are serving the Shadow. And the Shadow's greatest victory is making people believe he is some fanciful demon mothers tell their children about to make them behave."

"So, when I was here, and the mountain range was gone, and there was a mysterious person clothed in black, who wasn't the one who comes with the carriage?" Erik asked open-endedly.

He couldn't help but see the look Dewin gave the other man who sat under the tree.

"Is that the Shadow losing power?" Erik asked.

"I told you," Dewin said, "there is something else—another evil —rising up."

"A new evil?"

"Yes and no," Dewin said. "New and ancient at the same time."

"An ally of the Shadow?" Erik asked.

Dewin shook his head.

"It opposes the Creator, but also the Shadow?" Erik asked.

Dewin nodded slowly.

"That is bad," Erik said. "My battle isn't over, is it?"

"Oh no, Dragon Slayer," Dewin said with the hint of a laugh, "it has just begun. And it is about to become much more dangerous."

The distant thunder caused the ground underneath Erik to roll. He heard the air crack and felt the hair on the back of his neck stand on end. Purple lightning flashed, and Erik closed his eyes, sucking in a sharp breath. When he opened his eyes, Dewin and the other man under the tree were gone. The distant range of mountains was gone. The sun seemed to pale. And a cloaked figure stood in the middle of the vast field of grass.

Erik opened his eyes to darkness, the only light in the room the sliver of moonlight escaping through the smallest of cracks in the window's shutter. He sat up, Simone gently snoring next to him, her breasts beneath the covers moving slowly up and down as she breathed evenly. He swung his feet to the edge of the bed, putting them on the floor. A rug of bearskin lay there, and it felt soft and warm under his feet. He looked to the small table next to this bed. His sword, Dragon Tooth—the Dragon Sword reforged—leaned against it.

Erik grabbed his sword and unsheathed it. The green glow was soft as if somehow it knew his wife was sleeping and glowing brightly would wake her. The green flames, almost mere silhouettes, danced along the blade, and Erik rested the steel in his hand. It didn't burn him. In fact, it felt cool.

Erik stared at the weapon, as he did most nights when his wife was asleep. He didn't want anyone, especially her, catching him watching the blade longingly, lest she think him mad, so he did so at night. It worried him as much as it might worry anyone else—a man just staring, having a conversation with a sword in his mind as if it were some long lost friend. But there was no response anymore. The voice was gone—the elf, Rako. And it truly felt like Erik had lost a dear friend.

What do I do?

He dropped his chin to his chest.

I cannot leave my family again. More assassins will come. How can I work to stave off evil for the greater world if I am always worried about the ones I love?

He heard shuffling outside his window, heard the distant low growl of a dog, and the scratching and skittering of a mouse across the wooden veranda outside the house. He heard the chase and the squeak of the rodent as it desperately tried to avoid capture by a farm cat. He heard a hiss and then a louder squeak and a low growl. The hunt was done, and he or Simone would find an offering on their doorstep in the morning. A part of him wondered, hoped, that maybe it was a great snow cat outside his window, hunting mice. He smiled. It was a nice notion, but his ally was gone, living a life of freedom, and mouse would be much of a meal. Thought of the snow cat brought the elf to mind again.

I am sorry, Rako. I wish I could have saved you. I wish I were stronger.

He looked over his shoulder, making sure his wife was still asleep.

I feel lost without your guidance. I miss your presence.

Erik sat for a while longer, staring at his sword, inspecting the etching of a raven on one side and the dwarvish runes on the other. He thought it funny, the sigil of the raven. He had thought it a bird of death, but Turk had explained to him that the dwarves revered the raven as wisest of all birds, strong and loyal. He smiled.

Erik placed the tip of the sword in the scabbard and began to sheathe the blade. He felt the gooseflesh on his arms and stopped. He squinted as if he could see something on the blade he had never seen before. He tilted his head as he heard something faint and distant. A voice.

64

_____

Syzbalo walked through his dungeon, hands clasped behind his back, his witches and Isutan advisor trailing close behind him. He stopped before a cage. A shadow in the corner moved and he was pleasantly surprised his prisoner was still alive. He hadn't had the time to visit the scum and few people survived very long in these cells. He lifted a hand and snapped a finger and the bars that covered the front of the cell disappeared. He stepped in.

"Tarren," Syzbalo said, his voice hard and flat.

The prisoner stirred and groaned. Syzbalo lifted a hand and said an incantation in his mind, one he had newly learned. He knew the dwomanni's intestines had begun to twist and wrap themselves through the cavity of his body, constricting and tightening. The prisoner groaned louder. He was ready to scream. Syzbalo knew it.

"Are you ready to speak?"

"What?" Tarren Red Hair, Captain of the Shadow Horn Guard asked.

The Lord of the East lowered his hand and the magic stopped. The dwomanni slumped against the wall. Syzbalo pointed to the corner. A small ball of red light appeared. It was enough to illuminate the creature, enough to irritate him, but not enough to harm the wretched, pale-skinned, dwarf-kin. Tarren immediately threw up an arm, shielding his eyes.

"Oh stop," the Lord of the East said, rolling his eyes.

"Have you found the sword?" Tarren asked, scooting up against the wall and staring out at the Lord of the East with pale, blank, blind eyes.

The dwomanni was blind, a symbol of allegiance and loyalty to their dark gods, the Shadow, and their dwomanni ways, but despite being blind, his other senses were so heightened, he might as well have had his sight.

"No," the Lord of the East said.

The dwomanni looked upset, as if he had wanted Syzbalo to find the Dragon Sword. The Lord of the East found that odd, since he had no intention of giving it to, or even aligning himself with, the dwomanni. Him finding it was just as bad, maybe even worse, than the dwomanni not fighting it at all.

"We didn't find it," Syzbalo repeated. "In fact, Erik Eleodum found it and, apparently, reforged it as his own sword."

"What?" Tarren hissed.

The dwomanni pushed against the wall, sliding up the stone until he stood. He hissed.

"You fool," the dwomanni hissed.

The accusation took the Lord of the East aback. How dare this wretched creature call him any name, let alone *fool*?

"It will eventually fall back into the hands of the elves," Tarren said, sidestepping along the wall, towards the entrance to the cell.

"The elves?" Syzbalo asked, raising an eyebrow.

"We can still find the crown," the Lord of the East said, "the Dragon Crown."

"It is only one piece of the puzzle," the dwomanni hissed, seemingly more agitated with each passing moment. "It is nothing without the sword. The scroll, sword, and crown must be combined. And then the mistress and her master can rule."

"Are you speaking of this dragon?" the Lord of the East asked. "I will be the one controlling her."

Tarren gave a croaking laugh, shaking his head.

"No," he hissed, a mad smile spreading across his face. "You cannot control the right hand of the Shadow."

"I will," Sybalo said, even as the dwomanni slid closer.

"Fool," the dwomanni cursed.

The Lord of the East was about to speak the incantation again to twist the dwomanni's intestines when he felt a presence behind him.

"The Dragon Sword and Dragon Crown are nothing but trinkets forged by dwarves and enchanted by elves."

Syzbalo turned to see the cloaked figure, who had infiltrated his throne room, standing between he, his witches, and Melanius.

"You," Syzbalo hissed.

"Be careful," the man said.

The Lord of the East turned to see Terran lunging at him. The dwomanni should have been near death, but he came at Syzbalo with strength and fervor. He put up a hand and the dwomanni stopped midair. He flicked his wrist and Terran flew across the cell, slamming into the wall and crumpling to the ground.

"My master has been generous with his power," the cloaked man croaked.

The witches and Melanius all began to touch their magic, Syzbalo could feel it, and the cloaked figure laughed.

"Leave us," Syzbalo ordered.

"But master," the witches said in unison.

"I said leave us," and he snapped a finger. His three magical advisors disappeared and it was just he, the cloaked figure, and the unconscious dwomanni in the corner of his cell.

"The Dragon Sword is not some trinket," the Lord of the East said.

These tools are nothing compared to the power of Chaos! a deep voice boomed, low and methodical, so loud the whole dungeon shook.

The dwomanni began to move, pushing himself up into a crouch.

He groaned and hissed as the unseen voice rolled through the dungeon.

Do not waste time on trivial things, the voice said, deep and mechanical, *rather, seek me, and seek true and real power.*

"Lies," the dwomanni hissed. "You are nothing compared to the Shadow and the Mistress."

Rolling laughter rippled through the dungeon, causing the walls to undulate and crack. The cloaked figure unsheathed a black, long sword that seemed to drink up what little light existed. Syzbalo thought, for a moment, the shadowy figure meant to use it on him, but he stepped towards the cell. Before he could strike the dwomanni down, however, a surge of magic passed through the Lord of the East. It was like swallowing a mouthful of freezing water and it caught his breath. The dwomanni must have felt it too, as his body went rigid and his eyes went wide. The red light present in the cell brightened to a blinding intensity and the twisted creature screamed as he began to levitate.

Blood poured from his nose and mouth and eyes and ears. His screams went silent as his body moved, bones breaking internally, muscle tearing away from their tendons. His tattered clothes caught fire and his pale skin turned black. He crumpled to the ground, nothing more than charred bone and ash after only a few moments.

"What have you done?" Syzbalo asked as the magic subsided.

Do not question me, insect! the voice boomed, so loud the Lord of the East ducked, covering his head with his arms.

The hooded figure cackled, sheathing his black sword.

I can give you the Dragon Sword, if you truly wish it, but if you follow me, I will give you power beyond frivolous elvish magic.

Syzbalo waited a moment, collecting his thoughts and digesting what had just happened.

Do you desire power?

"Yes," the Lord of the East replied.

Will you follow me for that power?

"Yes," Syzbalo said without hesitation. The thought of such

power, something that could infiltrate his most magically guarded places, destroy a creature in such a way, emanate the kind of power he felt was almost intoxicating.

Bow to your new master, the voice said. *Bow to the Lord of Chaos.*

Syzbalo didn't know in which direction he should bow and, for a moment, he wasn't sure if he wanted to bow to someone...something. But the power he felt. The power he had been given as of late, was enough to bend his knee. He took a knee and bowed.

"Master," he said.

Good. It is time to find the Stones of Chaos. It is time to resurrect my beasts.

STONE OF CHAOS: CHAPTER 1

*E*rik Eleodum watched the setting sun reflecting off the frost-covered ground. It never snowed heavily in Northwest Háthgolthane, but as the winter waxed and the temperatures dropped, the frost that covered the grass and the branches of the bare trees each morning would remain all day. A flash of purple distracted him. He leaned to his left and raised his sword, blocking the oncoming strike.

Erik grinned at his cousin, Bryon Eleodum, who was breathing heavily, sweat glistening on his face despite the cold. The purple light of Bryon's elvish sword seemed to meld with the greenish hue of Erik's dwarvish one—Dragon Tooth—and, for a moment, his cousin's snarl was illuminated, making him look angry. Erik knew he wasn't, that was the look Bryon had when they trained. Obviously annoyed Erik had blocked his surprise attack, he kicked out, pushing Erik away with his boot. Bryon was better than most, perhaps one of the best with the sword, but Erik was better. It just happened that way.

There usually wasn't much to do on a farm in the winter except to raise a few hardy crops and tend their livestock. They would service their tools and make sure they had stocked enough seed for the coming spring, but that season had also been a time of rebuilding. Erik's father's barn had burnt down at the end of autumn, and Erik had expected to spend most of the winter helping his father rebuild it.

However, within a week of the fire, a hundred dwarves from the Gray Mountains arrived at the Eleodum farmstead and the barn had been rebuilt within several weeks. The dwarves arrival was testimony to their generosity and recognition that Erik and his family were now, as far as they were concerned, dwarves after he had been baptized into Clan Dragon Fire.

Erik had also wanted to spend time with his wife, Simone, but she her pregnancy had recently left her in bed most days and he had no idea how to comfort her. His mother and sister, Beth, did most of what was needed, often shooing him out of his own bedroom so Simone could rest. That left little more to do than train, and so that's what Erik and Bryon did, along with their dwarvish companions, Turk, Nafer, and Bofim, and even Andu, an Easterner who had once served the king of Hámon, a man named Bu Al'Banan, and now served the Eleodums as a head farmhand.

"Are you going to train or what?" Bryon asked, feigning a swing with his sword only to kick out again.

Bryon was tall and, even though he looked lean, was stronger than most. Their instruction had originally come from a man who once served in the Eastern Guard, the most prestigious military force in Golgolithul, a nation most these days referred to as the Eastern Empire. Wrothgard Bel'Therum was a good man and an even better teacher. Perhaps his most valuable lessons weren't about using a blade or weapon, they were the mental ones, about calming the mind, envisioning success in battle before it even happened. He taught them to understand their weaknesses and strengths, and using the latter to their fullest advantage.

"What does it look like I'm doing?" Erik retorted, swatting Bryon's foot away with the broad side of Dragon Tooth's blade.

"Day dreaming," Bryon replied. "That's all you do these days...

day dream. Do you miss the adventure that much? The fighting? The danger?"

Erik looked north, at the Gray Mountains. Low clouds covered the two tall peaks known as the Fangs. Snow covered the entirety of the mountains, even the foothills. He wondered how the people of Mayisha Maythia —once known as Fealmynster—were doing. Was Shu'ja'a as good a leader as he thought he would be? Erik shook his head, wanting to dismiss such thoughts.

"No, I don't," Erik replied. "I don't miss it at all."

Erik looked over his shoulder, back at his house, where Simone lay in bed. She would be all right, as would their baby. Erik's mother had experienced the same fatigue when she was pregnant with all four of her children—Erik, his now deceased brother, and his two sisters—but Simone spending most of her time in bed put more stress and worry on Erik.

"You're lying," Bryon said.

"I don't lie," Erik replied.

"You just proved yourself a liar," Bryon said with a smile.

"Do you miss it?" Erik asked.

"It's all I think about," Bryon replied without hesitation.

"Truly?" Erik asked. "What about your farm? Your parents? Your sisters?"

"I am grateful for my farm," Bryon said, "and father has been teaching me the business aspects more but, as much as I feel blessed for a renewed relationship with my family and the opportunity to run a successful farm, I find no true purpose in it."

They both looked to the Gray Mountains. Then, in unison, they looked east.

"I had purpose out there," Bryon said. "But what was it all for?"

Erik stared at his cousin, studying his face as Bryon continued to look east. The look that crossed Bryon's face could only be described as one of yearning as he remembered past days.

"What do you mean?" Erik asked.

Bryon turned to look at Erik.

"You know damn well what I mean!" Bryon replied. "What was the purpose of all of it? The dwarves? The dragon? That damned sword? Befel's life? What was it all for? So we could come back to Western Háthgolthane and live out the rest of our days as farmers? We could have done that without ever leaving. And Befel would still be alive."

There wasn't a day that Erik didn't think about his older brother, and so many things reminded him of the only man he looked up to as much as his father. From the smell of the farm to the sounds his pigs or cows made to the simple buzzing of a passing honeybee. He was a better man than all of them, loyal and strong, and he left this world the only way he would have expected to... helping someone else.

"Maybe it was to teach us to appreciate what we have," Erik said but he didn't sound convinced.

"Seems a harsh way to teach us that," Bryon replied. "I just feel like there is more for us. Out there."

Erik said nothing but he agreed. In fact, he knew there was more for them. He—they—were wanted men. The Lord of the East wanted Erik's sword, once known as the Dragon Sword and now reforged as Dragon Tooth, and therefore, wanted him dead. The north—Gol-Durathna—wanted him dead as well, for a reason Erik could only guess was to keep Dragon Tooth out of the hands of the Lord of the East. A rebel faction of dwarves, led by a politician named Fréden Fréwin, wanted him dead, thinking men were nothing but a disease. And, even though King Bu Al'Banan had stayed true to a word of truce he had given Erik, the latter still suspected the king of wishing him ill will also. Slavers from Saman—northern most city of Wüsten Sahil—wanted him dead. There were probably others, men he didn't even know existed, who wanted his life.

And if all these people wanted Erik dead, it meant they wanted his family dead as well. He would have to save his family, but what was it Dewin the ancient wizard had said? Something about winds of change moving swiftly and that Erik would be called. That's when he was to leave again. But called by who and how?

Save the world, you will save your family. Save your family, the world dies.

Those fifteen words Dewin had spoken rattled daily in Erik's mind. The old man had put the weight of the world on Erik's shoulders, but it was all riddles. Everyone spoke to him in riddles. Andragos. Dewin. His dreams even never brought clarity. Some damned mystery he couldn't figure out. He just knew he'd become mixed up in it all and that it somehow had to do with his sword—Dragon Tooth —and a crown and a spell... and dragons.

"Only the Creator knows," Erik finally muttered.

"What was that?" Bryon asked.

"The Creator," Erik said, speaking louder, "he knows what is in store for us. We just need to wait."

"I've been waiting," Bryon said. "We'll continue waiting and supposedly know what he had in store for us when we die and, according to you, go to meet him. I don't know that I want to keep waiting for some stupid sign."

Erik just shrugged. They continued to stare east, as the sun sat more than halfway below the horizon, and remembered a different time. Erik wondered which part of all that had happened was currently uppermost in Bryon's mind. For Erik, he couldn't shut out the last time he spoke to Dewin.

The sun was almost gone when Bryon turned to Erik, extending his hand.

"Tomorrow," Bryon said.

Erik nodded with a smile and shook his cousin's hand, but Bryon didn't squeeze back. His eyes were trained on the east.

"Bryon, give it a rest," Erik said, smiling and almost laughing. "The east will be there tomorrow."

"Hush," Bryon said, letting go of Erik's hand and squinting, leaning forward. "I see something."

"It's nothing," Erik said. "Dusk always changes how things look."

"No," Bryon said. "There's someone out there."

A year ago, Erik's untrained eye would have never seen it, or he would have passed it off as an errant ray of sunlight or a distant firefly. But now, it was unmistakable. The flash of a blade.

"I see it," Erik said.

As if still instructed by Wrothgard, Erik and Bryon crouched simultaneously, and began to move slowly towards the waist high fence that surrounded Erik's home. The movement was fluid, unhurried yet deliberate. Against the gently rolling hills the farmlands backed onto, a myriad of bushes and fences marked out farm and land boundaries. Despite the different fruit and nut trees—albeit leafless in the deep winter—and farmhouses and barns that could obscure a man's vision, Erik could see shadows, and he knew Bryon saw them too. Men were moving a step at a time.

"What do we do?" Bryon whispered.

"We don't even know who they are," Erik replied. "They could be anyone."

"Who would be slinking in the shadows?" Bryon asked. "Especially in the farmsteads. Especially around your farm?"

"Children," Erik offered.

"They don't look like the shadows of children," Bryon said.

"Older boys," Erik offered, even though he didn't believe his own words.

"No. It's probably that prick Bu, going back on his truce."

"It's only a matter of weeks since that lord of his was here talking of trade agreements."

"So what? He's a tricky bastard," Bryon said. "Maybe he's decided it's time to finally take away our free lands. I think they're Hámonian."

Erik's stomach twisted and something caught in his throat.

"If they are here to kill us," Erik said, "then they could be anyone."

STONE OF CHAOS: CHAPTER 2

"So, what do we do?" Bryon repeated.

"Sneak up on them," Erik said, "slowly."

"Get your hunting bow," Bryon said.

Erik nodded and crawled over to the gate in his fence and up onto the walkway made of polished flagstone leading to his front door. He stopped twice, his eyes trained on the shadows hidden in the night, as their unknown assailants still moved furtively. He opened the front door as quietly as possible, hoping he didn't alert his wife and the shadowy figures slinking in the darkness alike. The main living room of their home was dark and for the first time in his short marriage, Erik was glad Simone forgot to light the candles and lantern. He reached just inside the door, where he kept his hunting bow, and grabbed that and the quiver of arrows leaning next to the weapon.

"Are they still there?" Erik asked when he returned to his cousin, still crouched next to the fence. The sun had now fully set and it was harder to follow the shadows. The moon was low on the horizon and shedding very little light.

"They've moved," Bryon said, and pointed towards a copse of apple trees. They were closer now.

As his eyes became more accustomed to the darkness, Erik saw one of the figures—he surmised there were three of them—motion with an arm. Their paced seemed to pick up as they made their way across a wide road made of hard packed dirt that passed through the Eleodum Farm. He looked down at the hunting bow and nudged Bryon.

"What?" his cousin asked.

"Here," Erik said, giving him the bow, "you're better with this than I am."

Bryon nodded, took the bow, and nocked an arrow, waiting. The figures had disappeared into a dip in the road, only to rise up again. Bryon drew the bowstring back halfway.

"Shouldn't we wait to see if they're hostile?" Erik asked, looking at the half drawn bow.

"Why don't you go over there and ask them if they mean to shove a knife up your ass or just join us for dinner?"

Erik didn't answer. He ducked down as he heard shuffling and whispering, so quiet an untrained ear might have missed it.

"They're close," he whispered.

Bryon just nodded, breathing slowly and lifting the bow.

"Are you sure about this?" Erik asked.

"Nope," Bryon whispered, shaking his head.

Erik looked down at Dragon Tooth, still sheathed. If these men were as good as he thought they were, sneaking up on them by the cover of night, Bryon would only get one shot. He would have to move quickly. He plotted his course— around his wife's rose bushes and over the fence to the right of a wagon; that would take him south of where the men were last seen. He point for Bryon to move in the opposite direction and then circled his finger back the other way; they would converge in the middle.

Bryon nodded his understanding and breathed out, slowly and evenly. He pulled the bowstring as taught as it would go as one of the figures moved and then stopped again, low in the night. The unmistakable glimmer of the moon on the edge of a blade as the clouds shifted confirmed their expectations; they weren't friends.

"Do it," Erik said, deliberately, his voice now hard steel.

Bryon let go of the bowstring and headed right before he could even check what had happened. The arrow sounded like a quick gust of wind before Erik heard a thud and a quick cry. One of the figures stood about fifty paces away, then his body gave a quarter turn and disappeared from sight. Erik heard the unmistakable sound of a body hitting the ground.

Erik moved left around the cut-back rose bushes and leaped over the fence, head still stooped low. He ran to the left of a wagon, making sure to crouch low under its wooden sides. He inched his head around the end, and waited until he heard whispers in the darkness. The language sounded familiar and it reminded him of two soldiers from Gol-Durathna who had taken the Dragon Scroll from him, causing the dragon attack on South Gate, the poor suburb that rested against Fen-Stévock's southern wall. Another snatch of a few words confirmed to him these were Durathnans.

Their voices sounded concerned, their words quick and angry. As the moon rose higher, he saw there was one more than he had originally thought and confirmed that when he heard three distinctive voices. He presumed they were arguing over what to do next now they'd been discovered and one of their number was dead.

He ran south, hurrying past the trunks of the orange trees that ran along the eastern edge of his property; they weren't wide enough to give him coverage. He stopped again, this time behind another gray-leafed bush. The shadowy men were now quiet; they had stopped moving.

He slid under the lowest rail of the fence that separated his property from the road, slowly wiggling his back against the ground, and then turned onto his front and squinted. If these men were as trained as he expected them to be, they would see any sudden movements and had no idea if Bryon was ready to attack yet. In their haste, they failed to discuss a cue.

As if his mind was being read, Erik heard the hoot of an owl but the feigned sound didn't fool the attackers and, in the moonlight, he could see eyes darting around in the darkness. He heard another quick gust of wind, and something thudded into the ground several paces away; another arrow from Bryon. A miss. Was it on purpose? It didn't matter, because as the three figures stood, he saw a purple glow. The shadows shouted and the glint of steel flashed in the space between the three men and Bryon. The glow grew closer, weaving back and forth, bobbing up and down, trying to confuse. Erik unsheathed Dragon Tooth.

He didn't understand Durathnan, but when Dragon Tooth flared with its green flame, the men became excited. They knew about the sword, or perhaps it was because they were trapped between two magical blades. Whatever the case, their words were angry and hateful, regardless of the language. As he now rushed towards them, Erik saw one had turned towards him. The other two concentrated on Bryon.

The man's clothing was black and he seemed to be wearing a dark cloth mask as well as having smothered some blackening agent on the blades of his two short swords; Erik could only see their sharp-looking edges. The man moved quickly and precisely, but as Erik closed in on him, he could the assassin blinking wildly in the green light of his sword.

Erik rolled underneath the swipes from the short swords. He came up, blocking two more overhead strikes and kicked out, the heel of his boot crashing against the man's shin. The assassin gave a short cry and attacked again. He was fast and strong and stealthy. He said something, directly to Erik, but he didn't understand the words.

"I don't know what you're saying," Erik said, swatting one short sword away and then swing down hard, knocking the other one out of the assassin's hand.

The sound of metal scraping against leather told Erik that the assassin had drawn another blade. From the corner of his eye, Erik could see flashes of purple. He felt a fist in his ribs and an elbow to the side of his head. It wasn't enough to knock him unconscious, even daze him, really, but it did push him back. This assassin knew how to fight, with both weapons and hand, but it was a style Erik was familiar with. Wrothgard had taught him, but he also shown Erik to improvise.

He heard cloth flutter and sensed another fist, this one clutching a blade, flying towards his face again. He ducked, stomped his boot heel on the man's toe and brought his knee up into the man's crotch. He felt balls crush under his knee and the unmistakable sound of air leaving a man's lungs. He expected the assassin to fall into him, but rather, despite his obvious pain, he rolled backwards, coming up into a crouched position before lunging at Erik again. This one was rather persistent.

Erik felt the air move again as he ducked once more, a blade passing over his head. He leapt backwards when another blade tried to slash at his throat and then chanced a kick, connecting with a leather greave with enough force to send his attacker to one knee. He swung downward, his blade catching in the middle of the assassin's two crossed weapons. Erik pulled his sword through and then swiped up, knocking the dagger and short sword out to the side. He saw the flick of the man's wrist and instinctively jerked to one side, a knife barely missing his cheek. It probably wouldn't have caused much damage, if these men were truly assassins, it was likely to have been poisoned.

Erik kicked up again. The assassin blocked his foot with a hand, but at the same time, he brought Dragon Tooth down; and hard. The green flame around the sword flared and the assassin screamed as the blade cleaved through his shoulder and into his ribs, and some of his black clothing caught fire as Erik retrieved his weapon.

The Durathnan fell forward, dead, his burning clothes lighting up the scene of the fight. As much as Bryon's handling of a sword might not have been as good as Erik's, he was holding his own against the other two men and the smell of burning flesh—together with the green of Erik's sword—told them they were now on their own.

Erik faced Bryon and gave his cousin a quick nod, just enough of a sign that he was all right and Erik was there for him. The other Durathnans split their attention between their two opponents. The flames of burning cloth began to die, but in the dim light, Erik could see they were slight men, short and thin, wearing black clothing that hugged their bodies. Half masks covered everything but their eyes and they wore hoods.

The Durathnan assassin facing Erik squinted, his black eyes hateful. He flicked a wrist and a small, double bladed knife twirled at Erik, both sides undoubtedly coated with some sort of poison. He didn't know if the man meant for the attack to cause injury, or if he meant for it to simply distract Erik, but it did neither. Gripping Dragon Tooth with both hands, Erik swung down hard, but the lithe attacker rolled out of the way, flicking his wrists two more times.

One of the two-sided knives caught Erik on his left hand as he brought it up to shield his face. The weapon bounced away, drawing a small trail of blood, but the wound burned. Erik hoped it wasn't a deadly poison. The assassin did a back flip, kicking up at Erik at the same time, before landing in a crouch. He wheeled his foot around, trying to trip Erik, but he jumped high over the assassin's leg. The moment he landed, Erik slashed at the man's leg, cutting flesh and causing the black pants to catch fire.

The Durathnan stood quickly as he let out an involuntary yelp and slapped at his leg, trying to extinguish the fire. Erik took advantage of the distraction, and rushed in, ramming the assassin with his shoulder, grabbing his throat with his left hand, and thrusting upward with Dragon Tooth. The hateful eyes went wide and Erik could smell the sickening combination of bile and blood, trapped between the mask covering the man's mouth and his lips.

Erik felt a knee in his side as he pressed into the dead man and saw a flash of black run past him. He looked to Bryon, pushing himself up quickly from his knees.

"Are you all right?" Erik asked.

"Never better," Bryon replied, breathing heavy. "Don't let him get away."

They both gave chase, but the assassin was fast, and the road was dark, causing Erik to stumble over a rock or a small ditch several times.

"We're going to lose him," Bryon said.

"Here," Erik said, stopping and reaching into his boot, grasping the small handle of a small knife he always kept in his boot.

It was hardly a weapon, something meant as a tool around the farm, but it might be enough, if well aimed, to slow the assassin. Erik tossed the knife to Bryon who caught and in one motion, threw it. Despite the darkness of the night—the moon only rising a bit more and casting its white light on the farmsteads—Bryon had impeccable aim and the small tool flew blade over handle, into the center of the Durathnan's back. The yelped and stumbled forward, now tripping on the even ground until he was sliding along, face first. In moments, Bryon and Erik were on the man, kicking away his weapons and Erik dropped on their target, holding him down.

The man struggled, but Erik drove his knee into the assassin's neck as Bryon pointed his elvish blade at the man's face, the tip sizzling as it touched his flesh. The man fell still, but groaned loudly underneath his half mask.

"What do you want?" Erik asked.

The man replied in his native tongue, but with clear hatred in his voice.

"We don't speak your language, Durathnan," Bryon said, bringing the tip of his elvish blade closer to the assassin's eye.

"You," the assassin said, his accent rolling and fluid. "I want you."

"Me?" Erik asked.

"Both of you," the assassin added. "And the Dragon Sword."

"Why?" Erik asked.

He felt the man shrug under his weight.

"I do as I'm told," he said.

"It'll be to your death," Bryon said.

"Then I die fighting an enemy of the north," the man replied.

"An enemy of the..." Erik began to say.

He grabbed the Durathnan's shoulder and pulled the man up, so that he was kneeling. Erik tore away the mask, revealing a young man, clean shaven with a strong jaw. His hair was short and either black or brown, but he couldn't tell in the moonlight.

"Gol-Durathna?" Erik asked. "I don't know why Amentus hates me. I am no enemy of the north."

"Don't banter with him Erik," Bryon said, "He's not worth it."

Erik ignored his cousin.

"Speak," Erik said. He shook the man.

"You serve the Lord of the East," the assassin accused.

"I serve the Creator," Erik retorted, "and my family and friends. I have never *served* the Lord of the East."

The assassin shrugged again.

"The Dragon Sword is gone," Erik said, lifting up Dragon Tooth. "This is Dragon Tooth, and it is mine, no one else's."

"More will come," the assassin said. "The Atrimus never sleep. Whether you serve the Lord of the East or not, it doesn't matter. Alive, you are still a danger to my people."

"You can fight me all you wish, but leave my family alone. Take back that message, and I will let you live." Erik said.

The man looked up at Erik, the green light from Dragon Tooth reflecting across his face. He smiled.

"Never," he said.

As Erik lifted Dragon Tooth, the man threw his head back.

"Atrimus!" he shouted and Erik brought his blade down hard.

ABOUT THE AUTHOR

Christopher Patterson lives in Tucson, Arizona with his wife and three children. Christopher has a Masters in Education and is a teacher of many subjects, including English, History, Government, Economics, and Health. He is also a football and wrestling coach. Christopher fostered a love of the arts at a very young age, picking up the guitar at 7, the bass at 10, and dabbling in drawing and writing around the same time. His first major at the University of Arizona was, in fact, a BFA in Classical Guitar Performance, although he would eventually earn a BA in Literature and a BFA in Creative Writing.

Christopher Patterson grew up watching Star Wars, Dragon Slayer, and a cartoon version of The Hobbit. He started reading fantasy novels from a young age, took an early interest in early, Medieval Europe, and played Dungeons and Dragons. He has read The Hobbit, The Lord of the Rings, and the Wizard of Earthsea many times and heralds Tolkien, Jordan, and Martin, among others, as major influences in his own writing.

Christopher is also very involved in church, especially music and youth ministries, and is very active, having been a competitive power lifter since high school.

He thanks his grandmother for letting him waste paper on her typewriter while trying to write the "Next Great American Novel" and his parents for always supporting his dreams.

facebook.com/TucsonAuthorChrisPatterson

twitter.com/C_Patterson23

instagram.com/ChrisPattersonFantasyAuthor

ALSO BY CHRISTOPHER PATTERSON

Books in the Dream Walker Chronicles

The Shadow's Fire Series

A Chance Beginning

Dark Winds

Breaking the Flame

The Demon's Fire Series

Dragon Sword

Stone of Chaos

Demon Rising

Other Books by Christopher Patterson

Holy Warriors

To Kill A Witch